Published 2019
Waterville Inc. Publishing
watervilleinc@aol.com

Copyright © 2018 by Theo Czuk
All rights reserved.

ISBN 9780991287246

Cover fashioned by:
Michael Faris
aboutimepublishing.com

Layout and formatting:
Michael Faris
aboutimepublishing.com

Author's portraiture:
Margo Peacock

Although some characters may have been gleaned from historical records, the novel THE BLACK BOTTOM: The Measure Of Man is a work of fiction and comes with all of the warranty that a work of fiction can command.

AUTHOR'S NOTE:

The area known as Detroit's Black Bottom has undergone a number of manifestations in its history. From its earliest beginnings as a farming community noted for its rich and black soil (and where it got its moniker), through a landing spot for European and southern black refugees alike. Thanks to the urban planning of the '50s and '60s, the Black Bottom now lies buried deep beneath the cement of the I 375 freeway.

The Black Bottom and Paradise Valley were conjoining neighborhoods of poverty in Detroit through the roar of the '20s. Paradise Valley was playing host to the white Eastern European refugees – German, Polish, Ukrainian, Jew – who were escaping the poverty and political turmoil of their home countries while the Black Bottom was hosting the Negro refugees that were escaping the poverty and residual slavery mentality of America's southern regions. Each community, the white European and the southern black were migrating to the promise offered by Detroit's industrial jobs as a way out of poverty. A promise that a man could make bank on his own sweat. A promise of equality. A promise of hope.

But the roar of the '20s also was noted for a dark side. Prohibition. And Prohibition, the prohibiting of the sale of alcohol, created an environment ripe for the predator. Predators that prey on the weak and the disenfranchised. Gangs and hoodlums ran rife in these neighborhoods of poverty and Detroit's neighborhoods would not be excepted. Where prohibition served as a stimulant for the Mafia in New York and Al Capone in Chicago, Detroit was germinating the Purple Gang. The Purple Gang; America's Jewish version of the Italian and Irish mobs of Prohibition.

The poverty of the incongruently named Paradise Valley and Black Bottom neighborhoods, bubbling with this raw energy of hope and promise, were also bubbling with the artistic release so often found in communities of poverty. Musically, the Black Bottom and Paradise Valley were Detroit's breeding ground for this new and vibrant music called jazz. Much like New York's Harlem, New Orleans' Baker Street, and Chicago's South Side, these communities spread across America, and became notorious for their late night back-alley speakeasies that spawned America's great musical art form, jazz.

This novel concerns itself with the manifestation of the Black Bottom, and its sister neighborhood, Paradise Valley, during the tumultuous roar of the 1920s. Although many conditions contributed to the roar of the '20, the three most impactful conditions contributing to this roar were Prohibition, the industrial revolution, and jazz. While Prohibition was playing ugly and the industrial revolution offered promises, jazz, this most particular American art form, was finding its voice in the underground speakeasies, juice joints, blind pigs and honky-tonks of America's backside.

The Black Bottom was Detroit's contribution to this voice.

Much of the Black Bottom was gleaned from my father, Eddie Cowall. He was an old man then, I in my first year of college, when we would meet for our Thursday night Stroh's beer rendezvous in neighborhood taverns of Detroit. Some of this was difficult for him to talk about, and I am sure that there was so much more that he could not bring himself to share. When his father died in a train accident, the thirteen-year-old Eddie supported his mother, younger brothers, and sister as a paper boy for *The Detroit Free Press* during the day and a numbers runner for the Purple Gang by night. By the time he was eighteen, in 1931, he and an older buddy owned seven speakeasies around Detroit.

After a heroic tour of duty in WWII, which found him serving in both the Asiatic and European theaters, he returned home with a couple dozen medals and nothing left of the accumulated assets that had been left to the mismanaged care of his mother.

Dad, as Eddy, makes a cameo appearance in *The Black Bottom.*

Although every piece of history I attribute to 1927 Detroit happened in 1927, sticklers might take issue with exact dates. For instance, even though the reopening of the Ford plant for production of the Model A happened in the fall, I had it open in the summer to best accommodate the story line. Art happens at a much faster and more fluid pace than reality. This is what art does.

The photographic artist will sometimes create a double exposure, placing one negative over the other, to create the desired artistic expression. This is what art does.

When reading someone's life history, a biography, that biographical text does not take eighty years to read. The artist condenses the subject matter to the core. To the crux of the protagonist's storyline. This is what art does.

But I would like the reader to rest assured that the historical events attributed to 1927 Detroit happened in 1927 Detroit even though I sometimes needed to shift the canvas on the easel. This is what art does.

–Theo Czuk

This book is dedicated in loving memory to
Edward Theodore Cowall and Juliette Anais Gauthier.

Thank you thank you thank you:
Special heart-felt gratitude
goes out to, in alphabetical order,
Juliette Cowall, Linda Hartmann,
Karen Sarno and Susan Zanjani
for their counsel, insights, wisdom and editing
and whose contribution to this novel
could never be over-estimated or over-valued.

Theo's Opus:

Novels:
THE BLACK BOTTOM: The Measure Of Man
HEART-SCARRED

Music Albums:
THE BLACK BOTTOM: The Full Measure
TOO MANY SHADOWS
JAZZATOPE - out of print
MENSA'S AT PLAY - out of print
THE GAMUT
COLLAGE
VICTIMLESS CRIME OF LOVE - out of print

Poetry:
CHANNELING VENICE: Apparitions Of Light
PARISCAPES: Conversations With Paris

"Don't look back. Something might be gaining on ya."
—Satchel Paige

The BLACK BOTTOM:

The Measure Of Man

By Theo Czuk

1

Sometimes The Wolves Are Silent

With the dreams came the headaches. Long and lowdown headaches. Headaches that seeped from under the teeth and oozed out through every follicle of Kaleb's black and whorling tress.

The dreams, the nightmares, had haunted Kaleb's sleep all the while the coma lingered. When he stepped into the world of the lost, adrift on the vortex of amnesia.

The nightmares had begun slowly, beginning with just the street scene, the streetlamp diffusing its glow in an inverted V pattern over the city pavement. The flush of the lamp's light shone lonely on the street with an occasional wispy draft tumbling litter across the lighted asphalt.

As the days of the coma stretched into weeks, the streetscape nightmare was joined by a solitary man, silhouetted black against the night. Leaning back on the lamppost, he moaned sorrowful melodies on a saxophone to the moonlight that lay beyond the reach of the streetlamp's nightshade. The man wore a fedora tilted low over his eyes and he blew a sorrowful alto sax against the darkness that lay just beyond the reach of the lamppost's blush.

Silhouetted against the night, Kaleb Kierka could not decipher the size or the race of the man. But the music that the silhouetted man groveled was not a tune as much as it was poetry. Words. Words of verse were issuing forth from the bell of the saxophone. And the words made sense as only poetry mournfully droning from an alto saxophone can make sense in a dream.

As comatose weeks dragged on, the saxophone man playing poetry through his horn was joined by a black cat that sat dutifully at the edge of the streetlamp's glow. Like the man, the cat was silhouetted and burned black against the streetlamp's light.

In due course, this black cat would speak to the poetry offered by the sax-man. The black cat spoke in a bored and tired voice. Sometimes in a bored and pissed-off voice.

The silhouetted cat addressed the sax-man as *Blew* and, although the silhouetted sax-man never spoke, he addressed the cat as *Black*.

Black the cat and Blew the sax-man. Black and Blew.

The dreams had a repetitive theme. Set in a midnight cityscape

under the inverted V's glow of a single streetlamp, outlining the
silhouetted shadows of a black feline and a saxophone man. Blew
leaned slumped shouldered against the lamppost while playing a
mournful jargon through the horn. Beyond the reach of the soft
light of the streetlamp gathered the darkness.

***

*Black flicked his tail in irritation, caterwauling existence,
while Blew moaned the lowdown on the horn, waxing a poetic
idiolect through the saxophone.*
    "Ya hear 'em, no?" the cat-silhouette asked the sax-silhouette.
"...The same 'ol yowling every night."
    *Blew stopped playing and listened to the dogs moaning in the
darkness beyond the reach of the streetlamp's soft flush.*
    *Flickflickflick went Black's tail as he yowled in disgust. "Dogs,
wolves. Canines certainly. Constant crying. Crying at the moon.
Or crying because there is no moon. Crying for the sake of crying.
God damn wolves."*
    *Blew shrugged his shoulders in the shadowed outline and put
the saxophone's mouthpiece back to his lips.*
    *Black continued to flick his tail in irritation and, more to
the blackness outside of the lamp's glow than to Blew, Black
continued, "God damn wolves. Creep me out. Moaning on and
on about their existence. Their vanquish. Their nowhere world.
Strays astray."*
    *The silhouetted Blew stopped playing the saxophone again,
turned to look at the silhouette of the cat, thought about strays
astray, and turned his mouth back into the horn.*
    *When Blew blew his horn again the notes sounded like words.
They were words. The notes dispersed from the sax-man's horn
in a muted prose.*
    *Nattering over the saxophone, Black the cat ranted on about
the crooning wolves. "We all got our problems, ya know. We all
seen troubles, ya know. Don't none of us know who the hell we are
anyways. We all lost. We all got de Blues."*
    *Blew sucked wind deep into his chest, into his diaphragm. He
blew lowdown into his yesterday and deeper into his tomorrow
and he blew about strays astray. This is the tune that Blew blew
blue:*

SOMETIMES THE WOLVES ARE SILENT

1.
I listen to the howl,
Of the baying at the moon.
Suddenly somehow,
I've been singing that tune.
But sometimes,
SOMETIMES THE WOLVES ARE SILENT.

2.
I've been looking in the mirror,
At the danger and the fear.
I can't help but stare,
'Cause there's a stranger in there.
But sometimes,
SOMETIMES THE WOLVES ARE SILENT.

BRIDGE:
Sometimes I get so lost in shame,
'Cause when I listen to my song,
And all my inspiration and my pain,
Read like graffiti on a bathroom wall.

3.
There's an itching in my heart,
That I don't know how to scratch.
A torch in the darkness,
But I ain't got a match.
But sometimes,
SOMETIMES THE WOLVES ARE SILENT.

***

Waking from the dreams of the silhouetted cat and the silhouetted sax-man, Kaleb slouched over and rubbed at his temples, waiting for the headache to subside. And as the headache subsided, Kaleb yielded to the nightmare of the awake. Of the amnesia.

2

Ruins Of Reflection And Rubble Of Recall

The beating had been severe and the coma deep. Five weeks deep. But now the bandages were being unwrapped and light seared at the rods and the cones of Kaleb Kierka's eyes. It was a light that shuttled pain at 3,600,000 miles per second. A blazing light. The damn light.

Kierka had climbed from the long dark tunnel of unconsciousness a full week earlier, but only now were his eyes ready for the light. "Ready" being a relative term.

Doctor Stein stood on Kierka's left and the cop, Detective Morane, hovered on the right. Detective Morane had been interrogating Kierka during this aforementioned week of consciousness but with nothing to show for it.

The hospital's astringent smell hung in the air like a flavor. Chemical and bitter, clean to the bone and giving no quarter to any particular consequence of life or death.

Detective Morane addressed the doctor. "Ever see a beatdown like dis, Doc?"

The doctor, squeezing his brow in tight consternation, uncoiled the last of Kaleb's head wrap while answering, "Sure I seen beatings like this. In the morgue."

Kierka was in his own world. When the final strip of gauze was unfurled from his eyes, the pain of light seared at his forehead. A migraine on steroids.

For the past week, once he had regained consciousness, the nurses had been shepherding him around the hospital to break the stiff atrophy of his joints and muscles. From these meager ambles Kierka was well aware of the hitch he had acquired in his left leg, and the doctor had warned him of the shiny pink scar that dove under his left eyebrow. Now the blistering light flooding Kaleb Kierka's eyes made sight a painful proposition.

The gauze that had blinded Kaleb's eyes lo these many weeks had allowed other senses to step to the fore, and these other senses had become acute. Touch and hearing and smell and even taste had become the escort. Taste, even the chemical trail reaching Kaleb's tongue, provided environmental information. Kaleb could almost taste his route about the corridors of the hospital.

But the greater disgruntlement was not with the hitch in his step or the scar under his eyebrow or even this blinding light - this damned light - that seared into his cortex. The particular frustration that troubled Kaleb was reserved for the amnesia.

Kaleb Kierka was a man without memory.

Although Detective Morane was not convinced. Challenging the doctor Morane asked, "Whataya think, Doc, ya think this amnesia thing is real or is he playin' sport on me?"

The doctor ignored the question, instead studying Kierka's reaction to the light. He held a finger inches away from Kaleb's nose. "Can you focus, son? Can you make out my finger?"

Fighting through the cloak of pain, Kaleb Kierka tried to focus on the blurry digit that played before his eyes.

"Got it," said Kaleb. "Lest ways, I think so. You sure you've unwrapped all of the gauze?"

Doctor Stein smiled at that. "Yep, I'm afraid that gauze you're seeing now is of your own device. It'll begin to clear, give it time. Time."

And indeed, the gauze of light began to slowly lift and the doctor's digit detailed before Kierka's eyes. As it did, the doctor slowly drew his hand further from Kaleb's nose until the finger was a good three feet away. "And now?"

Kaleb Kierka studied the finger until it came into form again. "Got it."

The doctor smiled. "Good, now take a look around the room, son."

As the pain from the light subsided, Kaleb moved his head and took stock of his surroundings. The hospital room was much larger than he had envisioned when he only had his shins banging against the furniture to gauge its scope. And the doctor was much taller than Kaleb's aural experience had suggested. And Detective Morane was much uglier than he had hoped.

Mostly Kaleb was intrigued by his own body unfolding on the bed in front of him. When one does not have the luxury of memory, one's own existence is brought into question. Until he witnessed his own legs, he had no gauge to calculate his own physical being. Until he had vision he did not know his color. Until he had vision he did not know the three dimensional parameters of space that his body occupied.

Kaleb lifted his hands up before his eyes and slowly turned them back and forth, forth and back. Slender and strong hands. Longer fingers than the length of his legs would have suggested. He studied them, hoping to glean some memory from the lines and the veins. Nothing there.

"Took him a good god-damn long enough to wake up and now this amnesia thing, jest too handy is all it is," Morane grumbled.

If Detective Morane was a study in frustration, then Doctor Stein was a picture of fret and trepidation. Kaleb Kierka went from Morane's face to Stein's face and finally brought his eyes down to rest on his hands, looking away from the extraneous visual noise of their scrutiny.

Collecting his thoughts through the jumble of lost memories was like trying to negotiate through a city under siege of a carpet-bombing. Memory of the brain's debris was heaped in the ruins of reflection and the rubble of recall.

Closing his eyes against the clatter of the doctor's and the detective's surveillance, Kaleb drew within himself, searching his intellect for signs of recognition, of understanding. The memory cells of his cerebellum had been damaged, but the analytical had been left intact. Kaleb's eyes were closed, but his consciousness was wide awake as he rummaged around his synaptic gaps.

"You gonna sleep now, kid? Shit...." Morane was impatient.

The doctor was feeling Kaleb's wrist. "I think he's awake. Just overwhelmed is all. But he's awake."

Kaleb slowly churned in the thoughts, digesting the known from the unknown. He would need to begin a file, a digest, of these muddled musings on milled memory. A digest of the known. At present, the known was a thin volume.

"Oh, he's awake alright, Doc, I 'spect he's playin' possum is all. But he's awake alright."

Kaleb slipped from the conscious world into the unconscious and immediately he was met by the searing headache and the silhouetted cat and sax-man, Black and Blew.

***

Twitching its tail in irritation in the streetlamp's glow Black, the cat, bemoaned to Blew, "Awake? Awake. What the hell does awake mean?"

When Blew did not respond, Black ranted on. "Can light be measured by the blind? Can the noisy din be measured by silence? And just what scale measures 'awake' to a man with no memory?

"Sight, sound, touch, taste, smell; these are all filters used to discern, to calculate and to investigate the natural world. Devices to appraise our vital; tools to quantify our existence."

Blew blew lowdown but that did not deter Black.

"With sight we do not tumble from the curb. With sound we are forewarned by the siren's scream and our touch advises us against the sting of the flame. But what of awake? What of cognizant recall? What is awake to a man with no memory? Is memory not our foundation and our pilot, our signpost and the ultimate homing beacon?"

Blew growled deep into the saxophone, into the nether regions of the horn. But Black was mid-rant.

"Our eyes measure the light against the mélange of the dark, and our ears measure loud to the backdrop of quiet. Just as awake is measured by the quality of the memory."

Blew unplugged the sax from his mouth, adjusted the embouchure of the mouthpiece, wet the reed, and stuck the horn back into his face. He blew low and he blew gritty. Blew blew blue:

> *There's an itching in my heart,*
> *That I don't know how to scratch,*
> *A torch in the darkness,*
> *But I ain't got a match.*
> *But sometimes,*
> *SOMETIMES THE WOLVES ARE SILENT.*

***

"I don't like it," pronounced Detective Morane.

Opening his eyes again to his lap, his hands, Kierka ignored the cop as the doctor enjoined Kaleb's crusade. Scrutinizing Kierka's reaction to the light, the doctor only half asked the detective, "You don't like what, exactly?"

"I don't like that Kierka 'ere's got a convenient case of amnesia."

Kierka rolled his hands, resting them palm up on his legs, and turned to the detective. "Convenient for who?"

The cop had a puffy pink complexion and he was stumpy fat. A solid stumpy with fat stumpy fingers like the fat stumpy cigar that hung from his mouth, unlit, under a fat and stumpy nose. Fat and stumpy. The fat stumpy nose squinched in a silent snort. "Convenient for whoever the hell you're trying to protect."

"I'm trying to protect someone?"

Momentarily caught off guard, the detective shrugged his shoulders in the frumpy, threadbare suit jacket, the uniform of every overworked and underpaid honest cop of the Detroit Police Department. Not all of the cops of the DPD were beholding to the graft of the gangs of prohibition. "Protect *from* or protect *for* or protect *of* the goons you run with."

Kaleb knit his brow in confusion, which, in turn, irritated the pink scar under his left eyebrow. Lifting a finger to his eyebrow, Kaleb began to softly stroke the eyebrow, calming the tenderness of the wound. "Goons? I run with goons?"

The doctor cut in at this juncture. "Look Detective, this man may or may not be faking this memory loss. That's unclear at the moment, but...."

Detective Morane held the stump of a cigar in his stump of fingers and scolded them at Doctor Stein. "I know, I know, Doc. But, lookit 'ere, this boy's got a history. And it's a history of gangs and it's a history of vice."

Another soothing caress across the pink scar under his eyebrow while the light again began to trouble Kaleb's cerebellum. "Goons and gangs?" Kaleb repeated, trying to reconcile the words into the world of too-tall doctors and ill-suited detectives and fingers that were too long for the legs at the end of his own body. The only world he knew. "Goons and gangs?"

Detective Morane spit the words "The Purples."

The doctor turned now to the detective and said abruptly "This is just going to have to wait, Morane. I will discharge this boy in a day or two and you can have at him but until I do, you are not to question him anymore. You are not to challenge him and you are now going to leave this room."

Detective Morane plugged the unlit cigar into his face, shielding the slow smile that crept across his lips. "Sure. Sure, Doc. Couple more days." And then he turned to Kierka lying in the bed. "Get your story straight boy while this amnesia thing buys you time. I'll be back. This is what I do."

The cop made a grand gesture of putting on his hat and tipping the brim. He pointed his fat stumpy fingers, loaded with the fat stumpy cigar at Kaleb. "Be seein' ya, kid." And with that, the cop spun and toddled out of the room.

For a moment the doctor watched as the door flange slowly closed the door. When the door finally settled in its frame, Doctor Stein turned to Kaleb. "If you're playing at this amnesia thing, son, you're sitting in a hot pan on a flaming stovetop."

Kaleb studied the tall doctor carefully. "And if I'm not playin'?"

"Then you just jumped out of the pan and into the fire."

3

Get It While It Sizzles

Kaleb Kierka's apartment was on the border of Paradise Valley and the Black Bottom. It was Detective Morane who delivered Kaleb from the hospital to home and, for the most part, it was a quiet drive as Kaleb spent the time in study of the city. A city, Detroit, that Kaleb had grown up in. A city that Kaleb did not recognize.

For a rotund man, Detective Morane fit comfortably into the police radio dispatch car. His natty beige suit blended so well into the natty beige car seat that it was difficult to distinguish where the car seat ended and the detective began.

As for Kaleb, the ride home was an exercise in disorientation. He recognized the streets, the boulevards, the alleyways, but he could not associate context to the milieu. And even the clothes he wore, loose now from the five weeks of atrophy, were foreign and familiar at once. The jacket was a curious venture, cut more to action than to fashion. It was tailored loose under the arms and with an odd leather lining inside the side pockets. His billfold fit comfortably in his left inside breast pocket and he took it out to examine the contents. A driver's license without a photo. Sixty-seven dollars in small bills. Miscellaneous receipts. Nothing to spark memory.

Turning his attention back to the city that was whizzing by the automobile, Kaleb absorbed the enigmatic Detroit of 1927. A city in motion, in flex, vibrant with the vitality of a civilization, a culture, steaming headlong into the future.

"You seem to have the Doc believing in this amnesia thing, kid."

Kaleb turned his attention from the cityscape and studied the lines of the detective's face. Soft, puffy, lines. Smile-less lines. Lines creased by a vocation that toils on the seamy edge of humanity. Or, maybe, inhumanity.

"You don't believe I've got amnesia?"

Now it was the detective's turn to look into Kaleb Kierka's face. The scraggly beard that Kaleb had grown during the five weeks of hospitalization could not hide his youthful countenance. And a youthful countenance carries its own innocence. Deservedly so or not.

Morane had been traveling south on Woodward and he took a left onto Garfield; five blocks further, he turned south again onto Hastings Street. South toward Paradise Valley and the Black Bottom. South toward Kaleb's home.

Thought provoked deeper lines into the detective's crowfeet. "You're cute, kid. And I'll give you this much, you've got me half believing it. But if it's true, you are in for one hell of a ride."

Kaleb considered this. He had a lot of catching up to do. "One hell of a ride, how?"

Shrugging his shoulders in his beige jacket, Morane gave every appearance of a shrugging sack of potatoes. Pulling into a parking space in front of a yellow brick, three-story walk-up, he announced, "You're home, boy. Come on, I'll walk you up."

The apartment was on the third, the top floor, overlooking the bustle of Hastings Street. Kaleb Kierka opened the door with a key that was said to be among his items when his battered, lifeless body was delivered to Henry Ford Hospital. Kaleb stepped through the door first, but Detective Morane brushed passed him and gave the apartment a quick, professional, walk through. It was a small one bedroom with an efficiency kitchen opening to the living space.

As Kaleb stood in the center of the living room, taking in the space, the detective busied himself throwing open windows. "Smells like stale tobacco and burlap. I'll put some coffee on." He entered the kitchen and began the process of banging cabinet doors and pots.

A quick scan of the apartment gave Kaleb the impression of a fastidious man. Books arranged neatly on shelves, furniture smart but comfortable. Even the carpeting, Persian, and the drapes, French, seemed to have an easy rhythm to them.

The only incongruence, the only cluttered and chaotic spot in the room, was on a table overlooking Hastings Street. Here was a jumble of papers with scrawled script more attuned to the vagabond than to an exacting academic.

Kaleb decided that this table of cascading papers would demand further study, but for now, he would need to examine the bigger picture.

Moving with deliberation, examining the existence of an unknown being, Kaleb stepped from room to room, reacquainting himself with his life. The apartment felt familiar more than looked familiar. Not recognizing objects, the bed, the padded sofa, the easy chair, Kierka found more of a corporal link than actual familiarity with the environment.

Kaleb entered the bathroom and splashed water on his face from a small basin. He could feel the tightness of the healing wound under his eyebrow, and he calmed the irritation with a finger stroke across the brow. The stroke soothed the fresh scar's irritation. He opened the medicine cabinet and studied the salves and tubes for evidence of his life. Evidence of the aches and the pains and the stains of Kaleb Kierka's humanity.

The mirror above the basin offered Kaleb his first close inspection of the man who the world called Kaleb Kierka.

It was a foreign image. It was a familiar image. Kaleb studied the face staring back at him and tried to place it. It was like trying to recall a dream out of a sweaty and tousled sleep.

The eyes were a deep blue and were the draw of this façade's features. They demanded attention. The eyes looked as if they had studied too long and too hard for such a young face. The eyes seemed as if they could look deep into the past. But if the eyes were viewing deep into the past, it was a past beyond Kaleb's vision.

Morane came to the bathroom door and studied Kaleb while Kaleb studied the mirror. When Kaleb turned to Morane their eyes momentarily locked. Morane sniffed his meaty nose like a dog on a scent. Kierka turned back to the mirror.

"Brew's hot. Git it while it sizzles." Morane turned back to the living room.

One last look in the mirror - perhaps some small recognition? - and Kaleb joined the detective in the living room.

The detective had nestled onto the couch with his back to the window, to the street below, and sipped his coffee. There was another steaming cup of coffee on the small table next to the easy chair, and Kaleb took his direction from that, easing himself into the chair. The chair fit Kaleb like an old baseball mitt that hadn't been used since childhood. It was familiar and comfortable. Kaleb could turn a double play in the ninth inning in this easy chair.

Scrutinizing Kaleb carefully over the rim of his coffee, Morane gingerly worked on the hot potion. The old detective missed nothing.

In turn, Kaleb sipped at his brew and shared a smile with the detective. Smiles, as is their wont, gave new character to the face of Kaleb Kierka. It was a character that the detective appreciated.

"Look it 'ere, kid. Jury's still out about this whole amnesia thing, seems over the top to me, but just to ease my conscience, I'm gonna tell you where you sit."

Kaleb took this in, considered it, and sank a little deeper into the pocket of the baseball mitt chair, waiting for the pitch.

Detective Morane was not one to mince words and he laid it out in one breath. "Boy, here's what we know. You were born 27 years ago in the Ukraine. Came to Detroit as an infant escaping the Bolshevik Revolution. Your dad, Jewish, your mom, a Russian Orthodox Christian. Jew and Gentile. Didn't sit pretty with the Bolsheviks. They run your folks outta Russia. On the tip of a torch. Both of 'em now deceased."

After giving a moment for all of that to catch, Morane reached into his suit jacket pocket, pulled out a notebook and flipped it open. "Here's the skinny, son, jes in case you ain't shamming this amnesia thing." He began reading from his notes. "Kaleb Kierka was born in the Ukraine in March of the new century, 1900, makin' you 27 this year. Your folks escaped to the United States after watching your father's grocery store burn to the ground in the Bolshevik Revolution in ought-eight. Your father died in 1912 on a railroad crossing while trying to get a Model T in gear. No siblings. At twelve you supported your mama running numbers for the Sugar House Gang while hawking newspapers. Your mama died when you were 16 leaving you alone to run the streets of Paradise Valley.

"Story goes that as a teenager you were a founding member of the Purples. The Purple Gang. Split from them, don't know why or how. Don't care. Usually the Purple Gang exterminates Purple Gang ex-pats. But not you. Why? I don't know why you ain't dead and, now, *you* don't know why you ain't dead. But you come mighty close."

Morane looked up at Kaleb at this point, but the young man just looked over the rim of his coffee at the soft evening sky above the cityscape of Detroit. Morane continued to read. "You grew up with the kids in this neighborhood. They became the Purple Gang. Don't know why you left 'em, but they seem to leave you be in your speakeasy."

The curveball caught Kaleb's attention. "My speakeasy?"

"Your juice joint, your blind pig. Your speakeasy. Six blocks south of here on the border of Paradise Valley and the Black Bottom. You jive jazz piano at that same juice joint. Hear-tell you're pretty good on the ivories. No police record to speak of 'cept for small time juvee' stuff. But the speakeasy is playin' right on the outside edge of legal."

That was a mouthful of information to digest, and Kaleb set down his coffee and again studied the lines in the detective's face. No smile line in Morane's face.

Lots of information and Kierka was doubtful. He looked flatly at Detective Morane and called for a change-up pitch low and outside. "I own a speakeasy and I'm just on the outside edge of legal?"

The detective said nothing.

Kaleb lifted his hands and turned the long fingers back and forth in study. "...And I play piano?"

Detective Morane ignored the piano player and addressed the owner of the speakeasy. He did not like admitting this about the city of Detroit and discomfort showed in his face. "Okay, speakeasies pay off a few beat cops and they look the other way. City Hall wants to keep private enterprise in the city healthy so City Hall looks the other way. Looking the other way is good for city business. Liquor running through Detroit is a capital venture for this burg. You run a clean speakeasy and nobody gets hurt. And this I give ya: You've got the rep of runnin' one of the cleanest juice joints in the city. And God only knows how you do it considerin' the neighborhood you serve."

Kierka forced his eyes off of his hands and reached again for the coffee mug. After a moment of digesting the information, Kierka got up from the easy chair and walked to the bay window overlooking Hastings Street below.

"Has my speakeasy got a handle?"

"You call it The Temple Bar Speakeasy And Play Nice. Folks mostly jes called it 'The Temp'."

Standing at the bay window, Kaleb looked down on the Hastings Street of Paradise Valley and quietly mouthed "The Temple Bar Speakeasy And Play Nice?"

The potato sack of beige suit shrugged. "Mostly jes called 'The Temp'."

Six blocks south of this apartment in Paradise Valley was the border of the Black Bottom district. And The Temple Bar Speakeasy And Play Nice straddled the neighborhoods.

All of what Detective Morane had said sounded familiar in an ethereal way. Like walking into a movie that you maybe had seen before. Maybe not. But whether you've seen the movie or not, the ending is elusive.

After a moment of studying the jumble of the city's industry on Hastings Street three stories down, Kaleb turned back to Morane.

"Anything more I should know?"

"Just the obvious."

"The obvious?"

"Yep. The obvious."

Kaleb turned to face Morane fully. "I'm not real strong on the obvious right now."

Detective Morane set down his coffee and came up beside Kaleb at the window. Looking past Kaleb and down to the street, to Paradise Valley, Morane stuffed his hands into the pockets of his nattered suit, hunched his shoulders up against the worn potato sack fabric, took a deep breath, and let the air exhale slowly. "Somebody tried to kill you."

4

As Minutes Tick Like Chambers In A Gun

Where does one begin when trying to reassemble an unremembered life?

When Detective Morane left, Kaleb began to explore the apartment for evidence of this man named Kaleb Kierka.

Kaleb moved around the apartment, touching furniture as he went. He opened the curtains to let in the familiar sun. He picked up the book on the table next to his reading chair. Madame Bovary. Sniffing at the pipe that was sitting in the copper ashtray next to Madame Bovary, Kaleb smiled. The tobacco was Cavendish. And he knew it. That was something at least.

Moving into the kitchen, Kaleb decided to fire up the coffee, and he opened the correct cupboard housing the grounds. Luck or a recovered memory? Every achievement was suspect.

Two scoops in the coffee strainer and light the burner. The refrigerator was empty, but black was how he enjoyed his coffee in the hospital, and he had no reason to distrust that memory now. As the coffee perked, Kaleb continued to open and close cupboards looking for the familiar. Looking for something to spark memory. Looking for Kaleb Kierka among the saltines and the detergents.

When the coffee whistled, Kaleb poured a brown clay mug full - his favorite mug? - and sat down at the small table overlooking Hastings Street three stories below. On the table were the scrawling manuscripts of music notation in progress. Just as he suspected - just as he knew? - music was integral to who Kaleb Kierka was. Is?

There were scribbled music scores and there was scribbled poetry on the papers on the table. The music notation slanted to the right. The poetry slanted left. Different hands of script?

Wondering which script might be his, Kaleb picked up a pencil and signed the name that he was told was his name. Kaleb Kierka is what he signed. And he signed it again. It seemed to easily flow kinetically from his fingertips. Again he signed his name and then he copied the lyric that lay bare before him,

LAST CHANCE

Did you understand all the laughter,
Or did it go high over your head?
Do you really think it will matter,
When everything you think you know is dead?

Is there something pushing you faster,
Is there something pressing you on?
Do you see the clock as your master,
As minutes tick like chambers in a gun?

Are your senses suddenly reeling,
Do your feet feel anchored in clay?
Are you finally left with the feeling,
There's nothing left to do but walk away.

Nightingale

The sentiment was familiar to Kaleb and certainly pertinent to his present condition.

Kaleb's scrawl seemed to match the right slant of the music notation but not so much for the left leaning poetry.

The poetry manuscript was signed "Nightingale," and the left leaning scrawl on the page did not match his own cursive. A co-writer for his songs? A favorite poet?

Another piece of the puzzle to be unscrambled.

5

One More Shot Of Cold

It was a lot to digest.

First off, Kaleb was an owner of an illegal speakeasy on Detroit's lower east side. The Temple Bar Speakeasy And Play Nice. A speakeasy bordering Detroit's infamous neighborhoods of the Black Bottom and Paradise Valley.

Secondly, Kaleb was a piano player of some renown in Detroit's burgeoning jazz music scene. A new music, jazz, was yet in the process of defining itself.

And, not least, certainly, someone was trying to kill Kaleb Kierka.

Kaleb studied his hands, rolling the wrists back and forth, forth and back. Long and thin fingers. A long scar displayed across the palm of his left hand from pinky finger to thumb. Without access to his memory, his personal history, Kaleb could only speculate on the scar's origins. Was the scar a tattooed testament to the illegal hooch trade? Or maybe an innocent youth's escapade? Kaleb could only wonder. It was these little wonders, these lost episodes of time and place that filled in one's background. One's personal narration. And Kaleb was not privy to the chronicle.

Kaleb Kierka would need to identify Kaleb Kierka. Demarcate the boundaries that define Kaleb Kierka's province. Classify the character. Catalog the ego.

And with his own mortality suspended in the calculation, discovery must be quick.

Without a history, every step of Kaleb's life from here on would be a precarious step off a curb. Or a cliff. Or a six-foot hole in the ground.

***

After Detective Morane left and Kaleb went to the kitchen to busy the pot of coffee, he realized that he didn't know where anything was in the kitchen and began banging through cupboards and taking stock. He found the coffee in the cupboard above the refrigerator and the pans in the cabinet under the sink.

It seemed natural to use one scoop of coffee for every cup of water and that is what he did. The coffee was weak and he would note that for future reference.

When he had completed his survey of the kitchen and the living room, he moved to the bedroom. Clothes were neatly arranged in the drawers. Socks and underwear and laundered shirts were all aligned tidily in respective drawers. He reasoned that Kaleb must be a neat man, whoever the hell Kaleb was.

Another find in the sock drawer was a ring of keys. Four door keys and an automobile key. These would need further investigation and he stuffed them into his pants pocket.

At the closet he took his time examining the suit-wear. He felt the jackets for texture and studied the style. The fashion would say a lot about what kind of a man he was. He found the fashion to be smart but practical. Assuming the cut of the cloth was of the day, everyone on the streets wore suits, but the fabric tended toward the natty. Corduroy suits with patches on the elbows. Tweed with patches on the elbows. There were a couple of nicely made high-end suits that Kierka assumed were for special occasions, but mostly the clothes were practical. Like the jacket that he wore from the hospital, the inside of the side pockets of all of the suits were lined with smooth leather. For warmth, perhaps? To protect a pianist's hands? Odd, this leather lining of the side pockets.

The bathroom was the final mission. Rummaging through the medicine cabinet Kaleb again examined the razor and the shaving brush. The obligatory toothpaste and hairbrush. No particular drugs or salves to suggest ailments. He surmised that, when not dragging around the new hitch in his left leg, he was of reasonable health.

As he closed the medicine cabinet door his face caught and held onto the image in the mirror.

Certainly the face looking out from the mirror at Kaleb hosted Jewish origins; dark and curly hair, strong nose, tired eyes, darker complexion. But there was something else in there as well. Something more, something less. Something.

Although dark complected, Kaleb's skin was a shade lighter than the Jewish norm and his stature, just shy of six feet tall, stood taller than his Jewish brethren. But it was the eyes. Nordic blue with flecks of brown that set the eyes asparkle. Under clothing that hung loosely, given the five weeks of atrophy, fit a collection of muscle and bone that, even inert, lent itself to the impression of an athlete.

The eyes were familiar. Familiar like an acquaintance from a long and distant past. Familiar like a cane to blind man. Kaleb used the cane of recognition to steady himself.

Removing the shaving kit, the brush, the straight razor, Kaleb splashed his face and began working on his beard. He made use of the shaving brush and the razor, carefully finding the jawbones molded under the scraggy beard. He worked slowly, learning the geography of this terrain as he scraped at the stubble. With the task complete Kaleb found in the mirror a young, smooth-skinned man, more boyish than handsome, more soft than hard.

The rest of the facial terrain was youthful. Too youthful for the twenty-seven years that was his decreed age. The brow was high under a shock of wavy black hair worn much too long for the style of the day, owing, probably, to the hospital internment. The nose a little long but strong, noble. High cheeks that could weather a blow or host a smile.

Then back to the eyes. The eyes are where the attention was drawn and this is where he would find Kaleb Kierka.

The blue eyes had a life of their own. A sparkle like the blue of a rivulet splashing over laughing rapids as they gave way to deep, still, pools of reflection.

The single incongruent aspect of the young face was the crow's feet. Much too young of a face to sport crow's feet on the banks of those river-eyes.

The only thing that Kaleb could be certain of until, if ever, he regained his memory was of the here and of the now. He would need to deliberately reason his way forward. Friend or foe, fact or false, yes or no, would all need to be measured carefully. Somebody was trying to kill whoever this man in the mirror was, and if Kaleb had any hope of survival, then every length, every width, and every breadth would need careful consideration. Careful measurement.

***

Back in the living room Kaleb's attention was drawn once more to the table by the window with the smattering of papers. He drew up a chair and sat down at the table to examine the script and give closer study to the words.

The poetry was a sloppy, drunken, cursive. A quick and muddled cursive with *i*'s not dotted and *t*'s not crossed.

Kaleb picked up a pencil lying on the table and signed his name, Kaleb Kierka. He let his wrist muscles guide his signature, allowing the kinetic memory to shape the script. He wrote "To be or not to be, that is the question." and he compared this Shakespearean lament with the handwriting on the papers scattered on the table. They were notably different. Too different to be Kaleb's copy. Someone besides Kaleb had waxed poetic in these scribbles.

Shuffling through the papers, he found them to be poems or lyrics of some sort; Kaleb randomly lifted one and gave a read. The jumbled scrawl took a moment to get used to, like coming into a dark room and waiting for your eyes to adjust. When his eyes were accustomed to the scribble, to the light, Kaleb read:

ONE MORE SHOT OF COLD

1.
I don't want to keep guessin',
No more denials, no more confessin'
So raise your glass give a toast,
To ONE MORE SHOT OF COLD.

2.
No use being courageous,
Let's finish the chapter and turn the pages,
And when the book is closed,
I'll have ONE MORE SHOT OF COLD.

BRIDGE:
It's the nervousness in your laughter,
It's the chip up on your shoulder.
Give me ONE MORE SHOT OF COLD,
Before I go.

3.
For sweet love's epitaph,
Chalk up the heartache and a couple laughs.
Then on that lover's tombstone,
Write down, ONE MORE SHOT OF COLD.

Then pour me one for the road,
Make it a DOUBLE SHOT OF COLD.

Nightingale

Again. Nightingale.

Kaleb reread the poem. Somebody in pain all right. And they were signed simply, *Nightingale*. A pen name, Nightingale? But if Kaleb's own handwriting was any indication of the writer, he was not the author of these verses.

A cursory rifling among additional poems told Kaleb that the collection was of similar tone and script. Whosoever had penned these odes was a person who was intimately familiar with pain. And all of the odes of pain were signed, *Nightingale*.

***

Loss of memory is not loss of appetite and by 6:30 hunger was setting in. Kaleb needed to find an eatery. He knew that his speakeasy, The Temple Bar Speakeasy And Play Nice, The Temp, was due south six or so blocks along Hastings Street and he assumed that he would hit upon a restaurant between his apartment and the speakeasy.

Looking down onto Hastings Street from three stories above, Kaleb studied the people passing below to clue the outfitting for the appropriate apparel of the evening. Even in this poor working class neighborhood, men were in suits and ties, although, because of the paucity of this neighborhood, suits tended toward the threadbare and the frayed.

The street below had the energy of a bubbling river as it cascaded from the day into the evening. A bustling evening's discourse except, that is, for a singular sharp-angled, hatchet-faced man casually leaning against a dusty Model T on the opposite side of Hastings Street. The man was leaning on the T and facing Kaleb's apartment building while sucking on a cigarette. His hat tilted on the back of his skull made the protrusion of his sharply angled cheeks and nose all the more pronounced. The man was dressed in a finely cut navy blue ensemble and the new suit seemed out of place on the working-class streetscape below.

Except for this sharp-faced man, the general custom of street outfit was of a casual suit. So be it. Kaleb grabbed a fresh leather-lined-pocket coat from his closet, locked up the apartment, and descended to the street.

When Kaleb ventured onto the streetscape the smells and sounds were familiar in an ethereal and tactile manner. Only the sharp-faced, sharp-dressed man seemed to have disappeared. But that was befitting as he was out of place in the portraiture of Paradise Valley anyway.

It was exactly six and a half blocks south on Hastings Street to The Temple Bar Speakeasy And Play Nice and there was no restaurant on the way. There was also no spark of recognition in the streetscape. Nothing in the buildings, nothing in the shops, and nothing in the faces to give Kaleb a clue to Kaleb the man. Nothing.

**

The walk down Hastings Street was a revelation for Kaleb. Of sorts. Ethereal like a dream. Like a foghorn in the mist. Like the last train out to Never-Never Land.

The Detroit of 1927 was a city busting at its seams. Everywhere was the clang and clamor of industry and commerce. Pits were being dug for newer and bigger buildings. Girders for these buildings were being raised by the truck full, spider-webbing the sky with iron skeletons. More holes were dug and more girders were raised. Holes and girders. Girders and holes. The city could barely manage the bluster.

In the 1927 Detroit, after an unprecedented run of Model T success, Henry Ford was introducing the newest version of "the people's auto", the Model A. Henry Ford had fought his son, Edsel, tooth and nail to stop the Model A from production but Edsel had prevailed and the Model A went on to save the sinking Ford Corporation. And papa Henry quickly took credit for the Model A.

This 1927 Detroit had a brand new art institute open on Woodward Avenue that would come to rival the best art institutes America could offer. Ground was broken for a number of causes. Pilings were being driven for The Ambassador Bridge, a link between Detroit and Windsor, Canada. Out on 10 Mile Road, The Detroit Zoo was about to welcome a Noah's Ark full of animals.

The rag-tag warehouse district along the Detroit River's wharf found flourishing life as the funnel for Canadian liquor smuggled into a dry, prohibitioned America.

And chief among the noise and the clatter of 1927 Detroit were the factories that were churning out America's hardware, drawing workers from sea to shining sea with the promise of better tomorrows.

Joining the energies that fueled Detroit's financial drive, among the people that shifted the gears and pumped the accelerator of the churning engine that was Detroit, was the music and the music venues of Detroit. The sweaty, pumping force of music and the Detroiters that buttressed the music.

And The Temple Bar Speakeasy And Play Nice was a player in the music's abridgment of 1927 Detroit.

***

As Kaleb Kierka was about to enter The Temple Bar Speakeasy And Play Nice, he remembered the keys in his pocket. The keys he had found in his dressing bureau drawer. The first key he had identified as his apartment key. Now he dug on the key chain and tried keys until he found the one that slid comfortably into The Temps door lock. Spin went the key. Click went the lock.

Two keys down. Three keys left to provide a framework to Kaleb's world. Two house keys and one automobile key remained to ascertain.

If only memory were as easy to unlock as the twisting of a dead bolt.

***

The Temp was accessed through a walkway from Hastings, one storefront up from Gratiot Avenue. It was tucked between a pharmacy and grocers, and if you were not looking for it, you would not see it. Three discrete steps down from street level and a secreted thirty-foot walkway between the buildings, The Temp could not be more inconspicuous. If one were not purposely looking for this blind pig, it would remain very blind.

Even with a compromised memory, Kaleb was little surprised that an illegal operation would be so covert.

***

Before pushing through an unmarked door, Kaleb took stock of himself. This would be an important test.

Humans do not live in a vacuum. A man can only esteem who he is by the impact he has left on those around him. We cannot decide if we are good. We cannot decide if we are bad. And it is not in our judgment to say how we have affected, to the positive or to the negative, the people around us. It is only by the shadow that we cast on others that we can best estimate our value, measure our worth.

And Kaleb Kierka was now about to venture into that evaluation. Taking a deep breath, he pushed through the doors of The Temple Bar Speakeasy And Play Nice.

6

The Temp

A cumbersome moniker, The Temple Bar Speakeasy And Place Nice, was colloquially known simply as The Temp. Indeed, most folks who patronized The Temp did not know the full breath of The Temp's name and ascribed various meanings for the abbreviation. Many assumed that The Temp was labeled such because the booze and the party that was The Temp was such a grand temptation. Others thought the contraction owed to the idea of temporary as in, "I'll be gone Temp for a breather." There were even a goodly number of patrons who felt the name was best suited for temperate as in a place that they might find some moderation in the hectic world.

Whether a time frame, a temptation, or temporary relief against life's suffering, The Temple Bar Speakeasy And Play Nice was a juke joint that accommodated the diversities of lives offered in the Detroit of 1927.

***

There was a gradual turnover of clientele at The Temp as the sun slowly settled rays between the brick of Detroit's skyscape.

Wave after wave of patrons surged through The Temp's doors.

During the day The Temp was mostly empty, playing host to early morning drunks before turning afternoon over to a smattering of night laborers.

In the evenings, the second shift of factory workers gradually migrated into The Temp. Between the factory and home, the workers would come, knocking back quick boilermakers to shake the assembly line noise from their ears and the grit from their clothes. The boilermakers were a capable antidote to numb the throbbing redundancy of the assembly line from under their skin.

The next shift for The Temp, the night shift, usurped the factory staff. As the blue-collar contingent slid from the stools and their boilermakers, the pool hustlers and the hookers took over the barstools, warming up for their particular skills of the night.

The Temp allowed no gambling at the pool table, so the pool hustlers used the place as the batter's box to warm their pool cues for their evening ventures at other venues. And as The Temp permitted no prostitution on the premises, the prostitutes found the speakeasy to be a safe harbor for a fortifying shot of courage before they began their night rounds up and down the hookers' haven of Cass Avenue. The Cass Corridor.

***

The Cass Corridor ran along Cass Avenue where Clifford Street merged with Cass Avenue. This seven-block corridor provided the perfect proximity to the money that flowed through the Grand Circus Park.

Street corners hosted the ladies of the night and the blind pigs hosted the pool hustlers and the money from the Grand Circus Park upscale clubs channeled their way north through the corridor. The prostitutes wanted a piece of this money and the money wanted a piece of the prostitutes. It's all business. Supply and demand.

***

The final shift of The Temp's business began arriving at 11 p.m. or so. These were the revelers seeking temptation. Seeking temporary relief. Seeking a calming distraction against the squall.

The musicians would begin assembling on the stage somewhere between the blue-collar crowd and the gamblers and hookers and by 11 p.m. the collective of the house band, Jazz du Jour, had taken shape. Every night was a different collection of musicians in The Temp. From as small as a trio to as large as a small big band, Jazz du Jour was an ever evolving work in progress, an undulating gathering of miners with their picks and axes bared and ready to dig for another golden vein of jazz. Dig?

As the night played out, more musicians would augment the assembly as they finished their gigs in the uptown venues and sought an opportunity to cut loose. The ever-present Beethoven Jones could be joined by saxophonists or trumpeters or banjo pickers or accordion players. Any musician who wanted a piece of this new medium, this jazz, was welcome to the journey.

***

These late night speakeasies stank of dancing, sweaty bodies and stale beer and reefer and the occasional puke from hard liquor on weak stomachs.

But the salvation offered in these speakeasies overcame the stench of the sweaty bodies and the stale beer and the reefer and the occasional puke from hard liquor on weak stomachs.

Upon reemerging into the world outside of the speakeasies' doors, one could not but note the stink of reality.

7

Holes And Girders. Girders And Holes

When Kaleb stepped through the door of The Temple Bar Speakeasy And Play Nice he was unnoticed and he took those moments to survey the room.

The holes and girders of Kaleb's stroll down Hastings Street were now holes and girders of his memory. More holes than girders.

The atmosphere of The Temp was playing dodgeball with his memory. A toss of recall here, a dodge of recollect there. As Kaleb scanned the room, the dodgeball game of memory whirled. Chuck and duck, chuck and duck went the memories. Chuck and duck.

No memory stuck. None held a girder. Just the empty hole of muddle.

***

It was a double-wide room, probably two separate rooms at one time with the center wall knocked out. To his right was a long wooden bar. Dark wood. Etched but not gaudy and hewed with too many years of spilled drinks and dribbled faces. A couple dozen people were scattered willy-nilly about the room, and to the left rear, on a small riser, was a band rostrum that was hosting a small trio of musicians playing familiar tunes. Too familiar, thought Kierka.

Behind the bar was a skinny old man with a wrinkly puss spinning a beer mug on a bar towel. Fifteen or so barstools lined the old bar with half the stools supporting patrons.

At three of the tables sat couples who were focused on the trio playing on the stage. The three musical comrades were a hodgepodge of humanity. A little white man with a sailors cap was pumping a big accordion and a light skinned mulatto man was tapping the time on a snare drum center stage.

The third person, the focal point of the stage if for no other reason than his size, was a giant of a man, maybe seven feet tall, skinny as a rail and black as coal. With his head bowed to the instrument, he was thumping on a big upright fiddle. The black giant was laying down a bottom groove to the music like he was laying asphalt. Asphalt hot. Asphalt black.

The music was coaxing Kaleb on a level he was not in tune with as the asphalt groove inveigled his fingertips, insinuating the familiar.

***

Like a heartbeat, like a throbbing "tempoed" tick of time, Kaleb felt the rhythm. It was in him and it pulsed through him. It spoke to him in a language of cadence and pace and time and space. Appraised and gauged, qualified and quantified. A signature of time; bar to bar. Measured music. Measured time. Measured space of "rhythmed" rhyme.

***

With attention focused on the trio on the stage, Kaleb was able to survey the room at his leisure and he took his time to do so. This was Kaleb's speakeasy. Kaleb's domain. Memory beckoned from across the rift but only smoke signals. Smokey signals.

The bartender was first to recognize the interloper, and he ceased spinning the beer mug in the bar towel and starred at Kaleb.

A slow wave of silence drew across The Temp, starting from the right, at the bar, to the left, toward the stage, as people stopped talking and drinking and socializing and gawked at the figure framed by the door.

When the wave reached the stage, the musicians, one by one, took their turn petering out and looking towards the door. Towards Kaleb. Lastly, the room was left with just the low hum of the big black man padding on the bass. And then the black giant looked up, looked toward Kaleb, and all fell silent in the room.

The moment of recognition. The instant that one is appreciated for the good or the bad that is the sum of the man. The measure of a man.

When the apex of the shock of Kaleb Kierka's presence was reached in The Temple Bar Speakeasy And Play Nice, the faces in the bar broke. And they broke into grand and opened mouthed humor. Chairs were pushed back, scraping the floor, as people jumped to their feet to welcome Kaleb in all manner of joyful greetings. Back slaps and pumping handshakes, hugs and laughter. Even tears.

***

The Temple Bar Speakeasy And Play Nice was a black-and-tan club, so called for the brave mix of white and black people daring, against custom, often times against the law, to share a common space and a common language.

A space called the black-and-tans. A language called jazz.

Situated on the border of Paradise Valley and the Black Bottom, The Temp straddled the two foremost working-class communities of Detroit. The working black and the working white. These communities were also the two foremost playing-class communities of Detroit. For when the day's light closed its sleepy lids, the nighttime people took to the stage.

Paradise Valley was the safe haven for the poor European immigrant communities while the Black Bottom was the caldron for the Negro communities from all points east and south. They had come, these white and black refugees, from their respective histories of repression, be it Europe or the South, and they were all looking for the promise that was America.

And the confluence of Paradise Valley and the Black Bottom is where the true evolution of America's blue-collar workforce was generated. The workforce that would be the lifeblood of America.

Bestride these black and white communities of working men and women were the enterprises, the shops and depots of a new generation of Americans. And these mercantiles catered to this new generation, serving all manner of folk, the gentle and the brassy, the uptown and the downtown, the black and the white. And this new generation of commerce, these businesses that were blind to color, were the black-and-tans.

The Temple Bar Speakeasy And Play Nice was a black-and-tan speakeasy cum dance hall cum music mixer sitting seductively on the union of Paradise Valley and the Black Bottom.

***

As the bar folk spilled upon him in greeting, something began to choke in Kaleb's cognition. Too much palpable information coming in from too many directions and Kaleb began to feel dizzy. The people, the walls, were closing in.

Bucky, the bartender who had been swabbing the beer glass, recognized the disorientation in Kaleb's eyes and moved to reach him before Kaleb spilled to the floor in a threatening blackout.

***

The reunion in the bar had been awkward. Patrons in the bar had poured from the tables and the barstools, surrounding Kaleb with backslaps and "how-dos" while the band on the stage broke into "Hail To

The Chief." But it quickly became apparent that Kaleb did not recognize these well-wishers and was uncomfortable.

When Bucky caught sight of Kaleb's eyes fading from blue to black, he slid through the circle of patrons and reached him at the same moment as the blackness reached Kaleb. As Kaleb's knees began buckling, Bucky guided him toward the back office, clearing space with his free hand and telling the throng, "'ere, give the boss a little breathing space."

As Bucky guided Kaleb to the back office, he called over his shoulder to one of the patrons who had been sitting on a barstool, "Granma, man the bar for a few while me 'n the boss flap gums in the back." He ushered Kaleb through the well-wishers and into the back office.

Granma, spitting chaw into a pea can spit cup, said to herself, "Goddamnittohellandbackagain," and slid her chubby frame off of the barstool and behind the bar.

As Bucky escorted Kaleb to the office the well-wishers hushed in self-consciousness. Discomforted by Kaleb's apparent relapse, they filed back to their respective drinks and the band let a sad ballad guide their sentiment.

Beethoven Jones unobtrusively slid from behind the bass fiddle and followed the men to the office.

***

As Bucky led Kaleb to the office desk chair, the tall black man who had been wrapped around the bass fiddle slipped through the office door. He sat on a beer crate and leaned his back against the wall. Crossing his legs at the ankles, he let their length splay out into the room.

Kaleb had managed to hold off the headache and the blackout but at the cost of some coherency. The long black man studied Kaleb's face like he was studying a well-read book he had dog-eared for reference points.

Bucky was the first to offer, "It's good to have you back, boss. By the looks of you in the hospital, we weren't holding out no hope."

The office was a large room that doubled as the storeroom. It was filled with a variety of empty and full crates of illegal booze and miscellaneous bar paraphernalia. A small desk with a wheeled desk chair sat behind the desk while a natty green couch and a four-drawer oak filing cabinet completed the room's ensemble.

"You saw me in the hospital?" Kaleb was scrutinizing Bucky, trying to put a memory to this wrinkled old man with the overbite of a can opener.

The genesis of Bucky's nickname was easy to ascertain as the upper palette of Bucky's mouth jutted out like a cliff, pushing his front teeth out of his mouth so far that his lips never managed to fully cover the incisors.

"Sure, boss. We all visited you the first few weeks. Even set up a rotating vigil with some of the barflies from 'ere."

A small and skinny man, Bucky had a conundrum of a face lined with waves of wrinkles. Smile lines pressing into his cheeks wrestled with frown lines grooved deep into his forehead. The frown lines of Bucky's forehead and the smile lines of his cheeks were in a constant dance to shape his face to their bidding. The smile lines and the frown lines played a sort of hop-scotch around the bucked palette.

"A vigil?"

Bucky's face animated as it shifted back and forth between the smile lines and the frown lines.

Utilizing his forehead's frown lines Bucky explained, "Yep. A vigil. For the first few weeks anyhow. 'Til it looked like you might be there for the long haul. Then I decided that the best way to help you was to keep your club up 'n runnin'."

And then Bucky worked on the smile lines, pushing his entire face up at the edges, stretching the bucked palette to its brink. "But 'ere you are now, boss. Back 'ome."

Kaleb turned to the other man who was too long for the room. Too long for any room, quite probably.

Addressing the too-long-for-any-room man he asked, "And you? How do you fit in this operation?"

Bucky jumped in with a flap of wrinkles. "Why Jones, Beethoven Jones, 'ere is your partner, boss. You 'n him own The Temp."

"My partner?"

"Yep. 'N your bass player."

Kaleb studied Beethoven Jones, his frame slackened on the beer crate. "Do you speak Beethoven Jones?"

Bucky started, "Jones ain't one to get involved much, he...." Kaleb cut off Bucky while never taking his eyes off of Beethoven Jones.

"I'm asking Mr. Jones. Mr. Jones, *partner*, do you speak?"

Beethoven Jones had a slow and easy smile and he shared it with Kaleb. It was a smile that warmed and soothed. It was a smile that lay back in the cool shady grass under an old oak tree.

In a warm baritone rumble from under the shade of the old oak tree, Beethoven Jones, smiling, enjoined, "I speak at times. Don' like to get involved much. But I speak. Sure."

"And you are my partner?"

"Sure." The words were few but the smile bespoke plenty. This was a familiar smile to Kaleb. A smile that spoke of a shared history. A good history. And although Kaleb could not lay claim to memory of this shared history, he recognized it as a history of some significance. Of some worth.

Kaleb waited for Jones to continue. When Jones did not continue, "You take this silent partner stuff seriously."

Jones only smiled.

"And we've played music together?"

The baritone smile stretched out on the shady grass beneath the old oak tree and clasped its hands underneath its head. "Sure."

***

Bucky coaxed the conversation by asking. "Little confusing...?"

For Kaleb, Bucky was familiar yet not familiar. Like a déjà vu without the vu.

"So this is my Speak?"

"'Most three years now. Me'n you 'n Jones opened it when you broke up your band."

That, too, had a familiar ring to it. "I've been told that I play music."

"Why, sure. Piano. That's your band on stage."

Kaleb looked down at his hands and spread his fingers. "Piano. I play the piano." Kaleb studied his fingers - elongated and slender - but the amnesia was yet too deep for comprehension.

Bucky was exercising his smile lines around the protruding teeth. "Sure, boss, 'n I'm sure that Jones 'n the boys would like to have you sit in."

Kaleb thought of the three musicians on the stage of the bar. He let the offer pass and it lay there like an old and worn rug on the floor.

"Who was the chub in the navy blue threads? He was sitting at the end of the bar when I walked in."

Bucky thought, trying to recall "The chub?"

Kaleb added, "'Bout 6'2", wide shoulders. Hatchet-type face."

The wrinkle in Bucky's forehead sparked memory. "Right. Big guy. Trim. Too ugly a mug to fit in that pretty suit." And Bucky's wrinkles scanned his memory banks. "Now you mention him, I don't believe I'd ever seen that mug before. He mean something to you?"

Kaleb considered the hatchet-faced man who had slipped out of the back door when he slipped in the front. "Not yet."

Working the worried lines on his forehead, Bucky probed, "You okay, boss? You look whipped."

Now that Bucky mentioned it, Kaleb was feeling played out. "Yep. Tired. Guess I'm still in recovery mode. I need to get a bite and lie down."

"Look 'ere, boss, why don't I have Hollie take you home, and I'll send some food up to your place."

"Hollie?"

"Yep. Hollie. 'Member? He's the bar-swab 'ere "Cleans up the club, sweeps, mops 'n such."

"Sorry. Don't remember h…"

Bucky continued unabated, "Older guy, club foot, clef palette, kinda slow in the thinkin' department? Some call him simple."

Kaleb worked at the recall. Memory was flowing in and going out like the lapping of the water on a lake. A very small lake.

Kaleb worked out a memory. "Cleans the bar after closing 'n sometimes spends nights sleeping in one of the booths?"

Bucky's face lit up and his smile wrinkles stretched to his ears. "That's the boy, boss. You got it."

Tricky thing, these memories. Why would the bar-swab spark recollect and yet his partner, Beethoven Jones, not? This amnesia thing is some problematic business.

As soon as Kaleb had grasped the memory of Hollie, he lost it again. But the memory was there. And momentarily, it was a clear memory.

Bucky persisted, "I'll fix it all up. By the time you get back to your place I'll have kishke on rye waiting for you."

"Kishke on rye?"

"Kishke on rye. With horseradish. And a beer."

Kishke on rye. With horseradish. Kaleb's smile exercised his face in the memory.

"But the boys are gonna be disappointed in you not diggin' into the ivories."

Again Kaleb looked to his hands. "Another time."

"And Nika will be sorry she missed you."

Kaleb looked up to Bucky at the sound of the name. "Nika?

Nika a girl? Someone I should know?"

This time Bucky laughed outright. "Yep. Nika Nightingale. You know 'er all right."

Nightingale. The name caught. Nightingale was the name on the poetry on the table in his apartment.

"Do I know her professionally or socially?

Bucky's smile was to his ears, exposing the full complement of the bucked palette. "Yep."

Kaleb searched his memory for a Nika Nightingale. Nothing.

"Look, boss, you best slip out the back tonight. Avoid the well-wishers. Eat and get some rest. Come by tomorrow and I'll plug some holes for ya."

Holes and girders, girders and holes.

8

Clickety Click. Clickety Click Click Click.

Thought, thinking, deliberation: these were concepts that Kaleb was aware of as the swarm of well-wishers had pushed onto him in greeting at The Temple Bar Speakeasy And Play Nice. Although he might not be a man with access to memory and reflection, he noted that his gray matter was operational. And if he were to negotiate to the future, he would need the gray matter for assessment. He would need to measure each step forward, every connection, with considerable consideration.

The process of thinking, of reasoning, was an instantaneous process with the electrical charges jumping the synaptic gap faster than the speed of light. Wits, then, would be the chance, the tool, for Kaleb's survival.

Lacking the benefit of memory, of history, every step forward must be a considered step. Every contact must be a calculated quantity. Every word needed to be calibrated, and every breath needed to be measured and weighed.

As the unrecognizable throng rushed forward to greet Kaleb in all manner of good humor, Kaleb's brain had worked overtime.

With his brain firing at the speed of light, the darkness began. First a hint of nausea as the room began to spin. His knees became rubbery and he looked about for something near to grasp.

Too late.

***

Black and Blew were under the streetlamp. Blew blew blue while Black chattered away in his cat-yowl drone, flicking his tail like finger snapping to Blew's tune. Clickety click. Clickety click click click snapped Black's tail.

Clickety click went Black's tail. Clickety click click click.

As Blue blew blue, Black droned and yowled, yowled and droned along to the clickety click. Clickety click click click.

"Can one accurately gauge oneself by what others might see in us? By the reflection, bright or dark, of what the outside world will attribute to us.

"Our mothers, our lovers, our enemies and our friends? They have far too much at stake in us to accurately discern the full weight and

estimate the us of us. Their reflection of us can never be trusted as a scrupulous representation of our own id."

Clickety click click click.

"Can we ever be certain of a candid depiction that these exterior visions present? Our mother will likely reflect to us an image of good. Our partner's vision will be more of a belief in our potential. Our children will never come to recognize the human frailty in our cause, and our enemy will never acknowledge our finer attributes."

Clickety click.

"When someone reflects on us in a good light, we feel better about ourselves. But is it a false light? A voyeur's light?

"Conversely, when one is besieged with negative judgment from the external, it will make our ego respond with a protective coat, weighing us down in the process like the knight's maille."

Clickety click click click.

"But should these views from the outside, these exterior views of good and bad, be reckoned into the summation of who we are?

"Are these external visions to be trusted for an accurate representation, or are they a vision more akin to the image in a carnival fun house mirror? A warped mirrored reflection owing less to our id then to the reflectors own collection of distorted light."

Clickety click. Clickety click click click.

All the while Blew was deep within himself, digging into the low end of the saxophone. The horn's refrain drifting from the bell was in Morse code: SOS. SOS:

> *"I listen to the howl,*
> *Of the baying at the moon.*
> *Suddenly somehow,*
> *I've been singing that tune.*
> *But sometimes,*
> *SOMETIMES THE WOLVES ARE SILENT."*

Clickety click. Clickety click click click.

The blackness that had engulfed Kaleb, that had buckled his knees and sent his head swimming, was the domain of Black and Blew. It was a momentary lapse in Kaleb's consciousness, and, unless you were watching Kaleb's eyes, you would never know of the fleeting oblivion that had just passed through his cerebellum.

***

"How long are these blackouts going to last, Doc?" Kaleb had asked in the hospital.

Doctor Stein creased a bow over one eye. "I can't say that I know. I've never heard of them before."

"Whadaya make of 'em?"

The doctor shifted the creased brow to the other side, to the other brow. "I don't know. Your subconscious seems to be having a go of it. Or maybe it's your unconscious. Or maybe your used-to-be conscious trying to break through."

"Subconscious? Unconscious? Used-to-be conscious? That sounds like a bunch of hooey to me."

"Hooey is the best that the medical profession can offer. There's just no book on amnesia. Every case follows its own course. I've read of nightmares before but nothing about dreams with silhouetted cats and horn players reciting poetry through a saxophone."

"What do the dreams mean?"

"Don't know."

"How long will the dreams plague me?"

"Don't know."

"What can I do about them?"

The creased brow waggled back to the other side. "Don't know. But, whatever they are, you are going to have to let them play out."

Kaleb thought about letting these headaches, these blackouts, these nightmares, play out. "I don't mind the sax-man, Blew, blowing poetry so much but that cat Black rambles on and on."

Doctor Stein doubled down on his concern, creasing both eyebrows simultaneously.

***

Stiffly, Kaleb had accepted the warm welcome at The Temple Bar Speakeasy And Play Nice even as he wrestled with fitting this greeting into a definition of the man they called Kaleb Kierka.

There were celebrated words to accompany the mirth, but words were only words. This open-faced glee was gold and it was ubiquitous.

Ubiquitous, that is, except for the singular hatchet-faced man dressed in a fine, navy blue blazer who slipped out the back door of The Temple Bar Speakeasy And Play Nice when Kaleb stepped in.

9

A Wash Of The Familiar

After the back office meeting with Bucky and Jones and so as not to have to run the greeting gauntlet again, Kaleb slipped out the back door of The Temp and into the alley. He stopped a moment to let his eyes adjust to the evening light before walking around to Hastings Street.

Crossing Hastings, Kaleb took a seat on the top step of a building kitty-corner from The Temp to watch the comings and goings of The Temp. He sat on the top step of the porch, in the shadows. He needed time to process.

Sitting on a stoop of wood that jutted out from an old wood frame farmhouse, Kaleb tried to measure the street. To measure his world. The farmhouse was of late 19th century and would not be long of this earth. The structure was of a time when this neighborhood was farmland and the Black Bottom was row after row of corn and the soil was of the richest of black and where this neighborhood got its moniker. A basin of rich black dirt. The Black Bottom.

Kaleb sat on the stoop, sucking on a cigarette and surveying the club, watching the people come and go, studying faces for recognition as the darkening evening light stained the street with creeping shadows.

Pulling the sack of Bull Durham from his breast jacket pocket, he began working up a new smoke. Cupping the paper between two fingers of his left hand, Kaleb dusted the tobacco from the sack into the paper before pulling the string tight with his teeth. He rolled the tobacco unto itself in the paper and licked the edge. A perfect cylindrical roll that he flipped into his mouth and lit with a fingernail flick of a match.

His fingers knew what to do and how to do it. Kinetic memory. Any kind of memory was good memory.

As the evening darkened into night, the hustling bustle of the mercantile subsided and Hastings Street evolved from the day natives to the nation of the night.

The day people were worker bees, men and women with serious faces who drove the city's commerce. Somber people with calloused hands and lined faces supporting families in tiny apartments while

sending any spare pennies back home to support families from
whence they had come. Money to Alabama and to Europe and to
the Appalachians. Detroit was feeding the world.

Conversely, the night nation was a darker breed, wearing their
hat brims tilted lower and their coat collars tucked higher. This
night breed had a quieter step and was not thinking of faraway
shores. These night people were more immediate, walking in the
shadows of the encroaching darkness.

Drawing fume off of the hard sack tobacco of the Bull Durham,
Kaleb's mind wandered. He had lost most of the hitch in his left
step, his eyes were seeing truer, and his kinetic memory for simple
tasks seemed to be recovering exponentially. If only his memory
would catch up. It was like playing a game without knowing the
parameters. Without knowing the rules.

Stepping up from the three-step stoop that led down to The
Temple Bar Speakeasy And Play Nice came a small mulatto
woman. She was dressed for the street, flapper style, her kinky
hair hot-combed and bobbed. Her legs, long and lean, found their
headwaters at her neck before cascading down to her spiked heels.
She wore the prostitute's makeup - too much lipstick and red blush
and eye shadow - her face was a mascara marquee proclaiming a
fun ride on the roller coaster of love.

The stoop that Kaleb sat on was across the street and in the
shadows, so Kaleb used the shroud of the night to study the woman.

The girl tweaked some familiarity for Kaleb as he watched this
little mulatto girl busy her purse for a smoke, and he wondered if
he knew her. And how he might know her? As a friend? Maybe he
is a client of this lady-of-the-night. Was Kaleb that kind of a man?

The street scene in front of the blind pig shuffled past the
young prostitute as the evenings gray surrendered up its last bit
of light to the night. He snubbed out his second smoke, and looked
forward to the kishke sandwich that Bucky had promised to be
waiting for him at his apartment.

Kaleb pushed himself up from the stoop as a man approached
the mulatto girl, and it appeared that negotiations began. He was a
big man, clearing six feet and two-fifty on a light day. Kaleb could
not see the man's face from this angle but the woman's face was
moving side to side in the negative. The big man moved closer to
her, looming over her slender frame while her head picked up the
pace, frantically rebuffing the man's offer.

When the bulk of the man leaned into the girl and grabbed her wrist, twisting at the joint, the woman's face registered first anger and then discomfort. Then her face, looking into the big man's mug, registered fear.

Kaleb was crossing the street on a reflex. Kinetic memory again?

By the time Kaleb had reached the pair, the big yob had twisted the mulatto girl's wrist so that the woman's knees were beginning to coil and buckle.

Kaleb reached the lout just as he was screwing the woman down to the pavement. Grabbing at the oaf's wrist did not make him loosen his grip on the girl. But it did bring the man's head about to look into Kaleb's face. The man had a big block of ugly face and a smile of lecherous larceny. A nose that had had a battlement of scars from doubtless countless combat dominated a mug of mêlée. Angry and determined, the ruffian's face held the same intimidation that the beef of his body promised.

Dismissing Kaleb as he would a pesky mosquito, he sneered, "Shove off, bud, this one's mine."

When Kaleb did not let go of the man's wrist, the man turned his attention forthright to Kaleb while maintaining his grip on the woman's wrist.

"I said shove off, bud. If'n you want a piece of Kitty 'ere, ya kin get in line. An' the line starts behind me." With the thumb of his other fist he flicked in the direction over his back.

With the name "Kitty" came a wash of the familiar. Kaleb could not identify the particulars of the familiar of the name of Kitty, but familiar it was. He turned his attention from the beef and looked into Kitty's face, and somewhere deep in his memory bank, synaptic gaps were leapt to recall. Kitty's face had gone from fear to a sort of wonder as she recognized Kaleb.

"Kaleb?" questioned Kitty. "Kaleb, is that you?"

As Kaleb's brain sputtered memory, the big man let go of Kitty and turned his attention and his body full-front to Kaleb. With a flick of his arm he dislodged Kaleb's grip on this wrist, and with a poke of a fat finger he stabbed Kaleb in the chest. "If'n you're looking for a Charleston, buddy, I'll dance wit' ya."

Ignoring the oaf and looking past the stabbing finger Kaleb said to the woman, "You know me?"

This set Kitty's face on an exploration of all sorts of puzzlement. "Of course I know you! You're…" but she did not have the opportunity to continue as the beef, with his left hand, slapped Kitty's face, while his right hand stabbed his fat forefinger deeper into Kaleb's breast.

With more irritation than fear, Kaleb finally turned his full attention to the big man.

The man's finger raft digging into Kaleb almost collapsed Kaleb's chest and took some wind from his lungs. But Kaleb was surprised that he felt no fear, no panic. In fact, quite the opposite was true. As the lug's angry finger poked into Kaleb's chest, jackhammer-like, a calmness settled over Kaleb. A coolness. Somehow this big man's hostility was familiar territory. A routine affair.

Calmly, Kaleb wrapped his left hand around the prodding digit. With the lug's finger securely locked in his own fist, Kaleb twisted the finger backwards and down, corkscrewing the digit back into the oaf's wrist. It was a quick movement with minimum effort, surprising Kaleb himself, and it brought the ugly lout genuflecting in pain before Kaleb.

Instinctively Kaleb knew that if he relented and released the threatening lug, he would have hell to pay. As the man genuflected before him, Kaleb swung his right arm full force and slammed his elbow into the man's nose, flattening an already battle-tested beak. The boor slumped to the ground and he stayed there.

It was quick and it was clean and it was decisive. Kaleb stood over the unconscious bulk and studied his handiwork. This did not make him feel good. Nor did it make him feel bad. Kaleb felt more of a calmness. A calmness of routine. Of habit? Is this the man that Detective Morane suggested Kaleb Kierka was? A gangster? A hoodlum? A thug? Easy and practiced in the demolition of another man?

Kaleb certainly could give a full account of himself as a combatant, but was this his sum? His end game? Was he more or, god forbid, was he less?

As the thoughts raced to connect this exploit with any history that he might recover, Kaleb remembered Kitty and turned to face her.

But Kitty was gone. Any hopes of enlightenment about his history from Kitty were, at least for now, suspended.

10

Jazz Beckons Kaleb Home

Kaleb took his time walking home from the bar. The confrontation with the oaf and the vague recognition of the prostitute were a nebulous place to start. But they were a start.

As he walked north toward Paradise Valley and, home, Kaleb turned the memory of Kitty and the oaf over in his mind. Violence was a familiar and comfortable backdrop for him. And hookers seemed to be part of his history as well. But it was the image of the casual violence with the brute that was skipping rope on the street corner of his memory. Skipping rope with a hangman's noose.

***

Kaleb walked the streets of his home town, his Detroit, the city where he had spent his youth. These city streets where his mother had raised him. These city streets where he had played stickball. Where he had been educated in the schools and tutored in the alleyways. This cradle of asphalt, this suckle of adolescence.

These streets that were the only streets that he had ever known. And Kaleb was walking these streets for the very first time.

***

They were good to him at the hospital. Nursed him just fine. The scar that ran under his eyebrow had already lost most of its pinkness and was barely visible as it dove under his left eyebrow. And, as far as the slight hitch in his left step, well, Nurse Cathy assured him that he would again be running from the women in short order.

It felt good to walk. It felt good to walk outside. On the street. In the air.

At the hospital they had given him his name and address. His name was Kaleb Kierka and his address was in the Paradise Valley.

The neighborhood became familiar. Familiar, that is, in a vague, déjà vu way. Ethereal. Street names were recognizable but they had no context. Street noises, people in commerce, children playing street-ball, automobiles farting, it was all so familiar. And yet, these somatic connections were lost in a vague limbo.

As Kaleb walked from the Black Bottom up into Paradise Valley, he realized the misnomer of the name. This neighborhood was no paradise.

Gritty and blue-collar, Paradise Valley was more like an overweight, sweating, grunting plumber, wrenching at the piping of an ancient toilet with his ass cleavage hanging out of his trousers. Kaleb took in the streetscape with eyes and ears and touch like one would encounter an old and familiar friend who had gone off to war and came back a changed man. Everything was the same but everything was new again.

The odors were of fruit markets and sewers and Model T's burning rubber and cheap perfume masking bad hygiene and street urchins popping Bazooka Joe Bubblegum and strollers filled with dirty diapers and cheap whiskey and sweet pickles.

All of the street odors were there, in a bouquet of the living.

The sound as well, the sounds inundated Kaleb's senses like the weight of gravity.

A radio from a second-floor apartment, screeching tires, babies crying, mothers scolding, screaming street stickball, cursing motorists, and all manner of commerce from the grocers to the clock shops to the plumbers to the bakers. Voices of greetings and curses and exclamations and whining and all in languages both familiar and foreign.

Paradise Valley was Detroit's port entry for all manner of men and tongue.

Detroit was in its heyday as an industrial magnate, and workers of every bent, domestic and foreign, landed on these streets. The shards of domestic English; Appalachian, Irish, Bronx, Southern and Midwestern were bumping and tumbling with the broken English languages of Polish and Italian and Jewish and Ukrainian and Greek and Armenian. A hodgepodge of vernacular.

But the language that united these tongues of every language and every hue was the language of a hard day's work. These were men looking for a way up from the poverty from whence they came, domestic or foreign, and they were willing to put their backs and their blood into the chance of a more secure future for their families. And Detroit offered them that prospect.

And everywhere Kaleb heard music. Music poured from every cubbyhole of the streetscape. Music from the shops and music from the apartments and music on the street corners. The streets oozed music. Or could it be that the music is what Kaleb was most attuned to?

Imposing itself onto Kaleb's consciousness, every step seemed to bring another variation of song. Music had found its way from every corner of the planet as it piggybacked onto this contingent from the men and women flooding Detroit's streets. An Italian opera from a back-alley flat. A folksy plucked guitar from some wandering troubadour. A student's awkward scale plunked over and over on an out-of-tune piano from the window of a four-story walkup. A brassy trumpet in the wind. An accordion running button-bass lines. Every step into Paradise Valley offered Kaleb an ethnic opus of sound.

But the tuneful sounds that most imposed itself onto Kaleb's consciousness were the sounds of a wild and magical rhythm. Kaleb searched his memory for the name of the rhythm. Something new. Something vibrant. And something a little bit scary.

This was a new sound and it seemed to come from everywhere and nowhere. From fingers and throats and perspiration. It was honest and it was real and it spoke in a voice that was vital and pressing. Beseeching and earnest.

Kaleb searched his memory for the identification of this new music, and as he rummaged his memory, his fingers began to animate. The digits were dancing to the rhythm. Kaleb's fingers were trying to tell Kaleb something.

Jazz.

Like a bolt of lightning, the word jazz sparked Kaleb. It was jazz music that was bending Kaleb's ear. This was the first piece of information that Kaleb had somehow collected on his own since his reconstituted consciousness. The first piece of evidence that Kaleb had of self. Of identity.

Jazz was a part of Kaleb. But what part? What context did jazz have in Kaleb's life?

From Detective Morane Kaleb had learned that Kaleb was half-Jewish, a speakeasy proprietor, a piano player, and a probable gangster. But that was information that he was given. Jazz was the first piece of information that he had collected on his own volition.

***

Bucky was good to his word. The kishke sandwich and the beer were waiting on Kaleb's apartment stoop when he returned home. The smell of the kishke mingled with the apartment hallway and triggered an ambient memory. A tactile memory that eluded intellectual scrutiny even as it prickled the hairs on his neck. Scooping up the provisions, he climbed the three flights of stairs. Even the creak of the steps sounded familiar as he climbed. He could almost predict the stairs that would object to his step. Almost.

At the apartment, Kaleb turned the door handle and entered the apartment. Again. And for the very first time.

11

I've Been In The Flame

The sandwich was good. The beer better. Taste held a recall superior to his cranium. The kishke sandwich was good in the way that the familiar is always good. Satisfying. Taste is the place where the tactile senses and the olfactory senses pull together as a team to offer a distinct encounter with matter. Kaleb savored the savory and relished the relish.

After cleaning up the dishes, Kaleb went into the bedroom to lie down. There were a stack of books on the nightstand beside the bed and he scanned the titles. Pulp fiction and Westerns mostly, with a smattering of classics. Flaubert's *Madame Bovary*. Twain and Poe were represented. Kaleb flipped through the books, taking careful measure of the entertainment that Kaleb Kierka employed.

The top most book, *The Sun Also Rises*, was splayed open. Hemingway. Kierka could not remember the name. Published 1926. A newer writer. He turned the book and leafed through it. Punching the pillow to crop his head, he lay back and turned to a dog-eared page.

With the nourishment of the sandwich and beer came drowsiness. His body was yet recovering from the atrophy of the hospitalization and the rations were beckoning rest. Stretching out on the bed, Kaleb quickly fell to slumber.

In tussled sleep Kaleb had fits of dreams that he could not put an identity to. Dreams that he could not associate with his consciousness. If dreams are our psyche's endeavor to process information, a filing system for all of the information our senses have collected during the waking hours, what then if the filing cabinet has been damaged? If the lock is broken and the key is lost?

Tossing and turning in half wakened spasms, Kaleb's dreams wrestled with his meager collection of memories. Memories that had begun as recently as his awakening from the coma. From the comatose.

Kaleb had nary a key for the filing cabinet.

***

Clickety click. Clickety click click click, went Black's tail as he bent his ear to Blew's dirge.

Black was at the very edge of the streetlamp's glow, looking out into the darkness, out into the vagueness of Kaleb's consciousness. But he could see nothing there.

"I'll be a son of a gun," Black mused to the darkness beyond the streetlamp's glow. "…Is man nothing more than a smattering collection of memories? Of what came before? Is the future that we make solely contingent on whatever our personal history came before? And if no history, no man?"

Blew stopped blowing momentarily, looking from Black to the blackness beyond and back to Black again. Back to Black again.

Black continued to muse. "Are our fears built on our failures? Is our nerve constructed on our successes? Can our inner drummer only march to the beat of the rhythms of the familiar? Can one's pulse never throb in an improvised rhythm?"

***

The incident with Kitty and the oaf suggested that Kaleb was no stranger to danger. The confrontation did not alarm him. Rather, it served to calm him. It felt natural. But isn't fear a survival mechanism? And without knowing fear, does one not know one's limits?

Some suggest that plants feel physical pain. But physical pain is an evolutionary consequence of fight or flight. When a hand is burned by the flame, the hand instinctively withdraws. Flight, then, is the result of fleeing from the pain. But a tree cannot flee, and so it would be an evolutionary dead end for a tree to feel the flame of fire. There would be no purpose for pain to an entity that cannot flee.

But what about an emotional flame? What scars to the psyche from poverty? What blemish when one is raised in glut?

A history of fitness and vigor can command a much different outlook than a personal history of illness and disease. The loss of loved ones at a young age? Being bullied? These would contribute to the calculation of one's prospects. Of one's instincts of fight or flight?

And are these designs, poverty or glut, healthy or sickly? Are these then the collection of our history, and is our history the blue print for our future?

***

Clickety click snapped Black. "What does one make of Kaleb's calmness in the face of danger? What history does this suggest? What fight or flight trigger does it portend? What flame is this fight trigger responding to?"

Clickety click. Clickety click click click.

Blew blew blue:

I'VE BEEN IN THE FLAME

1.
I've worked in the warehouse of broken down dreams,
With row after row of what might have been.
But I never lost touch, I never lost faith,
'Cause I HAVE BEEN IN THE FLOOD,
AND I HAVE BEEN IN THE FLAME.

2.
I've bloodied my fingers on broken dream shards,
Working for ringers blowing smoke from cigars.
I've lost so much blood but I never lost face,
'Cause I HAVE BEEN IN THE FLOOD,
AND I HAVE BEEN IN THE FLAME.

3.
I've lived out some nightmares, I've lived without hope,
But the lowest I've been I've been able to cope
'Cause when push comes to shove, I come to play,
And I HAVE BEEN IN THE FLOOD,
AND I HAVE BEEN IN THE FLAME.
I'VE BEEN IN THE FLAME
I'VE BEEN IN THE FLAME.

***

Kaleb had no history, no blue print that he could put memory to. What criterion could Kaleb evaluate to design a forward direction? Without memoir, wherefore the pain and wherefore the flame?

Without a personal history of torched fingertips, wherefore the triggers of fight or flight?

Adolescence is nothing more than a series of reaching out to the flames and getting burned. A man without the benefit of these flames, these lessons, is a man without wherewithal. *Wherewithalless.*

Kaleb fell asleep wondering how capable he would be to meet the flame.

12

Another Round Of Coffee Grounds

Wakening, Kaleb had a splitting headache; the bedroom light was dark. A dim light from the kitchen seeped into the bedroom and he managed to crawl from the bed without skinning his shins on the unfamiliar furniture.

Kaleb felt better. Stronger. The hitch in his left leg had subsided to a barely perceptible draw, and the scar under his left eyelid had lost much of its pink shine. The general muscle atrophy receded with every step.

According to the watch he strapped on, it was almost 11:30 at night. He had strapped the watch on his left wrist and it felt comfortable there. Right-handed. Confirmation. A meager start but a start nonetheless. The smallest of clue for a man without a memory. Scant evidence, indeed, but until Kaleb was able to fit all of the pieces of his life together, no clue would be insignificant.

The coffee preparation felt natural this time, and as he waited for the pot to bubble, he walked to the living room bay window, summing Hastings Street three stories below. Although it was late, Hastings Street had much bustle left in it. The mercantile shops were closed, and the streetscape below offered a different sort of folk shuffling to and fro. Fro and to. The night people.

Taking special note, there was no hatchet-faced man with a navy blue suit in the street scene below his window.

The coffee pot screamed and Kaleb busied himself with the pot and the cup, taking some small measure of comfort in the familiar habit.

The steam of the coffee watered Kaleb's eyes as he lifted it to his lips. Sitting at the small writing table, he flipped through a few more pages of the rhyming cursive. One that caught his attention, in a sloppier scrawl, a drunken or drug-induced scrawl, was a poem that tapped him on the shoulder and whispered covert messages into this dark and solitary night high above 1927 Detroit.

SOMEONE LIKE YOU

1.
I can't believe this,
Feeling I'm feeling for someone like you.
Lost in the deepest,
Gloom and despair then there's someone like you.
Someone like you,
Someone to answer for me.
Someone like you,
A midnight dancer for me.
SOMEONE LIKE YOU.

2.
I thank the moonglow,
And I thank the summer for someone like you.
I sing this tune though,
There's nothing to sing without someone like you.
Someone like you,
Someone to listen to me.
Someone like you,
With vision to see through me.
SOMEONE LIKE YOU.

Nightingale

In secret and hushed tones the poem whispered into Kaleb's ear. Tones of a lover sharing furtive fears in the darkness of shared somnambulism. Tones of an intimate, a lover and a friend.

Setting down the poetry, Kaleb pulled the coffee again to his lips. Nightingale. Bucky had mentioned Nightingale. Nika Nightingale. Kaleb was told that Nika was his cuddle. His gal.

But the tangible memory of Nika Nightingale remained elusive to Kaleb.

Who the hell was Nightingale, and why the hell was her poetry busying up his desk?

***

Having gotten the coffee's equation right, Kaleb's headache waned. In the bathroom, he splashed water on his face and again studied the lines in the skin. He decided that although not classically handsome, he had a soft and attractive cut of façade. Wavy black hair, too long for the cut of the day. The high-brow musician cut.

The curliness of his locks kept the hair from falling onto the high-brow with a mid-nose catch, befitting his Jewish ancestry. The blue eyes were slightly offset, with the right eye seeming to have another target of focus. The scar diving beneath his eyelid had lost most of its pinkness and was beginning to settle into the warm toned flesh of his face.

In the closet he found a casual suit and size 10 shoes. The suit was a little loose in the corners, a consequence of the month of his body's atrophy. He surmised that he was just shy of 6 feet and somewhere in the neighborhood of 155 pounds. When he regained his fighting weight he would fill out this suit at a lean 170. Maybe. Although the body was mending well, the amnesia hung fast.

Hastings Street below Kaleb's window was darkened by the shadows of the night. The clock read 1 a.m., a natural awake hour for a piano playing owner of a speakeasy. A small piece of evidence but corroboration of the man he was reputed to be.

The street was quarter-moon lit with the occasional streetlamp aglow. The night's darkness encroached between the streetlamp's glow, sagging from lamp to lamp.

Coffee fixings and rolling a smoke from the Bull Durham bag were now part of Kaleb's kinetic memory, and he stood with coffee and cigarette in hand, overlooking the blackness of Hastings Street. He could not see The Temp, six blocks south of this perch, but he could feel the pull. Like a magnet. Like a homing pigeon to its home roost.

Kaleb felt an intuitive draw to The Temp but he could not pinpoint the reason. He was told that he owned The Temp but, why? Even so, it was an innate magnetism, and if he were to uncover his history, he would need to follow the lure. He needed to trace his steps as if he were standing on the outside of his life and viewing it as a voyeur. From the outside looking in.

Putting on a fresh jacket, again with leather-lined pockets, Kaleb slipped from his apartment and into the darkness of Detroit's lower east side.

13

The Black-And-Tans:
Hues, Views And Attitudes

Down on the street Kaleb headed south to The Temple Bar Speakeasy And Play Nice. Cloaked in the night he felt just about right. He was a night person. Another small clue to the man who was Kaleb Kierka.

Within half a block of the speakeasy Kaleb could hear the music straining against the closed doors of the bar. It gathered a muffled trumpeting as it pulsed through the passageway between the buildings and sneaked out onto Hastings Street.

It was a primitive music. It was a raw music. It was a music that seared the ear with yesterday's grief and tomorrow's hopes. It was a music that cried with laughter and laughed with tears.

It was jazz.

***

The beat.

Kaleb could feel the beat in his blood. In his pulse. The rhythm surged outward from his aorta through his arteries and spilled back through his veins. A tempo'ed pace, the blood-beat flowed to his furthermost extremities, to the very tips of his finger capillaries.

Looking to his hands, to his fingertips, Kaleb wondered at the sensation. Was this beat that coursed through his body - this rhythm of blood, this drumming in his bones - was this, then, the calculation of his value? Was Kaleb's worth tallied in the quality of the cadence? In the tap of the tempo? In the measure of the time?

In the measure of time.

***

Outside the doors of The Temple Bar Speakeasy And Play Nice Kaleb hesitated, listening to the thumping engine of the rhythm. Although he could not recover the tune's name, Kaleb knew the tune and was one with the pulse.

Lost in the rhythm, in the groove, Kaleb was surprised when someone slipped her hand under his arm and voiced, "Hey baby, is that really you?"

At the corner of Hastings and Gratiot a middle-aged mulatto woman was pacing her corner. Her office. Her place of business.

She offered Kaleb a full-lipped smile and tenderly slipped her hand into the crux of his arm. It was the mulatto woman from earlier. The painted street hooker. The woman who had slipped off into the night when Kaleb had brought her bully tormentor to his knees.

He studied the painted brown face, looking for sign, for recognition, for anything that might connect him to whom she was. To whom he might be.

Memory caught. And stuck. "You're the lady that was muscled by the beef, no?"

She smiled at that and the tone of her skin, cream chocolate, heavy on the cream, gave her smile a golden glow. "That was me, yes."

"Why did you run from me?"

She registered surprise and then confusion. "Not from you, Kaleb. *Never* from you, Kaleb. I had to fade 'cause I couldn't take no gamble on the badge showin'. It'd be my third run-in this year. 'N Judge Samuels don't take that real lightly like."

With understanding, her demeanor changed to a warmer brown. "Last time I seen you in the hospital you was lights-out, baby. Gone in goonesville." She smiled and her face lit into a warm, brown glow. "Can't say I cared for the beard much you was growin' in the hospital. Kinda hid that baby face." When Kaleb did not respond, she troubled her brow. "I'd heard that beatin' left you brain-crippled. You don't remember me, baby?"

Kaleb, embarrassed and confused, stammered, "I, I'm sorry. I can't reca..."

With her free hand, Kitty cuffed Kaleb playfully on the shoulder. "Don't you worry none 'bout that. My name is Kitty and we, me 'n you, we are the best of buddies."

Kaleb reviewed this pretty brown lady clutching fast to his arm. The low-cut dress, high heels and over-caked makeup could not disguise her age. The cut of her cloth belied her profession. The uniform of the street. Of the ladies of the night.

Trying to calculate his relationship with this woman, Kaleb Kierka, gingerly explored "We are, um, that is, you 'n me..."

But Kitty was kind and finished his thoughts. "No, silly boy, you are not my john." and an ever-so-slight pink blush played under her chocolate cream complexion. "Although, lord knows, I've tried. I've tried. But you 'n me, we are just the bestest of buds."

Guiding Kaleb to the speakeasy's door, Kitty said, "Com'on, let's go in and raise schnapps."

With that, Kaleb, under the tow of Kitty, entered The Temp for the second time since he left the hospital.

Kaleb allowed himself to be led into the speakeasy, into the soundtrack of a 1920s America.

Jazz. Kaleb entered a world that he had spent his entire life. For the very first time.

***

The band was pumping and The Temple Bar Speakeasy And Play Nice was rollicking.

Bucky was behind the bar flinging beers and highballs of Canadian 7 Crown and Vernors Ginger Ale. Granma was on her center stool trying to follow a Tigers game above the baying of the club noise, and the joint was filled to its shoulders with the multi-hued colors of the people of the city, dancing and playing pool and arguing about the Tigers. The general mayhem of an underground bash.

***

Beethoven Jones was the singular constant with the bands that cycled through the doors of The Temp. Tonight it was Jazz du Jour with August Pini on the keyboards and Billy Oldham on drums. Leon Barwood was sucking the saxophone and Jazz du Jour be rhythm burning.

Locking down the center of the ensemble, Beethoven Jones was wrapping his long black fingers around the bass fret board and tap tap tapping out the rhythms with two digits of his right hand. His body cuddled into the big bass fiddle like a lover as he caressed sweet sighs from the instrument's body.

Jazz du Jour was a quartet for the ages. A collective of diverse experience that came together to explore the canal to this new sea called jazz. And Beethoven Jones's groove was the wave that Jazz du Jour surfed upon in these uncharted waters.

Kaleb and Jones had resolved that The Temple Bar Speakeasy And Play Nice would be black-and-tan.

And Jazz du Jour reflected this assortment of tribes.

***

The black-and-tan venues were exactly what the name suggested. These were the cabarets, theatres, restaurants, and blind pigs that catered to the black and the white clientele alike. Whereas most of America, and much of Detroit, was yet suffering through a racism of color and an elitism of money, the blue-collar ghettos of America were creating a new point of view.

In neighborhoods like the Black Bottom and Paradise Valley, where the southern black refugee was rubbing shoulders with the eastern European refugee, color was mitigated by poverty. A community bonded in hunger.

But black-and-tans were not ubiquitous. The mixing and milling of races was frowned on in most quarters of 1927 Detroit. Uptown clubs stayed white and the Black Bottom clubs stayed black. But the black-and-tans were another matter. Peopled by folks of mixed and mixing bloods, the black-and-tans offered respite from the racism of a 1927 America.

And the music of these black-and-tans bubbled with a new breed of musician and a new breed of music. Jazz.

Hunger will always recognize hunger and these neighboring communities of poor white men and poor black men were hungry for a new vision, a new conduit, and a new definition of community. The black-and-tans offered a fresh and exciting channel for America and jazz gave it a voice.

The black-and-tans: hues, views, and attitudes.

The Temple Bar Speakeasy And Play Nice, situated as it was on the neighborhood junction of Paradise Valley and the Black Bottom, was in a prime location for a black-and-tan establishment. And The Temp offered the channel.

Detroit's progenitors of jazz from the uptown white bands like the Graystone Orchestra and the Book-Cadillac Orchestra mixed with the colored bands represented by such ensembles as McKinney's Cotton Pickers, Billy Miner's Melodeons, and The Chocolate Dandies, and they converged in this black-and-tan. They had common ground, a common language, and Kaleb's bar offered the channel. The sharing of divergent musical licks and tricks was at the heart of jazz music.

The vaudevillian venues cycled fresh blood throughout America and The Temp was always ready for a late night transfusion.

***

August Pini, an Italian Jew, was a classically trained pianist who made a decent living with The Detroit Symphony. The drummer, Billy Oldham, was a good ol' hillbilly boy who tumbled out of the Appalachian Mountains to sling nuts and bolts in Ford's River Rouge plant. And Leon Barwood, well, you couldn't exactly tell what race Leon belonged to. Leon could have been a kinky-haired Greek boy, or he could have been a light-skinned black boy; or by the way he made that saxophone take flight, he could have just stepped off of a space ship.

Then there was Beethoven Jones. There was very little mixing of the races in Jones's heritage. Long and black as a mid-winter's night, Jones's groove was the constant that locked down the stage at The Temple Bar Speakeasy And Play Nice.

Any given night was a new world for Jones. Beethoven Jones would play with the country western swingers who came through town from Texas. He played with the southern colored folk fresh off the plantation fields, and he played with the Gypsy bands with their strange Balkan stringed instruments and exotic modal meanderings. Beethoven Jones could and would play with any and all comers of music. Even Krikor, the little Armenian accordion player with the syncopated Mediterranean rhythms, found a brethren in the bass fiddle of Beethoven Jones.

But as solid a lock down as Jones delivered in the groove, his bass solos were tapping into a realm deep into his African ancestry. Beethoven Jones would build his bass solos with the skill of a Don Juan making love to the music. Like panting lovers in the troughs of passion, Jones gently enticed the music out of the bass. Tenderly at first, he would lovingly coax the bass in its lower registers, slowly tempting sweet murmurs from it crevasses. As the passion of the music swelled, Jones quickened his touch, skimming his long black fingers across the neck faster and higher until finally the bass exploded in a crazed orgasm of sound and fury.

Jones was one with the bass and the bass was one with the band and the band was one with the club and all was right with the universe.

Tonight, Jazz du Jour was pumpin' 'n thumpin' and the joint was partying like the Devil on a weekend furlough.

14

Catgut Your Tongue?

The music spilled from the stage and the multi-hued dancers swirled on the dance floor to a tribal beat. The men and women, black folk and Jews, and Poles and Germans, pulsed like blood. Blood in an artery of a commune of the spirit splashed on the dance floor of The Temp.

The band was mid-gospel and the dancers were in a jazz frenzy when Kaleb and Kitty pushed through the doors of The Temp. Just another mixed-race couple coming through just another door in just another black-and-tan.

A quick scan of the speakeasy brought Kaleb to the stage where he became transfixed on the music and with the musicians on the stage. Kitty saw this and, holding fast to his arm, guided him to one of the few tables that did not have drinks waiting for their respective dancers to return.

Kaleb recognized Beethoven Jones on the double bass from his earlier visit. Jones was now joined on stage by a hodgepodge collection of multi-hued musicians. A white trumpeter, a black drummer, a white accordionist, a mulatto sax-man and a trombone player who Kaleb could not discern from a dark Italian or a light-skinned black man. The upright piano sat empty, pushed tight, stage left.

Parking Kaleb at the table, Kitty went to the bar and returned with a beer for Kaleb and a peppermint schnapps for herself. As for Kaleb, he was transfixed on the music and did not notice Kitty's departure nor her return. When the song stopped, Kaleb saw the beer in front of him on the table and smiled at Kitty.

"Thanks," exercising his atrophied smile muscles. "I'm guessin' I like beer." In the dim light of the speakeasy he studied Kitty anew. Her features played petite, small nose, more Caucasoid than Negroid, with cheeks almost too delicate to support the weight of the hooker's thick mascara. From what Kaleb could discern from the exposed skin, and there was plenty of that in her hootchie-girl attire, Kitty's soft brown tone played consistent over her body.

Kitty, in turn, appraised Kaleb. "That's a pretty little scar you collected."

Kaleb touched the mark just under his left eyebrow. "Like it? I'm thinking 'bout getting a matching set for over the other eye."

Kitty's smile pushed out the caked mascara, cracking at the outermost reaches of her smile lines. "Bad humor's intact."

The music whirled into a crescendo and came crashing down to a pulsing finale with a cascading drum roll that led into the final smack of the full band leaving the dancers in mid-gasp. Clapping as they caught their breath, the dancers began shuffling back to their tables from the dance floor, and Kaleb was beginning to be noticed.

Head nods of "How do." and "Welcome back." visited Kaleb and Kitty's table. But this time it was more reserved, careful to not intrude on their space. Many in the procession of well-wishers asked Kaleb if he would be sitting in with the band tonight, "Ticklin' keys?"

Kaleb, embarrassed, said, "No, not tonight." He had gotten the gist that he was a piano player, but he couldn't remember ever touching the apparatus and doubted if he would know what to do with the beast if he sat down to it.

When the well-wishing subsided, Kaleb turned to Kitty. "So, I guess I'm some kind of a musician, eh?"

Kitty laughed, again caking the mascara to the edge of her smile lines. Then she noted that Kaleb was not kidding. "You really got that amnesia thing bad, boy, huh?"

By now Bucky had a break at the bar and he came over to Kaleb's table. "Nice seein' ya, boss. You sure you ain't pressing your mendin'?"

Kaleb ignored the question and nodded towards the bar. "Looks to be a good crowd tonight."

Bucky surveyed the room. "Yep, pretty solid Friday."

So it was a Friday night.

Kitty said to Bucky, "Our boy 'ere don't 'member that he play piano."

Bucky studied Kaleb and frowned. "Is 'at right, boss? You don't even know you paint the keys?"

Kaleb was embarrassed to not know who he was, absently he stroked the new scar over his eye. Stroking the scar was becoming a new tick in Kaleb's deportment. "Popular consensus seems to make me a piano player."

Bucky snarked, "I'd say you is. Jazz, big dog, jazz."

It's an odd circumstance and a humbling experience when others know more about you than you know about yourself. Or maybe that's how it always is. We just don't recognize that to be the case. Kaleb was slowly learning who he was from those who knew him better. From the outside looking in.

Kaleb looked down at his hands and, rolled them back and forth. "I was good?"

Kitty and Bucky snarked together this time. It was Bucky that offered, "Boss, that's your band up there."

***

It was break time and the band began their slow mosey from the stage; They followed the well-wishers across the dance floor to Kaleb's table with "Welcome back." and "Come on and sit in with the band." Awkwardly, Kaleb demurred and offered, "Another time."

Only the long black man wrapped around the bass fiddle held tight to the stage, plucking at notes while tuning up the instrument.

Kitty noticed Kaleb studying Beethoven Jones and said, "You best go say 'hey' to your partner."

"Don't want to bother him."

Kitty eased her grin down but a trace of mascara remained at the edge of her smile. "Bother 'im? You 'n 'im is grown up together, same 'hood, same Bishop High School, and you two started you music careers together. Playin' boy duo."

"How come he don't come say 'hey'?

Kitty shook her head, "Boy, you got a lot of catchin' up to do. Jones don't say nothin'. Don't get involved with nothin'."

"Nothing?"

"Nothin'."

"Okay then." and Kaleb gave a little more weight to his study of Jones. "...Be right back." And he pushed off from the table.

As he approached the stage, Beethoven Jones looked up from his bass and gave Kaleb a tentative smile.

Kaleb began, "So, Beethoven...."

"Jones." Not looking up, Jones corrected. "Jes Jones."

Kaleb thought this over. "Okay, then. Jones. Partner. I hear we're best bud's, huh?"

Jones twisted at the bass tuning peg. "Suppose so."

"And you don't come say 'hey'."

Jones stretched the catgut strings into pitch. "You really don't 'member?"

"Not a lick."

Screwing the string into pitch Jones answered, "If 'n you don't remember me, then how kin I trust you with our link?"

Kaleb listened for a moment. "Your D string's flat."

Jones twisted the D string into pitch, and without looking up at Kaleb asked, "If you ain't got no who's who, how you know it's a D string?"

This thought stumped Kaleb and he absently reached to stroke his eyebrow. He just didn't know. When Kaleb failed to answer, Jones continued, "You ain't got no memory until you do. Is you is or is you ain't got recollect?"

Kaleb did not know the answer. He was as perplexed about how amnesia works as Jones was. As the doctors were. Nobody knew. There was just no good rhyme or reason to when a memory would pop up. "You don' trust me with our link? Our association? What does that mean?"

"I jes don't get involved."

"Yes. That's the legend alright." Kaleb, referencing Jones's quietness, nodded at the bass strings. "Catgut your tongue?"

That broke Jones's face into a smile. "Sure, catgut my tongue. Ha."

Again Kaleb nodded at the bass and said, "Now you've tuned too high."

Onto the next string, Beethoven Jones twisted the tuning pegs, stretching the catguts into pitch. "I 'spected you'd come up when you was good and ready. I guess you're good and ready."

"That the best you can do?"

Jones quit tuning the bass, gave Kaleb full consideration, and then made a grandiose head bow. "Sure Massa, it sure be good to see you back on the plantation, Massa. Missed you. Love you. Sometin' like that?"

Kaleb chortled, "Sure, that's pretty good. All warm and fuzzy like."

And they stopped right there for a moment, esteeming their connection. Kaleb stroked his eyebrow. "Coulda said hello."

"I just did."

The two men looked at each other, face into face. Beethoven Jones studied with memory. Kaleb Kierka studied for memory.

Kaleb said, "D string is still flat," and turned back to his table.

Jones spoke to Kaleb's back as he was walking away. "Hey K…" and Kaleb turned back toward the stage. "Welcome home, boy."

Kaleb hesitated a moment and turned to face Jones. "Thanks, man."

"When you ready, that box be waitin' for you." With a tip of his head, Jones indicated the piano.

Kaleb looked at the piano and then he looked back at Beethoven Jones. "Sure."

Jones extended an open hand. Kaleb looked at the hand and then gave it a back hand tap, knuckle to knuckle, in the manner of the Black Bottom. Kinetic memory?

"Thanks, man... " Kaleb nodded to Jones. "...But the D string's still flat." And he returned to Kitty and to his beer.

15

Chug Chugging Into The Future

Kaleb sat transfixed on Jazz du Jour, deep in study of the modes, of the fashion, of the groove, of this music called jazz. He was so transfixed by music that while Kitty was working on her third schnapps, Kaleb had barely managed half of his first beer. After a time, as the band wound through its last tune of the set, Kitty again took Kaleb by the arm and rose to escort him out of the club.

"We don't want you swamped with well-wishers, 'gain. Let's amble a bit."

Kitty knocked back her schnapps and Kaleb left half of his beer on the table and together they left for the nightscape of the city.

***

With the rise of the industrial revolution, Detroit had developed an ambient hum. A hum that aurally delineated the borders of the city from the country as keenly as the streetlamps delineated the starlight.

Although Detroit's hum quieted with the oncoming night, the low drone was omnipresent. It was a background rhythm of factories and electric lines and traffic and the bustle of bodies. A constant backdrop of trucks coughing smoke and streetcars screeching to stops and police cars whining alarm and always the factories, purring in a soft undertone. The hectic chatter of a city in progress. A city chug-chugging into the future.

***

Kaleb put his arm around Kitty's shoulder. "Where do you live, I'll walk you."

Kitty smiled at this innocence. "'Course I live in the Black Bottom but soldier..." and she held her small chocolate hand to Kaleb's cheek, "...I've yet got a good piece of work to do tonight. I'm a working gal, you know"

Again Kaleb took note of the hooker's uniform and shared a flush. "Right. Sorry." They were walking east toward the Cass Corridor and the red light district.

Kitty was kind and changed the subject. "When you going over to see Nika?"

"Nika?"

"Yeah. Nika. Nika Nightingale. Your flame. Your gal. The woman you flip-city for."

Nightingale was the name on the poems on the table in his apartment. Apparently, Nika was the name that went with Nightingale. Nika Nightingale.

The name Nika sparked something in Kaleb but he wasn't sure where to tender the flame.

"You don't recall Nika?"

Kaleb reacted with his new tic, tugging at the eyebrow and newly acquired scar, and Kitty laughed at him and punched his arm. "You don' remember Nika? Ha! Maybe now's my opportune ta make my move on you."

Embarrassment? Anger? Resentment? What is the proper reaction when the world knows more about you than you know about yourself? Kaleb went with embarrassment.

"Kit, whyn't anyone visit me at the hospital?"

Kitty stopped their stroll and turned, facing him straight on, searching his face for recognition. Some way to get through. To be on familiar terms.

Taking hold of his hands she said, "Lookit 'ere Kaleb, git that silly notion out of your head right now. That first week you was in the hospital your friends, me 'n Bucky an' Nika, and the band 'n others, we all kept a 24-hour vigil at your bedside. You never stirred a finger. The second week, same vigil 'n same result. We cut it back to daylight long visits. By the fourth week, it became plain that you were into that coma for the long haul. That coma, boy, that coma jes wore us plum out. They said you might never be back. The hospital, the doc, the nurses, they was gonna tell us of any signs of improvement and...."

"And?"

"And the notice never come."

Kaleb thought that through, smoothed the scar, and then changed the subject. "Tell me about Nika."

Amusement was back in Kitty's voice and she tucked her arm back under Kaleb's elbow as they resumed their stroll towards the Cass Corridor. "Like I say, Nika is your flame. Your special squeeze. Your go-to gal."

Fitting pieces together, Kaleb knew now that the poetry on the table in his apartment, the poetry signed only "Nightingale" was that of this woman, Nika. Nika Nightingale.

Kaleb was desperate to reconnect with who he was and this would be a big piece of that reconnect. "Where can I find her?"

"Her and me share a 'partment over on Sherman jes cross Gratiot."

"Share an apartment? Is Nika...?" but he couldn't collect the appropriate terminology to not offend Kitty.

And Kitty was going to have some fun with this. "Is she what?"

"You know, is she, is sh...?"

"Tall?"

"No. No."

"Is she pretty?"

Kaleb was in full flush now. "No, I mean, you know, is she...?"

Kitty would not let him off the hook. "Is she *colored*?" Kitty spoke the word colored like an eight-cylinder engine pulling a trailer. Uphill.

That wasn't where Kaleb was going and Kitty knew it. Finally she let him off the hook, but her tone turned serious. "No, Kaleb, Nika's not a chippy. She don't hook much no more."

Kaleb caught the darker tone Kitty had affected. "Something else? Something more?"

Searching for words, Kitty absently pouted to the fullness of her lips while a cloud descended on her humor. "Jes no kind way of sayin' this, I guess... Nika's dopey on the needle."

"Drug dopey?"

"Ridin' the horse. Heroin. She beginin' to clean up, but then your beatdown sent her tailspinnin' an' she been trackin' her arm heavy-like lately."

Kaleb had nothing to say and, letting that lay there, Kitty went on. "Lately she got 'erself mixed up with the Rubbles."

The Rubbles. Kitty noted that the name struck familiar to Kaleb and she continued. "Mizzy Rubble an' 'er gang."

This was sounding familiar and Kaleb stretched for the memory as his tongue fumbled. "Who's Mizzy Rubble? Who's her gang? What's 'er game? Do I know 'em?"

"Sure. Sure you know 'em. They been givin' you grief 'bout takin' over The Temp. Gang's small time goons, mostly Mizzy Rubble an' her boys, Jimmy-Jimbo and Fat Tony. They rent extra brunos when they need more muscle but mostly it's Mizzy Rubble and 'er boys. They small time gangsters what's got a much bigger design for themselves. They been pressin' you hard to get they fat mitts on yer juice joint."

Kaleb rolled this information around, trying to get a grip on the history, the evidence.

"You say that Nika got herself mixed in with this gang."

"Through the drugs."

"Just the drugs?"

With that, the cloud hanging over Kitty's demeanor shadowed darker. "Jes the drugs that I know of but...."

Kitty hung that "but" suspended like an empty hangman's noose, until, finally, Kaleb stuck his neck in and asked, "But what?"

Pulling Kaleb into her lithe frame, Kitty gave a tender squeeze. "Not sure how Nika's payin' for the dope but sure 'nough Jimmy-Jimbo and Fat Tony ain't no hock shop."

Long minutes passed while Kaleb reflected on this. He seemed hesitant to follow up with the obvious question, so Kitty saved him the trouble and said, "They ain't no hock shop... I 'spect the Rubble boys are takin' payment out of 'er hide."

More long moments while Kaleb let that sink in as nothing remained to be said. They resumed their stroll silently, Kitty and Kaleb, arm in arm, as he worked out the angles. There is no free ride in the drug trade and the implication was clear as to how Nika was paying the toll.

Coaxing the thought into another direction, Kitty offered, "An' she's the canary wit' Jazz du Jour."

The distraction worked and it was welcome. "She's a singer? Nika's the singer in my jazz band?"

"Mostly. And a damn fine warbler."

Kaleb thought about the band playing at The Temp, about Jazz du Jour. "Where was she t'night?"

Kitty's darkly clouded demeanor shaded black with thunderclaps brewing in the distance. "Lookit Kaleb, you got to understand, this horse stuff, heroin, you know, she don't warble so well all the time."

***

After Kaleb left Kitty at the corner of Cass and Henry Street, he strolled a wide loop back to his apartment on Hastings Street.

He needed the air. He needed the amble. Detroit's night air was refreshing and the churning industrial white noise of the city's resonance was familiar and calming.

Kaleb felt kindred to the city. To Detroit. It was a familiar that came from the streets and from the alleyways. The familiar rose from the cement like welcoming arms that cradled Kaleb in their limbs, rocking him gently on the purr of the city's ambient hum.

At his apartment he dug into his pocket for the door key but he would not need it.

The apartment door had been flung open and the rooms had been tossed.

16

Let Me Ease Those Tired Shoulders

It took Kaleb Kierka some time to put his apartment back in order. Whoever had tossed the room, tossed it with a colander. Having done a thorough once over of the apartment before leaving earlier, Kaleb did a memory inventory of the rooms but could not identify anything missing. This was evidence. Even no evidence was evidence.

Kaleb knew that somebody had tried to kill him. But that could have been a robbery gone wrong or just a disagreement that had escalated into violence, and Kaleb was on the losing end of the dispute. But this was a confirmation; here was evidence of ongoing criminal intrusion into his life. Into his world. Intrusion into a world that, to Kaleb, was yet unmapped.

Apparently Kaleb was involved in a dangerous pastime that needed attention. And if this narration, this probing of his apartment, was any indicator, immediate attention was required.

Kaleb took stock of what he knew, which was slight. He was a young man, 27 according to his Detroit ID, whose business it seemed was the operation of a speakeasy. An illegal but, for the most part, tolerated enterprise in the Detroit of 1927.

The Temple Bar Speakeasy and Play Nice was tolerated. Why? Was he paying off cops? Did he have uptown friends at city hall? Did he have downtown friends in the gangland? What was being sought in the rummaging of his apartment and to what account could he reckon his near-death battering?

Why, Kaleb wondered, hadn't the apartment been tossed while he was in the hospital? Whoever the transgressors were, they had plenty of time while he was comatose and absent.

Whatever Kaleb was involved in was an active condition, contingent on his being alive and animated.

The only piece of Kaleb's apartment that had not been jostled was the table by the window with the scribbling of Nika Nightingale's poetry. The interlopers were, evidently, not poetry enthusiasts.

Rearranging his apartment, replacing items to their original spot as best he could remember, took Kaleb the better part of an hour. At half past 2 in the morning Kaleb's adrenaline was bubbling in his veins.

***

Hastings Street was quiet now, subdued by the late hour and the darkness of the shadows. The hitch in Kaleb's step, in his left leg, was becoming less and less pronounced. The muscles were beginning to remember. But kinetic memory did not enhance cerebral memory. And the memory in the firing synaptic charge was crucial if he were to figure out the puzzle of Kaleb Kierka.

It was 2:45 in the morning and he assumed that The Temp would be closed tight. And, indeed, the front door was locked. But a raucous pulse of jive jamming was challenging the constitution of the walls of the juke joint. There was a band wailing full tilt behind the locked door of The Temp.

Using his key, Kaleb slipped inside, unnoticed. Leaning back against the door to close it, he took stock of the bar. Earlier when Kaleb had entered the club he was flashing on the adrenaline of memory. This time through the club's doors Kaleb took a careful study of the layout.

To his right was the long draw of the bar with squared red stools, empty now, forming a line like soldiers to the ready against the bar counter. The bar counter itself was a simple shelf of worn wood with a solid tapered lip to support the weight of the drinkers' elbows leaning into their drinks. Likewise, the bar back was a simple affair exhibiting the variety of liquors available - a rather generous variety considering the illegality of the product - with a big brass cash register taking center stage among the liquor display. The radio that played the Tigers game now sat silent next to the cash register.

At the farthest end of the bar was the door to the hallway of the two restrooms, then the office, and beyond the office, a passageway to the alley door. To his left were a dozen or so tables, four chairs apiece, and the small dance floor. In the left-most corner of the bar was the small riser serving as the stage.

Maybe twenty people sat about the tables, more than a locked bar door would suggest, and they were intent on following the musicians jamming note for note. A lumpy little man was pushing a broom across the floor near the restrooms. Lights were dimmed low and the smell of reefer hung heavy on the air.

The jammers on stage were a different collection of black-and-tans than the ones he had seen earlier in the evening. Different players all but for the long and lithe black man plucking on the double-bass. Beethoven Jones.

Kaleb flashed on recognition of this scene assembled before him: the stage, the song, the black-and-tan ensemble. There was something somewhere tucked deep into the recesses of his mind. A flicker of sunlight on a cloudy day. A spark of déjà vu.

And then it was gone.

At one table sat Bucky, the barkeep; a woman was sitting beside him. Kaleb did not recognize her and from the side view estimated she was on the shy side of twenty-five, petite, and exotic dark.

The dumpy man in ragged attire who was pushing the broom was focused on his task, floor sweeping as a singular vocation. It was this dumpy little man sweeping the floor who first noticed Kaleb, and he dropped the broom with a crack on the floor. Bucky and the girl looked to the bar-swabber, then to what the bar-swabber was looking at. And they found Kaleb.

The woman was on her feet with a rush and before Kaleb could respond, tucked herself into the crux of Kaleb's arms, holding fast and cooing a lover's greeting. The woman's rush confused Kaleb, but somehow, some way, the embrace of this petite, exotic woman with black hair and blacker eyes felt right in his arms. Felt very right. Even, familiar. And familiar was a welcomed novelty for Kaleb.

Bucky stayed in his seat and let Kaleb and Nika have a moment.

On the bandstand the musicians were focused on the music and did not become aware of Kaleb's presence for quite some minutes. As realization came, the players nodded and smiled to each other and then refocused their energies into the task, into the tune at hand. The tune was familiar to Kaleb. The song, *Stardust*, the first composition written by a young Hoagy Carmichael, had been a favorite of Kaleb's and it coaxed an aural memory.

Kaleb was not sure what to do with this woman in his arms, with this Nika Nightingale, as they stood there, locked together for long moments, familiar yet foreign.

Holding fast to Nika, to this wraith-like memory cozied to his chest, he swayed gently as the band medleyed from tune to tune, from measure to measure. As they clung to each other, Kaleb was drawn more into the sound, into the timbre. *Blue Skies, Me And My Shadow,* and then Blind Willie Johnson's *Dark Was The Night, Cold Was The Ground,* resonated to Kaleb on a subterranean measure.

As the music triggered memory, it detonated Kaleb's body. He could feel the music radiating from deep within his breast to his very fingertips. Slowly he swayed with Nika. They danced. Holding tight, here was evidence of an organic memory, more organic than reason or intellect. Each measure of the music offered a measure of memory. A measure of Kaleb Kierka in 12/8 time. He was lost in the aural memory. In swing time. After awhile Nika tugged Kaleb to their table and Bucky called out to the bar-swab, "Hollie, get us some beers."

***

There was something about her, this woman Nika. Pretty and petite and mysterious, certainly. But something dark as well. Something foreboding. She carried a sadness that weighed on her shoulders and shadowed her bearing. She wore a black draped dress that clung to her bones, cut low exposing the thin line of her clavicles and bound tight to her nipples as it slid down to the pelvic crest of her waist.

Kaleb had just met, re-met, this woman and there was already the urge to rescue her from this undefined darkness. Something in him that wanted to save her. Protect her. Deliver her from the glum that shadowed her steps like an echo.

***

Blew blew blue:

LET ME EASE THOSE TIRED SHOULDERS

Let me ease those tired shoulders, let me help you with that load
There'll be plenty time tomorrow to scuffle down that road.
You've picked some mighty lessons on the path that you have chose,
But for now come sit beside me, ease those shoulders from that load.

I don't believe I've known someone to take on such a task,
To stand your ground against the pounding weathering the blast.
As troubles like a Northern storm billow sails of your mast,
Let me ease those tired shoulders, for the moment let you rest.

If just for but a moment I could somehow help you see
That the world will keep revolving without your company.
And though I'd never keep you from the lessons that you seek,
Let me ease those tired shoulders momentarily.

The heaviness you carry, the sadness that you know,
Will walk beside you constantly until you let it go.
But it's something you must learn yourself, you must pay the toll,
But let me ease those tired shoulders, before you go.

***

It was a sorrow that Kaleb did not know and could not fathom. He reached across the table to hold her arm against the shadows, against the dark. It was when his hand gently enclosed about her forearm that he felt the tracks. He turned her arm upward to the light.

The needles had knit a tapestry on Nika's forearm. An embroidery that bespoke of self-medication. A medication but not a remedy. Certainly not a remedy.

At best this medication offered a temporary relief from the pain, from the sorrow. At best.

***

Kaleb Kierka and Nika Nightingale cooed to the backdrop of Jazz du Jour, to Kaleb's band, until The Temp shut down at daybreak. Musicians and audience, weary from the long night of rehab, dragged weary bones to the early morning flux of the cityscape's daybreak.

Fatigued by the hour yet refreshed by the music, Nika offered, "Can't take you home, baby, Kitty's workin' our habitat t'night. 'Bout now, she's needin' to rest her carcass but if you wanna roll-on to your crib, I'd be much charmed."

Kaleb looked into this little Jewish minx with the pouty lips and the eyes that smoked tender. This woman, this lover, this friend that he had known forever and yet had just met. By all indications, this was his lover and his best friend. By all indications, that is, except for his stifled memory.

Until he regained memory, Kaleb would need to be wary and circumspect. His fortress was under attack and he would need to stay vigilant against the siege. The sentries would need to stand watchful and the gates barred to the blitz.

All of this Kaleb reviewed while straddling the border of the Black Bottom and Paradise Valley in the quiet city drone of a 1927 early morning dawn.

The nebulous boundary between the Black Bottom and Paradise Valley. Between the black bottom and paradise valley.

At some juncture Kaleb would need to trust somebody and Nika was as good a place as any to begin.

Maybe better.

17

Baby Can Dance

Kaleb and Nika strolled arm in arm up Hastings Street as grocers rolled their carts of fruit and vegetables to storefronts. Unfurling awnings in an early morning yawn to the curbs, to the city's dawn of the clatter and the clamor of commerce.

Up and down the block urban folk began spilling to the streets while Tin Lizzies coughed awake under the twist of the crank against the backdrop of newspaper hawkers crying, "First Edition! Gitcha First 'ere. Henry to reopen Ford plant in the fall! Gitya firsted 'ere!"

Kaleb took in this fresh, somehow familiar, rolling portrait of Detroit's early morning cityscape. With Nika's hand in the crux of his arm, they strolled in unison to the beat of the metropolis. There is some comfort offered in the familiar, and Kaleb felt the tweak of comfort as they ambled through this early morning Detroit.

Whether remembered or not, this scene, this setting, with Nika at his side and the city under his feet, felt right, and Kaleb breathed in the affair with the ease of habit.

Nika's dark locks cascaded to alabaster shoulders and framed a face anchored by smoky green eyes. Or were they blue eyes? Or were they hazel eyes? Depending on which way she turned her head, which way the light angled, Nika's eyes played a color game of hide-and-seek. Although a little long in the Jewish tradition, just enough to give her face character, her nose tapered tight and gave her lips a reason to pout. A tight package, on the thin side, she was encased in a taut, dark dress that did not offer her figure much sanctuary.

***

Black scoffed to Blew, "Love at first sight? Oh, pleeeeease..."

But Blew blew blue as Black flicked his tail in irritation, becoming more reflective. "Is love at first sight possible? Maybe, maybe not. But certainly there is attraction at first sight. Infatuation at first sight. A chemical link as old as the human saga. A pheromonally charged magnetism indebted more to biology and genetic codes. A DNA code searching for a symbiotic link in the elemental brew of chemicals bubbling in our veins."

Blue was busy trying to find the right overtones in the saxophone's low notes.

Black was not distracted. "Or is this feeling, this attraction, that Kaleb felt for Nika more owing to a recovered recollection of the sentiment that he had held for Nika before the coma left him memory sloppy?"

The overtones were not working for Black. He tried the undertones. Black's tail clicked to the beat. In swing time.

"Is love an intellectual experience? Could love actually transcend the physical battering of Kaleb's brain? Is love not endemic in the brain? But how does a dog, with its limited analytical capacity, love its owner with zeal if love is analytical?

"If love is not located in the brain, then where? Are the poets closer to the rub of the truth when they speak of love in correlation to the heart? To the physical center of our mass?"

Clickety click…

"Or is love a product of neither the mental nor the physical body at all?

"Could it be that neither the brain nor the heart plays host to the dynamic we attribute to love? Maybe love exists in some ethereal specter that hovers just outside of our plane of consciousness. Maybe love is not of the matter nor of the consciousness."

Overtone to undertone, back and forth, Blew blew. Overtone to undertone. Undertone to overtone.

"Maybe love is neither a knowledge cultivated in the brain nor a pulse churning in the heart but, rather, is outside of an understanding that our simple little human condition is not privy to."

Blew blew deep into the saxophone. He blew down into the lowest register, into the forlorn trough of the horn. Blew blew into the lowdown:

LAST CHANCE

1.
Did you understand all the laughter,
Or did it go high over your head?
Do you really think it will matter,
When everything you think you know is dead?
Last chance, roll the die.
Last chance, for the sky.

2.
Is there something pushing you faster,
Is there something pressing you on?
Do you see the clock as your master,
As minutes tick like chambers in a gun?
Last chance, roll the die.
Last chance, for the sky.

3.
Are your senses suddenly reeling,
Do your feet feel anchored in clay?
Are you finally left with the feeling,
There's nothing left to do but walk away?
Last chance, roll the die.
Last chance, for the sky.

***

Wherewithal that love might resonate, it was doubtless tweaked when Kaleb was introduced, re-introduced, to the nightclub singer, Nika Nightingale.

***

They made Kaleb's apartment before the 2nd Edition hit the streets and, laughing and teasing their way and juiced from the night of carousing. This was all new and unknown to Kaleb. Yet so familiar.

Tonight they would make love again. Make love again for the very first time.

***

At first the touch was tentative. Like dipping a toe into the pool. But, once tested and found to be agreeable, the plunge was a wild splash into the deep end.

The lovemaking was profound. New and wild, they explored their respective peaks and valleys with the exhilaration of a Lewis and Clark Expedition.

Their Lewis and Clark lovemaking passage of passion led them across the golden plain states, up the crest of a Rockies summit, over the Great Divide - lordy lordy what a Great Divide! - then, finally, to a climaxing cascade down the rush of the Snake River.

***

Nika lay sleeping in the crux of his arm. The lovemaking had been rigorous, impassioned, and now she lay quietly, love-spent, her dark locks cascading onto his chest while her nostrils softly whistled a tune of contentment.

There was something that stirred deep in Kaleb's chest when he was with Nika. The stirring gave warmth and tenderness and a sense of belonging. A sense of right. A sense that he had been here before and a desire to be here forever.

Had love transcended the amnesia? Had love reached across the great divide of his memory loss to remember a sentiment that his battered cranium could not access? Was this feeling, this memory, this love, of a higher caliber than the simple reflections of thought?

Gently, so as not to stir the woman in his arms, Kaleb traced the outlines of her face, her sharp cheekbones and the small knot, mid-nose, that gave character and strength to the Jewish elf in his arms. Gently his fingers followed her thin neckline down across her small breasts, lingering at the dark and hard nipples only long enough to get a quiet sigh from Nika's lips. Down across Nika's column of ribs, pressed tight against stretched skin and down again past the belly button that delivered her mother's sustenance to a child yet unborn.

At the brim of Nika's pubic kink, Kaleb rested his hand, not wanting to reawaken the frenzy of her passion. He would let the girl rest.

With his free hand, Kaleb tilted her head gently toward him and kissed her lightly on her forehead. Her scent, her trace, the sweet sweat mingling with the vulva's loving lubricant, stirred Kaleb physically and emotionally.

***

Black said to Blew, "Could this scent, this woman's personal bouquet, be the progenitor of the familiar that Kaleb recognized in Nika? Can olfactory memory transcend the limits of intellectual deliberation? Is scent then, this flume of fragrance, this pout of pong, a reliable conveyance of memory?"

And Blew blew blue.

***

In quiet sleep Nika whispered an unintelligible bubbling hum. Kaleb drew his hand from her nether regions, reaching across her body and enfolding her tenderly into his arms. As his hand reached her forearm it fell across the pitted track lines of the needles trace. Rough and rutted, the skin flared with testaments of dull spikes and rancid infections.

Instead of withdrawing in horror at the ugliness of the diseased forearm, Kaleb let his hand set softly against the wounds, petting the spiked craters with the tips of his fingers. Kaleb wished to heal the wounds, to smother the fire that burned in her veins. He wanted to wrap Nika forever in the safety and the sanctuary of his arms.

Love is not found in the passion but rather in the mission.

***

Sleep came deep and it came hard to Kaleb and the dreams were only able to slip in toward the end of the slumber, but when the dreams came, they came on a gale of urgency. Muddled memories of music and mayhem with too many colors and not enough light, the images poured forth from Kaleb's unconsciousness offering insights that were out of sight, out of reach of recall.

Dreams of a little Jewish lover and a tall hatchet-faced man and long black fingers caressing a bass fiddle and painted mulatto prostitutes. Hookers and harlots and whores, oh my!

But there were deeper-welled dreams as well. Dreams of a boy crouched at third base with a battered baseball mitt intent on the crack of the bat that would send a small hard sphere blistering the gravel to his face. Dreams of a hobbled old lady, perhaps mother, scolding his ineptness in a Ukrainian tongue. Dreams of clean hands on dirty streets, of dirty hands awash with liquor and blood and beer. Dreams of too many shadows and too much fog.

Twirling dreams, swirling dreams. Smoky whorling, curling dreams.

Dreams might well be the conduit of memory. Unfortunately, the storage filing system for dreams is not organized in a Dewey decimal system.

***

When Kaleb awoke Nika was gone. But she had left a cautionary note on the table. A poem. A song of foreboding? An ominous warning?

BABY CAN DANCE

Prologue:
I can't remember when she walked out of the door,
But I could still taste the night before.

1.
From the cut of her ankle to the hollow of her cheek,
She keeps throwing angles 'til you're spinning on your feet.
Baby can dance, baby can dance.
Still taste the sultry sweat of sweet romance,
BABY CAN DANCE.

2.
Like a strangers shadow on a long and lonesome night,
The trophies on her mantle of the lovers in her life.
Baby can dance, baby can dance.
Still taste the sultry sweat of sweet romance,
BABY CAN DANCE.

3.
There's trouble to her swagger, there's torment to her sighs
With the piercing of a dagger there is danger in her eyes.
Baby can dance, baby can dance.
Still taste the sultry sweat of sweet romance,
BABY CAN DANCE.

Nightingale

***

Nika also left a used needle on the bathroom sink.
Hell of a thing to wake up to.

18

A Disturbing Collective Of Adversaries

Nika and Bucky and Kaleb sat at the table in The Temp long after the band had broken up for the night. Even Beethoven Jones, the ubiquitous bass player who seemed an appendage of the stage, of the bass, had packed up his fiddle and left. Hollie had finished the sweeping and the swabbing, leaving Kaleb to the task of quizzing Nika and Bucky. To investigate his life.

Nika and Bucky seemed to be in agreement over one point; Kaleb had never been a man prone to his comfort zone. Never a man of habit. A man of habit is a careless man. A man of habit is a man becoming complacent in his world and is an easy mark just waiting for the curtain to drop.

According to Nika and Bucky, Kaleb was a careful and studied man. Kaleb needed to know what was behind the closed door and under the rock. A man of caution. Attentive and vigilant.

Bucky explained, "We don't know who or why someone tried to kill you. You left the bar after chord cuttin' with the band in the wee hours. But the band always broke up at different times. Sometimes late night, sometimes early morn. The breakup time was as unpredictable as the jazz. Whoever got to you knew where you would be and what you would be doin'. It was an easy hit."

Nika was lightly stroking the new scar under Kaleb's left eyebrow.

Bucky continued, "'N lord knows you gots 'd enemies. Coulda been the Rubbles. Coulda been the Purples changin' they mind 'bout your value. Coulda been a dozen drunks you bounced outa 'ere. Coulda even been Capone."

Somewhere, somehow, a familiar name in the fog. "Capone?"

Nika's attention to Kaleb's scar was becoming a distraction from the task at hand, and he gently took her hand away. "Flush 'em out, Bucky. Who are these enemies? "

"Well, for starters, the Rubble gang."

"Mizzy Rubble's gang?" This was the first time that a name rung and stuck. And stuck hard. Kaleb rolled the name Mizzy Rubble around in his mouth like a bad taste.

"Sure," Nika put in, holding on to Kaleb's hand now after he had removed her hand from his brow. "They've been trying to push you out of this club for better'n a year. Mizzy Rubble wants this place for her boys."

Filling in blanks, Bucky added, "Yep. She's wanting to expand her province out from the boonies. She's got an ol' farmhouse blind pig out in the sticks an' been eyein' this hub as a nudge into Paradise. And you are in her way." Bucky leaned back in his chair and looked to the ceiling in thought. "Sure. Mizzy Rubble. She could be the foil all right. She 'n Capone been wantin' your ticket into the Canadian hooch."

Again a name that registered alarm. "Capone? Al Capone from Chicago?" He recognized the name, but Kaleb seemed to have no memory about issues involving Al Capone.

"Yup. The Capone gang has been threatening a number of juice joints in Detroit. You being just one of 'em. See, if he muscles a foothold in Detroit, he will have a first class ticket to the good hooch pourin' out of Canada. He'd love nothin' better'n to git a direct pipeline from the Canucks. And The Temp is the foothold that he wants."

***

Al Capone had tried a number of times to muscle into the Detroit booze market. The illegal alcohol contraband coming in from Canada, a short hop across the Detroit River, was brewed in legal factories in Canada and was of the highest quality. Besides the good Canadian liquor it produced, Canada proved to be a convenient conduit for European and Caribbean contraband. From German schnapps to Jamaican rum, Detroit was the Midwest port of entry for the finer liquors and liqueurs on the world market.

Detroit was a pipeline for illegal hooch and Capone wanted direct access to it. The problem for Capone and company was that the Purple Gang maintained an iron grip on the Canadian entryway, and Capone found out the hard way that the Purple Gang was every bit as violent and ruthless as the Chicago gangs. After a short-lived war, Capone found it easier to contract with the Purples than to try to usurp their grip on the trade.

Capone conceded the point, cut a deal with the Purples, and bought the incoming booze to Chicago from the Purple Gang. Al Capone would market this good booze under the Log Cabin label.

But Al Capone was always on the lookout to cut out the middleman.

Kaleb took a moment to digest this. Rivalry from the Rubbles within Detroit and from Capone outside of Detroit. This was shaping up to be a larger portrait than Kaleb had reckoned.

But Bucky was not done. "And then there's the Purples." The Purple Gang.

Like Al Capone, the Purple Gang was another outfit that Kaleb seemed to have memory issues around. But unlike the memory of Al Capone, the Purple Gang had an emotional attachment affixed to it. Recognition of the Purple Gang was more of an intimate recognition. Innate.

The Purple Gang was not just a business connection nor a rival's bond. The synaptic firing of Kaleb's memory surrounding the Purple Gang was personal. And it held a charge that Kaleb could feel in his yesteryear.

Mizzy Rubble's gang. Al Capone's aspirations. And the Purple Gang. A disturbing collective of adversaries by anyone's measure.

And maybe, someone somewhere who had nothing to do with The Temple Bar Speakeasy And Play Nice.

***

More players, more equations, than Kierka had reckoned for.

Kaleb Kierka had not been a man of habit. Never a man so comfortable in his skin that he had become careless. But with so many enemies, so many people wishing him ill, it was only a matter of time before Kaleb would again become a mark.

As careful a man as Kaleb had been before, even greater vigilance was demanded as he proceeded forward.

With a fuzzy memory for a map, signposts of good and of ill would be difficult to recognize, and a course of action would be tricky to navigate.

Kaleb would need to sum the equation of this man named Kaleb Kierka. As the outcome was perilous, the calculation would need to be quick.

19

The Ballad Of Kaleb Kierka And Nika Nightingale: Rummaged Remnants Of Ragged Reminiscence.

They never came on the same way twice, the memories. But whether with a flash or a dull thud, the onset of memories would leave Kaleb shaken and numbed.

Try as he might, Kaleb could never be confident of holding fast to a memory. He could never be certain if the memories would gain a foothold and stay with him or if the memory would crawl off to another dark crevice to again hide against discovery.

Memories could slip in barely noticed, tip-toeing around the periphery of recall like a feral dog at the outer margin of a Neanderthal fire, never certain whether it was being coaxed to the fire to share in the meal or to be the meal.

There were times the memories would come roaring in on the shoulders of giants with clubs hammering at Kaleb's cortex with fury and ferocity, busting down the barred doors of forgetfulness. Other times memories would sneak in softly, quietly, with the stealth of a pickpocket slipping deft fingers into the pocket of yesterday.

Memories were often accompanied by the vision of Black and Blew as the streetlight pair endeavored to pry reason from the recall. When Black and Blew shepherded in the memories, they splashed the recall in on a pool of sluggish air of pain and blackness, sending Kaleb to his knees, to the murky shadow of the comatose.

***

The memory of Nika had found Kaleb in the Black Bottom. He had been driving the T and when the headaches came on he pulled to the curb.

The memory of Nika came on in tattered clothes and worn shoes with cardboard inserts at the ball of the feet to hold back the slap of the concrete. Of the concrete.

Kaleb peeked at Nika's memory through the knothole of a gray and weathered-wood fence that stood between two empty fields.

Rummaged Remnants of Ragged Reminiscence.

***

You never knew what you were getting by way of the pianoforte when you toured the country honky-tonks and the rural blind pigs. Some establishments took great care of their pianos, keeping them well tuned and primed as the centerpiece of the stage. Others barely gave the piano a second thought. In these latter establishments the piano might well be out of tune and missing teeth, missing keys. A pianist was at the mercy of the club's ownership and at the mercy of whatever piano was gracing the rostrum.

Kaleb Kierka and Beethoven Jones were barely out of their teens but were already seasoned veterans of Detroit's club scene. They knew the clubs and the theaters and the granges of the greater metropolitan Detroit area, and they knew what to expect from the venues. So it was no surprise when the young men showed up to play the dance hall at the Howell City Town Hall with the piano in a tattered condition.

Even though Kaleb had become very good at finger hopping over the broken keys and the out-of-tune keys, this piano at the Howell City Town Hall suffered so many mangled and malformed keys that Kaleb packed along his portable keyboard. The portable piano that every good keyboard jockey of the day kept handy for just such an occasion, the accordion. Kaleb hung the accordion over his shoulders, and he and Beethoven Jones would have at it.

Three sets into the gig, halfway through the night, and the duo of *"The Jew Boy and The Colored Boy"* were rocking the house. Three straight up-tempo tunes had the crowd hoppin' and boppin' on the dance floor when it was time to give the feet a rest. Breaking into a mournful ballad, Kaleb laid back on the squeeze box into a slow shuffle, and Jones began dragging his bow across the big bass fiddle with a soul that dug deep into his African derivation.

On occasion, a local musician would take the stage with the boys, singing or playing the instrument of their calling. In this manner, the boys would at times find themselves accompanied by banjos and bugles and bagpipes and hurdy-gurdies. All manner of musical mayhem.

The boys loved this venture, as they would get a taste of the regional musical flavor. Often enough though, these rural honky-tonks served up amateurs without enough time spent woodshedding their chops. Much like the toothless pianos, the musicianship in these backcountry honky-tonks was a hit-or-miss proposition.

She was a little girl, Nika was. She was dressed in a flower print rag of a dress with her hair disheveled. She tottered on scuffed heels that lifted her up to a grand height of maybe five feet tall. Maybe.

The black, curly hair and the slightest knot on the bridge of her nose gave away her Jewish heritage. Her smile was tentative as she took to the stage, her nervousness evident.

Jones nodded to Kaleb and Kaleb looked at the girl with some reservation. Too often a local singer would join the boys on stage, pumped up on the adoration and their parents' blind belief in the talent of their tone-deaf offspring.

Kaleb and Jones had become well versed in nursing a pitch-crippled singer through an arrangement. They braced themselves for the worst.

Softening their instruments to accommodate the vocals, Kaleb found the girl's key and the boys readied themselves to jump in on the first measure that this pretty young vixen began to falter.

But the falter never came.

The little girl opened her mouth and belted the blues in a voice that was well acquainted with the blues. She was acquainted with the blues in the first person.

Her voice was raspy and warm and powerful - where the hell did she get that power in that little frame! - she sang with a vision that could see to the greatest depths of a tortured soul - where the hell did she get that vision! She sang with the authority of a spirit that had been bruised by the worst, and she sang with the character of the survivor.

Nika coaxed the life from the tune as she nursed the song's pain in her tender, throaty tone.

Kaleb and Jones shared pleased, relieved smiles and slipped their accompaniment under this little philosopher of croon.

Singing over the blues progression, Nika shared a blues poem that the boys had never heard before:

WORLD OF WOE

Turn the lights low, so they can't see the scars,
Then tuck your body in the darkest corner of this bar.
Well there you go, another World of Woe.
There you go, another World of Woe.

He's got bravado, he measures every word,
But he tilts his hat low so you cannot look into his hurt.
Well there you go, another World of Woe.
There you go, another World of Woe.

You see the sufferin', you see the pain in her eyes
You want to help her but it's best just to let her cry.
Well there you go, another World of Woe.
There you go, another World of Woe.

20

Nika Would Be No Different

When Kaleb and Beethoven Jones opened their speakeasy they sought out Nika to join them as part of the house band. But she was not easy to find.

Shortly after the boys opened The Temp, Granma and Kaleb were bonding over a brew and a Tigers game on the radio when Kaleb happened to mention the long lost Nika to Granma.

"You mean that little Jew girl what shot dead her ol' man?"

"She shot her partner?" Kaleb was confused.

"Partner? No no. That girl shot her pap. Her dad."

"Shot her dad? What...? You know her?"

"Know her? No. But I heard-tell 'bout her. Her pap was a raping her and her sisters, and she brought him up on a charge of gunpowder. Blew a couple of holes big as the Liberty Bell into the man. Gotta love a kid like that."

"She killed her dad?"

There was a crack of the bat on the radio and now Granma's attention was waning. "Goddamnittohellandbackagain."

***

She was built like an icebox. With a head. Granma was.

Assimilation was the cause for the day and Granma was the icon. Whether they were escaping their homelands' political, social or religious persecutors, the European migrants were done with bullshit.

America offered a new point of view and a new beginning.

When migrants arrived on America's shores in the early part of the 20th century, they were not looking to maintain their culture. They were looking to join, assimilate, into the culture that was the promise of America. A promise of liberty to personal views and unity of community.

Granma was among the throng who landed on America's shores with this promise. When Granma left the European tribulations, she knew that she would never see her homeland again. Never walk the streets of her youth or visit the graveside of her parents. This was the price of admission to this new culture offered by America.

It was a hefty admission to pay, but considering the alternative, it was worth the cover charge.

She was the number one fan of the Detroit Tigers and her default expression was "god-damn-it-to-hell-and-back-again." The phrase had become so easy at rolling off her tongue that it became a single word in Granma's vernacular. Goddamnittohellandbackagain.

Granma also had a taste for chaw. Rolling a wad of tobacco 'twixt her cheeks, she carried a tin can spittoon with her to discharge the brown sap.

The 1927 Detroit Tigers gave Granma plenty of opportunities to exercise this unique vernacular and plug the spittoon. Goddamnittohellandbackagain.

Much like her vernacular, Granma's disposition was Goddamnittohellandbackagain.

Ty Cobb was Granma's favorite ball player, and Granma's disposition was modeled in the Ty Cobb mold. Whereas Ty Cobb slid into second base with razor-sharp cleats raised high to carve up the shortstop's tag, Granma wore her cleats on her tongue.

With a chaw of chewing tobacco and the godamnittohellandbackagains, Granma held center stool in The Temp.

Granma could not afford a radio in 1927 Paradise Valley, so every Tigers game found her having a beer and sitting center stage, that is, center barstool, planted in front of the radio that sat on the bar-back of The Temp.

From the first crack of the bat to the final out of the game, Granma would sit her roost on The Temp's barstool drinking a beer. Drinking beer and exercising her unique vernacular.

And the 1927 Detroit Tigers had given Granma plenty of opportunities to exercise her vernacular.

Goddamnittohellandbackagain.

***

Kaleb was pressing Granma. This was the first solid whiff of Nika Nightingale that he had had, and he was not about to let the whiff dissipate.

Pushing on he asked, "Nika killed her dad?"

Granma was getting irritated by Kaleb's insistence that there might be something else in the world as important as the Tigers baseball game. "What? Killed her dad? No. Yes. That is, officially they called it a suicide, I guess. But…," and with another crack of the bat she shouted at the radio, "Goddmmittohellandbackagain! That's the third hit this inning! Take that little shit out and put in a arm!" Turning to Kaleb she added, "That Augie John's ain't more'n a batting practice arm. Don't know why they don' trade 'is ass, Goddamnittohellandbackagain."

Ignoring that, Kaleb pressed on. "Where can I find her?"

"Find who?" Granma was engrossed in the Tigers game.

Kaleb snatched Granma's beer from in front of her. This had Granma turn her full attention to Kaleb, swinging on her barstool to face him directly. "What the hell are you talking about?"

"Nika."

"Nika? Oh, right, Nika. Nika Nightingale. Whadayawant to know?" Augie John was pulled from the game and Jim Walkup was on the mound taking his warm-up tosses. "Another little shit arm, Goddamnittohellandbackagain." Granma finally gave Kaleb some attention.

"Where can I find her?"

Granma snatched back her beer, "Last I heard of the girl she got messed up with junk. Shootin' goon juice out with that Rubbles. Miz Rubble 'n the boys. They been stinkin' her up with heroin and whatnot 'n boys been usin' her for they private party."

Kaleb had had some exchange with the Rubbles. Mizzy Rubble and her boys, Fat Tony and Jimmy-Jimbo, had wanted in on The Temp, and when Kaleb rejected their offer, all manner of mayhem was threatened upon Kaleb.

Kaleb pressed through the ballgame. "They got a blind pig somewhere, no?"

"They got a blind pig somewhere, yes. Out west. In the boonies."

"In the boonies?"

"Sure. Out inna farmhouse out Livernois way. 'Snames Rubbles Bubble or sumthin'. Not so much a blind-pig as it is a pen-yen."

"Pen-yen?"

"Yep, pen-yen. Opium den. Heroin house. Dope house. The Rubbles got Nika hooked up deep in the juice."

With another crack of the bat, the Tigers game had resumed and Granma was lost again to Kaleb.

"Goddamnittohellandbackagain."

***

When Kaleb headed out for the Rubbles he asked Beethoven Jones if he'd have the inclination to come along.

"I don't get involved," said Jones.

"I'm off to find that canary, Nika, for the band."

"I don't get involved," was the Jones mantra.

Kaleb studied Jones for a moment and then turned to the door.

***

Transit to Rubbles Bubble was easy enough. Northwest out of town on Grand River, turn north at the dirt road Livernois, past a big dairy farm on the right for about two miles to a shabby old farmhouse on the left, the west side of the road.

But Kaleb never got to Rubble's Bubble. As he jiggled along on the washboard strip of dirt that was Livernois, Kaleb drew up to a shabby and almost naked young lady tottering alongside the road toward town. As he drew closer he slowed his buggy down for safe passage.

The young woman was dressed in a flimsy gown, barefoot on the hard dirt road with hair disheveled and dirty. Eyes glazed catatonic, she did not notice Kaleb's T stop, nor did she respond when he grabbed her by her arms and attempted to jiggle her to consciousness. She was not cognizant when he gathered her into his Model T and whisked her away.

The young woman was Nika Nightingale.

***

It was three full days of sleep and food and hot coffee before the veil was eventually lifted from Nika's stupor. Three days of sweating and malaise, anxiety and depression, insomnia, cold sweats, nausea, vomiting, diarrhea, cramps, chills, and fever. Three days of endless walking to and fro from the kitchenette to the bedroom to the kitchenette to the bedroom. Walking walking walking against muscle spasms that rattled the girl's bones.

Cold turkey is not fun to watch and it's hell to suffer.

For three days Kaleb kept vigil on Nika in his third-floor apartment above Hastings Street in Paradise Valley, nourishing her with hot chicken soup and cooing promises of recovery.

And Nika did recover. And she cleaned up well. And Nika became the third staple of the house band at The Temple Bar Speakeasy And Play Nice. Kaleb Kierka and Beethoven Jones and Nika Nightingale: Jazz du Jour. But heroin addiction is like an enemy's shadow that has latched on to your own profile. A shadow that stalks you when you are happy and beckons when you are sad. It is there when things are good and when they are bad; always vigilant, always in wait for the opportunity to overcast your being and drag you once again into the blackness of its silhouette.

Nika Nightingale would be no different.

21

General Miasma

"Ya got any ideas 'bout who's playin' my shadow?" Kaleb was looking for information.

They were sitting in Detective Morane's Buick again. Morane's body had once again assumed itself into the car seat as the detective's suit and the bench seat blurred into a single vision.

"Someone's shadowing you? Following you?"

Kaleb watched Morane's face for a tell but none was forthcoming. "You don't know nothing about me being tailed?"

When Morane shook his head to the negative, his body jiggled with the movement and for a quick moment, Kaleb could detect the contours of the detectives shape against the seat bench.

Morane was sitting in his car when he had intercepted Kaleb on his way to The Temp, calling to him and then waving a fat finger for Kaleb to join him. They were sitting in the police unmarked cruiser parked along the alleyway between Brewster and Wilkins streets.

Kaleb flushed it out. "Tall, slim, maybe six-four, sharp angles to a thin face, seems to have a fondness for chic threads of the dark blue variety."

Again Morane's head shook a negative. "You sure he's on your track?"

"Seen 'im a couple of times now. First time he was playing statuette on the street across from my apartment. Next time he was sliding out the back door of The Temp while I was entering the front door."

Morane looked down the alleyway then half rotated his body to look around the street. His movement momentarily demarcated the detectives outline from the Buick's bench seat. "He with us now?"

"No."

"A periodic shadow? That would be a new twist." Morane gave Kaleb a moment to respond and when he didn't, he asked, "You certain about the tail?"

Kaleb shrugged his shoulders and Morane finished it. "If it is a shadow, I mean *if,* I don't know nothin' about it. And the city don't encourage our department to spend money on such extravagance, neither. All the big graft money is going to rotating regimes. Not a penny for men in chic blue threads."

Kaleb thought about that and then let it go. "So what do I owe this visit? You want to see me about something or are you just on holiday in the Paradise Valley?"

Morane took his time plugging a cigar butt into his face, and Kaleb took the moment to roll and fire one of his own. It was not a tight roll and Kaleb could taste the bitterness of the raw tobacco on his tongue. He spit shards of tobacco out of the car window into the alley.

The two sat quietly, filling the car's cab with blue haze. Then Morane scrunched his face into a serious frown. Concern did not look natural on the jaded detective's face. "I'm gettin' chin-wag 'bout the Purples movin' hard on the competition. Gun hard. You could be in for a wild ride."

"I didn't know you cared." When Morane let that lay, Kaleb continued. "I thought you said I was tight with the Purples?"

"Allegiances change, battle lines shift. I'm just telling you to know your pond before you take a dive."

Kaleb had nothing to say to that and he kept on not saying it.

Morane was done talking as well. They sat there in the old Buick in the alleyway and let the blue smoke curl out of the car windows to join the general miasma hanging over the summer swelter of 1927 Detroit.

22

Pockets Full Of Mayhem

There is an element of street smarts that is cultivated in poverty. Street smarts is knowing where to make a stand and when to lay low. Street smarts can recognize danger in the tilt of a hat and menace in pocketed hands. Street smarts allows one to disappear on a whisper into the alleys and into the clefts of the boulevards. Street smarts is at once in the flow and against the grain.

The night before Kaleb reacquainted with Nika Nightingale at The Temp. Tonight, when he made the street, it was close to midnight, and he spent time wandering the neighborhoods to get a feel for the streets, for his home.

Feeling the pains of hunger, Kaleb found a 24-hour eatery on Woodward and slid into a back table, sitting with his back to the wall so as to watch the comings and goings of the establishment.

Paradise Valley was teaming with European flavor. Each restaurant held fast to a native cuisine and custom representing the nation's origin. Polish and German and Italian and Jewish and Ukrainian and Armenian recipes were prepared in the traditional techniques of the country that they were representing.

Perusing the menu, Kaleb found that he had landed in a kosher eatery. The menu read like a tribute to the letter *K*. Kugel, knish, kreplach, kashrut, kasha, kishke. The dietary law of Kosher, noted Kaleb Kierka.

The meal was heavy: kishke and kreplach and latke and coffee. He had angled his chair to watch the door, the street, but the night was late and the city was quiet, allowing Kaleb to bond with the familial foods of his DNA's ancestry.

Finishing with a babka, Kaleb lingered over a third cup of coffee and torched tobacco.

Detective Morane had once again linked Kaleb to the Purple Gang, and it might be nigh time to sum their integer into this equation.

But where would he start? Without his memory, his history, the Purple Gang was as foreign to him as the moon. Kaleb did not know people, he did not know the gangs, and he did not know the streets. He would need to be a quick study on the boulevard of street smarts.

***

It was close to three in the morning when Kaleb walked into The Temp. The speakeasy was quiet. This night there was no band and no dancers and no revelers. The Temp was still except for the little limping lump of a man tirelessly pushing the broom across the floor. Hollie. Clubfooted, cleft palette with a blue tint to his complexion, a blue baby at birth, Hollie had not been done many favors by the fates.

"No party t'night, Hollie?"

Hollie did not break from the task of sweeping to answer Kaleb. Speaking over the swooshing of the broom, he replied. "Don' know." Then, looking around the bar, he added, "Guess so."

"Go home, Hollie."

***

Kaleb Kierka locked the speakeasy door behind Hollister Pericles Rockefeller. Hollie.

It had been suggested to Kaleb that Hollie was slow, dim-witted. Kaleb found that Hollie was not necessarily slow, rather, Hollie had an otherworldly interpretation of the world. Physically he was a little potato of a man, unkempt, with a sour odor that clung to him like an overcoat.

When Hollie spoke, mumbled, the language malignment was a study of linguistic riddles.

Hollie spoke quietly, garbling words deep in his throat so that the sound barely passed his lips. And whatever resonance tumbled over Hollie's tongue was open for interpretation. What might sound like "I'll go wit' the gloom," was, in reality, nothing more than Hollie saying, "I'll go git 'da broom." When Hollie offered to, "...wretch up yer teeth like toffee," he was merely offering to "...fetch up yer cup of coffee." For those who didn't know Hollie, or didn't care to know him, a conversation could be a very disconcerting exercise in exorcism. Language exorcism.

Most saw him as a crumpled and dirty little man, this Hollie. That is, if they saw him at all.

Most of the crumpled, disheveled, street people like Hollie went unnoticed by society at large, chiefly ignored by the industrious elements of society. Abandoned, isolated, and neglected by society they waft through their lives as an ambient visual noise.

If not for the clubfoot giving his gait a bobbling drama, Hollie might never have caused a ripple in the affairs of humankind.

Where Hollie came from was anybody's guess, as he didn't have the vocabulary to share his biography. Those who cared to ask, Granma for instance, were left with a befuddling compost of syntax.

But push his broom Hollister Pericles Rockefeller could do. Hollie pushed his broom with the fervor of the obsessed. He had found his mark in time, in humankind, and he went about this business of broom pushing with a single-mindedness.

"Where are your people?" Granma would ask.

What Hollie mumbled was, "Folks are dead." What Granma was able to decipher was, "Forks for bread."

Granma spit chaw into her tin can and mumbled back at Hollie "Goddamnittohellandbackagain."

***

Once Hollie shuffled off into the night, Kaleb turned his attention to the office. Although his apartment had been tossed, the club's office had not been touched and Kaleb wanted first spin with the room.

Somewhere, somehow, Kaleb had become a target and it would behoove him to figure out the whys and hows of this affair. And the whos. Especially the whos.

Owning a speakeasy did not speak well of who Kaleb might be. An illegal liquor establishment was not an establishment to brag to mom about. But Kaleb recognized that in the Black Bottom of 1927 Detroit, an illegal juice joint was not necessarily a wicked mission. Indeed, The Temple Bar Speakeasy And Play Nice seemed to be operating wide open and playing by a slightly tarnished golden rule. Patina on gold does not make it less gold.

Bucky had given the combination of the bar's safe to Kaleb and he began shuffling through the contents. He found deeds for the building, contracts for booze coming in from the distributors, the gin runners, and contracts going out for distribution.

The Purple Gang's name did not appear in the contracts. Nor did the Rubbles. Kaleb Kierka was an independent contractor, securing and selling booze on his own terms from the hodgepodge of rumrunners flitting Canadian booze across the Detroit River.

Booze coming in and booze going out. Some of the receipts of outgoing booze were labeled "Log Cabin" and flowed in the direction of Chicago. The Log Cabin was Al Capone's brand. There must have been some nefarious underworld goings on.

Contracts. Honor among thieves? So the bar served not only as a vendor of illegal hooch but as a distributor of the contraband booze as well. Importer and exporter, The Temple Bar Speakeasy And Play Nice gave as good as it got.

Kaleb sat down at the seven-drawer desk. The desk was pitted with age, and edges of it were scorched from burn lines of cigarettes that had been left to fend for themselves. The desk had three drawers to either side of the chair and a thin pencil drawer center top.

Kaleb could well understand how an illegal rumrunner would find himself mixed up with unsavory company. He was finding things out about himself that were leaving a bitter taste in his mouth. Kaleb pulled out the top drawer on the left. A bottle of very fine brandy presented itself, and popping the cork, Kaleb sniffed the contents and then took a stiff draw. The brandy was the good stuff. He examined the bottle. French brandy from the Cognac region of France. It tasted right. Maybe beer wasn't his drink of choice. Another wrinkle in the character of this Kaleb Kierka fellow.

Rifling through the rest of the desk offered typical bar commerce. Typical but illegal bar commerce. There were receipts for chairs and broken mirrors and taxies and payroll. Payroll for Hollie and Bucky and Granma and a collection of musicians.

Kaleb rummaged through names and dates and amounts of transactions. The tally of commerce.

Could this be the reason that Kaleb Kierka was a hunted man? Could he know too much and have the paperwork to prove it? Was he a blackmailer? Could he be putting his foot down on the wrong neck and the wrong neck was pushing back?

Pulling open the final drawer, the bottom right drawer, Kaleb found two ready revolvers, a big Colt .45 and a smaller Smith and Wesson .38. Both guns had short barrels and filed triggers. Pocket armaments.

Kaleb sucked on the bottle of brandy and looked down at the drawer of artillery. So this was Kaleb's life. Guns and contraband. He was not so much surprised as he was saddened.

Looking into the drawer, Kaleb studied the guns. He lifted the .45 into his right fist and it felt right. It felt comfortable. It felt familiar. And when he fit his left fist around the .38, the package was complete. The big kick of the .45 would be at ease in his right hand, his strong hand, and his left hand could easily accommodate the kick of the .38.

Standing, Kaleb flicked open the guns and spun the chambers, fully loaded, and he balanced the weight of the artillery into his hands. He slid the hardware smoothly into the side pockets of his sport jacket, and they nestled comfortably into the leather-lined pocket pouches.

This, then, answered the question as to why the side pockets on all of his jackets were lined with leather. Pocket holsters. The leather-lined jacket pockets were scabbards designed to support the conveyance of guns.

But these guns posed more questions then they answered. Why wasn't he carrying the hardware when he suffered his beatdown that left him five weeks in a coma? Was he meeting someone that he trusted? Had he been set up?

But this much was clear: Kaleb was a man of contraband and a man of violence. A man who needed two fists full of fury to execute his affairs.

Chagrined and with pockets full of mayhem, Kaleb sat down and took another long draw of the cognac.

***

So this was it then. Kaleb could trace his personal track back to this. A crook. A criminal. A reprobate.

There was much that Kaleb had to work out in his own mind. He did not savor himself the criminal element, but more and more, evidence of an unsavory life presented itself.

Guns and booze and hookers and violence seemed to be endemic to his existence. At every turn, at every discovery, Kaleb found further evidence of a man of violence and illicit ventures.

Kaleb did not feel the part of the criminal world. It felt wrong. It felt foreign to some place deep within his breast. But the evidence was there, clear. Could he really be of a delinquent constitution? It felt like an unfamiliar prospect but the data seemed overwhelming.

Kaleb wondered what turn his life could possibly have taken to demand this life of mayhem. He had read that a severe concussion can drastically change a man's demeanor, can radically alter a man's attitude. This criminal activity certainly felt unfamiliar to Kaleb's core. Could the blows that Kaleb suffered to his head modify his synaptic discharge so that morality would dance to a new tune?

And now, which way forward?

As Kaleb ruminated, a familiar smoke of a distant fire was imposing itself on his will. Blackness was again encroaching on his consciousness and he recognized the comatose beckoning from the shadows.

Kaleb slumped back into the chair as the nausea of the concussion reasserted control. Down he went into the blackness. Into the numen.

***

Black was arguing with himself while Blew blew blue:
"Is a man the summation of all the work he has done?" Black argued.
"Of his deeds? His performance? His manner of conduct? And is a man's
history the only path forward? Is man nothing more than a smattering
collection of memories of what came before? A tumbling bumbling
assembly of the sum of his experiences of the good and of the bad?"
Blew sucked wind and dug deeper into the horn but Black was not
distracted.
"Is one's future solely contingent on whatever one's personal history
has designed? Are our fears nothing more than products of our failures
and are our confidences but the result of our triumphs? Is an individual's
potential limited to what has come before?
"Hopes and desires, these designs on the future, where do these place?
What to destiny? To chance and to fate?
"Does our history hold sway over what will become? What will be?
Does one's past dictate one's future?"
Mid-rant Black stopped to consider this. Then he continued, "Or
should a man be measured by his behavior in the private moments? The
moments when only he and his selective maker are the sole witness to the
action?
"Howsoever you measure this man, is this the sum total of a man?
Should consideration be given to the future? The potential for him to move
forward in the direction of his choice?"
Blew blew blue:

> *Are your senses suddenly reeling?*
> *Do your feet feel anchored in clay?*
> *Are you finally left with the feeling,*
> *There's nothing left to do but walk away.*

***

Whatever the yardstick that Kaleb Kierka decided to use as a
measurement from this point going forward, he was still presented with the
fact that somebody was trying to kill him.

23

Kaleb's Spaceship

Kaleb slept late, arising with the sun warming the bed. Lying still, he ruminated on his life as he knew it. Not a lot. Working his way backwards, he needed to find what had made him become what he had become. That is, whatever he had become became.

He did not enjoy the prospect of being a criminal, if that was what he was. Nor a gang member, if that is what he was. And he certainly wasn't enamored with the idea of being a target.

Today would be a day of investigation, of filling holes and recovering data.

Crawling from his bed, he used the bathroom and, in front of the mirror, was transfixed by the image it reflected. The presentation was slender and taut. The tight curls of hair on his head suggested motion and the V design of his body's angles implied action. Although he could yet feel the tug of the atrophy, he was becoming aware of the elasticity of energy lying dormant in his muscles. Kaleb tallied the vigor of his body and came up with a good equation.

A stronger brew of coffee was on this morning's menu. He did not know how the former Kaleb drank his coffee, but he decided that he enjoyed his coffee strong. No sugar and no cream. Cradling his cup of coffee in his hands, he stood before the window high above Hastings Street, a podium perch over the Paradise Valley, and calculated tactics to move forward.

The sky was clear and the Saturday bustle was bubbling in the markets on the streets below. Model T's, Tin Lizzies, of every variety were chugging up and down the thoroughfare. Model T coupes and Model T pick-ups and Model T delivery wagons and Model T sedans and they were all black. The Model T was ubiquitous and proletarian. An integral part of the energy that was the Motor City. While other parts of Detroit were awash in Buicks and Mormons and Jordans and Packards, the working class neighborhoods were black with the Model T ("Any customer can have a car painted any color that he wants so long as it's black." Henry Ford).

How simple would his task be if his world, his history, were Model T simple, thought Kaleb.

Draining the last of his second cup of coffee, Kaleb set the cup down on the shelf of the bay window and glanced onto the street scene below. His eye caught on a solitary figure leaning on a Model T directly across the street from his apartment.

Although resting casually against the automobile, the solitary figure was a tall and hard man who would be quick to trigger. And he was wearing a dark navy blue suit and had a sharply angled and thin face. A hatchet face.

Kaleb threw on his clothes, last night's natty sport jacket, and flew out the door. Despite his gimpy left leg, Kaleb took the three-story staircase two steps at a time. Bursting out onto the bustling Saturday morning of Hastings Street, he sprinted across the street, dodging the traffic, to the Model T where the hatchet-faced man had been leaning.

The man was not there and could not be detected in Kaleb's quick scan up and down Hastings Street. On a second, slower scan of Hastings Street, Kaleb studied the individual foyers of each storefront and apartment building but could not find the figure.

Facing his apartment building again, Kaleb leaned back into the exact spot against the Model T where the hatchet-faced man had been. Looking up to his apartment, he tried to reason what the man was looking at. For?

Three times now Kaleb had seen the hatchet-faced man. Twice across from his apartment and once slipping out the back door of The Temp

Kaleb casually slunk his hands into his coat pockets, and his hands touched on the guns he had taken from The Temp the night before. The .45 in his right pocket, the .38 in his left. They rested comfortably in the leather lining of his jacket pockets.

The guns were a reminder of his circumstance, a reminder that he was the center of a violent arc whose trajectory he did not know.

Suddenly he had the thought that perhaps this automobile was connected to the hatchet-faced man. This was, after all, the second time Kaleb had seen him leaning against this very same Model T across from his apartment. He pushed off the fender he had been leaning on and went to the driver's side running board. Reaching through the car's window, he lifted the clip off the visor and read the automobile's registration. The registration tag informed Kaleb that this Model T was registered to a Kaleb Kierka who resided on Hastings Street in Detroit, Michigan.

Memory was flickering as Kaleb reread the registration card. And he read it again. And with each reread, his brain's motor coughed as if the choke was pulled out and the crank wrenched. Suddenly, a sputtering ignition.

Kaleb reached into his pants pocket and retrieved the chain of keys he had discovered in his apartment. He opened the automobile's door, stepped into the cab, and sat on the leather bench seat. It felt right. He jingled the five keys, coming up with the automobile key between his thumb and forefinger. Fitting the key into the ignition, he twisted. The engine sputtered, but the battery did not spark and the engine whirred to silence. Feeling under the bench seat, Kaleb found the crank. Leaving the ignition on, the transmission disengaged, and the choke pulled out, he climbed from the cab.

The first five twists of the crank gave little response but on the sixth the T coughed. Two more hard cranks and the T gasped. Finally, on the ninth screw of the crank, the engine sputtered and spit, and then it sparked. Ignition.

Sitting behind the wheel as the T rattled awake against its own version of comatose, Kaleb took stock of the meaning behind this collection of keys.

One door key fit his apartment, one door key to The Temp, and the third was the Model T's ignition key. Two door keys and the one automobile key were now identified. That left only two door keys to detect.

***

Maybe the keys fit Nika's apartment? It could be a girlfriend's apartment key. Or Bucky's apartment. Certainly it could be a friend's apartment key.

Kaleb pushed the T's choke in and gunned the accelerator to warm the cold engine. The motor began to purr easily, easier than Kaleb would have assumed after sitting dormant for better than a month. Slipping the lever into gear and easing the Tin Lizzie out of the parking space, he made a tight U-turn, dodging the cluttering traffic of Hastings Street, and slowly drove the six blocks to his speakeasy.

The Temple Bar Speakeasy And Play Nice seemed to be the cosmic center. The center of his universe. This Model T would serve as Kaleb's spaceship in his probing orbit of the cosmos that was Kaleb Kierka.

24

Joey Louis Barrow

It was late morning when Kaleb pulled up to The Temp. He slid the Model T into a parking space on Gratiot. It was a warm, pleasant day but Kaleb could not attest to it. His focus was on who he was. And who he needed to be.

Once through the double doors of The Temp, Kaleb stopped to examine the scene. Bucky was again behind the bar twisting a shot glass in a bar rag and the lumpy Hollister Pericles Rockefeller, Hollie, was again pushing the broom back and forth. Forth and back.

Beethoven Jones had the music stage to himself and was bent over his bass fiddle, plucking a minor pentatonic scale with a flat 5. The blues scale.

Although the radio was across the room and behind the bar, it was easy for Beethoven Jones to follow the drift of the Tigers game. Jones only needed to monitor the exhortations of Granma, sitting center stage at the bar in front of the radio, to follow the course of the game.

With every crack of the bat or thump of the glove Granma would exclaim the direction of the baseball game. A big "whoop" for the good, a sulky "Goddamnittohellandbackagain." for the bad. This was the only language that Granma allocated game-time as she held center stool in front of the radio. The whoops, the goddamnittohellandbackagains, and the sputter of tobacco plug were Granma's world when the Tigers game was on the radio.

Besides being the baseball guru of The Temp, Granma was also the bar's pinch-hit bartender. But now Granma's world belonged to the Detroit Tigers ballgame that was broadcasting on the radio on the bar-back.

A big whoop for Charlie Gehringer's leading off the inning with a Texas League floater over the shortstop. Another whoop when Heinie Manush singled him over to third base. Then the cascading "Goddamnittohellandbackagain" and a spit of chaw when Warner, Woodall, and Heilmann drew two pop-ups and a strike out.

When Granma was in front of the radio with the Tigers game, her beer warming in front of her, the rest of the world faded to black. "Whoop, whoop whoop" and "Goddamnittohellandbackagain" was Granma's world.

Kaleb crossed the room and with a tip of his head, signaled Bucky to join him in the office.

Bucky had been gifted with a rolling tumble of wrinkles for a face. The waves of his wrinkles would animate in the direction of mind-set, rolling upward in mirth, downward in woe.

Bucky's face waved to Granma. "Watch the suds, Granma."

Granma was mostly in the radio with the Tigers but she managed a "Goddamnittohellandbackagain."

***

In the back room office, Kaleb swung into the office chair and got to the point. "Give me the yam on Miz Rubble's gang."

The wrinkles on Bucky's face danced with thought. "Yea, the Rubble Gang, Miz Rubble, welp, she and her sons been trying to take over The Temp. First she tried to buy you out, cheap like, then she 'n her boys threatened you."

"My beatdown come from the Rubbles, maybe?"

The wrinkles in Bucky's face did a somersault as he thought this over. "Maybe. Maybe, boss. Mizzy wants this place almighty bad. This is a happin' juice joint in Paradise Valley that she and her boys wants. Sure, I guess she would want you slabbed."

Kaleb thought this over. "Then, why, do you think, the Rubbles didn't move in on The Temp when I was five weeks down?"

Bucky's furrowed face was having trouble with that question. "Don't know, 'xactly. Maybe 'cause Jones was still here manning the fort."

"But most folks don't know that Jones is half owner of The Temp, and those that do, know that Jones don't much get involved anyway."

More rolling of the wrinkle folds. "'Nother reason could be the Feds."

"What have the Feds got to do with it?"

Bucky explained. "Well, they seem to have gotten mighty busy in the past couple of months. And the Rubbles have been the target of most of their attention."

"Okay, maybe, I guess that can explain it. But why do you think the Feds are zeroed in on the Rubbles?"

"Could be their opium reputation. Or maybe just coincidence. Either way, they've been too busy to make a move on The Temp."

The office chair had a squeaking pivot and Kaleb leaned back into the squeak, thinking this over. When his eyes refocused, Bucky continued. "The Rubbles, Miz and the boys, got a place out in the boonies. Rubble's Bubble. More of a dope house than a speak, really. But she gots designs on movin' downtown. Looks like her designs are on The Temp again."

Again Kaleb's eyes unfocused and drifted toward the ceiling as he played this thought through Kaleb asked, "How big is her squad?"

This time Bucky's wrinkled forehead creased a V between his eyes. "Hmmm, well, there's Miz Rubble, she's the boss, and her two sons, big boys with a streak of mean. Other than that, Miz Rubble jes picks up the mercenary goon as needed."

Kaleb let that settle. "And what about the Purple Gang?" Even the name Purple Gang rolled off Kaleb's tongue easily, like a natural fit. "Tell me 'bout the Purples?"

This time Bucky's forehead wrinkles lifted his scalp. "The Purples, boss? You really don't remember the Purple Gang?"

Kaleb was getting a foggy recollection somewhere deep in the recesses of his gray matter but he said, "Noooo. Not really. Something about…."

"You used ta run with the Purples, boss. They was your classmates at Bishop High. They was your playmates and your buds. You come from the same Paradise Valley streets as those boys; boss, you *was* the Purple Gang."

"Flush that out a little 'bout me 'n the Purples, Buck."

"Only know what you told me. You boys were all part of the Jewish street urchins that scampered the streets of Paradise Valley. Started as a neighbor baseball squad but eventually a contingent moved on to harassing the neighborhood. Petty crime stuff at first. Purse snatchin', rolling drunks, that sort of thing. A contingent graduated to working for the Sugar House Gang and full-blown gang warfare. Eventually that young Jewish street ensemble evolved into the Purple Gang. Don't know when you broke from them or why. If you weren't half Jewish yourself, they probably never would have let you play with 'em."

Somehow Kaleb was not surprised. Disappointed but not surprised. The more Kaleb learned about himself, the more he was not surprised at an illicit narration. The criminal element drew a steadfast gravity over the orbit of Kaleb Kierka.

"Anyone else comes to mind that I might best concern myself with?"

"You mean 'bout your beatdown?"

"I mean 'bout my beatdown."

"Jesus, boss, there must be half a.dozen no-goods you crossed one way or t'nother. You never did give much leeway to red-hots and goons. Even crossed Capone's gang a time or two." Kaleb thought back to the receipts he had come across in his earlier search of the office. There were plenty of sales receipts for Capone's Log Cabin Whiskey, so Capone was a buyer.

"Al Capone."

Bucky only nodded.

"From Chicago?"

"The same."

It was odd what stuck to Kaleb's recall. The name Al Capone rang the bell and the ringing resonated. He knew of Al Capone and he knew of the Chicago mobs. But the closer to home he got, the closer to Detroit and deeper he dug into the man named Kaleb Kierka the less the shovel hit pay dirt.

Bucky was flushing it out. "'N buying hooch from the independents running the Detroit River never gained you much glam from any of the gang dealers."

"So I bypassed the gangs like the Purples and stocked my shelves with private-party hooch?"

"Sometime right off'n the boat."

A lot to consider but Kaleb had to start somewhere. Absently he pulled softly on his eyebrow, on the scar, and rocked a squeak out of the chair. "Where can I find Miz Rubble and the boys?"

With his face rolling on waves of wrinkles, Bucky thought this over. "Rubble's got a Rubble's Bubble dive out west. She's on an unincorporated farm out on a dirt road. Livery-somet'ing."

"Livernois?" The memory was playing hide and seek with Kaleb. Somehow he knew the dirt road Livernois.

"Sure. That's it. Livernois."

"And what about the Purple Gang? Where will I find the Purples?"

Bucky's face broke into a Charleston, his wrinkles barely keeping up with the tune. "I don' know boss, you never let them boys into the club. I think that you had a falling out of some kind. Anyway, you got no use for those boys no more."

When Kaleb didn't say anything, Bucky continued, "Everybody buys booze from the Purples 'cept you. You go independent, buyin' the hootch from your own collection of local rumrunners. Suprisin' thing is, the Purples leave you be."

"Why, do you think that is?"

This question made a mess of Bucky's face. "Can't say. Mostly they're a mean bunch and don't cut slack to outside competition. You? Don't know. They just let The Temp be."

When Kaleb said nothing, Bucky continued, "Sure boss. Everybody gets their booze from the Purples in Detroit. But other than that, you and Jones keep 'em out of the club."

Kaleb rocked a squeaky rhythm in the chair while he thought this through.

"You say I was tight with the Purples, but now I'm on the outs with them?"

Bucky shook his head back and forth in thought and the wrinkles followed a centimeter behind with each roll. "My understandin', sure. But I wouldn't know where to find 'em. They keep a tight profile. Maybe the band can help. They git around to the different clubs, you know. Maybe they know. Or maybe one of the newspaper hawkers. They're all over the streets."

"Newspaper hawkers?"

"Sure, boss, those newsboys are all over the city streets. They's everywhere. And they got eyes and ears. You want the legit news, you buy a newspaper. You want the underbelly news, you buy the newsboy."

***

When Kaleb and Bucky emerged from the back office and into the bar, musicians were beginning to join Beethoven Jones on the stage. A drummer. A trumpet player.

Sitting separate, toward the front glass-block windows of The Temp, an old man with an accordion was working with a black child, maybe 12 years old, who was clawing out notes on a violin.

The child was dressed to the nines, and although the suit was old and worn, it was crisp in its cleanliness and the necktie was tied tight and high to his neck. The boy was dressed in his Sunday best on a Saturday afternoon.

The child was awkwardly chinning the violin while the accordion player pointed out finger placements to him. Squawk squeak squawk went the dressed-to-the-nines boy on the violin. Squawk squeak squawk.

The stage was a fifteen by ten foot affair and rose about two feet above the dance floor. The extra height gave the audience good sight lines to the musicians. It also elevated the musicians into the miasma of the cigarette and reefer smoke that hung along the ceiling of a full club.

When Kaleb approached the stage, he was again greeted warmly and enthusiastically. Thanking them for the greeting, he apologized and asked that they should reintroduce themselves. "…Memory muddle," he offered.

The introductions awkwardly went around. August Pini was the trumpet player, a tiny little white man with a big nose that rivaled the span of the trumpet. A chunky black man with lightly salted hair, Billy Oldham, was keying his snare drum into tune.

Turning to the bassist, Kaleb nodded, "Beethoven Jones."

Even as he sat on the bar stool, Beethoven Jones loomed above the assembly.

Jones did not make eye contact but acknowledged with a tip of his head and said, "'Flattered you 'member me."

Kaleb nodded back, noting the hard and tight muscles in the elongated, lithe black arms. "You'd be a hard one to forget."

Jones threw Kaleb off his track by nodding toward the front of the club in the direction of the accordion player and the young boy. He offered, "Up there ya got Krikor. He been teachin' young Louis the violin."

Kaleb rolled the name around in his mouth, repeating it under his breath, *Krikor*. "Krikor. And who's the boy? Louis? What's the boys last name, and what's his business in The Temp?"

August Pini lowered the trumpet from his lips, from his nose. It must have been his extraordinary proboscis that gave Pini's voice the heft. In a deep baritone, the diminutive Pini offered, "Barrow is the boy's last name. His first name, I think, is Joey. Yeah, Joey Louis Barrow. Least ways that's what his mama calls him when she gets mad at 'em. He gets his Saturday violin lesson from Krikor right here. In The Temp."

"Every Saturday?"

The baritone continued, "Like clockwork. Right there. His mama's a stickler for that boy to be something beyond the streets. Don't never see that kid in any less than his Sunday best."

Billy Oldham set down his tuning wrench from his drums and enjoined, "Waste of two bits, iffin' you ask me."

August was quick to rejoin, "The boy's a good kid."

"Sure, he is a good kid, alright. His mama makes him a gentleman, that's for sure. Jes that the kid is tone-deaf is all. That boys been takin' lessons for close to a year now, and he can't hear a hoot from a holler."

Kaleb took a listen to the music lesson playing out at the front of the bar, and sure enough, if this boy was a year deep into these violin lessons, he would have to agree with Billy Oldham's estimation.

"Where's the boy's family from?"

"South. 'Bama I believe. Got run out by the Klan. Been in Detroit 'most a year now. Live up on Catherine Street."

Billy Oldham added, "Funny thing is, one time little Joey come in and open his violin case 'n out pops a pair of boxin' gloves?"

"Boxing gloves? What's the boy doing with boxing gloves in the violin case?"

Oldham had to laugh. "I 'spect he's keepin' hidden from his mama. That Mama Lillie Barrow don't want Joey growin' up to be nothin' but a gentleman."

August nodded toward Beethoven Jones. "Meybe if'n Jones 'ere was teachin' the kid. 'Sides bass fiddle, Jones play the violin fiddle too."

Kaleb turned again to Jones. "You play the violin?"

"A mite."

"Why'n'cha helping teach the boy."

Beethoven Jones set to tuning his bass. After a moment he said quietly, almost to himself, "I told you. I don't get involved." He then turned the conversation away from the young Joey. "You be sittin' in with the band t'night?" he asked of Kaleb.

It caught Kaleb off guard, and one by one, he looked into the hopeful faces of August and Billy. When Kaleb looked back at Jones, Jones nodded in the direction of the piano. "We got a fresh tunin' on it and it's ready to ride."

The piano was a Steinway, an upright grand. Strung like a grand piano and tipped up for space conservation. An upright grand piano.

Somewhere deep in Kaleb's core stirred a recognition of the piano. However deep the recognition, it was a vague recollection to Kaleb's consciousness. "I, I don't think that I will."

The baritone Pini offered, "Do you some good to set down and bang away. You always called it therapy."

And Billy Oldham added "Yep. 'N do us some world of good to have ya sittin' in."

"'Nother time," Kaleb said and he turned the conversation. "What can you boys tell me about the Purples?"

That colored the musicians' mood. Black. Whistling through his teeth, Billy tendered "Whew, boy, Kabe, you sure got one ugly segue."

"You know 'bout the Purple Gang?"

Uncomfortable on the topic, Billy shook his head, "Personally? No. Know about 'em? Sure. Everybody knows about the Purples. Ugliest collection of rumrunners Detroit ever stockpiled. But I thought you was out of that game now?"

"I didn't know I was in it."

It was apparent to the musicians that Kaleb was at a loss, and Jones came in and said, "Kaleb, look man, you used ta run with dose boys. You 'n me both when we were kids. But they was a fallin' out with 'em an' it left you on the outs. We don't mention 'em much no more."

So maybe this was it, maybe the Purple Gang was his tormentor.

Over the din of the squawk squeak squawk, Kaleb pressed on. "Where can I find those boys?"

Billy, August, and Jones exchanged cheerless looks.

Billy offered, "You don't want to find them, man."

If Kaleb wanted to retrace his life, he would need to follow the path. "Yes. Yes, I believe I do."

Billy Oldham, shaking his head said "I don' think it's healthy but if'n yer bound and determined....well, you might try that little newsie comes in 'ere. Little Eddy I think the name is."

"Little Eddy?"

"Sure. Little Eddy, scrawny little kid, 14, 15 years old. Comes in 'ere most every day selling newspapers and runnin' numbers for the Purples. He was in 'ere earlier takin' bets on the Tigers game."

"For a juice joint, we sure get a lot of kids runnin' through here." Again Kaleb took a turn around each face, "And this boy, Eddy, he runs numbers for the Purples?"

"Sure. He's a numbers runner for 'em. He's got ta link up wit' 'em at some turn. I 'magine he knows how to find 'em"

"Know where Eddy is now?"

August's rolling baritone put in, "'Bout this time a day, the boy sells newspapers over on Madison in Kunsky's Circle. He got a regular newsstand there...." August was shaking his head back and forth, his big beak leading the way. "...But I don't know how wise it is ta be huntin' up the Purple Gang."

Kaleb looked from face to face of August, Billy, and Jones. Anxious and apprehensive faces all.

At that moment Joey Louis Barrow struck a shrill note on the violin that sent a shock up everyone's spinal cords.

Wincing, Beethoven Jones concluded, "Those big brown bomb fists need to find another enterprise."

Kaleb cringed at the sound of Joey's screeching fiddle, nodded a sympathetic salutation to Pini, Oldham, and Jones, and then he turned to and walked through the door of The Temple Bar Speakeasy And Play Nice.

***

When the Tigers game ended, Granma would slowly come out of her baseball trance. She'd look around the bar to see who had shared the game with her, and then she would spit chaw into her tin corn can. As she slid her stout frame off of the barstool, she would give a quick wave and say, "See ya, Buck…"

Turning off the radio, Bucky waved his wrinkles to her, "Behave yerself, Granma."

As she slipped through the door she cursed under her breath, "Goddamnittohellandbackagain," and Beethoven Jones knew that the Tigers had lost the ball game.

25

Jazz

There is a place for every mark-up of man in a music ensemble. The happy and the sad and the good and the bad. The tortured and the saved and the fallen and the brave. There are musicians who are studious, giving great weight and study to each note probed, and then there are musicians who are cavalier and mischievous and tease every note as a coy cherub.

Every style and personality can be found in a music ensemble. Can and will.

As incongruous as it might seem, there is even plenty of space for the loner, the isolated spirit, in the company of the music ensemble. Reserved and withdrawn souls smoldering in a private flame. Solemn and somber and solitary souls.

Jones carried this aloneness. This sadness. Whether a solitary stature, coaxing forth the somber voice of the bowed bass or finger thumping the strings in a ferocious groove in the midst of a full throbbing ensemble.

Beethoven Jones bore lonely like an illegible scrawl on a weathered tombstone.

Reclusive, Jones spent long days on the stage with his bass fiddle, forlornly dragging the bow across the catguts, across the deepest notes of humanity. At times the low notes spoke soothingly with a tenderness of compassion and empathy. Other times the muted tones spoke with the chilled shade of the down and the dirty and the forsaken.

Whether tender or chilled, each voice confided to a private haven deep within the bass fiddle of Beethoven Jones.

***

Jazz du Jour was stompin' The Temple Bar Speakeasy And Play Nice. In full swing, they powered the dance floor with a music that sweat sweet. Jazz. Sweet and sweaty jazz.

Oldham was kicking the drums into the groove and Beethoven Jones was pumping the wellspring of jive juice while Krikor comped chords on the accordion, and Doctor Dan growled the saxophone six feet into the dirt.

The patrons, cutting the rug, cutting the night, splashed the dance floor with their troubles and their woes and left them there, stomped to nothingness, stomped into oblivion. Stomped to oblivion if only for the night, if only for the dance.

For even oblivion has its limits.

***

At fourteen years of age Beethoven Jones stood a foot taller than his compatriots and even in the blue-collar neighborhood of the assorted human hues of Paradise Valley, he stood alone. Due to his height, Jones was recruited to Detroit's premiere high school, Central High, at Cass and Warren Streets, to play for the school's fledgling basketball team. As it would turn out, Beethoven Jones was a terrible basketball player, but the recruitment did allow Jones access to one of the finest educational outlets that Detroit could offer, and he quickly became a fixture in the school's music department.

Jones, Jonesy, Too Tall, Stretch, the Colored Colossal, whatever moniker that was hefted upon Jones never seemed to stick, and as cumbersome as the name Beethoven Jones might be, many folks gave full breadth to the name Beethoven Jones when addressing him. Even so, the full girth of the name Beethoven Jones did not give a full account to the physical length of the man.

Jones teamed up with his classmate pianist, Kaleb Kierka, and the boyhood duet became a local mainstay in the Detroit entertainment circuit. Billed as The Jew Boy and The Colored Boy, Kaleb and Jones were minor celebrities about Detroit and were adopted almost as pets in the bourgeoisie circles. The duo and their music gave the boys options rarely afforded to the youth of Paradise Valley, as they became the cause célèbre of the upper class.

Although the boys were too young to tour the national vaudeville circuit, they became a core opening-act in the entertainment stronghold of Detroit's vaudeville bastion of the Grand Circus Park theaters.

Grand Circus Park was Detroit's uptown entertainment nucleus. A four-block cut of land with Adams Street to the north and Witherell Street doing a half-moon circle along the east, west, and southern borders of the park, the park itself was a green respite during the day. A playground for toddlers, a gossip mill for young mothers, and a lounge where old men could sit on park benches and share foggy memories about the big war that got away. At night it became Detroit's theater district.

John Kunsky built more than twenty theaters in the Detroit area with most of them circling the Grand Circus Park. This collection of hopping nightspots included movie houses, restaurants, taxi dance parlors, and vaudeville theaters and became known as Kunsky's Circle, Detroit's entertainment Mecca.

The Jew Boy and The Colored Boy were one of the hottest local acts to grace Kunsky's Circle.

With the money that Kaleb and Jones made in the local vaudeville clubs, they were able to open The Temple Bar Speakeasy And Play Nice. The boys envisioned The Temp as a musical outlet where they could host music compatriots, and explore this newest and wildest of a music medium. Jazz. The Temp became a late night hot spot of musical discovery.

The boys' music compatriots in Detroit and the touring musical acts from the vaudeville circuit soon found their way through the doors of The Temple Bar Speakeasy And Play Nice. As for the illegal booze aspect of The Temp, well, that was just what one did in this roaring decade of 1920s America.

Noted as a safe place to hear the best music that Detroit could muster, The Temple Bar Speakeasy And Play Nice quickly became a fixture in the underground entertainment scene of Detroit, circa 1927.

The Temp became notorious as a place of refuge for national touring acts. After finishing their engagements on the vaudeville circuit in Kunsky's Circle, the touring musicians would inevitably find their way to The Temp, sharing their musical wares deep into the night. The Temp became a pilgrimage, a mecca that national touring musicians would pay homage. Acts from shore to shore would genuflect toward Kaleb and Jones's speakeasy as they toured America on the vaudeville entertainment circuit.

In this manner The Temple Bar Speakeasy And Play Nice became a melting pot of musical styles of jazz. Jazz in its infancy. Jazz as a rough sketch. Jazz as it was yet defining its very nature.

The speakeasy hosted musical explorations as divergent as New Orleans swing to the blues of the rural plantations to the country pickings of the Appalachians to the European gypsies fresh off the boat at Ellis Island.

All of these styles and much more found their confluence in the reefer drenched early hours of the corner stage at The Temple Bar Speakeasy And Play Nice.

Kaleb Kierka and Beethoven Jones, The Jew Boy and The Colored Boy, played host to this late night confederacy of America's original art form: jazz.

26

Sylvia Botter

The white woman had two children in her fists and came straight up to Kaleb as he sat at a table watching the band tune up. One child, a girl, was in a tattered dress and just shy of waist-high to the woman. The little girl was holding a bundle wrapped in plain brown paper with a twine fastened tight.

The boy was just as natty, sporting holes in the knees of his pants, coming thigh-high to the woman. Both children were barefoot. The woman's clothes fared no better than the children's garb. Although the trio's clothes were shabby and worn, the clothes were clean and the children were tidy.

Sylvia Botter wore lipstick like an amateur. The lipstick spilled over the edges of her mouth like it was on unfamiliar terrain. The lipstick did not want to be there, and it was trying its damnedest to get away.

When Sylvia Botter reached Kaleb's table she smiled graciously, but the lipstick had already caught the Midnight Zephyr to the coast.

Kaleb smiled back, looked over the children and the woman with the nomadic lipstick, and offered, "Hello, can I help you?"

Sylvia took the package from the little girl and set it on the table in front of Kaleb. Her smile opened up and showed a patchy collection of abused teeth. Maybe the reason for the lipstick's attempt at escape.

But the smile was very beautiful and it was genuine when she spoke. "I heard you wasn't keen in the memory department. You don' 'member us?"

Kaleb looked into each of the three faces but there was nothing in there for him. "I'm sorry. I don't."

Concern scowled the woman's forehead and the lipstick caught a streetcar to anywhere else. "I'm sorry too." She tried to mold the lipstick into a smile again. "But, leastways, I'm glad to see that you are healthy in yer body. These are yours," she said and indicated the package she had set down.

Kaleb looked at the package and then at the woman's face. Nothing stuck so he looked back to the package she had set on the table.

And simple as that, Sylvia Botter turned and led the children right back out of the door of The Temple Bar Speakeasy And Play Nice.

Sylvia's lipstick had to run to keep up.

***

"Goddamnittohellandbackagain." and Granma spit chaw.

The Yankees were in town, Holloway was on the mound, and Granma was on her roost, center barstool, in front of the radio. The Tigers were down by half a dozen and Granma's "Goddamnittohellandbackagain" oven was cooking with gas.

New York's murderer's row, Ruth, Gehrig, and Meusel, were pounding Detroit's pitching, and the Tigers were well on their way to their worst thrashing of the season.

Tentatively, Kaleb untied the twine on the brown paper package that Sylvia had set down before him. Shirts, pants, underwear, socks, towels. All clean and neatly folded. There was an invoice on the top of the clothes that read "Clean and fold, 25 cents per pound. Three pounds total." Scrawled across the invoice, in big red letters, "Paid In Full."

The sound of the bat smacking the baseball slapped from the radio on the bar, quickly followed by the pinging of spit tobacco juice in a tin can. The exclamation of "Goddamnittohellandbackagain" was the inevitable clincher.

Maybe this would be a good time to pick Granma's brain.

***

Granma appreciated the distraction from the Tigers game gone wrong. She studied Kaleb up and down squeezing one eye in her examination. "You really don't 'member nothing, eh?'

"Some stuff is wheedling in. Not much."

"Not your ol' Granma?"

He studied Granma's face, the lazy eye, the iron-gray hair, the dark, southern European complexion, the mole on her cheek sprouting three wire-like hairs. The tobacco chaw had stained the corners of Granma's mouth a juicy brown, and the mouth lines, tilted down, bore the memory of more frowns than smiles. "Nope, Granma. Sorry."

Granma was not offended. "And that washer woman, Sylvia..."

"Sylvia?" He let the name play on his tongue before he pressed his lips together and shook his head slowly to the negative.

"Right. Sylvia. Sylvia Botter. You don't 'member her a'tall?"

"No. Not really. Sometimes I get a feeling I know someone, some thing, but I just can't seem to finger the mark."

Granma answered with "Goddamnittohellandbackagain," but the exclamation was referencing the Tigers game that was droning on in the background. Holloway had just given up a sixth run to the Yankees, and Ownie Carroll was coming in as relief. Granma had no faith in Ownie's curve ball. Goddamnittohellandbackagain.

Granma reached over and turned down the radio. "You, boy, you don't 'member Sylvia Botter and her brood of babies?"

"Not any longer than meeting her ten minutes ago. Were we something to each other?"

"Somethin'?"

"Was she my, my, that is, was she my special gal sometime?"

Granma laughed to herself. "No, Kabe, she weren't your sheeba and you weren't no lovers, that's a fact." Granma studied Kaleb with her good eye while her lazy eye went on a sightseeing tour of the ceiling. "Boy, you were something to behold in that ass-kicking."

"I kicked Sylvia's ass?"

Granma laughed earnestly and her lazy eye watered in delight. The laughter bubbled up a swallow of brown juice and Granma spit it into her corn can spit-cup. "No, Goddamnittohellandbackagain, boy, you didn't kick Sylvia's ass. You kicked Sylvia's no-account husband's ass."

Again with the violence. Guns and gangsters and brawling beatdowns. The more that Kaleb learned about himself, the more his life seemed to be steeped in violence.

"And you really can't 'member it?"

"Nope. Seems I've had a crossing with this Sylvia woman, but my memory can't argue the point."

Granma's lazy eye unfocused to a corner of the ceiling as she recalled the event. "This woman, this Sylvia, was not much more than a girl of nineteen or so. Three children had already taken turns suckin' on her teats and a fourth child was fatiguing those breasts again. She married young to an older man. Abusive man. Tommy-John Botter. A no-account that Tommy-John Botter was. Lots of good men coming up from those Appalachian Mountains but not that Tommy-John. Tommy-John was a mean one. A bully and a belligerent and a buffoon. Tommy-John Botter kept Sylvia and the babies in rags while he caroused and drank hisself a fit. Beat that poor child-wife aplenty."

Kaleb grasped for the image but there was nothing there. "What was my draw with this Tommy-John Botter?"

"First off, you banned him from drinkin' at Temple Bar."

Kaleb's brow, the eyebrow with the new scar, tugged gently on the fresh skin, and he stroked the brow with fingers, soothing the scar absently as he considered Granma's account.

"And this is why the woman tweaks so hard at the edge of my memory? Just because I banned her husband from the bar?"

Granma threw back her head and laughed again. It was a hardy laugh without a single Goddamnittohellandbackagain to be found.

"Nope. It started at a Christmas party 'ere at The Temp."

"We have Christmas parties here?"

"Sure. An' you were here. An' Jones. An' Bucky an' Nika an' Hollie an'..."

"Nika was at the Christmas party? But Nika's Jewish, Jesus ain't her God."

Granma was chagrined and spit a chaw. "First off, Nika was celebrating the darkest day of the year with her friends. But outside of that, God or no God, Jesus was a Jewish man doing heroic works. What's not to celebrate?"

Kaleb played with the thought until Granma pushed on "You wanna hear the Sylvia Botter story or not?"

"Right. Sylvia Botter. What is Sylvia Botter and her kids to me?"

"Okay then. Listen up boy, 'ere's how it played..."

***

Sylvia Botter would walk the streets with the children when Tommy-John was in his worst drunks. These drunks of Tommy-John's would leave her children cowering in the corners and Sylvia's face beaten and bloodied. Later she would tell people that she had walked into a door but people knew. People knew. There just weren't that many doors for her to walk into. People knew.

So she would bundle up the children on those days of liquor and whippings; she would bundle up the children in their rags and baby in the stroller with the bent axle and squeaky wheel. She would bundle up the children and walk the streets of Paradise Valley. And the Black Bottom. And beyond. For hours she would lead her brood about the corridors and the boulevards of Detroit while her provider drank himself to oblivion until he passed out in his stink of booze. Sylvia and the children would walk the streets until it would be safe for Sylvia and the children to return home.

Scorching sun or blizzard cold, no weather was a deterrent for Sylvia and her brood when Tommy-John was on one of his drunks. People knew.

The Tommy-John Botters were the best argument that the Prohibition League could muster for their crusade.

People knew.

You could hear the raggedy collection of mother and children coming, and you could hear them going as the bent axle on the stroller thumped a beat with every turn of the pin, and the squeaky wheels kept a droning chorus of sympathy to their plight. *Squeak-squeak-squeak-thump. Squeak-squeak-squeak-thump. Squeak-squeak-squeak-thump* went the pageant of mother and child. *Squeak-squeak-squeak-thump.*

On the coldest of days, when the chill froze fingertips and the ice crystals from frozen breath chilled the face, you could hear the sad march of displaced mother and children as they made their way around the neighborhoods of Detroit. Up one street and down the next. *Squeak-squeak-squeak-thump.*

On occasion the drunken slot, Tommy-John, would track them down. He would hunt them, stalking his own family - how dare they walk out on him? - and if he found them there would be hell to pay. Sylvia's only hope would be to keep moving. To keep walking and turning corners and walking to the next boulevard and turning the next corner. A moving target is a difficult target to hit.

People knew. The neighbors knew. The neighborhoods knew. Everyone knew and nobody called him out. Nobody dared the wrath of the bully.

The bully, Tommy-John Botter, was immune to account until...

It was Christmas Day and The Temple Bar Speak Easy And Play Nice was having a Christmas party for the souls left alone on the holiday of Christ.

Bucky was there. And Nika was there and Beethoven Jones was there and Krikor and Kitty were there and Granma was there. And Kaleb was there as well. Celebrating a communal cheer to pass the dark solstice just as man has celebrated it from time immemorial.

As they raised their glasses to toast this community, this celebration of unity and love, even as their tumblers clinked in seasonal joy, from the street came the familiar and forlorn squeak-squeak-squeak-thump of the collection of rags on their flight from terror.

On Christmas Day.

Granma spit a wad and went to the front window to watch Sylvia and the procession of rags as they squeak-squeak-squeak-thumped past The Temp. It was a hard thing to watch.

"It's the Botters alright," Granma announced over her shoulders. "On Christmas Day." And she turned back to the club because she could not watch the sad procession of mother and child. "Goddamnittohellandbackagain."

Nika reached across the table and rested her hand on Kaleb's. "Isn't there something we can do?"

"It's really not our place."

Giving Kaleb's hand a soft squeeze, Nika said, "Maybe just invite 'em in to get warm?"

The sad procession outside troubled Kaleb, certainly, but it was Nika's entreating smoky black eyes that made him cede. She pushed on, "It's Christmas Day."

When Kaleb went out to bundle the brood of refugees into the warmth and community of The Temp, it was at that precise moment that the bully found his clutch. And Tommy-John was drunk and his eyes were red with rage.

Tommy-John did not see Kaleb as Tommy-John's sights were set on Sylvia. It was she who led the clutch and she would be the first, although not the last, target of his fury. But Kaleb saw Tommy-John all right. And Kaleb stepped between the bully and his family.

It took a moment for the drunken slot to understand the situation but when he did, when he grasped the meaning of Kaleb's interference, a full measure of squall was directed at Kaleb, and he charged with both fists flying at this impetuous interloper.

Kaleb put up both hands, open and empty, and commanded, "Wait."

The demand and gesture, Kaleb's open and raised hands, surprised the drunken Tommy-John, and he stopped in his tracks with wonder, confusion and anger splashing his face in turns.

A contingent from the bar, Nika and Hollie and Kitty and Bucky, had followed Kaleb to the street. Granma waited on her barstool roost. Jones stayed in the bar and did not get involved.

Kaleb needed only nod to Nika and Kitty and the women collected the bundle of exiles, Sylvia and her children, and escorted them inside. Squeak-squeak-squeak-thump went the parade of rags into The Temple Bar Speakeasy And Play Nice.

When the last of the bundle of bruises crossed the bar's threshold, Kaleb again turned his attention to the enraged Tommy-John.

Hell would be paid and the tab was open.

Granma had not followed the partiers to the street so she could not attest to what happened next. But this much Granma did know: when next she saw the drunken bully, Tommy-John, he was not a drunk and he was not a bully.

It was two days past New Year's Day when Granma again encountered Tommy-John Botter on the street. The bully wore the same manner of violent bruises that he had so often tattooed on his family. His left leg was bent at an odd angle, and when he walked down the street his body went squeak-squeak-squeak-thump.

***

Granma had barely finished the story before the distraction of the Tigers drubbing demanded her attention. Goddamnittohellandbackagain.

***

Again with the violence. Again with the mayhem.

Once again Kaleb learned that he was a man of violence. Of carnage. Every story of Kaleb's past that unfolded, every chronicle of his history, was littered with violence and mayhem. A man comfortable with warfare and easy to the battle.

Was this, then, this man of violence; was this the man who accounted for the self that wore the moniker of Kaleb Kierka?

Kaleb's shoulders betrayed an uncomfortable shudder at the prospect.

***

"Goddamnittohellandbackagain," ranted Granma.

Ownie Carroll had given up six runs and the Tigers went down to their worst drubbing of the season, 19-7, against these damn Yankees.

"Goddamnittohellandbackagain."

27

The Recipe Of Man

Nika and Kitty sat in the kitchen area of their studio apartment. Their third roommate, Tia, was working her day gig as a nurse at Parkside Hospital, the colored hospital, over on Brush Street.

The three women, Kitty the prostitute, Nika the nightclub singer, and Tia the nurse, shared a studio apartment in the Black Bottom. The single bed would accommodate their rotating schedules. Often their schedules would overlap and they would share the bed. Two to the bed was comfortable. Three to the bed was tricky.

The Murphy bed, blankets jumbled, was let down and assumed itself over half of the living space of the apartment. They sat in the only two chairs offered in the apartment, Kitty in the pillow easy chair and Nika at the kitchen table on the Windsor back dining chair. Nika was nipping at a steaming cup of coffee while Kitty, sitting upright on the sofa chair with her legs tucked under her, was tilling her nappy tresses with a hair-pick. Even bobbed and ironed flapper style, Kitty's hair fought every tooth of the comb.

The studio apartment was no frills, a kitchenette, a living area that housed the Murphy bed, and two windows. One window view overlooked the brick wall of the neighboring brick building a mere eight feet away. The other window had a view of Mullet Street three stories below and might offer a nice perch for a suicide. The toilet and shower were down the hallway and was shared by the entire second floor.

"Better skip to the loo 'fore 'partment 29 wakes," offered Kitty as she plowed through the nap of her hair. "Once he sets to the pot the place ain't habitable. That boy leave that bathroom smellin' worse'n a outhouse in a 'Bama swelter."

It was seven o'clock in the morning and Kitty had yet to make bed-fall. The mussed blankets on the Murphy were Nika's doing.

Nika held the coffee to her lips, letting the aroma swirl to her nostrils, letting the heat of the cup warm her hands.

Kitty's cup of brew was supplemented with the sleep enticement of a shot of peppermint schnapps.

The one room studio apartment that the three women shared was cluttered with the photographs of Kitty's children. Despite the grainy black and white of the photos, one could tell that the children spanned an assortment of racial identity. Her children bridged the color spectrum from light, even white, to black as coal. The array of shading of prostitute Kitty's offspring testified to her service to the white community and the black community.

***

For Kitty, babies were a commodity that came easy. A mother at fourteen, a double mother at sixteen and her third child by the time she was seventeen, Kitty had followed the black labor movement migrating north toward the industrial promise of a better living. Kitty was fast on the movement's heels as part of the service trade that supported the industrial industry. Employment options were limited to a black girl in the rural South and Kitty did what Kitty had to do to feed her babies. To survive.

Like her mama and her mama's mama and her mama's mama's mama, Kitty worked the cotton fields until her womanhood liberated her from the fields. And enslaved her into another commerce.

They didn't call it slavery anymore. They called it sharecropping. Whether slavery or sharecropping, the upshot was the same: more babies and less food.

Sharecropping. Sure. Sharecropping. Kitty shared her crop all right and her field proved to be very fertile. Four babies in thirty-five months fertile.

That was the way. That was how it was in the poverty of the rural Alabama. But Kitty wanted more for her babies. What exactly more meant she had only a vague notion but more is what she wanted. There had to be more. More of *something.*

Leaving her babies in the care of extended family and with a satchel full of rags and tenuous dreams, Kitty made her way to the North. North to the promise of jobs and equality and freedom. North to the future. North to Detroit.

In Detroit Kitty did find better wages and greater freedom and though equality was yet ambiguous, the promise of equality was robust. As for profession, her lot had been cast, and though the pay was better and the promise nearer, Kitty found herself yet sharecropping the same crop in Detroit that she tilled in Alabama. Prostitution.

The plan was for Kitty to secure enough of a foothold in Detroit to bring her babies north to a better life and a future of promise. Until then Kitty would scrimp and save and send as much money to her babies as she could glean from sharing her crop.

***

As for Nika's family pictures about the apartment, there were none. Hers was not a history that she wanted adorning the walls. Her memories of Bliss Gate and Big Joe would have been a taunt hanging on the walls of this studio apartment.

Nika sipped on the warm brown brew and felt it slide past her tongue and down her throat, chipping away at the flatness of her tired black eyes. "What's on your map today, honey."

Kitty was tugging on a snag in her locks. "'Git some rest, mostly."

"Tough night in the cradle?"

Kitty gave a small, sour laugh. "'Member Kenny Picka?"

"Picka? Picka. That big oaf up by Perrien Park?"

"Yep."

"Kinda smells like carrion?"

"Yep. Same. The carrion from Perrien."

"Christ. He's a tough one."

"Three hours under that stinkin' carcass. An' I swear he's got a railroad spike for a sconge. And that wasn't even the worst. He brought along that beady Billy that's got more fingers than brains. Just ain't right how that little fellow can prickle those digits. Like having sex with a porc'pine. An' he tastes like skunk. Porc'pine and skunk. I jes thank the good Lord above for the schnapps." She hoisted up her cup of coffee'd schnapps in a toast, knocking back a generous gulp.

Nika set down her coffee, went over to Kitty, climbed on back of the pillow chair that embraced Kitty, and straddled Kitty's shoulders with her legs. She took the hair pick from Kitty and began gently working out the knots in her kinked hair. "You need to get some sleep today, baby. You been up 'most twenty four hours now."

Kitty cozied under Nika's touch and relaxed her back into the crux of Nika's thighs while Nika picked at the knots on Kitty's head. "Soon's I git to the post. I need to send off jack to my 'Bama babies."

Nika could feel Kitty settle in between her legs as she busied the knap. It warmed Nika in a woman's way to have Kitty nestled so close, so tight. "How old's your youngest baby, now, Kit?"

Kitty thought about this while she sipped at her coffee and schnapps. "Le's see, she 'most one years ol' when I come up 'ere and I been up 'ere best of two years, so's she'll be three next November. November 24. She's my Thanksgiving baby."

The warmth of the drink, the cozy of Nika's thighs, and the gentle hair picking were bearing on Kitty's countenance and her body began to relax. Weariness from the night of sharecropping was beginning to weigh on her bones and her eyelids sagged with the fatigue. She shuddered her shoulders to keep herself awake. "I gots to get the money off to the post."

Nika set down the pick and began massaging Kitty's neck and shoulders. "Lookit 'ere, baby, I'm runnin' up Willis Street way 'n meetin' Kaleb for lunch. I can drop by the post."

Kitty tilted her head back and looked up to Nika. The schnapps gave Kitty a warm pinkness under her milk chocolate cheeks. "You take some good care of me nice, baby, better'n no man never did," she said. Kitty set the coffee mug down and turned around toward Nika, cuddling against Nika's thighs.

Returning a tight embrace, Nika caressed and kissed Kitty's forehead. The sweet bouquet of Nika's perspiration diluted the tang of a night with Kenny Picka. Pulling her tight to her chest, Nika held Kitty's face to her breasts. Holding fast, Nika held Kitty until Kitty fell asleep in her arms.

A measure of kindness. A measure of love. A dash of grief, a pinch of hope. Measurements of humanness. Part of the recipe, the measure, of man.

Nika retrieved the blanket and the pillow from the Murphy and fussed the slumbering woman into a comfortable position on the pillow chair. She topped off the coddle with a kiss to Kitty's forehead.

Finishing off the last of her coffee, Nika grabbed her bath towel and went off to brave the lavatory at the far end of the hall. She knocked back the remainder of Kitty's schnapps-spiked coffee to steel herself against the bouquet that awaited her in the community bathroom.

28

A Fiver For Your Time

It was dusking a soft amethyst when Kaleb left The Temp, and it was shaping up to be a warm evening with an early sliver of a moon hanging low in the sky. A cool draft from the Detroit River was wafting about the streets of Paradise Valley, tumbling yesterday's newspapers like urban tumbleweeds and whispering sweet nothings to nobody.

Kaleb needed to find his tormenter. Tormentors? Deciding that his best course would be a direct course, he would hunt up the Purple Gang first. Apparently the Purples were known to Kaleb and Kaleb was known to the Purples. Somehow, someway they were connected, and be it to the good or be it to the bad, this connection must be explored.

To hunt up the Purple Gang, he would first need to hunt up the kid who ran numbers for the Purple Gang, the newsie kid, Eddy.

Bucky had mentioned to Kaleb that the newsie Eddy had a regular newspaper corner on Monroe Street in Kunsky's Circle in Grand Circus Park. Kaleb surmised that Eddy would need a place, a rendezvous spot, to relay the numbers and drop off bets to the Purple Gang.

Whether moniker was paperboy, paper-hawk, paper-pusher, ink-dole, or newsie, these deliverers of the newspapers were the ubiquitous news purveyors of the streets and the lifeline of the press. These boys were the bond of all things metro. At a time when the daily newspaper would offer as many as five editions of copy a day, it was the newsie's job to take the ink to the streets. While The *Detroit News* and the *Detroit Free Press* were battling for dominance, the newsboy was the artery that circulated the ink.

Although the dailies offered multiple editions throughout the day, it was the last copy of the day, the 5th Edition that would be the moneymaker. At six in the evening just about every street corner hosted young hawkers shouting out the headlines in hopes of shaking nickels from the throngs. Four cents to the newspaper and one cent in the newsie's pocket. If the kid sold a hundred papers he'd go home with a buck in his pocket. That would be a good day.

The tougher the kid, the better the corner. The better the corner, the bigger the income.

Eddy had a prime corner in Kunsky's Circle in the Grand Circus Park, a premier location for a newsie. From the description that Bucky had given Kaleb, Eddy was a diminutive boy, and if the bigger news hawkers were turned away from Eddy's corner, it would attest to another, higher, authority. The Purple Gang maybe?

The 5 Star Edition would be hitting the street about now and Kunsky's Circle would be the place to find Eddy.

Climbing into the Model T heap, Kaleb turned the vehicle east on Adams and slowly cruised the six blocks through the rush hour traffic in the direction of Grand Circus Park. Traffic lights were a sporadic phenomenon, and once out of the working class neighborhoods, Kaleb guided his T among experimental automobiles, bicycles, and even the occasional horse drawn wagon.

Making a left onto Witherell Street, Kaleb drove the half circle around Grand Circus Park, slowing at the Monroe Street corner. He spotted Eddy on his corner hawking the 5 Star. But Eddy was too busy dealing press for Kaleb to talk to the boy.

Witherell Street was a half loop around the southern rim of Grand Circus Park, and as Kaleb drove the half circle, it returned Kaleb right back up to Adams Street. Driving straight across Adams onto Park Street, Kaleb caught sight of a café where he could grab a quick dinner as he waited for the 5 Star crowd around Eddy to thin.

Guiding the Model T to the curb, Kaleb pulled up to Minnie's Café. Minnie's Café was a half building diner and bustling with a dinner mob. The six tables were full, but of the eight counter stools, only two were occupied, and Kaleb mounted a lone seat at the end of the counter in the back, near the kitchen.

Kaleb's amnesia was like being at the bottom of a deep well that, although he could see light high up to the aperture, he could not see over the lip of the orifice. Each piece of familiarity lifted him ever so slightly from the floor of the well and widened the aperture at the well's summit. Deep in his subconscious there were places, people, and things that rang familiar to Kaleb. Places, people, and things that were buried somewhere deep in his psyche and rang a note of the routine, of the known.

Minnie's Café was not ringing familiar.

Kaleb ordered his burger rare and got a cow on a bun that was still grazing pasture. Minnie's coffee was hard, bracing, like a backhand across the face. A blue-collar coffee with a screeching factory whistle for a wakeup call.

Passing on Minnie's desserts, Kaleb reviewed his circumstance over a third cup of the buttressing brew.

Sifting the players through his mind like a sieve, Kaleb considered Nika and Kitty and Bucky and Beethoven Jones and the band and Detective Morane and Mizzy Rubble and her boys and the Purple Gang. Kaleb gave special consideration to the hatchet-faced man in the navy blue suit. With each pass of these characters through his gray matter, the fog of amnesia was dissipating incrementally.

Somewhere in the cacophony of these characters, and the sundry streets of this very city, existed a man named Kaleb Kierka. A man, it would seem, of some influence, of some talent, of some good and of some bad. A man determined by his deeds. Quantified by his actions. Measured by his manner.

A man he was slowly coming to know.

***

Leaving the jalopy in front of Minnie's Cafe, Kaleb walked the two blocks across Grand Circus Park to the corner of Madison. The hitch in Kaleb's step was becoming less pronounced with every stride as the damaged nerve endings reconnected routes to his brain.

The newsie, Eddy, was there all right, hawking the final edition of the *Detroit Free Press*. From half a block away Kaleb could hear Eddy heralding, "Git cha news 'ere! Retooling complete! Ford opens manufacturing! New Model A gets lines rolling!" Something and something and something was lost to the crowd noise, and then he heard the kid holler, "Ford recalls workers! FORD RECALLS WORKERS! Git cha latest!"

The Ford plant shutting down for the retooling of a new model was big news for Detroit. The Model T had a solid eighteen-year run but a change was a coming at the Ford plant in 1927. Shutting down the Ford plant in May of '27 had laid off 60,000 workers, but with the retooling just about complete, the full complement of line workers was gradually recalled and preparing for the October 20 release of the Model A. After running its course, and selling 15 million Model Ts, Ford reopening the plants with the Model A was manna to the suspended workforce.

"Extra, extra. FORD RECALLS WORKERS. Git cha latest."

Eddy was dishing newspapers like he was dealing cards. Kaleb found an empty park bench facing the newsboy and sat back to watch the boy work the swarm.

As Kaleb watched the boy hawk the daily, he noted that there were certain buyers who lingered longer with Eddy. These customers used dollar bills instead of coin to pay for the newspaper. And they were not receiving any change. It would seem that, in addition to collecting bets on ponies in the bar circuit, Eddy was using his newspaper perch as a till to gather the gamblers' stakes.

When the evening bustle waned, Kaleb got up from the park bench and moseyed over to Eddy's newspaper stand. Eddy continued barking even as the crowd thinned and the papers dwindled. Kaleb, laid down a five–spot and said, "Gimme a paper," interrupting the boy's bark.

Without looking at Kaleb, the boy dealt a *Free Press* off of the top of his stack, took the fiver and began counting out change.

Flipping the boy a nickel for the paper, Kaleb added, "And five on the Tigers."

Still without giving Kaleb anything more than a cursory glance Eddy asked, "Which game?"

"Tomorrow's game. Sunday."

Without looking at Kaleb, Eddy flipped the nickel into a canvas sack hanging from his belt and slid the five-dollar bill into a jacket purse. "Mister, tomorrow there are two games. A Sunday double-header, you want that I split the five 'twixt the games or roll all on one ride?"

"Surprise me."

Now Eddy looked up and into Kaleb's face and then he looked up and down the street with some caution. "You bein' funny mister? I got no time to play games." Then recognition sparked. "Say, I know you. You got that speakeasy joint over Hastings Street." Recognition turning to wonder he said, "But I thought you was dead."

Kaleb smiled at that and absently tugged at the eyebrow that semi-concealed the scar. "Not dead yet, son. Leastways, not that I remember."

Another customer flipped Eddy a nickel and grabbed a newspaper in passing. Eddy snatched the nickel out of the air and slid it into the bag on his belt. Turning his attention again to Kaleb, he asked, "You never pursed the games before; what's the big spin?"

Kaleb took a quick survey of the street and said under his breath, "How about we turn that fiver into information?"

Worry furrowed the boy's brow. "Look mister, yer tootin' the wrong ringer. Eddy don't yam 'bout nothin'." He retrieved the five spot from his belt purse and pushed it back at Kaleb.

Kaleb looked at the bill but did not accept the money and pressed on. "I need to connect with the Purples."

Eddy nervously shifted from one foot to the other and back again. Again he looked up and down the street to see if anyone was listening in before he rejoined, "Mister, if, and I mean IF, I knew where and how to reach the Purple Gang, what makes you think I'd dial you in? What kinda pigeon you take me for?" Eddy again pushed the five-dollar bill at Kaleb.

Kaleb looked at the anxiety in the boy's face and thought it over. "Look 'ere, Eddy, you just let the gang know that Kaleb Kierka is huntin' 'em up."

"I don't know what gang you talkin' 'bout."

Kaleb laughed. "Okay, son. Just let 'em know Eddy. That's Kierka. Kaleb Kierka," and adding a smile for the boy, "And keep the fiver for your time."

29

Memories

There was a healthy crossing of water vessels from Windsor, Canada to Detroit, Michigan in the wee hours of the night. All manner of watercraft from yachts to row boats to tugs to ferries and all loaded stem to stern with good Canadian hooch intended to satisfy the booze appetite of the prohibitioned 48.

The system of warehouses set up to net this oncoming flood of alcohol stretched from Toledo, Ohio to Port Huron, Michigan, but most of the action was taking place right smack dab in the center of Detroit's warehouse district between Riopelle Street and Mount Elliott Street. The multiple shipping canals and myriad docks made this an impossible quarter for law enforcement to patrol. Not that Detroit was interested in stemming the tide. Trafficking was the commerce of 1927 Detroit be that the traffic of the auto industry or the trafficking of booze. The money made from contraband alcohol ran a close second to the commerce of the automobile.

Dodging the three main ferry lines that crossed from Windsor, Canada - the Grand Trunk, the Michigan Central, and the Canadian Pacific - the Detroit River was a hemorrhaging artery of contraband commerce that no amount of police picket could possibly clot.

The Purple Gang was the main cog in this paddlewheel boat of booze crossing the Detroit River, and Kaleb would need to uncloak the Purples if he were to discover his history.

***

Retrieving his automobile, Kaleb slid the jalopy into a parking space on Adams Street where he had a clean sight line to Eddy's newsstand. When Eddy closed up shop, when the working class evening throng had given way to the nighttime revelry in Kunsky's Circle, Kaleb slipped the car into gear and followed the boy.

Eddy crossed the park and jumped on the streetcar at the turn around on the north end of Grand Circus Park at Woodward Avenue. Following the trolley along the chaotic Woodward Avenue was a tricky affair. Kaleb dodged coughing traffic, click-clacking horses, and harried pedestrians in a mad dash to navigate Detroit's main artery heading north.

While the black Ford Model T was ubiquitous in the blue-collar working neighborhood of Hastings Street, the main strip of Woodward Avenue was a different affair entirely. Chevrolet and Bugatti and Morris and Dodge and Cadillac automobiles in a vast array of colors and designs ignited the boulevard. The three-color traffic signal, created by Detroit cop William Potts in 1920 to alleviate congestion was a sporadically used device along Woodward north of Grand Boulevard. Traffic navigation became more of a game of chicken as automobiles darted to and fro across the side-street veins crisscrossing Woodward Avenue.

But the streetcar that Eddy rode never deviated from its tracks, and dodging traffic, Kaleb managed to follow the trolley until, at Holbrook Street, he saw the boy leap from the car and walk east toward Hamtramck, Detroit's Polish quarter.

Abandoning his car, Kaleb hoofed the eight blocks into Hamtramck, into Poletown, shadowing Eddy at a comfortable distance. The smells of this working class immigrant neighborhood teemed with factory oil and sauerkraut and horse manure and beets bubbling to borsht. The neighborhood, originally German, now Polish, hummed with the foreignness of an Eastern European enclave. English was the second language in this district. If English was spoken at all.

Left on Lumpkin Street, right on Comstock, Kaleb kept a comfortable half block behind Eddy. Half way up the street on Comstock, Eddy turned between two houses and disappeared. Kaleb slowed his stroll and walked on, continuing past the house while he slipped a glance between the two houses that flanked Eddy's path. The sideway that Eddy had followed was empty now, but it opened at a gate to the house on the left. A two-story red brick affair with two residential flats, one upper, one lower.

Continuing down the sidewalk, Kaleb counted the houses to the corner. Turning right on Dubois Street, Kaleb walked the half block to the alley that ran behind Comstock and turned up the alleyway. As he walked the alleyway, Kaleb recounted the houses until he found the house that Eddy had turned into.

Finding his mark, Kaleb opened the back gate and walked along the pathway next to the garage behind the house. Between the garage and the house was a small yard with an apricot tree and a plum tree, and though this should be the season of the trees' greatest fruition, there was no fruit on the trees.

The grass on the lawn area between the buildings was worn to dirt, and there were implements of childhood - a baseball glove, a rusty scooter, a skipping rope - littered about the yard. This was a yard that had seen the abuse of children's play. Many children. An empty clothesline hung limp over the yard, and the empty fruit trees bore witness to the impatience of youth.

Kaleb leaned on the garage and stroked the scar under his eyebrow in thought. Eddy was his link to the Purple Gang. Eddy had been collecting bets at his newsstand all evening and now, somehow, he would need to transfer the funds and the bets to the Purple Gang. Maybe he could try to reason with Eddy again. Or maybe he should just follow him.

As he stood there surveying the circumstance, Kaleb did not hear the alley gate open nor did he hear the soft footsteps coming up behind him. But he heard the sharp click of the switchblade as it snapped open.

Swinging around, Kaleb was confronted with the business end of a six-inch switchblade. The blade was connected to a boy's hand and the boy's hand belonged to Eddy the newsie.

It was a simple reflex that jerked the guns out of Kaleb's suit jacket. The .38 in his left hand and the big .45 in his right. The pulled guns fit naturally, effortlessly, into Kaleb's hands.

The sight of the guns brought horror and panic to Eddy's eyes, and Kaleb just as quickly shoved the guns back into his pocket. He did not want to harm this boy and he did not want to scare Eddy.

But now Eddy was confused, and as he stood there with the switchblade held fast to his fist, his forehead went through a ballet of fright and befuddlement. Slowly, finally, Eddy lowered the switchblade and pursed his lips, forming the thoughts, forming the words, "Look, mister, what you want to be hound-dogging me for? What's your game?"

Kaleb, nodding toward the knife and said, "My game ain't to play with needles, Eddy. Go ahead and put that away."

As if he had forgotten that it was in his hand, Eddy looked first to the switchblade in his fist and then up into Kaleb's face. Almost shyly he clicked the blade closed and lowered it to his side.

Eddy was a small boy for his age, not much more than a tuft of black hair on a stick-frame. But Eddy was hard, street-urchin hard, and his face angles were chiseled in pig iron with a dull blade.

Kaleb continued, "Like I said before, I need to get a hold of the Purple Gang."

Eddy was remembering now. "But why me? Why you want to go through me?" Eddy's forehead had now ceased to tango, but there was yet some slow waltzing going on.

"Because you're the only one I know with the connection. I need you to help me get to them."

Eddy laughed out loud. "Firstways, Eddy don't yam on nobody. And second-like, you own a goddamn speakeasy for god's sake! Give 'em time. The Purples will be 'round."

Kaleb certainly saw the humor in that but said, "I don't know how much time I got, Eddy."

Eddy studied Kaleb's face for any sign of a terminal disease. "What? You dyin' or sometin'?"

Kaleb laid it out. "Seems like. Seems someone has been encouraging my dying, leastways. I got a bump on my head that kinda tells me that my living hasn't been real popular."

Eddy studied Kaleb's face for humor and found none. "Are you dizzy?"

"Nope, not dizzy 'xactly. I've got something called amnesia. My recollect is tapped out."

"I thought you said you was Kaleb Kierka, owner of The Temp speak?"

"So I've been told."

Eddy thought on this for a moment. "So's you got that amneesceea?"

"Amnesia. Yes."

"And you really don't know who you are?"

"I get hints occasionally. Flashes of memory. But nothing I can hang my hat on."

Again Eddy considered this. "Well, what is all the rush to jump into the fire? Why'n'cha flick a match, easy like at first? The Purple Gang is like jumpin' in a firestorm."

"Don't know if I've got the time, Eddy, to sit at the back of the bus. Someone seems to be stalking me."

Eddy slipped the switchblade back into his pocket. "Stalking you how?"

"The Temp has been tabbed, my apartment was tossed, and let's not forget that someone's allotted me a near-death beating. I'm just not confidant that time is a luxury I enjoy."

Eddy thought this over carefully. "But, Jesus, mister, the Purple Gang? Those 'r some big torpedoes to discharge."

"But you know how to find 'em?"

"Sure. Maybe. Kinda. I know where to drop the bets and the money. But that's a sacred cover."

"Lookit, here, Eddy, I don't want to set you up, so I'm not gonna press you on taking me to them. I just want you to relay to the Purple Gang that Kaleb Kierka would like a pow-wow."

Eddy thought this over while his forehead sat out a dance. "Guess I could relay the message, alright."

"That's all I'm asking. I just need to hope that they'll find me."

In marvel, Eddy's eyebrows made high inroads up his forehead. "Oh brother. They'll find you all right, mister. They'll find you, all right."

***

It was yet pre-dusk when Kaleb Kierka made it back to his heap. To Woodward Avenue.

Sitting in the T, Kaleb pulled the guns from his pockets and studied them, the .45 in his right hand, the .38 in his left. The guns came to his fists too easily when Eddy pulled a knife. They came to his fists naturally, like a man taking a breath. Kaleb was learning that he was a man familiar with guns. With violence. And comfortable with all of the wickedness that this violence would imply.

Like astringent bile in his mouth, Kaleb was repulsed by the revelation of this violent man. This Kaleb Kierka. Shoving the guns under the automobile seat, onto the wooden floorboard, Kaleb deigned to leave the guns be. Whoever he had been, he was not that person now. He would never again pull this kind of firepower on a fourteen-year-old newsboy.

***

As the evening bore down, Woodward Avenue became a calmer affair. Delivery trucks had completed their tasks, and the automobiles had distributed their commuters to the outlying neighborhoods. Even the streetcars, which had been bursting with bodies hanging from poles, were running barely half full now. Horse drawn carriages, mostly milk, junk and garbage wagons, which had been relegated to the alleyways during the day, were now making their appearance along the drag. The equestrian buggies offered a more tranquil kind of driving challenge and Kaleb eased the Model T to the flow.

Woodward Avenue was bursting to the curb with progress as it stretched a tentacle north. Kaleb eased down the avenue, weaving between the horses and the trolleys and the automobiles, meandering amid the nineteenth and the twentieth century. The streetscape offered trifling memory igniting sparks at the periphery of Kaleb's wits.

There was a time, before the reign of the asphalt, that Detroit hosted arteries of streams and creeks that fed into larger rivers. The Rouge River to the south and the Clinton River to the north each flowed long and clear before they emptied into the mighty Detroit River. Springs and streams bubbled up clean and clear in Detroit's dells and glens long before their cement entombment under the progress of the twentieth century.

At Woodward and Mount Vernon, Kaleb flashed recognition on a sandlot where he had played baseball. A solid memory. A foothold in Kaleb Kierka's history, to his recollect. He pulled the Model T to the curb and he let the memory play out.

***

Thirteen years old and Kaleb Kierka was a ball player. A third baseman, the hot corner, and he played the position tight, closer to home plate than most third basemen. Playing this close to home plate, to the batter's swing, giving every pitch a special menace. Tight to the baseline, to home plate, was like playing goalie in hockey and either you had the reflexes for it or you wore the baseball in your teeth. Kaleb liked the challenge and the focus of playing third base, in the batter's lap: Kaleb Kierka savored the memory. A real, honest-to-god memory.

Looking beyond the baseball field, where Woodward Avenue pushed across West Grand Boulevard, he saw the cratered foundation for the upcoming Fischer building, Detroit's first skyscraper. But Kaleb remembered that very spot as a spring-fed gravel pond where he would swim naked with schoolmates while playing hooky in the warm spring rains.

And as quick as these memories appeared, they vanished. But they were there long enough for Kaleb to begin piecing together a memory. A history.

Honest-to-god-memories.

***

Following the memories, Kaleb turned the Model T into a long sweep around the city, west on West Grand Boulevard and then south as the boulevard made its western arc around the city. Left at Michigan Avenue and straight down to Randolph Street and City Hall. There was another memory blast at City Hall. At the Hall Of Justice, the jailhouse. A foggy déjà vu about jails and badges and guns and gangs and courts, but he could not cleanly recapture the memory. Maybe some things were best left unrecalled.

Following Congress east brought Kierka to Hastings and he turned the T north on Hastings Street, north toward home, north toward Paradise Valley.

This route took Kaleb through the heart of the Black Bottom.

30

Baldy's House Party

Paradise Valley served as the principal landing pad for the flood of refugees from Eastern Europe and the Appalachian Mountains while the Black Bottom served as Detroit's primary enclave for the black men who were escaping the poverty of the America's southern reaches. While the rest of America was dueling it out along the battle lines of race, the hodgepodge collection of humanity that overlapped the conjoining sister neighborhoods of Paradise Valley and the Black Bottom had come to a judicious alliance.

Poverty is a great equalizer.

Paradise Valley inclined toward the Eastern European: Italians, Greeks, Poles, and Jews escaping the food deprivations, political turmoil, and religious persecutions of Europe. Paradise Valley was also the refuge for America's homegrown immigrant, the Appalachian hillbilly escaping America's rural poverty and repression. Paradise Valley was just the opposite of everything that its moniker could conjure: slums that housed the poorest of the poor, miniscule two-room apartments bursting at their walls, hosted families and extended families. There existed equal amounts of suffering and pain with an international collection of languages united in America's promise of tomorrow.

The Black Bottom served the black community. Named for the legendary rich black soil of a time when Detroit was a young and prosperous farming community, the Black Bottom was the neighborhood that offered sanctuary for the black men and women escaping racially divided America, with the promise of good jobs and a righteous livelihood in the smoke-belching factories of Detroit.

But the line between the Black Bottom and Paradise Valley was nebulous. A black-and-tan community. Of the two communities, the Black Bottom was the more desired neighborhood if for no other reason than it housed professionals. Real professionals. Black doctors and black dentists and black writers and black engineers. Men at the top of their profession who were denied access to upper-class neighborhoods because of the color of their skin.

If a black doctor could not ply his trade in the white communities, he opened a practice in the Black Bottom. If one's color kept a black engineer or plumber or pick-your-profession from living in the white neighborhoods, he or she landed in the Black Bottom. Detroit hosted a healthy measure of black professionals, indeed one of the leading professional black populaces in early 20th century America. Unfortunately, due to America's racism, these professionals were relegated to working and living in the poor neighborhood, the Black Bottom. But the presence of these professionals in the Black Bottom made it one of the more desirable locales for the disenfranchised.

Running north and south through the communities of the Black Bottom and Paradise Valley, Hastings Street was the main drag of the hustle and the bustle of the commerce that defined the community. Conjoined communities full of people of every hue and united in their aspirations to escape the poverty and the repression of the respective destitution from whence they came.

Kaleb Kierka's speakeasy overlapped the five-cornered intersection of the convergence of the three streets, Hastings and Adams and Gratiot.

The Temple Bar Speakeasy And Play Nice straddled the kinship of subjugation that was the Black Bottom and Paradise Valley.

***

It was after nine o'clock as Kaleb cruised north on St. Antoine through the Black Bottom on his way to Paradise Valley. Kaleb's Tin Lizzie was purring.

The T, the Tin Lizzie, the Liz, the go-getter, the jitney, the flivver, the heap, the gas buggy, all good handles for the Henry Ford's Model T. Maybe the most appropriate nickname was the Universal Buggy, for not only was it built and priced for the everyday man, but also because the Model T was flex-fuel capable, burning everything from gasoline to kerosene to alcohol.

And what greater symbol for America could there be than this proletarian vehicle running on the same fuel that fueled the Roaring 20s? Alcohol.

Kaleb spun the T over to St. Antoine Street. A co-main drag, one block east of Hastings Street, St. Antoine Street ran parallel, north and south, through the Black Bottom. A few blocks deep into the Black Bottom, Kaleb guided the T into a parking spot, and turned off the vehicle so he could listen to the neighborhood. Sitting still in the vehicle, he pulled out the cotton muslin bag of Bull Durham, opened the drawstring and poured a couple of pinches of tobacco into the paper. Kinetic recall spun the perfect cylinder of tobacco.

Flicking the cigarette ablaze with a thumbed match, Kaleb sat back in the T and took in the mundane sounds of the Black Bottom.

Shaking the match out, Kaleb watched a thin trail of smoke rise to the window of the T and slip out into the ambient environ of the Black Bottom. As the smoke swirled away, Kaleb wondered at this kinetic memory of smoke and ash. At the myriad ways a man moves through this world, through this plane. These collective kinetic anthologies organized by the body to keep one standing upright and moving forward. To breath and to eat and to shit and to laugh and to cry. It was the body's kinetic memory, not the brain, that thrust the human onward. Onward to the future.

Kaleb's mind was envious of the way his body was able to move to its own memoir. Maybe, he thought, just maybe, the magnitude of a man's measure can be calculated on the collection of his tactile recall.

***

Commerce had settled along St. Antoine Street and the habitat was flexing toward the nightlife. Kaleb sucked deep on the tobacco as the sounds of a neighborhood in transition seeped towards the night.

Above the now silenced mercantile of St. Antoine Street were the sounds of people settling in for the night. The chatter of children over mothers' scolds, the protestations of love, babies yowling for the nipple and always the constant hum of the white noise of the factories. And the smells - smells of too much perfume over too much body odor, of collard greens sizzling in the flat iron, of decaying muck collecting along rudimentary sewage trenches.

Kaleb's brain sucked in the sights and sounds and smells of St. Antoine Street like he was reading a vaguely familiar book. Although he could not recall the title of the book, nor the plot, nor the characters, and certainly not the resolution, Kaleb knew he had read this pulp before.

He had smoked the cigarette to its nub before he heard the music. It was coming from one of the brick buildings opposite where he sat in the T. Muffled and muted, the music seemed to be bubbling from under the buildings themselves. Under the pavement. Under the Black Bottom.

Eyeing the buildings, Kaleb caught his mark. A brick stairway alongside one of the shuttered storefronts and barely visible at street level, there was a descending flight of steps beneath a staircase. It was from this descending stairway that the music crept. The music beaconed Kaleb like a curling forefinger to 'come-hither.'

Climbing from the T and tossing his cigarette butt with one motion, Kaleb crossed the street to the descending stairway, to the music.

At the top of the stairs Kaleb heard not only the music but also the general hubbub of a party in full swing. Of a speakeasy speaking easy. Descending the stairs to the cellar house party and to the music, Kaleb pushed through the doors to find the blind pig hopping with bodies. Black bodies. This was not a black-and-tan club. This was a black club in the heart of the Black Bottom.

***

What Kunsky's Circle was to uptown jazz, the Black Bottom was to the lowdown. Clubs such as the Koppin Theater on Gratiot Avenue became mainstays for the black entertainment in Detroit, featuring touring blues artists like Bessie Smith, Ida Cox, and, of course, Ma Rainey, "the mother of the blues."

Mostly it was the house parties in the Black Bottom where the most roughhewn of jazz was explored. Places like Hattie-Bell Spruel's house on Alfred Street where Hattie-Bell sold liquor upstairs while the revelers partied down below.

The music ensembles of the Black Bottom were noted for a freer, improvised rendering of jazz. The bands in these black clubs and house parties were smaller versions of the orchestras favored by the high-society venues and the music's emphasis was less about the arrangement and more about spontaneous improvisation.

***

Innocuous enough, the house party cum speakeasy that Kaleb had infiltrated did not suspend its party for the lone white man who sidled in, but there was a breath of acknowledgement in partygoers. Kaleb was quick to be judged threatless, to not be of the legal variety, and the whoop carried on.

The party pulsed with the music and dancing as shouted conversation fought to be heard above the general aural mayhem. Black men and women in the boogie of life. In the pirouette of love. Of jazz.

***

Again the undertow of the rhythm pulled Kaleb into the deep waters of the music. A submerged undertow of undertones beckoned deep within his breast. A beckoning beacon of steady tidal rhythmic waves to the shore.

Breaker to breaker, wave to wave, the swell was cadenced and metrical as the rush of the music's surf calmed him and excited him with every surge.

The music's tide paced and measured the very blood-flow of Kaleb Kierka.

***

At the bar, Kaleb noted that the club's drink of choice was the boilermaker. A cognac would be nice but pretentious in this raucous setting. Kaleb tipped his forehead at a boilermaker down the bar. "Set 'er up."

The barkeep, a short and stocky black man, bald except for a strip of hair doing a half circle around his dome, gave Kaleb a quick review. He had the look of a man who had seen it all and really didn't care to see it again.

The bar man set a shell of beer and the shot of whiskey in front of Kaleb and said, "Two bits."

Kaleb flipped the quarter on the bar and picked up the whiskey glass.

A boilermaker is often referred to as a shot of whisky with a beer back. Local boilermakers plop the whisky shot glass, shot glass included, into the center of the shell of beer. The mix allows one to sip on the blend as a single brew.

Kaleb dropped his whisky into the shell of beer, the plunk splashing the bar top. Sipping on the potion, Kaleb again marveled at kinetic memory. His body certainly seemed to have its habits and the whisky-beer boilermaker reinforced the ritual.

It only took a taste of the boilermaker to know that the booze had been cut. The whiskey was cut and the beer was cut and it made for a watered down boilermaker. Even as the first swallow was making its way down his throat, the hot sear of the whisky and the cool rime of the beer, he knew that these were not blends that he shelved in his own establishment.

As the barkeep was leaning down, working on something under the bar, Kaleb addressed the bartender's wide, bald forehead. "'Lestways I won't be driving drunk." When the bartender looked up, Kaleb tipped his glass in salute and took another pull of the imbibe.

"Funny'" said the barkeep. He smiled sideways and added, "You a funny Ofay." And that was all.

Kaleb pressed casually, "Whose your hooch bank? This stuff is cut so deep it needs sutures."

The bartender drew up and studied this white man sitting at his bar and asking about his booze. "An Ofay with humor," he countered. And then the barkeep began to scrutinize this white man who had walked into his bar. "Who's askin'?"

"'Jes an uptown rival." And Kaleb gave his best impression of a warm smile.

The barman continued to study Kaleb suspiciously until the spark hit. "Right." And he echoed Kaleb's smile as he said again, "Right. You that white boy that got that Temp joint up Hastings 'n Gratiot." The barkeep's smile reached almost to the slat of hair running around his head as he recognized Kaleb. The brotherhood of hooch.

"Watcha smokin' out this joint for?"

"Reconnaissance. Jes a little recon."

The barkeep drew another beer and placed it with a shot in front of Kaleb. "Here's one on the house, brother," and added, "The Bernstein boys is my booze bank."

The Bernstein boys. The Purple Gang. The name Bernstein caught traction in his memory and Kaleb sucked a quick breath. To himself he breathed, "The Purples."

The band onstage, a banjo player, a piano player, and a drummer ended a song, catching the room's conversations in mid-holler. As voices calmed to the silence, the bartender got busy with the dancers coming to the bar for boilermaker reboots. When the band resumed the jam, the bar again became an empty plank, and the barkeep returned to the white man.

Quietly, so the conversation remained between himself and Kaleb, the barkeep asked, "You run wit' those boys, the Purples, right?"

"I run with the Purple Gang?"

"Is this news to you?"

Kaleb did not answer and the barkeep's light went on. "Say, thet's right, you got messed up and lost your who's who. Street news, last edition, says you got your bell back on. Not so much, eh?"

Kaleb ignored the newsflash. "I ran with the Bernstein boys? The Purple Gang?"

"Well, you used to anyhows. Heard tell you had some kinda row 'n got chucked out. Some kinda murder or som'ting."

This was all news to Kaleb. "Murder... or something?" Spinning a shell glass in a towel while keeping his voice low, the bartender answered, "All's I know is that you used to tie tight wit' the Purples. Now you don't."

Kaleb let this settle in as the barkeep moved down the bar to service another customer.

Everyone seemed to be clued in that somewhere in Kaleb's past, distant or recent, he was some part of the Purple Gang. A member? A liaison? And now he is not a member of the Purple Gang. Could this be why he does not buy his liquor off of the Purple Gang's shelves?

And could it be the Purple Gang that had tried to beat him to death?

When Baldy walked down the bar to service a patron Kaleb turned his attention to the stage and the groove of the tune.

***

There it was again. The underlying rhythm. The beat in his bones. A gospel in his marrow that was drumming to an intuitive chorus. It was there. It was always there. The primal drumbeat of blood pulsing in rhythm and in rhyme. Iambic pentameter palpitating a shuffling triplet to the backbeat of four-to-the-bar.

Beat me daddy beat me daddy four-to-the-bar.

***

Interrupting this link, Kaleb was joined by a couple of black men on either side of his barstool.

The man on his left cozied up and asked, "Say, ain't you 'de cat that digs on ivories up Hastings Street way?" The man on his right, slapping Kaleb on the shoulder added, "Why sure, you that keys boy, awright. I pumped my t'bone wit' ya when I been slummin' north. Ya gonna sit in wit' our troop t'night?" and he thumbed over his shoulder in the direction of the stage.

Kaleb was awkward with this acknowledgement and it was obvious. Again folks seem to know more about Kaleb than he knew about himself. The bartender recognized this, and like all good bartenders do when a customer is in distress cut in. "Why'n'cha leave the man alone. Can't ya see he just dropped in de 'stablishment for a little git away." The men surrounding Kaleb caught the barkeep's cue. "Why sure. We on'y meant to say 'how do'." And the second man added, "Yep. On'y meant to say 'how do,'" and then he added with a gentler cuff to Kaleb arm, "Say, man, I looks forward to a jimmy-jam wit' you again. I'll be pumpin' my bone up to your joint 'gin soon."

Kaleb, discomfited responded, "Nice, man. Real nice."

"Sure. Sure. I'll bring my t'bone next I'm up."

As the men melted back into the general pulse of the speakeasy, Kaleb addressed his second boilermaker.

Looking down at the bar, not looking into Kaleb's face, the bartender said under his breath, "You know you'se been followed inna 'ere?"

Kaleb looked at the barkeep and realized that the barkeep did not want eye contact. Kaleb answered with minimal lips movement, "I've been followed in 'ere? How do you know?"

Still not looking at Kaleb, the bartender suppressed a laugh. "Lookit 'ere, boy, when two white mens comes into my 'stablishment within minutes of each other, somebody's followin' somebody."

Kaleb did not want to turn to search the club. "A hatchet-faced man?"

This time the barkeep's smile almost reached the slap of hair over his ears. "Ha! What do I know about a hatchet face, boy? What's a hatchet face mean? I guess he's got a long sharp nose on a skinny type face, but mostly you white boys all look the same, you know." And the black man added, solemnly, "But he's big, boy, real big."

Kaleb looked up to the mirror on the bar back and surveyed the room.

Spinning a glass in his bar rag and looking everywhere but at Kaleb, the barkeep added, "Back ta your left. Under the Stroh's sign."

Kaleb shifted his gaze up to the left, under the Stroh's Ice Cream sign.

And there he was. Same hatchet face. Same big shoulders threatening the uptown cut of the same navy blue jacket. His eyes seemed a little beadier in the light of the speakeasy as they flit about the joint like a flea seeking blood.

Kaleb nodded his appreciation to the barkeep, and the barkeep slid down the bar to draw another beer for another patron.

A waitress was just setting down the big man's boilermaker, and Kaleb watched as the man first sipped at the whisky and then sipped on the shell of beer. He did not plop the whiskey into his beer. This was a tell. This man was foreign to the shores of the Detroit River.

Kaleb knocked back the last of his boilermaker, taking care not to chip his teeth on the whiskey glass as it slid to the lip of the beer glass.

He intended to push away from the bar quickly, take long and fast steps to cross the barroom floor, and confront the stranger before the big man had a chance to unfold his long legs.

As he began to turn he was intercepted by the trombone player, again slapping his shoulder in familiarity. This time the man was dragging a woman with him. "See ya Mabel. Told ya it was 'im. This is that Kaleb man, the piano man, from up Temple Bar way."

And Mabel was all smiles. "Why I am surely pleased ta meet cha acquaintance." All smiles and she had more teeth than a piano has keys.

Distracted but trying to be gracious, Kaleb took her hand and forced a smile. "My pleasure, Miss, uh, Miss Mabel?"

Holding tight to Kaleb's hand, the woman continued, "Mabel is right. Mabel Strickland. But you can call me Mabel. Seems like every time I meet a musician I gots ta fin' out how he do what he do. Some playa's like to have a little needle juice 'fore they blow, some's like a drink. Some neva speak 'bout it, ya know and...." Mabel continued a soliloquy, but Kaleb had lost the thread as he was trying to locate the man who had followed him into the bar.

Mabel's friend cut off her rambling, and holding up his trombone for Kaleb's inspection offered, "I gots my 'bone right 'chere if'n you want to splash some boogie."

Mabel was not ready to let go of Kaleb's hand. "And I sings a bit."

Kaleb Kierka felt an urgency to extricate himself from the clench of these well-wishers. "No, I'm sorry, not tonight." And he pushed away quickly from the bar, clipping past Mabel and the trombone player and into the direction of the Stroh's Ice Cream sign.

"Well! I never!" exclaimed Mabel as Kaleb brushed by.

"He's jes a busy man," defended the trombone player.

The table under the Stroh's Ice Cream sign was empty except for the drained whisky glass and half of a shell of beer.

Ten long and quick strides through the churning bodies of the house party and Kaleb took the cement steps two at a time up to street level. On St. Antoine Street Kaleb looked north. Nothing. South. Nothing. He turned to his sense of hearing and focused on the neighborhood sounds.

Except for the music bleeding from the house party below, there was nothing.

31

When Nika Sang The Flat 5

To call blues music "the blues" is not a misnomer. The blues offered the beaten, the downtrodden, and the lost some small comfort in their world of hurt. The blues carry a gutbucket of angst. Filled to the brim.

The pentatonic minor scale is a five-note scale: root, minor third, fourth, fifth with a flattened seventh note. But the minor blues scale offers further anguish to the pentatonic minor scale, additional ache and auxiliary angst. Beyond the 5 notes of the pentatonic minor scale, the blues scale offers a sixth note, the flat 5.

A pentatonic minor scale with a flat 5. That is the blues scale. A scale that is rooted deep in the African continent, deep in the African people.

Africa, the continent that mothered a planet and fathered humanity. Africa, offering a prehistoric music scale that was chanted around the earliest primate campfires, warding off everything from prides of lions to the prides of men.

It is in that flat 5 that you will find the blues voodoo. It is in that flat 5 where hearts are broken and souls are rounded up and branded. Like a flicker of a feeble fire on a dark and starless night, the flat 5 offers sanctuary against the blackness of the howling and the growling in the furtive shadows.

The flat 5 of the blues scale does not offer redemption, only tolerance. The flat 5 does not offer forgiveness, only sanctuary. When you awake from the spell of the flat 5, you will still be brokenhearted. Or poor. Or suppressed. Or whatever your ill. The flat 5 cannot save your life, but it will offer some measure of liberation to your soul.

The pentatonic minor with the flat 5 will offer you transient relief, some acceptance, and fleeting shelter from the storm.

***

The drugs were surging through Nika's veins now, giving her body a rush and her psyche some bravado. It was this synthetic bravado that brought her to the stage, to the microphone. It was this bravado that allowed access through her voice to her pain. To her minor blues with a flat 5.

Rich and deep and smoky, her voice was an echo. A sonorous echo that resonated from her personal pain and ricocheted around the collective pains of humankind.

Nika's echo was a pain that had an upbringing on a rural dairy farm in Houghton, Michigan, on a dead-end dirt road called Bliss Gate. Hers was a pain that witnessed her father die, crushed on the overturned Allis-Chalmers tractor in a cornfield. It was a pain that beheld her mother remarry Big Joe, a violent drunkard who molested Nika and her younger sisters.

Nika's pain was a pain that stood watch at too many beatings suffered by her mother at the hands of Big Joe. It was a pain that, at ten years old, suffered through her deflowering under the sweaty and alcoholic stench of Big Joe. It was a pain that, at seventeen years young, took the family shotgun, her biological father's shotgun, and blew a hole in Big Joe's chest the size of the Liberty Bell. Let freedom ring, let freedom ring, good God almighty, let freedom ring.

Through her dark and cavernous voice, through her flat 5 voice, Nika championed the ration of the abused, the forgotten, and the disenfranchised. At the microphone, Nika sang for the beatings endured by her mother, and she cried for the rape of her sisters. It was a misery purchased on chastity's loss; and it was a misery that the black-and-tans knew well; and it was a misery that gave voice to their own disenfranchisement. In the company of misery.

Nika sang and the walls of The Temple Bar Speakeasy And Play Nice seemed a little wider. The roof a little higher. When Nika sang the congregation breathed a little deeper, their personal crucifix lightened on their shoulders. Nika's voice was a voice that rang ancestral. Her voice chimed with grief and sorrow and the agony of the common bonds that united the souls of the European serfs and the African slaves.

When Nika belted the blues, the heavens cried in angst, and when Nika softly sang of love and hope, hell was humbled.

***

Laverne Nightingale, Nika's mother, had tried to intervene again, but Big Joe had knocked her unconscious with two swats of his big mitts. When Big Joe grabbed tiny Leslie, a scant eight-years-young, by her wrist to drag her to the bedroom, Nika took hold of her biological father's shotgun and blocked the door to the bedroom. Nika was seventeen now, and for eight years it had been Nika's lot to service Big Joe's incestuous lust. But now he had set his sights on Nika's youngest sibling, Leslie.

Barring the door, Nika had the stock of the shotgun tucked under the crook of her scrawny armpit, using her shoulder as leverage against the shotgun's weight, keeping the duo-barrels level to Big Joe's chest.

Big Joe looked at the child Nika standing in front of him with the shotgun, a gun as long as Nika was tall, and he laughed. An ugly, rotting-teeth laugh. With tiny Leslie's wrist clamped in one hand, Big Joe slammed his other fist into Nika, catching her square in the throat and crushing her larynx.

The boom of the shotgun in the tiny house, in the tiny room, shook the walls.

Nika's child-size hand could only finger one of the triggers of the two-barreled shotgun, but that single barrel blew buckshot into Big Joe's torso.

Letting go of Leslie, Big Joe stumbled backwards. Shock marred his mug as he grasped at the gap in his belly.

It was the pull of the second trigger, the second barrel blast that was not a reflex of the punch to Nika's throat. The shotgun's second trigger was deliberate, purposeful. The second barrel's blast was a blast of liberation. Deliberate liberation. Let freedom ring, let freedom ring.

Nika's purposeful pull on that second trigger was the flat 5 of the blues scale. Nika's emancipation.

Momentarily holding to his feet, Big Joe's forehead creased in wonder, and his ugly maw gaped an absurd torture before he folded into himself and heaped to the floor.

***

Constable Pete Towney of the Michigan State Police was the first on the scene. Houghton, Michigan was a small farming community and suspicions ran deep about what was happening at the Nightingale homestead.

Constable Pete Towney had heard the rumors. Constable Pete Towney had seen the blackened eyes that Laverne Nightingale wore to church, and he bore witness to the young girls shuddering, frightened and cold, under their Easter rags.

And now Constable Towney, pursing his lips, stood in the Nightingale's ramshackle house with the battered mother and the three tiny, trembling girls. Nika was unable to speak because of the crushed windpipe from Big Joe's fist, and all color drained from her face in the shock.

On the floor, in the center of this collection of pain and horror, lay the lumped body of Big Joe in a pond of his own blood.

Constable Pete Towney had witnessed his fair share of murder and of suicides in his 22 years of law enforcement in Houghton. Big Joe had taken the shotgun's blast square in his belly. A painful way to die by any measure. But the long barrel of the shotgun would have made suicide prohibitive, as Big Joe's arms were just not long enough for the equation.

Nika's faded, flower-print dress was stained black with the blowback gunpowder from the doubled-barrel's blast and blood splatter from the chasm in Big Joe's gut. Her cheeks were lined with the flood of terror and of relief, but the frail seventeen-year-old's eyes were not in the room of this little house at the end of the dirt road named Bliss Gate.

Constable Towney tried to reconcile suicide. The length of the shotgun barrel would make it implausible for Big Joe's reach to have pulled the trigger. The separation of the holes to the gut and to Big Joe's chest bore witness to the triggers of the double barrels having been pulled at separate angles. If the triggers had been pulled simultaneously, there would be one massive hole in Big Joe's chest. Instead, one hole had blown out the lower left side of Big Joe's belly, and the second barrel had blown out the upper right hand side of his chest. Either shot would have been fatal. If Big Joe shot himself the second time, this second shot would have been triggered after he was already dead. These were not self-inflicted wounds.

To a cop of Pete Towny's experience, the length of the shot gun barrel, the separation of the entry wounds, and Nika's gun-powdered and blood-splattered dress told the story in detail.

With his thumb and forefinger, Pete Towney pulled on his bottom lip as he reconciled the angles of the event. The entire crime scene. Laverne kneeling with the two younger girls, weeping and huddled tight together, cascading tears of torture. And Nika, waiflike, stained and bloody from the blowback, her eyes glazed and focused on nowhere.

Big Joe's bloody cadaver, Laverne Nightingale and the sobbing girls, and the little shell-shocked and bloody Nika were the totality of the crime scene that Constable Pete Towney appraised. An easy estimation for a seasoned lawman.

"Suicide," Towney decided.

Eyes blank, seeing nothing and still in shock, Nika could only softly echo the words, dimly knowing their meaning. "Suicide?"

"Sure. Suicide." Pursing his bottom lip with his thumb and forefinger, Constable Towney completed the thought. "It 'pears to me like Big Joe was holding that gun 'bout eight feet away from his body when he took the blast. 'Pears to me like he's been holding that gun angled out like that for too many years now. 'Pears to me like the trigger finally went off." Looking from the huddled girls on the floor to the vacuous Nika, Constable Towney concluded his thought. "Only surprise is it took so long for the gun to go off."

Again Constable Pete Towney pulled and pinched at his lips and let them flap back into the thin line that served as his mouth. "Yep, suicide. A long time coming suicide but a suicide nonetheless. It was just a matter of time."

It was a suicide that Big Joe had been designing for himself with every beating he delivered and every molestation he consigned.

Sometimes suicides take years to commit and are executed vicariously.

***

Nika Nightingale sang the blues into the depths of the microphone that few souls dared. A depth that did not judge nor critique. A depth that could only acknowledge, recognize and accept.

Nika sang perched unyielding on the flat 5 of the blues scale. She sang from the mountaintop of the flat 5 and she sang from the valley of the flat 5. Nika sang with the intimacy of knowing the flat 5 was exposed bare, raw, with its pants to its knees.

The hoarse texture that Nika's voice had purchased at the cost of collecting Big Joe's fist to her throat conferred upon her voice the honesty and the identity of the flat 5.

Bottles did not clink and chairs did not scrape the floor when Nika sang flat 5. Voices fell silent when Nika sang the blues. When Nika sang these subterranean blues.

When Nika sang flat 5.

When Nika sang the blues.

Let freedom ring, let freedom ring. Good God Almighty, let freedom ring.

32

A Harbinger To Music
Decades To The Future

It was a new club and a new attitude when Kaleb and Beethoven Jones opened The Temple Bar Speakeasy And Play Nice. They were young, brash, and full of themselves, and they played this new music, this jazz, with abandon. It was a new era and a new music in a new club and the boys were living every moment like it was the last.

When the boys discovered Nika and brought her into the fold, The Temple Bar Speakeasy And Play Nice had the planet that their moons could orbit.

When Nika first joined Jazz du Jour as the band's singer, she was shy and introspective. She did not understand or trust her talent; she only knew that singing gave her some relief from the pain inside. Like many introverted musicians of the time, Nika discovered heroin, and the drug allowed her to playfully wink at her self-consciousness.

At first the drugs had been a crutch. Then they became a requisite.

***

The drugs gave Nika some measure of bravado, and she had a ballsy bearing in the first set, the midnight set, at The Temp. It was an opening set to prepare for the night's guest artist, Ma Rainey, who would be gracing The Temp after her vaudevillian tour around Kunsky's Circle.

With the drugs in support, Nika began the night wailing her way through the songs. Playful and silly, Nika went from table to table, cooing into ears and sitting astride laps as she belted and torched her way through the tunes.

The first set was elongated as Ma Rainey had been delayed at the Adams Theater. Normally an hour set, this first set had gone half again as long and there was no end in sight. The band was rocking and rolling the rostrum and the dancers were swinging full bore on the floor.

The band's ensemble held groove and the bodies on the dance floor held sway, but the long set was proving to be taxing for Nika as the surge of the heroin began to wane. Her energy wilted and her complexion slid quickly from radiant to ruddy. The lyrics, those that Nika could remember, became a muddy slur of unintelligible syllables, and what had once been sultry became sloppy.

The set ended with Nika slumped like a wet coat on the piano bench while Jazz du Jour ripped off a raucous instrumental version of Bix Beiderbecke's "At The Jazz Band Ball."

At set's end, Kaleb confronted Beethoven Jones. "Where's she getting her junk, man?"

Jones looked up from his bass and to the heap of a black garment that was Nika Nightingale. He looked at Nika but he could not look Kaleb in the eye. With some sadness in the nod of his head he affirmed, "I don't get involved, man. I don't get involved."

***

The Roaring Twenties: This was the decade that the blues, escorted by the flat 5, established itself as a force to be reckoned with on the American musical landscape. Although the blues had been making inroads across the country for many years, it was during the Roaring Twenties that saturation was completed, and Detroit would not be denied its place in the annals.

In 1919 Jelly Roll Morton wrote "The Black Bottom Stomp" as a tribute to Detroit's Black Bottom neighborhood. Tonight Ma Rainey was gracing the stage of The Temple Bar Speakeasy And Play Nice. Ma's own band, Assassinators Of The Blues, had done the milquetoast Grand Circus Park circuit, and now it was time to cut loose the catguts. Backbeats were slammed and saxophones growled and Ma Rainey bent and contorted the flat 5 to her bidding.

Walls bowed and rafters lifted as The Temp *rocked* and The Temp *rolled*, a harbinger to a music decades yet to the future.

***

Kaleb found Nika in the alleyway behind The Temp. He kneeled beside her and held her head off the ground and out of her vomit.

With the heaves came convulsions that quaked Nika's small bones from stem to stern. During a break in her body spasms, she looked up at Kaleb through eyes that had sunk into dark sockets of swollen flesh. She could only manage a weak, "It's getting old, baby, it's getting old."

33

Fat Tony And Jimmy-Jimbo

"Blowoffs" were a traveling collective of partygoers: musicians and dancers and general merrymakers who converged on one establishment or another, bar-hopping from speakeasy to speakeasy in a sort of rolling thunder of revelry.

That night's blowoff was at a house party on Champlain Street, and The Temp was empty. Empty save for Bucky manning the bar, Beethoven Jones holding court on stage, and a love-struck couple sitting at a table with highballs in their glasses and the moon in their eyes.

Jones, alone on stage with his bass fiddle, breathed blue into the bass. Sonorous and foreboding blue, Jones drew the bass bow across the catguts to the empty stage, to the empty house. Without the benefit of a band, the full breath of the sadness could only be esteemed in the bottomless breath of the bowed bass.

The couple at the table were moon-eyed and eye-locked and had been nursing their drinks for the better part of an hour. They were a black-and-tan couple, he white, she colored. It was just past midnight, and Bucky was waiting for Hollie the broom tender to arrive so Bucky could shut the club down early.

Beethoven Jones had curled his long and loose-jointed frame around the double bass, becoming one with the instrument. Like a burl that forms on a wounded tree, he merged into the bass and one could not discern where the bass ended and the man began.

The interlopers walked into the club in single file with their trench coat collars up and their hats slung low. Once inside the door they fanned out. Each man had fists dug deep and heavy into his trench coat, and the bulging pockets advised more occupancy than just their hands.

Bucky saw them come in, saw the bulge of their coat pockets, and moved slowly toward the end of the bar, toward the shotgun.

But the interlopers' draw was quick and the guns slid out of their pockets with an ease that bespoke practiced proficiency.

"Suppose you just leave that blaster be." The one who spoke was short and fat, but his quickness belied his fat as he raised the gun at Bucky. His trench coat hung around the fatness of his belly like a tent, leaving a couple of skinny legs reaching to the floor.

The other gangster, much taller than the first, leveled two guns covering the room. The couple looked up from their moon-eyes and Jones made a quick assessment of the gangsters.

Moon-eyes had been holding hands across the table, across their highballs, and they clasped tight against the gunplay. Jones gave a cursory recognition to the hoods, and then resumed drawing the bow across the woe of the bass.

"Shut the racket," the taller one demanded. Jones stopped playing for a moment, looked the gunner in the eyes, tucked back into the bass and resumed stroking the strings.

The short fat goon, holding his guns on Bucky said, "Let the jig be, we got bigger stew to bubble." Speaking to Bucky he asked, "Where's the boss?"

"Boss?"

The goon was short, fireplug short and fireplug fat, but he moved quickly for his weight and slipped behind the bar, smashing bottles along the back as he went. Pressing a gun against Bucky's diaphragm he spewed through gritted teeth, "Don't git wise smart guy. Where's the owner of the hooch-joint? Thet Jew boy." Bucky could feel the iron prodding his guts.

The second gunman had moved to moon-eyes' table and shared a sickly smile with the lovers. Picking up the woman's drink and knocking it back it one swill, he addressed the man, "Boy, whatcha want wit' dis roach pussy? Ain't cha got no dign'ty?" He then turned his attention to the woman and smirked. "... But I'm a gotta be true, baby sure got some pretty brown mouth." The girl looked away but the lout persisted. "You a good sugar mouth, mama? You sure got the lips for a good sugar mouth."

Beethoven Jones stopped playing and looked at the thug. When the bass playing stopped, the lout turned his attention to Jones and said, "Ya got some issues we need addressin'?"

Jones looked from the gangster's gun to the woman and back to the gun. The moon had waned from the woman's eyes as she stared at the floor.

Jones looked again at the gun in the hood's fist and said sadly, "I don't get involved." and turned back into the bass.

The thug grinned, ear-to-ear, "You a smart colored boy. Why'n'cha play me some more sadness on thet big fiddle." He then turned his attention back to the girl. "Me, I like a good jig mouth now 'n then. Maybe me 'n you need to take dose puffy lips for a ride, whataya say?"

The fireplug with Bucky was all business. "Shut up, you pussy fool. We got agenda 'ere." Turning back to Bucky he demanded, "Where we find the kike?"

Bucky barely shook his head just before the fireplug slammed him across the face with the barrel of the gun. Bucky went down on one knee, leaning for support against the bar-back.

"Git up."

When Bucky lifted himself to his feet, the left side of his face wore the imprint of the gun barrel. "Beatin' me won't make me know where Kaleb is."

The logic of this stuck with the goon and he smiled. "Sure. I guess thet's right." Thinking this over, he took a moment to survey the room and he liked what he saw. "I like what I see 'ere. Me 'n Mama gonna make this little joint a nice home." To Bucky he said, "You play your cards right, boy, we might jes keep you on as the hooch gusher."

Bucky had nothing to say to that and that's exactly what he said.

When the fat hood had had enough of the silence, he called over his shoulder to his partner, "Let's lam." Addressing Bucky again he growled, "You be sure to tell the kike thet he had him some visitors a-callin'."

Bucky rubbed at his swelling welt on his face. The puffing was already giving his wrinkled face some fullness, puffing out the folds with blood under the skin. "Got a name with the calling card?"

"Jes tell 'im the Rubbles stopped by to say hi. Antony, thet's me 'n over there," he waved the gun in the general direction of the other man, "over there is my little brudder, Jimmy-Jimbo. Mama says we gonna to take over dis den of kikes and jigaboos. Make a respectable establishment out of it. Tell your kike boss thet."

Still rubbing the bruised folds of his wrinkles, Bucky said, "Sure, I'll let Kaleb know that fat and skinny came by to say hi."

The smile leeched from the fat man's face. "You jes lost future employment boy," and he slammed Bucky across the face again. This time he slammed him with the full weight of the revolver and Bucky went down and stayed down.

The fireplug man, Fat Tony, came around the bar and moved toward the door.

The tall gangster at the couple's table, Jimmy-Jimbo, reached down and cupped the girl's cheeks in his fingers. Squeezing gently, he pursed the girl's lips. "You sure got yerself some party lips, sweet stuff. Candy lips. Jig lips is the best. Maybe we meet agin when I'm not working,"

Fat Tony said, "Cut wit' the wooing, let's lam." Turning to Beethoven Jones he said, "You be sure to tell the kike thet we was here. Tell 'im we are serious businessmen makin' serious negotiations. Tell 'im these are our negotiators," and he waved the gun about the room.

Jimmy-Jimbo Rubble ignored the man at the table. With hard fingers he again pursed the black girl's cheeks, gently rubbing the gun barrel across the fullness of her lips. "Ya'all have a good time t'night, ya hear? Cuz, soon enough, we'll be sanitizin' dis joint of kikes 'n coons 'n jigs 'n Jews."

On their way to the door, the Rubble boys spilled tables and tossed a chair over the bar, smashing a row of bottles. After one last appraisal of The Temp, the Rubbles shoved their guns back into their pockets and backed out of the bar. All smiles.

***

Kaleb was addressing Beethoven Jones incredulously. "You mean, you didn't do nothing?"

"I don't get involved."

Kaleb was hot. "You don't get involved never?"

Jones stopped playing the bass and looked directly into Kaleb's eyes. "I don't get involved. Never. Never did. Never will. If'n you get your memory back, you'll know that. I never did get involved. Never did. Never will. Never." And he turned back into his bass.

Bucky was nursing his face with a wet bar cloth. "Let 'em be, Kaleb. They got the drop on us. They led with their guns. Warn't nothing nobody could do."

Kaleb did not like that his speakeasy was invaded by goons. And he didn't like that Bucky and his customers were assaulted. These were not circumstances that Kaleb could readily accept.

If these gangsters were hunting up Kaleb Kierka, hunting with guns to the ready, Kaleb would yet be in their sites.

And Kaleb Kierka would not make it a difficult hunt.

34

Goddamnittohellandbackagain

By the time that Granma had arrived at The Temp for her morning beer, Bucky had already begun cleaning up the damage.

"Goddamnittahellandbackagain, what happened here?"

Bucky looked up from his broom. "'Nother love note from Rubble and 'er boys."

Granma's good eye surveyed the scene while her lazy eye surveyed the ceiling. "Mizzy's gettin' frisky a'gin."

Bucky stopped and scrutinized the damage to the speakeasy. "Looks like. I'll getcha a beer." He slid behind the bar and drew Granma a beer from the tap. Granma came in twice a day, once in the morning for her beer breakfast and once later in the day to listen to the Tigers game on the radio. With beer.

Granma hauled her heft onto the center barstool. This center barstool had become her regular perch. Right in front of the radio on the bar-back. Right in front of the Tigers game. Granma was barely five feet tall, but she made up for her lack of height by being equally wide.

"Mizzy's got a big hunk of ugly 'bout her?"

Bucky shrugged and resumed sweeping up the smashed bottles. "It ain't all personal. They're hunting a shelf to ply their product in the city. They want to move Rubble's Bubble uptown from their dump out in the sticks. They already smashed up Lee's Grinning Duck Club on 2nd. Lee's considerin' pullin' in his awning. Been working on Kendrick's Song Shop Stop in the Corridor. But they got a special place in their black hearts for The Temp. Don't like Kaleb no-how, no-ways and 'sides..." looking down, "... oh shit, they smashed the schnapps. Kitty's gonna raise hell."

"'Sides what?" said Granma.

"What?"

"'Sides what 'bout Kaleb and Mizzy Rubble? You were 'bout to say."

"What? Oh. Yeh. Mizzy Rubble and 'er boys have been wantin' to move in on The Temp long time now."

Granma let this sink in as she crammed a plug of chaw into her jaw. "The Rubbles ownin' The Temp?" Granma gave a shudder with the thought and spit brown juice into the tin can she carried with her.

Bucky commenced cleaning the spilled schnapps. "Guess so. I guess 'sides bein' tired of runnin' a gin joint out the boonies, they got a special place in their black hearts for Kaleb."

"Goddamnittohellandbackagain." Granma thought this through and spit again. "What I hears, Rubble's Bubble is more of a needle joint than a gin joint they gots."

"Damn!" Bucky had cut his hand on a broken bottle and Granma threw the bar rag at him. He wrapped his hand and continued the thought. "Yep. Wouldn't surprise me none if'n needle joint is the design thet they got for The Temp."

"Wouldn't surprise me none neither." Granma nipped at her beer, spit a gob and finalized the thought, "Goddamnittohellandbackagain."

***

As the premier location for liquor, Detroit had a plethora of speakeasies, juice joints, blind pigs, roadhouses, and house parties.

Windsor, Canada, a stone's throw across the Detroit River, was not under Prohibition and offered easy access to good booze. Real booze. Whereas the rest of America was settling for whatever booze might be concocted in bathtubs and garage stills, Detroit was awash in top of the line Canadian whisky gleaned from the finest distilleries that Canada offered. And beyond. Canada was also a ready conduit for European imbibes.

The Detroit River, the thin line of water separating Detroit from Windsor, offered an easy channel for conveyance of the best distilleries that Canada and Europe could distill and dispense.

Speakeasies flourished in the prohibitive years of Detroit. They were protected by graft money to the police and to the city governance. The plusher the speakeasy, the further up the chain of command in the city governance the graft was to be rendered.

Any extra space that could fit a plank board bar and a few barstools was a candidate for a speakeasy during Detroit's Prohibition years. Shacks, basements, garages, carriage houses were all, likely as not, hosts for the speakeasies. During the height of Prohibition, every bare cupboard was a nominee for a speakeasy. These improvised beer taps serviced mostly the blue-collar of Detroit's young industrial trade and were so plentiful that they were generally ignored by the law. If not ignored, then they were bought off.

The Temple Bar Speakeasy And Play Nice was nicer than many, boasting a full bar, a singular pool table, and a small stage in the back corner. Situated on the border of Paradise Valley and the Black Bottom, it was a localized venue flying under the radar of the police force. While the rest of America was reconciled to cheap booze from backwater stills and dirty bathtubs, Detroit was enjoying the finest contraband that Canada and Europe could smuggle. America's Prohibition proved quite lucrative to Canadian and European distillers. Canadian distilleries like Carling Brewing, Labatt and Canadian Club were thriving while Irish whiskey, French champaign, and the occasional German schnapps found ways through the sieve that was Canada.

***

Granma sipped on her morning "vitamin B," her shell of beer, and exercised her lazy eye about the room. "Whataya think Kaleb is gonna do 'bout it?"

Bucky pulled up the broom. A small man, Bucky had always been a good target for bullies. And he hated bullies. Pointing to the baseball bat in the corner he said, "Don't know what Kaleb will do, but if it comes to me, I'd take that bat there and bust up Rubble's joint. Eye for eye, hooch for hooch."

Granma took another pull on her beer and studied Bucky. "That moose-herd of boys she's got is not the kinda troupe to tangle wit'. Them some big boys, Jimmy-Jimbo 'n Fat Tony."

Bucky smiled, set down the broom and walked over to the baseball bat. Choking the bat handle like Ty Cobb slapping a single to right field, he said, "First I'd take out they knees. Then they's my size."

Granma was not impressed, and she pinged her tin cup with a wad of tobacco juice to prove it. "Mizzy's got more than those goon boys of hers."

Bucky considered that. He shrugged his shoulders, set down the bat, and resumed his cleaning, picking up a couple of chairs that had been knocked about.

Granma knew what Kaleb would do and Bucky knew what Kaleb would do and neither of them wanted to put voice to what they knew.

The small stage was empty now save for the old piano and the double bass. The double bass looked odd without Jones's long knotty bones wrapped around it.

Granma surveyed the room. She sipped at the beer and watched as Bucky finished the cleaning. Kaleb's internment in the hospital had coincided with a stepped up harassment by The Bureau of Prohibition, The Feds, on Rubble's Bubble. Now that Kaleb was back among the living and the Fed hounding had eased, the Rubbles were stirring the waters again.

Granma finished her vitamin B and slid from the stool.

Bucky looked up from the broom. "Game times' 3:30."

"Yep. See ya," she answered.

As she reached the door, Granma turned and gave her lazy eye one more tour of the busted up bar.

"Goddamnittohellandbackagain," she said.

35

Satchmo's And Nika's Blowoff

One might well argue that it was the radio that gave jazz a national voice, when, in 1926 and 1927, NBC and CBS were founded and radio programming became a nationwide phenomenon uniting America. From sea to shining sea.

But the jazz offered by radio was a diffused, milquetoast version of a jazz rendering that would not offend delicate ears nor affront the provincial of the status quo. More so than radio, it was the vaudeville circuit that was responsible for the dispersal of the musical style of jazz throughout North America as it circulated the musicians and their unique regional music renderings from city to city.

Kunsky's Circle in Detroit's Grand Circus Park was the stronghold for vaudeville in the metropolis, Detroit style.

When acts came through town, be it Fats Waller or Red Skelton or The Rip Van Wrinkles, they would enter the vaudevillian rotation of the theaters in Grand Circle Park, Kunsky's Circle. These acts would run from 10 minutes to an hour. The ten-minute acts might be able to play seven, eight, ten clubs around Kunsky's Circle circuit in the course of a single evening.

But vaudeville could only do so much. The vaudeville circuit cycled these national acts through a town, but it was the wee hour blowoffs at the local dives that gave shape, gave voice, to the medium that became known as jazz.

This new-fangled sound got some traction in the uptown theatre cycle, but it was a watered-down and timid variety of jazz. Kunsky's Circle was pop entertainment for the common man and the music found in these upscale establishments of vaudeville were rendered to not offend the innocent ears of the bourgeoisie.

Conversely, blowoffs were all about the down low, and they were found late at night and tucked away in the back alleys of civilization. Most cities, large and small, that had touring vaudeville acts, had these alternate venues.

Speakeasies, juice joints, blind pigs, honky-tonks, all hovels of harmony, were where the touring musician could make a few extra bucks late at night after vaudeville closed up shop. More important, these late night dumps and dives allowed the touring musicians to swap dialects with the local musical dialect, trading licks and tricks with the native tongues.

In this way, the language that is jazz was developed, disseminated, and dispersed across the full breath of America.

When Kunsky's Circle shut down, the performers - comics, singers, novelty acts and band ensembles - would hit the local venues and cross-pollinate with the indigenous entertainers in this bubbling new brew of jazz.

Deep in the witching hour the dark and smoky clubs of the back streets on Detroit's Lower East Side would be swamped with these performers. These very same entertainers who offered up a milquetoast brand of jazz that reamed the masses of the upscale venues hit the dive clubs to cut loose with the spirit and the vigor of a Darwin expedition. This uncharted American expedition was called jazz.

Appropriately named blowoffs, these late night revelries of touring and local talent were the hot spot of the fusion that was the world of jazz. A world of music that was sweeping America. Sweeping America on the down low.

The Black Bottom was a Mecca for these blowoffs and The Temple Bar Speakeasy And Play Nice was a temple of worship.

***

The Temp was abuzz when word spread that Satchmo would be jamming with the house band. All of the familiar local cats were there with their respective instruments in the hopes of being invited to share their chops with the underground legend that was Satchmo. This would be a blowoff that none would blow off.

***

Like many of the early jazz bands cycling through on the vaudeville circuit, Louis Armstrong and His Hot Five played the uptown circuit of Detroit's Grand Circus Park for the paycheck, but after the uptown gigs, Satchmo landed lip-first in the local watering holes of Detroit's Black Bottom. Jamming with the local talent, Satchmo, with his New Orleans southern drawl of licks and tricks, cross pollinated with the local inflection of his northern music brethren.

Louis's day-gig ensemble was comprised of Johhny Dodds on clarinet, Kid Ory on trombone, Johnny St. Cyr on banjo, and Louis's wife, Lil Hardin-Armstrong, on piano.

In Kunsky's Circle, Armstrong's group stuck to the written page, to the music that did not challenge and did not offend. Uptown, Armstrong and His Hot Five settled into watered down arrangements with a sound that was much more in line with the familiar minstrel show bands popular in vaudeville. Arrangements were careful not to offend the meek of ear, not to challenge the music status quo.

But Satchmo's after-hour blowoffs were legendary in their provocation. Tonight Jazz du Jour was laying down the grooves at The Temple Bar Speakeasy And Play Nice and Satchmo was trumpeting a taunt with the band. And if Gabriel trumpeted for the saints, Satchmo was there to save the sinners.

Krikor and his accordion had joined Jazz du Jour for this special night, and he and Beethoven Jones were swapping riffs when Satchmo and St. Cyr entered The Temp.

Louis's wife, Lil, rarely went to these after hour jams, spending her spare time on the business end of The Hot Five, keeping the books in the hotel room. Kid Ory and Johnny Dodds were busy sampling the local women.

In these earliest manifestations of jazz there were no rules and no standard player. Jazz was exploring new realms and the only rules were that rules were not allowed. If the music sounded good, it was right. If it sounded bad, it was wrong.

In these earliest of jazz jams, when jazz was yet defining its voice, a southern banjo plucker like Johnny St. Cyr could find a kinsman in Krikor, the accordion player.

The Temp's rocking rostrum had a distinct flare as the Armenian accordion player and the New Orleans banjo picker swapped rhythmic comps underneath Satchmo's flame.

As for The Temp dance floor, it was shoulder to shoulder in sweaty anticipation of unexplored horizons. Kaleb had his seat anchored at the end of the bar and Bucky was pitching brew. Jazz du Jour, having already played a set, was tuned, warmed and primed for their jam with Satchmo Armstrong.

For this special occasion, Beethoven Jones was wrestling with new catguts on the bass, Leon Barwood was spitting up a new reed on his saxophone, and Nika Nightingale was in the alley, spiking her arm with courage.

As Satchmo and St. Cyr unpacked their instruments, the club began to murmur with expectation, and when they tuned their tools to August Pini's piano, a respectful hush fell upon The Temple Bar Speakeasy And Play Nice.

Once tuned, Satchmo looked out from the stage to the black and white and brown and yellow faces in the black-and-tan club, and with a laugh he croaked, "Mama warned me 'bout night's like dis."

With a smile full of endless teeth Louis rasped, "Let the revelry begin." At that he began the festivities by playing a solo soliloquy of the Calvary's "Revelry" on his trumpet, leading the charge into the night. As Satchmo's solo call to arms waned, the entire band, on cue, launched into Armstrong's hit song, "Heebie Jeebies."

Satchmo got the heebie-jeebies and Jazz du Jour got the heebie-jeebies and The Temple Bar Speakeasy And Play Nice got the heebie-jeebies and the joint was jumpin' with "Heebie Jeebies."

Satchmo's world of this new fangled music called jazz was a cornucopia of jazz. Satchmo's trumpet was a horn-of-plenty.

When Satchmo trumpeted jazz there was beef in the pauper's porridge and there was light at the end of the tunnel. In Satchmo's aural world of jazz there were no lonely hearts and no broken bones and there were no lost souls. In Satchmo's world of jazz there was God in heaven.

When Satchmo trumpeted "When the Saints Go Marching In," Gabriel conceded the pulpit.

***

The blowoff was blowing off and Satchmo was blowing off and Jazz du Jour had blown off The Temp when Nika was invited to the stage. Bound in a hip-clingy flapper drop-waist black dress and T-strap three-inch spikes, Nika Nightingale looked like the exclamation point at the end of a suggestive limerick.

The stage itself was a dais in the back corner of The Temple Bar Speakeasy And Play Nice and raised two feet over the dance floor. Stage left, near the piano, offered the singular step onto the platform. The longer legged players would often skip the footstep and just stride directly up onto the rostrum. Little Nika always used the step.

"We gonna have a local number join us for a swing or two," Satchmo announced with his gravel grin. Satchmo was the contracted name of "Satchelmouth," a tribute to his ever-present display of beaming teeth. Sharing the flash with the house he announced, "Ya'll know her as Nika Nightingale." Then he rasped to Nika, "Com'on up 'ere, baby, 'n give us a throw."

Nika was fresh from the alleyway and the heroin was surging a warm rush through her veins. She made the footstep okay but the step up onto the stage reached out and grabbed her foot and she stumbled headlong toward the platform floor. She would have made it, too, if August Pini had not swung around on the piano bench and caught her mid fall.

The speakeasy went silent as Nika righted herself and twitched the angles of her dress back onto her curves. Only the heroin swamping her veins mitigated her embarrassment.

Quick to recover, Satchmo put the house at ease, smiling with a satchel full of teeth. "The little lady's ready to explode with the drone," and the patrons laughed. And then to Nika he added, "Come on over 'ere, little one, let's me 'n you fill us up a decanter of jazz'em."

The band was full tilt in two measures. St. Cyr was bouncing banjo licks off of Krikor's accordion, and Beethoven Jones was thumping out the groove on new catguts. Billy Oldham snapped the snare while August was hammering on the piano. Louie Armstrong was center stage of the cacophony beaming full and toothy.

This jam played like an aural poem recited by Jazz du Jour with the stanzas being meter-monitored by Billy Oldham's drum slaps. Beethoven Jones was underlining the sonnet with the bass groove while Nika provided the exclamation point. Satchmo edited the composition with trumpeted scribbles of improvisation.

Nika Nightingale was on her best game. She was in the moment. She was in the place one gets to in meditation and in prayer. Nika was universal and she was of the singular moment. She was singing the full history of mankind. Nika was chanting the first-ever ancestral words around a dank fire pit, and she was crooning the future chronicles of humankind's prospect.

Nika was singing on high. On high.

***

Nika Nightingale sang from the highest of highs to the lowest of lows, letting her voice channel the full breath of the pain and the ecstasy of the human experience.

When Nika sang on high:

It was pure like the first snow and real like a grandmother's fable and it had the energy that tapped the shoulder of angels and cooed sweet nothings into their wings and the colored girls standing stage-side felt mist for their fellow gender trekker and said things like, "Jesus hisself a-gonna snatch thet girl aloft," and "…give thet child air 'fore she spark…." and every voice in The Temple Bar Speakeasy And Play Nice rejoiced the rapture and joined in the ecstasy.

And when Nika sang on the lowdown:

The pain and the agony oozed from the melody with a pitchfork and a hammer and the cries rang so deep that memory dug down to the dawn of man and Eve was thrown from the garden to bear the monthly blood cycle with babies at her feet and wolves at the door and the misted colored girls cried, "…forgive them Father for they know not what they do…." and Nika's voice was one with the moon and sister to the shadows.

***

When Satchmo jumped into Nika's moment, into Nika's deliverance, he lifted her high on the wings of his golden trumpet, and her voice was delivered naked like honesty and pure like the child of Joseph and Mary to the salvation that waited on the banks of the Jordan River.

The revelers cried in their joy and they wept in their sorrow and every soul in Temple Bar Speakeasy And Play Nice filled with the wisdom of the holy sacrament. Prayers were offered and answered in the same breath, in Nika's and Satchmo's blowoff.

This was a blowoff for the ages. This was a blowoff of every forbears' spirit, of their plight and their rapture, that had ever tread the rich soil of the Black Bottom and beyond.

Time is a manufactured concept that humankind has designed to give chronology to the human condition. Outside of man's contrived reality, time does not endure.

Jazz du Jour, with Nika leading the charge and Satchmo trumpeting the cause, stepped outside of the contrivance of human time and became one with the cosmos. One with the universe and one with the heavens.

One.

***

If not for Bucky throwing open the doors of The Temple Bar Speakeasy And Play Nice and washing the club with dawns early light, this blowoff, this revelry of Louis Armstrong and Nika Nightingale and Jazz du Jour and The Temple Bar Speakeasy And Play Nice, might well have persisted to this very day.

Awaiting the Rapture.

36

Kaleb Meets The Purple Gang

They met Kaleb as he was coming out of The Temp. Their long overcoats on a muggy day with fists dug deep into the pockets suggested trouble.

They were young, barely out of their teens, but they had the look down pat. The trench coats hung loose on their small frames, the low slung fedoras, shoulders hunched forward in menace, the practiced scowl. Stock gangster. It was all the rage in the Detroit of 1927.

They intercepted Kaleb on the sidewalk but said nothing. They just stood there, giving Kaleb plenty of time to admire their gangly-hood.

Finally the smaller one, the one with the tell-tale Jewish nose, said, "You don' 'member me?"

Kaleb had been appraising the boys from the start, but the appraisal had yielded no memory and his silence confirmed it.

When Kaleb had nothing to say the boy continued, "Heard you was dumb-clocked. S'at so? You ain't got no who's who?"

Again Kaleb had a whole lot of nothing to say and he continued not saying it.

Shrugging the shoulders of his gangly-hood, the boy-goon went on. "I got my skeptic on you ain't got no recollect."

This made Kaleb laugh. "You're not unique in that skeptic, son."

The word "son" made the boy wince. He didn't like it. It didn't give proper respect to the authority of his gangly-hood.

Warily, watching Kaleb like a boxer looking for a sucker punch, the boy continued. "I'm Izzy. Izzy Bernstein. This 'ere's Steiny. Hear tell you been huntin' us?"

The name Bernstein tinkled a bell, but there were no Big Bens ringing. Kaleb asked, "Who is us?"

Even in the oversized trench coat Kaleb could detect Izzy's chest inflate with some kind of lost pride. "Us? Who is us? Us is the Bernstein boys. The Purples. Us is the Purple Gang. Us is what rules these streets."

Kaleb was not impressed. "I'm looking for more'n a couple of street urchins playin' tough. Where's the top Roscoe?"

Izzy stiffened at the insolence. "I got all the roscoe I need right 'chere" and he pumped his hands on the bulge of his trench coat pockets.

The kid Steiny spoke for the first time. "Easy, Iz, ain't no time to let the mark ing-bing you to a fit."

Kaleb's insolence was goading Izzy who sputtered, "'Oughta jes fill 'em full 'a daylight 'n be done."

"Ray's wantin' ta chit-chat wit' 'em. Can't hardly do that if'n he's full of daylight."

This seemed to cool Izzy for the moment. "Sure. Ray wants ta pow-wow," but he added to Kaleb, "maybe another time we play cowboys 'n Indians, eh Kabe?"

There was a big Buick with all the trimmings sitting at the curb and Kaleb tipped his head toward the car. "I suspect we go for a ride now?"

Izzy and Steiny looked at each other and then they looked up at Kaleb. "How da hell didja know this was our ride?"

Kaleb nodded toward the street as he smiled at the boys. "This neighborhood's lousy with Model T's. 'Cept that one big black Buick. The Buick, the fedora, the trench coats bulging pockets of iron, the kitschy lingo. All part of the standard mob costume, ain't it?"

The boys did not blindfold Kaleb for the ride. This meant that they trusted him enough to not worry about his betrayal.

Or they were going to kill him.

***

Steiny drove. Izzy sat in the back seat next to Kaleb, and saying a whole lot of nothing. Kaleb watched the cityscape whiz by as the Buick swung west along Congress Street, then south onto Griswold Street toward the Detroit River. Toward the shipping and warehouse district. Toward the dock. Toward the Purple Gang.

Kaleb had been piecing together his history with the Purple Gang with the help of his acquaintances. Detective Morane and Bucky and Granma and Kitty and Nika and Beethoven Jones - although Beethoven didn't want to get involved - had all been able to provide some small detail to his memory of the Purples. And with each nibble of information came a brighter wattage on the light bulb of his memory.

As young Steiny squealed corners in his best imitation of what gang driving must be, Kaleb scoured the history that he had been collecting.

Kaleb had known the Bernstein brothers from his youth. From a time when they were kids hawking newspapers on street corners, playing baseball in the sand lots adjacent to factories, and raiding farmers gardens on the east end of the Black Bottom.

Izzy was the youngest of the Bernstein brothers, and Kaleb did not run much with the boy, but he had gotten on swell with brothers Abe and Raymond and Joey Bernstein.

***

Detroit was a hustling and bustling industrial nerve center for America and everybody wanted a piece of it. Honest and crooked national politicians alike journeyed through Detroit to gain political and, especially, financial support. Engineers and designers from across the globe came to study the cutting edge of the industrial age in Detroit's factories and architecture.

The blue-collar contingent, the blood and muscle that drove Detroit's engine, was flooding Detroit's inbound arteries. Appalachian hillbillies and southern black men and Europeans - Polacks and Germans and Ukrainians and Jews - were streaming into Detroit by car and by train and by bus and by foot, all seeking bread for their babies and the promise of the better life that was America.

America's criminal element was well represented in prohibition Detroit as well.

***

As the Buick crossed Congress Street at Woodward Avenue, Kaleb could look north, past City Hall, and see the east-west dividing line that was Woodward Avenue. A glorious testament to what Detroit's place in the world had become. A city of energy and light and growth and a city that made the 1920s roar.

As one looked north along Woodward, past the Grand Circus Park, one could make out the new intellectual hub of Detroit as Henry Ford's *Detroit Museum of Art* and the *College of the City* were sprouting on opposite sides of Woodward Avenue.

Further north still, the gold-gilded tiles of the Fischer building lit West Grand Boulevard. Designated as America's "largest art object," the Fischer Building would be the newest, and most glorious standard for the world's skyscrapers.

Steiny looped the Buick into a parking space on Griswold at Larned, and the boys walked Kaleb the two blocks down to the warehouse district on Atwater. Slipping though the cut in the chain link fence, Steiny first, next Kaleb with Izzy following, they entered the warehouse through a door at the rear. Once in the building they made their way to the iron-grate stairs along the back wall and then up to the loft office with glass windows overlooking the vast and empty warehouse below.

The office was sparse. A metal desk, a few hard-back oak chairs and an old 1918 calendar hung on the soiled wall. The smells of this unused warehouse, rancid oil and mold, hung in the air like a membrane. This was not an office in regular use.

Entering the room, the boys slid along the walls, Steiny going left, Izzy to the right. Raymond Bernstein relaxed behind the desk in an armed office chair on wheels. Abe Bernstein straddled a reversed hard-back chair with his arms folded over the chairs back. Joey Bernstein was not present.

He was friendly enough, Raymond was, but guarded and to the point. He gave a familial nod to Kaleb. "Same ol' mush, Kabe. Like ol' times," and then he went right to business. "I hear you been buzzin' for us. What's the yammer?" Raymond was Kaleb's age, the eldest Bernstein brother.

Looking about the office, Kaleb exchanged nods with Raymond and Abe. Izzy remained behind Kaleb, pressed against the wall, his hands dug deep into his heavy pockets.

Kaleb waved his hand toward the big, empty warehouse below. "What's with the Taj Mahal? Jew boys going Hindu?"

Ray laughed, Abe smiled, but Izzy was not in the humor.

"Our 'club house du jour'. You like?"

One of the idiosyncrasies of the Purple Gang was that they kept their home base mobile. Where other gangs might maintain one or two permanent sites, the Purple Gang changed haunts regularly. The scheme was to be a moving target from rival gangs and the law.

From behind Kaleb, Izzy was impatient. "You jes here to bump gums or you got some batter to mix?"

Kaleb kept his smile on Raymond as he spoke to Izzy. "You the red-hot, now, Iz? You do the buzzin'?"

Izzy was turning red-faced with the impudence. "Ain't sayin' I'm the mokker, jes want to know what blood track you on and why you huntin' up the Purples. What blood, exactly, are you huntin'?"

Kaleb turned from Raymond to give full measure to Izzy. Looking Izzy square in the eye he said, "Iz, the day I can't find my blood is the day I die of anemia."

Izzy glared at Kaleb. Kaleb returned a fixed eye to Izzy but the slightest of smile betrayed Kaleb's lips.

The Purple Gang was run much like a band of Indians with multiple chiefs but no boss.

When Kaleb spoke, he spoke to the room. "Seems I've been the object of the hunt. If it's the Purple Gang doing the hunting, I want to make it easy for you boys."

Again Izzy responded, "If it was us doin' the huntin' your head would already be taxiderm'd to the wall."

This time Abe enjoined, "Easy Iz." Then to Kaleb he said, "You understand Kabe, after you cut us out of The Temp thetaway, you left some hard feelin's 'mongst your old pals. 'N now you come askin' us to s'plain it? That make any sense to you, do it?"

When Kaleb was slow to respond, Abe continued, "You got your own way, Kabe, we got that an' we respect you for that. We owe you," and he threw a thumb in Izzy's direction and added, "an' nobody owes you more'in Iz owes you."

Izzy jumped on that. "I don't owe 'im jack-squat."

Abe continued, "We all owe you so we let you be. We let The Temp be. We let you walk away from us, Kabe. We let you walk away from the Purple Gang."

"'N it make us look like chumps," Izzy had to add.

"Shut up, Iz." And then back to Kaleb he said, "Here's how you stand with us, Kabe. You got your own ways. You got your own club and you get your own booze. We don't ask why or where or nuthin'. We let you be 'cause you got a deep history with us. A history that we are beholden to you. It ain't the Purples that been knockin' on your dome. Never did. Never will. You got too much capital in this posse."

Kaleb took this in. He had heard some vague anecdotes about his time with the Purples, but he was more concerned about the future than the past. "Whataya know about the Rubble Gang?"

Abe and Raymond exchanged looks and now it was Izzy who smiled.

Izzy venture, "We hearin' that Rubble's got her boys all over your club."

Kaleb looked from face to face.

Izzy followed up. "The Rubbles seem to have a issue with yer caterin' the jigs and roaches. No skin off'n our nose. Why'ain't cha askin' yer clientele for help? "

Again Kaleb directed his conversation to the room. "I ain't here to ask for help. I'm huntin' information."

There was some strain in Kaleb and Izzy's relationship that Kaleb was not privy to. The strain did not seem to extend to Raymond and Raymond redirected the conversation's tone.

"Speakin' a' jigs, how's that big jig, Jones?"

Kaleb appreciated the change of temperature. "Beethoven's still scrapin' the ceiling with his low tones."

Abe joined the conversation. "I 'member thet colored boy playin' baseball. B'fore you 'n him got all uptown with your boogie. That boy sure could play some ball. Shame they don't let the darkies in the big leagues."

"He got an offer to circuit that Negro league, 'member?" Raymond said.

"Yup. But he'd have to leave that bass fiddle at home. He warnt gonna do that. 'Sides, that boy ain't been the same since the Elmwood rumble."

The mention of the Elmwood rumble struck a chord for Kaleb and his eyes glazed trying to grab at the memory. "The Elmwood rumble?"

Raymond and Abe each noted Kaleb's eyes glaze as Kaleb tried to catch the memory of the Elmwood rumble and they exchanged knowing nods.

Abe Bernstein offered, "The Elmwood rumble. Sure. Elmwood Cemetery. You were there and we was there and little Sammy Cohen sheathed a shiv in his belly there. You don' 'member?"

"There's sometin' there, all right," Kaleb muttered as he wrestled with the memory.

Abe continued, "An' the jig, Beethoven Jones was there too, I 'member. An' that colored boy ain't never been the same since. No more come out to hang after that. Jes kinda kept to his own self. Don't get involved in nuthin'."

Raymond brought the conversation back on point. "Mizzy Rubble's beef is not our beef. She blown 'cause you let those colored boys and girls play with white boys and girls in your club. Says it ain't natural. Can't say as I'm particularly warm to the idea myself. But I appreciate you stickin' to what you judge right."

Kaleb nodded to that but Raymond continued, "But more'n that, Mizzy Rubble wants your club. She wants to set up her boys with their very own juice-joint and she wants The Temp to be the setup."

Abe added, "And she'll kill you to get it."

Izzy was itching for a fight. "White is white and black is black and we should'n be mixin' it up."

Ray cut Izzy short. "Let it lay, Iz," and then he said to Kaleb, "Rubble's been here already. She's askin' for help to move on you. Or, leastways, for us to lay out of any move she pulls on you. She's a real sweetheart."

Kaleb studied the Bernstein faces and spoke very slowly. "I ain't here askin' for nothing'."

Izzy cut him off. "Then why'd ya come?"

Again Kaleb took his time. "I jes come down here to ask you boys to stay in the dugout of the game."

Abe asked, "You don't want our help against the Rubbles?"

Izzy was quick to follow. "You ashamed of us?"

That hurt and the wince in the corner of Kaleb's eye was the tell. "I ain't never been ashamed of my roots."

Izzy would not let it go. "Getin' too uppity for our swarm?"

Raymond had enough. "Shut up, Iz." And then to Kaleb Raymond asked, "You think that you can handle those Rubbles okay?"

"My business. My handle."

"Who's got your back?"

"Bucky's with me."

"Bucky's a good boy but that little man ain't exactly intimidating. That all you got?"

Kaleb smiled at the thought of the 38-inch baseball bat in Bucky's fists. "We're good."

"You know we owe you, Kabe. Big owe."

"I don't know that you owe me anything."

Raymond looked to the floor while he considered this, but Abe volunteered, "If you want us out, Kaleb, we're out. But we got muscle if you want it."

"Second that," added Raymond. "You got safe passage on our turf anyhows. We owe you that much." Raymond shrugged his shoulders and nodded to the door. "Your heap's out at the curb, I 'spect you know the way home."

"My T's outside? But the keys are in my pocket...."

Even as the words left his mouth, Kaleb realized how ludicrous that sounded.

They all got a good laugh out of that one.

37

The Purple Gang Moniker

There were flashes of memory, flashes of light. The amnesia was like that. First would come a speck of light, a pale and far-off memory in the distance, like the infamous train entering the far end of the tunnel. When Kaleb focused on that memory, on that distant point of illumination, he could draw that glow to his senses, firing his synaptic gaps with electric charges. If enough charges fired, if enough synaptic gaps were leapt, the speck of light, of memory, would increase wattage.

As Kaleb drove the streets of his youth, across the tracks of his history, sparks would flicker yon and glimmer hither. Seizing the flickers and the glimmers, he tried to connect the points of the light to a common memory trace.

Grinding through the gears of the Lizzie held its own memory, and Kaleb seized the kinetic memory to enhance recall.

The muscle memories of Kaleb's fist as it slammed through the T's gears were flickers of light, and the streetscape and alleyways that Kaleb navigated were glimmers of glow. Connecting these flickers and glimmers created a brighter beam, and synaptic gaps were bridged and memory coaxed from the darkness.

As Kaleb made his way along the boulevards of 1927 Detroit, he clutched at the T's gears as he clutched at the memories.

The meeting with the Bernstein boys had jarred loose a smattering of memories, a collection of dust and rust from another life long ago and far away. Memories of street baseball and street hockey and knuckle-down street marbles: cat eyes and aggies and red devils and boulders.

Memories of boys being boys. Black boys and brown boys and white boys were united in their poverty and were yet to be divided by the distinction in the hue of their skin.

As he drove among the warehouses of Detroit's waterfront, the trickle of light became a stream and the stream became a river and the river became a flood of memory. Memory of the Bernsteins - of Raymond and Abe and Izzy. A flooding saga of the Purples washing Kaleb's darkness in a torrent of recollect.

Kaleb was barely able to guide the T to the curb before he lost consciousness to the searing blast of memories.

***

They were not always called the Purple Gang. Before the Purple Gang they were members of the Oakland Sugar House Gang and before that they were just a loose collection of disenfranchised Jewish boys running the streets of Paradise Valley. Just another collection of raggedy street urchins.

Kaleb and the Bernsteins were from these same ghetto streets of Detroit. He spoke the language of these young misfits. He went to Bishop School with these boys; he worked the Eastern Market with these boys; he played baseball with these boys. Mostly Kaleb played baseball with those boys.

But while the Bernstein brothers and the Keywell brothers and the Fleisher brothers, the future core of the Purple Gang, employed their idle time as petty street criminals, pickpockets, and muggers, Kaleb was plinking accordions in tandem with Beethoven Jones's double bass. While that budding Purple Gang graduated from petty street crimes to hijacking and strong-arm work, Kaleb and Jones were busking street corners with their hats out.

And then there was baseball. Baseball. The one communal pursuit that the Jew-boys of Paradise Valley and the colored boys of the Black Bottom had was baseball.

Every neighborhood of Detroit had its sandlot baseball teams. And it was always a big to-do when the Lower East side played the Outer Drive Squad or the Highland Park Posse would play the Hamtramck Polacks.

The Lower East Side baseball team was a peculiar collection of Jew boys from Paradise Valley and colored boys from Detroit's adjacent Black Bottom neighborhoods. Detroit's first and only mixed-race boys' baseball team.

The Bernsteins were part of this boys' baseball team. Kaleb was a part of this baseball team. And so, too, was Beethoven Jones.

Beethoven Jones towered above the heads of the other boys. He had a beanpole frame with hard muscles running the length of those long arms. Even though he had to stand four feet away from home plate to cover the strike zone, his swing was powerful. And ten long strides covered the full breath of centerfield.

But the childhood games had to end; the poverty outside of baseball, off the field, had made the Bernstein brothers and the Keywell brothers and the Fleisher brothers bitter rivals. Rivals in the craft of street thuggery.

Long before the Bernsteins, and the Keywells, and the Fleishers united as the Purple Gang, they were blood competitors. The boys were competition in Detroit's enterprise of small time thugs and pickpockets.

The best booty was to be found along downtown Woodward Avenue, and it was inevitable that these brothers' criminal paths would cross.

This turf war among these brother gangs was a constant irritant and it eventually would reach its culmination in fists and blood and winners and losers.

***

The rumble was scheduled for 10 p.m. on the northeastern most slice of the Elmwood Cemetery. This was in the backside of the cemetery. It was an empty, unplotted land that rose to a small knoll at the rear of the graveyard.

The dust-up would be the Bernstein boys and whoever they could muster against the Fleisher and the Keywell boys. Each side would bring a collective of street urchins who would rally to their cause.

This was an "in-house" party and only Jew boys were invited. No guns. No knives.

Word had gotten to the Bernstein brothers that the Fleisher/Keywell gang would be bringing a dozen bodies strong to the rumble. The Bernstein brothers numbered six and were looking at a good whooping.

But the Bernstein brothers would never back down. They were determined to be the toughest of the tough of the Jewish street thugs.

As the collection of Bernstein boys headed to the Elmwood Cemetery, they recruited bodies along the way. Walking north on Gratiot they collected little Sammy Cohen to their tribe. Sammy was a small boy, young. But the Bernsteins needed the bodies.

On Waterloo Street they collected Asheim "Shim" Gatstein into the fold.

With Sammy and Shim along the Bernsteins numbered eight bodies, still short of the Fleisher/Keywell contingent, but bravado was carrying the day.

The Bernstein gang chanced upon Kaleb and Beethoven Jones as they were returning from a Negro League baseball game at Mack Park on the east side.

Abe entreated the pair to join their ranks; but this was not Kaleb's fight and it was not Jones's fight. Although buddies to the Bernstein boys on the baseball field, Kaleb and Jones were not natural joiners, and they were not of the delinquent mindset of the Bernsteins, the Keywells, and the Fleishers.

But Abe was a great cajoler. "The Fleishers and Keywells are idiots and you're gonna have to walk their walk if they're the mokker. You may not like our methods, but lest ways, you know where we stand. And we let you be. Don't 'spect the same courtesy from those boys."

Kaleb was not of the constitution to take to gangs. But Kaleb did know the Fleisher and the Keywell boys and he took no pleasure in the thought of them enjoying dominion over the lower east side streets. He'd had a dust-up or two with the Fleishers and the prospect of paying the boys a neighborhood tariff was not an attractive prospect.

Izzy Bernstein should not have been in this row; he was too young. All of twelve years old but the Bernsteins needed the bodies. It was Izzy who aimed a taunt at Jones. "An' the Keywell boys hate jigs."

Although Kaleb was not the biggest boy in the 'hood, he was one of the toughest and Abe wanted Kaleb in the row. "Look 'ere, Kaleb, you 'n Jones help us now and I'll consider it a personal loan. You can cash in at will."

Kaleb did not want nor need the Bernstein boys to be in his debt, but the thought of nasty little Heimy Fleisher leading the lower east side corps left a sour taste.

Abe pressed the point. "You dust out now an' you be payin' your beans to the Fleishers. Lest ways wit' the Bernsteins you get a fair shake. Whataya say?"

Kaleb looked to Jones for advice and the tall black boy merely shrugged his shoulders at Kaleb. Kaleb and Jones did not need words to discuss the ramifications. They squared their shoulders into the direction of the Elmwood Cemetery.

They counted ten boys in the mix now. Ten Bernsteins against the twelve Fleishers. The Bernstein collective entered Elmwood Cemetery from the north, through the cut in the chain link fence along Waterloo Street. The dozen Keywell/Fleisher boys came from Mt. Elliott Street to the east.

They met on an empty collection of grave plots that would one day house some of Detroit's most notorious characters. And some of these very same boys.

Quiet settled on the graveyard as the gangs glared across the rise of land at the rear of the Elmwood Cemetery, sizing up each other's worth.

No one could account for how exactly the rumble began. It could have been a look. It could have been a word. It could have been a bird winging by. But it did begin and it was ugly and it was bloody and it would be a battle of legendary status of the Jewish gangs of Paradise Valley.

Even though outnumbered, the Bernstein boys were giving much better than they were getting. After a good 20 minutes of battle, the mêlée took a definitive turn for the Bernsteins when three of the Keywell/ Fleisher gang had had enough, jumped the fence at Mt. Elliott, and ran off toward the Michigan Central rail line.

As the outcome was becoming clear, Kenny Still of the Keywell/ Fleisher boys drew a knife. Kenny Still, older than the other boys, was a neighborhood bully, and it was not a surprise that the shiv appeared in his fist when he found himself on the losing end of the rumble.

Kenny was older, bigger and meaner than these street urchins and had bullied the best of them. He had bullied Raymond and he had bullied Joe and he had bullied Abe. And he had bullied Kaleb.

Kenny was also the first boy in the neighborhood to play with drugs. Reefer and heroin. The maniacal look in Kenny's eyes tonight suggested heroin.

The shiv was a thick butcher knife from his father's slaughterhouse.

The brandishing of knives was not on the program for this rumble, but Kenny Still was a bully and bullies do not follow the rules.

Kenny was a big boy and he swung the knife hard and stuck it deep into the chest of little Sammy Cohen.

Blood slowly oozed around the knife's blade as it stuck out of little Sammy's chest cavity. Sammy's face twisted from surprise to pain as he looked up into Kenny Still's face. Sammy's skin went ashen, his eyes glazed and he slowly slumped onto Kenny Still's extended arm, digging his body deeper onto the blade.

Kenny let go of the blade, leaving the knife to hold fast into Sammy's chest cavity. Slumping to the ground, Sammy curled into himself before sagging to the dirt.

The rumble halted in mid-combat. The little knoll at the back of the Elmwood Cemetery went quiet. Death quiet.

Even Kenny Still was held in a shocked stillness by his action. This was not part of the agreed brawl and it signaled that the Keywell/Fleishers had had enough. It was a capitulation symbol to the assemblage that the Bernsteins had prevailed.

But the victory did nothing for little Sammy Cohen with a butcher knife stuck deep into his chest. When Sammy slowly folded to the ground, he held a genuflecting position momentarily before falling face-first into the graveyard dirt.

Kaleb was the first to Sammy. Kneeling down and cradling Sammy in his arms, Kaleb felt the final gasp of breath slip from the small boy's lungs.

The Elmwood Cemetery held silence for long moments. The gentle drone of the nearby factories' swing shift held sway in the warm night air. It was Izzy Bernstein who pulled his own blade from his trousers. He was the smallest and youngest of the Bernstein brothers, and if the Bernsteins hadn't needed the body to fill out their ranks, Izzy would not have been at the rumble.

Isadore, Izzy, Bernstein forever carried a "just-in-case" switchblade. And this was the just-in-case.

Like a magic trick, a second butcher blade leapt into Kenny Stillwell's fist. A butcher's son would come well equipped with armament.

"You son-of-a-bitch," Izzy shouted as he squared off with Kenny Still. Kenny had just proven his proficiency with a knife. "You son-of-a-bitch, I'm gonna kill you," little Izzy cried.

As the big boy squared off with Izzy, the size disparity between the diminutive Izzy and the bully Kenny was unambiguous. The big boy towered his six-foot height and 250 pounds over the pint-sized Izzy.

Kenny smiled down at the pocket-sized Izzy and his pocket-sized switchblade. Izzy returned the smile. But Izzy's smile was a sickly smile as the full realization of the gauntlet he had just thrown down smacked him in the face.

As Izzy and Kenny began their death pirouette, everyone knew that Izzy had been invited to his final tango. The realization read on Izzy's face which paled to a pasty pallor.

Slowly the two boys circled. The butcher knife heavy in Kenny's fist against Izzy's toothpick switchblade.

Jabbing here, prodding there, the boys flicked their shivs at each other, testing for the opportunity for their knives chance.

Kenny made his move. Feigning left, the big boy lunged forward with his death stroke. Bigger, quicker, and with the skilled practice of a butcher's son, Kenny stabbed the blade at the small boy's chest.

But Kenny's stab whooshed at empty air as Izzy was swept off of his feet, slapped to the ground, by a blow from Izzy's blind side.

Kaleb had stepped into the fray. Landing a clout flush on little Izzy's jaw, Kaleb sent Izzy tumbling unconscious to the dirt.

Once Izzy was dispensed with, Kaleb squared to the brute, to Kenny Still. Kenny, his scalpel gleaming in the moonlight, now faced Kaleb with fists hard and to the ready.

Knocking Izzy to the ground and taking Izzy's place in front of Kenny's blade was unexpected and it took Kenny a moment to process. When the realization that Kaleb had taken Izzy's ground, without a knife, Kenny relaxed into an ugly smile. Kenny and Kaleb had history. Mean history. A history of the bully and the bullied. And this would be where the chronicle would end.

As the boys circled, Kenny with his knife, Kaleb with his fists, the silence of the dead echoed among the tombstones of the necropolis. Of Elmwood Cemetery.

It was Kenny Still who lunged first, but it was Kaleb Kierka who landed the blow.

Nimbly sidestepping Kenny's knife, Kaleb's clout came from over the top. It was a roundhouse blow that came from Kaleb's ankle with the full power of a follow through as Kaleb swung through the punch.

***

Swinging through a punch: A pugilist's power does not come from the boxer targeting an opponent's chin. No. True power comes when the boxer targets his blow to go through an opponent's face, to the back of the skull. When the blow targets the face and the punch lands on the face, that is where the jolt ends. But when a boxer directs his blow to the back of an opponent's head, through his face, that is the jolt that rocks.

In the pugilist parlance, that is called "swinging through" the punch.

***

Deftly sidestepping the shiv that Kenny Still had thrust at him, Kaleb targeted his clout to the back of Kenny's skull, through Kenny's face.

Kaleb's clout rolled from his ankles, met Kenny's nose, and drove deep into the back of Kenny's cranium. The quiet of Detroit's humming industry was pierced with the crack of Kenny's face as the boy crumbled to the dirt in a lump of unconsciousness.

Again, quiet, with the soft, ambient hum of the city in the backdrop, the rival gangs stood stock-still and considered these developments.

From the dirt, Izzy was moaning to consciousness. Pushing himself from the ground, he took stock of the scene. When his focus allowed him to understand the meaning of Kaleb standing over the lump of Kenny Still, Izzy seethed at Kaleb, "You mother fucker, you shoulda let me kill the bastard."

But everybody knew who would have done the killing. And as much as Izzy resented the interference, Izzy knew as well.

And Izzy resented Kaleb all the more for it.

***

This was the bruised and bloody battle that would decide the hierarchy of the Jew boys of the Paradise Valley street thugs. Never again would the Bernstein brothers be challenged in the pecking order of the street gang that would one day become Detroit's premiere gang, the Purple Gang.

That night, on the knoll at the back of the Elmwood Cemetery where little Sammy Cohen lost his life, would leave its scar on every boy present.

The Bernstein brothers, Abe and Raymond and Joe, were now the undisputed leaders of the pack. Top dog. Kingpin. Ticket master.

Izzy would always resent his small size. And resent Kaleb.

Kaleb Kierka turned away forever from these street roots.

Beethoven Jones would never again get involved.

And little Sammy Cohen lay dead.

***

Now the Bernsteins and the Keywells and the Fleishers were one gang in the brotherhood of blood.

In a homage to this final and deciding battle on that quiet night in the Elmwood Cemetery, the street urchin collective of the gangs, bloodied red and bruised purple, would adopt the single name the "Purple Gang."

Purple, the color summed of red and blue.

Purple, the imperial hue.

Purple, for the bruises that bind.

Purple, for the blood that dried.

Purple, for the boy who died.

The Purple Gang.

38

One Less White Boy In Bumville

Light was waning when Kaleb awakened in his T. He was in a cold sweat. He did not know how long he had been in the mini-coma, in the blackout.

But he remembered: Kaleb remembered the Elmwood Cemetery. He remembered the Purple Gang and he remembered the death of little Sammy Cohen. Kaleb remembered.

Although everything else in his memory was yet in splinters like splattered glass, these recalled memories of the night in the Elmwood Cemetery held fast. A solid footing. A place to lock into. Tangible evidence of a personal history.

Kaleb had pulled to the curb when the blackout began and he must have turned off the car. Reaching down to reignite the ignition, Kaleb felt the keychain and remembered that he had yet to identify two of the keys. One of the keys turned the bolt to his apartment, another key to The Temp. And the automobile key was to the heap he was sitting in. Two more keys, two more clues to Kaleb's who's who.

Earlier Kitty had slipped Kaleb the address to the apartment that she shared with Nika and Tia. Now he had another destination. Another goal. When the T coughed awake, Kaleb turned the car to the women's apartment. To Nika's home. To the Black Bottom.

***

The key fit, turning the tumblers in the lock, and the door creaked open. Kaleb followed the slow swing of the door into the room. The room was dark, the curtains pulled tight against the light of the evening. Stepping inside the room, he leaned his back against the door, closing the door with a silent click. Reaching to his left, he found the light switch and gave it a flick.

As Kaleb's eyes adjusted to the light, he found himself looking down the barrel of a .38 Colt revolver. Long barrel.

"Move real slow and easy mister, if you don't want a chest full of lead." It was a woman's voice. Not Nika's voice and not Kitty's voice.

Kaleb raised his arms in the universal symbol of surrender. "I'm not here to harm. I thought this was Nika's…"

"My god Kaleb! Is that you?" The gun was lowered, "You gonna get yerself shot sneakin' up on a body like that, boy!"

Following the gun's arc, Kaleb lowered his arms. Behind the gun was a tall woman, all legs. But for the short black kinks of her locks and the full lips, Kaleb would have assumed a white woman.

"I'm afraid that you have me at a disadvantage, ma'am. You seem to know me but do I know you?"

When she had heard the key turn the bolt, the woman had jumped from the bed, grabbed the gun, and, except for the gun, now stood naked before Kaleb.

She was a classic beauty of a race that was not black or white, not African or European. A mulatto woman with the skin tone of the Caucasoid and a body structure of the Negroid. Quite fetching in her nakedness, she was long and lean with a face that testified to how beautiful the mixing of races could be.

As he lowered his hands, Kaleb nodded towards a robe that was lying across the sofa chair. "As charming as it may be, maybe you'd like to accessorize the armament's attire?"

The woman first looked at the gun in her hand and then at the robe. Blushing in the realization of her nakedness she said, "You might have the courtesy to turn around."

Kaleb turned to the door and he heard the shuffling of the woman's feet to the chair and the soft rustle as the robe was synched to her waist. "Okay, you can turn back."

Kaleb turned back to the woman, now in a robe. The robe did little to mitigate her shapeliness.

Still with some measure of anger, she scolded, "You white-ass fool. You gonna get yourself shot sneakin' 'round like that." When she noted Kaleb's confusion as he leaned back against the door, she softened. "Well if you coming in, come in then. Sit down 'n I'll brew up some coffee." She went to the stove of the studio and busied up the coffee pot.

When she looked over her shoulder, Kaleb was still leaning against the door. "I said sit down."

This was a woman accustomed to giving orders and Kaleb followed her direction, planting himself in the sofa chair next to the bed.

When the coffee pot was outfitted, she pulled up a kitchen chair and sat down next to Kaleb. Long, silent, minutes passed as she studied Kaleb's face.

Still in a muddle with the epiphany of a solid memory, the memory of the Purple Gang and little Sammy Cohen's death, Kaleb folded his hands in his lap and sat silently. Kaleb had nothing to say and he repeated nothing, over and over and over again. When the coffee pot began to scream, the woman patted Kaleb's hand and said, "Boy, you gonna get yourself killed wanderin' inna 'ere like that."

Kaleb had pulled the pack of Bull Durham from his jacket pocket and absently set it on his lap. Tia took hold of the fixings and worked up a cigarette. She lit it and put it between Kaleb's lips. "Here, work on this while I fetch the coffee."

***

Tianna Strickland, Tia, shared the single-bed studio apartment in the Black Bottom with Kitty and Nika. Their nighttime professions, Kitty the hooker and Nika the nightclub singer, meant that the bed was usually empty at night and this fit with Tia's schedule.

A nurse by day at the Parkside Memorial Hospital, Tia had been with the hospital before it moved to the intersection of Brush and Illinois. Before that, it had been the Dunbar Hospital and, like the Dunbar, the Parkside Memorial continued its service as "the colored hospital."

The Dunbar Hospital, named after African American poet Paul Lawrence Dunbar, was founded by two Negro doctors, James Ames and Alexander Turner, with the purpose of serving the neglected colored community of Detroit. But the Parkside Memorial Hospital was a "take all comers" in the poor communities of the Black Bottom and Paradise Valley and nary a sickly soul would be turned from the doors because of the tint of the skin.

Tia Strickland was a creature of beauty by anyone's measurement. Long and lean bones from her African heritage merged with a white, almost pink, completion. The lightness of her skin tone allowed Tia to move smoothly between the various cultures of the Detroit communities with only a wig to cover the kinkiness of her locks, Tia could pass as white.

But Tia was hard-bitten by the way she had witnessed the subordination of her fellow colored folk. She gave no quarter to a white man's subjugation. Although she might have tolerated white people, Nika for instance, she carried a "colored folk" chip on her shoulder clearer than the Emancipation Proclamation and longer than a lynch mob's noose.

"You lucky I didn' shoot you jes for being white, fool."

***

"I know I was clear. Very clear. We don't give out keys to no boys. Especially no white boys." Nika was apologetic but Kitty was defiant in her response. "Don't be like that. You know Kaleb. Kaleb be a right gee."

"White boys always got ulterior motives." But even as Tia said this, she knew that Kitty was right. Kaleb was one of the right gees. "Sho 'nuff he seems upright enough but it's the principle of the thing."

Nika apologized again, "Sorry sorry sorry. You want that I should take the key back?"

Kitty jumped in at that and said, "It was my key and I ain't takin' it back. Kaleb may be Nika's squeeze, but he's my friend."

Tia thought this over. "Okay. Lookit 'ere. As much as a white boy havin' a key to our 'partment creeps me out, he can keep it. But you tell him that he knocks before entering a lady suite. He knocks hard and he knocks long."

Kitty could see the sense in that. "I'll tell 'im."

Waving her hand in dismissal, Tia summed up saying, "Next time maybe I come up shootin' instead of talkin'. One less white boy in this bumville don't make no matter to me."

39

Cigarettes And Schnapps

The band was pumping and The Temp was rockin'.

Bucky was behind the bar flinging beers and highballs of Canadian 7 Crown and Vernors Ginger Ale. Granma was on her center stool trying to follow a Tigers game above the baying of the club noise. The joint was filled to its shoulders with the multi-hued colors of the city, dancing and playing pool and arguing about the Tigers. The general mayhem of an underground ball.

***

Kitty wore her hair flapper style, iron-pressed like black enamel to her skull. The smoke hung in soft curls around Kitty's brown skin in an ethereal glow. She sat at the end of the bar on Kaleb's stool and watched the old Armenian accordion player have at it on stage. Folded over his accordion, Krikor was bouncing the ancient European Byzantine scale in his right hand against a Boogie Woogie bass line on the left hand bass buttons of the accordion. The Byzantine scale, the gypsy scale, gave an eerie and ghostly resonance to the groove.

It was mid-week hot at The Temple Bar Speakeasy and Play Nice. Granma had long since retired from her perch – the Tigers had lost again, "Goddamnittohellandbackagain."

It had been a slow night on the street for Kitty and she had clocked out of her street corner early for the lack of johns. Bucky was killing time drying out beer shells and chatting up Kitty.

Chain smoking, lighting her cigarettes ember to ember, Kitty said, "Be a sweet, Buck, hit my beaker."

The buck in Bucky's palette unfolded the word, "shffnapps?" Reaching under the bar-back and pulling out the bottle of clear liquor, he tipped a double shot into Kitty's glass. Bucky's question had been rhetorical. Or maybe mechanical.

Peppermint schnapps was expensive in these Prohibition years but Kitty always drank peppermint schnapps. The real stuff. It was the only booze that would cut the taste of the sexual sap from her mouth. Most peppermint schnapps in prohibition America was a peppermint-candied whisky, but The Temp kept a bottle of smuggled, genuine Austrian schnapps under the bar especially for Kitty. It was expensive, yes, but to Kitty, worth every penny to untaste the pong of her client's release.

Nipping at the syrupy schnapps in one hand and sucking up her cigarette in her other hand, Kitty nodded in the direction of the stage at Krikor. "The Greek's hittin' on all fours t'night. Different somehow."

Bucky smiled, stretching his top lip over too much teeth and resumed twisting the bar rag through the beer shells. "You know Krikor's Armenian, right?"

"What?"

"You called Kreek 'the Greek'. He's Armenian."

Kitty's laugh sputtered through the schnapps. Her full lips puckered and her brown eyes shared a twinkling giggle that tickled toes. "All you white boys is Greek to me."

***

Kaleb came in late, near closing. Krikor was manning the stage and Bucky was wiping the beer shells. Kitty still maintained her perch on Kaleb's stool at the end of the bar with her mitts full of cigarettes and schnapps while the cigarette smoke continued to curl about her.

Kaleb nodded his greetings to Bucky and Kitty. Pointing at his stool he asked Kitty, "Like the view from that roost?"

"Jes keepin' it warm for you."

"I like your hair cut that'a'way. Short 'n crisp."

With that sweet laugh that curled toes and tingled the spine, Kitty said, "Always don my toppers for you. 'Sides, short like this makes it easy to plant wigs."

Kitty was a medium-light mocha-skinned-woman but in a bad light and a good wig she could pass for white. If Kitty could pass she could work the white streets across Woodward, the Cass Corridor. With a good wig and dark light Kitty could turn one john on the white side of town for the same money as two johns in the Black Bottom.

On stage Krikor was playing the accordion with dynamic flourishes and its rising tide cut across the chitchat. Kitty, Kaleb, and Bucky turned their attention to the stage and admired the old man with the squeeze box.

Running bass lines on the left-hand buttons of the accordion, Krikor counter harmonized on the keyboard under his right hand. It was a melody and a harmony that sang back to the old country. To a time in serfdom where a man lived in clay huts on feudal plantations. A time when the serf was owned by the land and the land was owned by the lord. Slavery. European style.

The accordion soared to a high crescendo that transcended generations and sang of stories of fishing villages on rocky Mediterranean coasts with the women mending the fishing nets while the children played in the sand next to the bountiful sea. Then contorting the gypsy scale downward, Krikor twisted the music to the lowdown. Down into the low dirge of the songs of sailors lost at sea as women and children woefully threw flowered wreaths at a merciless sea.

Krikor squeezed all of the colors of human joy and sorrow into his squeeze box. And when Krikor finished his aural prism, Kitty, Kaleb and Bucky broke into applause.

Looking up, surprised that folks had been paying attention, Krikor sheepishly smiled and nodded to the applause. But the nod was all he would acknowledge, and just like that, he tucked back into his accordion and began another epoch journey into his pedigree. This time it was a rousing up-tempo misadventure of rollicking women and wine and song.

Kitty snuffed out her cigarette. "That white boy got some black bone in thet squeeze box," she said and her laughed twinkled to the tune.

As Krikor's music subsided into the background Bucky turned to Kaleb and asked, "You see Raymond and Abe?"

Kitty interjected, "You talkin' 'bout the Purples?" Then to Kaleb she said, "You don't want to be messin' with them, honey."

Flicking his thumb in Kaleb's direction, Bucky indicated, "Our boy Kaleb 'ere has a special place in their hearts."

Kaleb tried to silence Bucky with a look and a shake of his head but it was a no go.

Kitty said, "'Sat so? You tight with the Purples?"

Uncomfortably, like he was trying to fit into a coat two sizes too small, Kaleb responded, "I don't know about tight..."

Cutting him off, Bucky offered, "'Jes part of the ol' crew."

With some surprise, and sizing Kaleb up and down, Kitty was making a grand show as she tucked into her southern belle. "My, my, Masta Kaleb, why little ol' me woulda neva taken you for a bone'fide gansta type. How you *do* exhilarate." She fanned her neck with an invisible fan.

Kaleb tightly cut off the game. "I know the boys, is all. We sold newspapers and played some baseball as kids. I wouldn't say we were tight."

Bucky wouldn't let it lay. "Story on the street is that you saved Izzy's ass."

"That's the partial story. I saved Izzy's ass by knocking him on his ass."

The tinkle in Kitty's voice went into overdrive. "A saved ass is a saved ass, honey. Take it from the one in the ass business."

40

The Color Of Receiving

Nika was singing with the band and everybody in the club was hanging on every note of every word of every song she crooned. Petite to the point of elfin, her stature belied her voice as Nika sang with a raspy passion and power that defied physics.

Nika sang with a pain and the wisdom that transcended genre and gender and it transcended even time. Nika's voice harkened back to the primordial and cried of dark fears of black nights and wild beasts at the mouth of the cave. She sang with the bawl of every broken heart, and she sang the terror of every lost soul that filled the shadows of time immemorial.

Some have argued that the drum was *Homo sapiens's* first musical instrument when primordial man pounded away on tree trunks with sticks and stones. But even the sticks and stones put an extraneous tool between the musician and the instrument.

The voice, however, has no interloper between the musician and the pain. The creaks and croaks and squeaks and chokes in the vocalist are the creaks and croaks and squeaks and chokes inherent in the singer's body. In the singer's history. In the singer.

The punch that Nika received to her throat when she fended off her stepfather's rage gave her vocal tone an earthly color, and the cigarettes she chained smoked added burn to her timbre. Nika's authority came from her truth.

August Pini, the Italian piano hound, hypothesized that Nika had the Italian crooner's blood in her DNA. Doctor Dan, referencing his tenor sax, figured that Nika had the growl of the saxophone embedded in her DNA. Beethoven Jones's theory held that Nika Nightingale got her power because her lungs went all the way to her toes.

Whatever the source of Nika Nightingale's voice, it was Nika who now held center stage. And when Nika held the stage, the bar door would swing only one way. In. The joint was packed and nobody was going anywhere as she chanted her primal incantations of love and love's loss.

Bucky was behind the bar enjoying the show. Tending bar was an exercise in timing when Nika held the stage. With the room held captive, enraptured with Nika's sermon, Bucky would have nary a soul order a drink, but like a bronco busting out of the gate, the bar was rushed and the imbibe orders came fast and furious between the tunes.

Kaleb was sitting at his table to the left of the stage leaning with his back against the wall and enjoying the show. It would be a good night for The Temple Bar Speakeasy And Play Nice.

As Kaleb watched the svelte vocalist chant her joys and cry her pains, he held little wonder why this had been the woman he loved before he lost his memory.

Nika was honest in a raw way. Honest in a take-no-prisoners way. Although she offered plenty of sway in that tiny frame, her attraction came from the honesty she offered. The honesty she exposed. Honesty like the period at the end of a promise. Honesty like the exclamation point at the end of a cry.

Kaleb knew this woman. How? Was this honesty in Nika's vocals the thing that sparked recognition for Kaleb? A physical memory of the woman? Maybe a neurological memory of the woman? A memory ingrained in Kaleb's DNA.

Kaleb could not remember the reason, but the recognition was irrefutable.

***

Black was reflective, flick-clicking his tail, the sound echoing off the edge of the streetlamp's glow with a ghostly reverb. "Giving is receiving. Receiving is giving."

Blew stopped playing the saxophone and considered this.

Black continued, "Giving, receiving. Two sides of the same coin."

Blew turned this over in his mind as he tongued the reed of the saxophone, wetting the bamboo's rigidity against the vibration of the tongue.

Black resumed his commentary. "Giving does not exist without receiving."

Blew blew a tentative note. Indigo blue. Indigo blue was not the blue that Blew was seeking.

Black was working out the thought. "Selfless giving is receiving. Selfless receiving is giving."

Blew tried a cobalt blue in the saxophone. Nope. Blew continued working out the color as Black was working out the thought.

Blew blew a cerulean blue. That'll do:

Prepare yourself,
Then dare yourself,
To take a fall.
It's better to have loved and lost,
Then never have paid the cost,
At all.

Black continued flick-clicking his tail to Blew's rhythm. The rhythm flared into the darkness far beyond the reach of the lamppost's dull glow.

41

For The Love Of Ma Rainey

The women, Kitty, Nika and Tia, met at the Kresge five and dime store on Woodward at State Street. The lunch counter was not busy and the girls perched on the red swivel stools while the ceiling fans hummed white noise overhead.

Kitty sucked on a sarsaparilla and Tia was nursing a chocolate sundae. Nika's elbows were braced on the countertop to keep her face from dribbling onto the tabletop.

Tia was wearing her nursing-whites sans her nurse's cap as nurses were not allowed to wear their nurses' caps in social settings. Kitty was without makeup and casually dressed in a middy blouse, a loose pleated skirt, and short-heeled pumps. Nika wore an assembled tangle of knots and snags. Nika had been outfitted by a loaded syringe.

Tia was excited as she poked at the sundae. "Ma Rainey will be performin' t'night. T'night!"

Kitty slurped on her peppermint sarsaparilla and studied the lunch counter menu. She spoke absently to Tia, "Where's she performin'?" Before Tia could answer, Kitty added, "Can't afford nowhere, no-how."

Nodding against the marble-top counter, Nika was maybe following the conversation. Maybe. The knots and tangles of Nika's dress did not cover the fresh tracks on her arm that were seeping diluted droplets of blood. Her elbows were on the countertop with her hands dug deep into the whorls of her hair, propping her head against the countertop. She was having some measure of trouble keeping her butt centered on the swivel stool.

Tia was bursting. "She'll be at The Adams. T'night. Ma Rainey! T'night at The Adams!"

Kitty kept the conversation flowing. "Lord chil', I can't 'fford that. 'Sides, t'night's weekend. Us comfort gals got to make a livin'. 'N 'sides agin, the colored section of The Adams is nose-bleed section. You ain't gonna see 'n hear much up in the colored section."

Tia turned her energy onto Nika. "That's where you come in, Neek."

Nika looked at Tia under half closed eyes. Maybe. She was looking in Tia's direction anyway.

In her enthusiasm, Tia pushed on. "Nika's gonna be our cover, girl. We gonna don wigs 'n me 'n you 'n Nika is gonna sit right up under the stage. I already got the tickets. Three of 'em!"

Kitty laughed at the prospect and burbled on the bottom of her sarsaparilla. "You, yeah, maybe you can pass but ain't likely I get away with it. Uptown, they smell me out like a hound on a blood-track."

"You've passed before," Tia persisted.

Burbling, Kitty offered, "Sure. With the drunks and their raging testosterone under dim streetlamps." *Burble.* "...But uptown in the bright lights?" *Burble burble.* "No sir, not me." *Burble burble burble burble.* "'Sides, I already tol' you I got to work t'night. I got babies to feed, Ma Rainey or no Ma Rainey."

Sucking hard on the sarsaparilla bubbles in the bottom of the glass, Kitty flourished an exclamation of burbling burbles.

Frustrated, Tia stirred the chocolate syrup into the vanilla ice cream and reasoned out a new angle of attack.

With her head still in hands and her elbows still keeping her face off of the countertop, Nika spoke up. "I'll go 'long with ya."

Kitty and Tia were both surprised that Nika had been following the conversation. At least it *appeared* that Nika was following the conversation. Maybe. They looked at each other, then at Nika, then at each other again.

Kitty was the first to put voice to the thought. "Good luck with cleanin' her up 'fore t'night."

Tia turned her full attention onto Nika now. "Ya mean it, Neek? You'll go with me?"

Kitty sipped at the sarsaparilla bubbles and threw a thumb at Nika. "You'll need more cover then a hopped-up Jew girl."

But Tia had found new life in the idea and said, "I'll sober 'er up. I'm a nurse, 'member?"

Kitty was not convinced. Shaking her head and looking Nika over she muttered "Still...."

Tia slowly swiveled Nika back and forth on the stool, examining her face, her arms. "Gonna be a chore, alright."

Kitty sniggered, "Sure. A chore 'lright."

"But it's Ma Rainey!"

Her face lighting up, Kitty snapped her fingers. "Hey, I got it! Why'n'cha get Kaleb to go wit' you? He know his way aroun' that downtown class. He been workin' dose playhouse' since he's a boy. 'N he's gaga for Neek."

Tia shuddered at the thought. "He's a white boy. Can't stand bein' 'round white boys. White boys creep me out."

"Sure he's white but he ain't pure white. Half Jew, that buys him some credit, don' it?"

Tia spoke like she was trying to spit bile from her mouth. "The boy's white. White. Jew's same as white in my book."

Kitty smiled at that and asked, "Does yer book got a chapter on seein' Ma Rainey t'night?"

Tia thought this over while Kitty sucked the last of the sarsaparilla out of the beaker, playing the remaining burbles at the end of the straw for all of the burble she could get.

Tia thought about bringing along Kaleb and scrunched her face like she was whiffing a bad stench.

Kitty finished burbling the residue of the sarsaparilla and added, "I ain' goin'. Ya got 'n extra ticket, right? An' ya want ta see Ma Rainey."

Nika was following the drift of the conversation. Maybe.

***

Decked out in a blonde wig, Tiana Strickland, the pink-skinned black woman, looked more Caucasoid than the Jewish couple she accompanied.

Tia was dressed to the nines with change left over. Her drop-waist flapper evening dress clung low to her hips as the dress cut sharp at the very top of her knees, suggesting scandal. Four-inch spikes stretched Tia's already too-long legs to the moon.

Nika looked smart all right, but her acid green moiré dress with V-neck and taut hip could not compete with the mischief suggested by the long and blonde Tia.

Subtly dressed in a light brown suit with two-toned white and brown shoes, Kaleb was the canvas that the women were painted on.

Tia had sobered up Nika with coffee and reefer. Coffee to wake up the girl's neural lethargy and reefer to ward off the nausea. Nika's naturally cascading black locks framed her gaunt and ashen complexion, exuding the want of mystery.

Tia really didn't mind having Kaleb come along. For a white boy, he was okay. He had helped Kitty out of a few legal jams and gave Nika a job with Jazz du Jour. And Kaleb had never tried to hit on her. Christ, she couldn't stand it when the white boys tried to fuck her one day and nigger-her-out the next. Kaleb wasn't like that. He was okay. For a white boy.

Besides, this was the night for Ma Rainey. Ma Rainey!

Tia could stomach a bucketful of white boys for a thimbleful of Ma Rainey.

42

Kunsky's Circle

Certainly Tia's motive for a night on the town at the Adams Theater in Kunsky's Circle was to see Ma Rainey and The Rabbit Foot Minstrels. That was a given. Rag to the 4, baby.

But Nika's motive was a bit more textured.

Nika held out some small hope that taking Kaleb to Kunsky's Circle would ignite a spark in his memory. After all, these clubs and theaters in Kunsky's Circle were a big part of Kaleb's history. A history of a young celebrity as a piano player in the novelty duo with his boyhood pal Beethoven Jones. The Jew Boy and The Colored Boy.

Tia was wearing a blonde wig and she was passing. Passing with honors. She was taking a chance on passing to get into the better seats, the white seats, but this was not uncommon for the light-skinned mulatto of 1927 America.

Although the stage might be well represented with black entertainers, Ma Rainey and The Rabbit Foot Minstrels for instance, the audience was still kept segregated. Colored folk were relegated to the balcony in the uptown entertainment houses and the Adams Theater was not an exception. But with her pink complexion and blond wig, Tia was able to sit down stage, front and center.

Kunsky's Circle was a collection of theater houses centered around Detroit's Grand Circus Park. The entertainment industry was roaring through the 1920s with vaudeville and silent movies. The Kunsky's Circle collection of entertainment houses - the Madison, Colonial, Capitol, Adams, and State Theatres - were buzzing with patrons.

Before The Temp, Kaleb had irregular gigs in Kunsky's Circle. He was all over the circuit. As young men, he and Jones became somewhat minor celebrities, almost pets in Kunsky's Circle, as they played a duet of piano and bass between the touring vaudevillian acts. And their band, Jazz du Jour, was often booked to back up the touring singers while the movie houses employed Kaleb to accompany the silent movies on the organ.

Nika reasoned that if the Adams were to spark a memory for Kaleb, this would be the night.

This was a historic night for another reason. Tonight the Adams Theater was featuring the movie, *The Jazz Singer,* America's first ever full-length feature "talkie." This movie was a game changer. Kunsky's Circle was aglow in the radiance of being a part of history in 1927 Detroit. The Grand Circus Park was a circus of music and movies and merriment.

***

They were both big and they were both beefy, the two gangsters, and they were dusting close up on the heels of Kaleb and Nika and Tia.

***

The Jazz Singer was the main draw for Kunsky's Circle tonight but Tia was atwitter for another reason. Blues belter Ma Rainey was making the rounds of the vaudeville circuit and she was scheduled for a set after the movie. Nika had once had the opportunity to sing with Ma Rainey on a late night blowoff in the Black Bottom.

But for Tia, Ma Rainey was the banner. A fellow home-town girl from Columbus, Georgia, Ma Rainey was the tip to Tia's top.

Ma Rainey had a fresh new hit on the radio airwaves of 1927. The song "The Black Bottom" was a tribute to Detroit's lower east side, and Ma Rainey was one of the hottest tickets on the circuit.

Ma's lyrics had scandalously shaken custom when she equated: "The black bottom stomps and the Jew baby prances..."

***

The Adams Theatre was an "alley jumper," so called because the entrance was on Grand Circus Park while the Adams Theater was located one block over on Elizabeth Street. The patrons would need to walk up a flight of stairs and cross an enclosed sky-bridge over the alley to get to the theater's auditorium. A Grand Circus Park address was at a premium and this sky-bridge allowed John Kunsky to maintain the address on Grand Circus Park without the high rent that came with the address.

***

The two brunos who had been across the park when Kaleb and Nika and Tia had slipped under the Adams Theater marquee worked their way through the crowd until they were directly behind the trio when they climbed the staircase and crossed the sky-bridge.

Kaleb had noticed them earlier and sized the hoods against his own build. He figured they must each have been on the high side of 250 pounds. One was short and stocky, the other tall and beefy, and they were decked out in tilted fedoras and long trench coats. Their hands were dug deep into the trench coat pockets. Goon fashion.

In excited talk about *The Jazz Singer* and Ma Rainey, Nika and Tia failed to notice the imposing figures as they elbowed their way to their backsides. But Kaleb noticed and his neck hairs prickled.

As they walked across the sky-bridge from Grand Circus Park to the Adams Theater, Kaleb excused himself and went to the restroom down a side hallway. Halfway down the hall Kaleb stopped and casually leaned against the wall. He had rolled a collection of Bull Durhams earlier, and he pulled out a cigarette case and flipped a twig in his mouth. As he lit the butt, he stole a look over his cupped hands and, sure enough, the toughs had followed him towards the restroom.

The goons had not expected Kaleb to stop suddenly and they feigned conversation as they passed him. Sizing them, Kaleb carefully studied the men as they rumbled their way down the hall.

This was good and bad. The bad, of course, was that Kaleb was being tailed by a couple of goons. The good was that the women did not appear to be the object of their interest.

Kaleb slipped back across the alley-jump and out into the milling crowd in Grand Circus Park. He would lead the goons away from Kunsky's Circle and away from the women.

For Kaleb, *The Jazz Singer* and Ma Rainey's performance would need to be entertainment reserved for another time.

***

The crowd in Grand Circus Park was busy with the festivities of a Saturday night and Kaleb had to take care not to lose the gangsters. These were not seasoned shadows, these hoods following Kaleb, and, more than once, Kaleb had to make his trace obvious so he wouldn't lose them.

Kaleb slowed his pace as he crossed Witherell Street, eliciting an angry honk from a Buick, and when he stopped for a newspaper at Eddy's newsstand, Eddy recognized Kaleb immediately.

Kaleb picked up a newspaper and flipped Eddy a nickel and nodded at the headline. "Evenin' Eddy, world still spinnin'?"

In one smooth motion Eddy snatched the nickel mid-spin and slid it into a coin changer on his belt "So far so good. You ever catch up wit' the Purples? Or, more likely, the Purples ever catch up wit' you?"

"Sure, Eddy. We had a little pow-wow."

"Did I put your meat in the grinder?"

"No. Not much." As Kaleb tucked the newspaper under his arm and turned to go, Eddy added in a soft, hoarse whisper, "You know you got a couple a big bumpers on your caboose?"

Without looking back and with the corners of his lips suggesting just the slightest of humor Kaleb said, "Two big uglies?"

"Yep. That's 'em."

"That's a blessing. Thought I lost 'em."

Eddy's brow knit in puzzlement as Kaleb winked at Eddy and turned south on Woodward Avenue in the direction of John R Street.

Eddy watched the brunos lumber down Woodward after Kaleb.

43

The Black Bottom Stomp

A beautiful, lithe blonde woman could turn a lot of heads and open a lot of doors in 1927 Detroit. And Tia was as beautiful as she was lithe. And tonight she was blonde. Throw a sultry little Jewess in a black clingy number in the mix and heads were spinning on swivels as the ladies were escorted to their table.

The women were guided by the maître d' to a table alongside the dance floor. Front and center. Management understood the value of eye candy and Tia and Nika were prominently put on display.

The Adams Theater was one of Kunsky's gaudier affairs, and elegance showcased from the cut-glass chandeliers dripping from the ceiling to the tuxedoed boot-black in the lavatory who was quick with a spit shine and an ego boosting, "Yes sah, you look fine, sah. Mighty fine, sah."

Barely had the women's butts hit their seats before dance card hopefuls began arriving. The maître d' was kept busy delivering messages to the girls. "The gentleman at table C would like to buy the ladies a drink," or "The tall fellow at the bar requests the company of a dance." The offers were coming fast and furious and Tia blushed rose under her pink cast.

While Nika was uncomfortable with the attention, Tia was eating it up.

The Rabbit Foot Minstrels were already laying down the grooves as the ladies were seated and anticipation of Ma Rainey's appearance was palpable.

Distracted and scouring the entrance doors, Nika asked anxiously, "Now where did that boy get off to?"

Tia, looking around, found a dozen pairs of eyes trying to make contact with her and said, "I 'spect Kaleb will join us by 'n by. You worry so much."

Comforted only slightly, Nika smiled at Tia. "Maybe I do. Maybe I do."

"Sure. Lookit 'ere Nika, we came here to dance 'n have a good time. Let's dance and have a good time."

***

The Rabbit Foot Minstrels began shuffling to the opening bars of Rainey's signature tune "The Black Bottom" and everybody knew the moment had arrived. All eyes and bodies leaned toward the stage like a gravitational pull as anticipation of Ma Rainey took a turn to the frenzy. And she didn't disappoint.

In 1927 America, Detroit's Black Bottom neighborhood was dominating the new and expanding radio airwaves of America. Ma Rainey's bluesy ballad "The Black Bottom" was competing with the newest dancing rage by Henderson, DeSylva, and Brown also titled "The Black Bottom." "The Black Bottom" dance had usurped the "Charleston" as America's foremost dance craze. Dancing to the "The Black Bottom" was the boogie-du-jour while the "Charleston" was yesterday's news.

Taking the stage in an outlandish ostrich-feathered bonnet and a leopard-skin dress, Ma Rainey came on bigger than life, belting her signature shuffle, "The Black Bottom."

"Now you heard the rest, ah boys, I'm gonna show you the best..." Ma Rainey was off on a sizzle.

Ma Rainey had been at The Temple Bar Speakeasy And Play Nice on many occasions for after-hour blowoffs and when she recognized Nika sitting stage side, she gave her a wink as she crooned through the number. First, casually glancing at Nika's companion, Rainey gave a cursory nod to Tia and when recognition of Tia in a blonde wig caught, she choked on the song's words, almost giving up Tia's cloak as she laughed out loud.

Recovering herself, Rainey returned to the rowdiness of the song.

"Way down south in Alabamy
I got a friend, they call dancin' Sammy
Who's crazy 'bout all the latest dances
black bottom stomps and the Jew baby prances..."

With the words, "Jew baby prances," Rainey spun and blew Nika a kiss.

As The Rabbit Foot Minstrels segued into the dance "The Black Bottom" Tia and Nika were caught up in a swirl of boogie as the music sucked the pulsing throng of floorflushers to the dance floor.

44

"God Damn Black And God Damn White And God Damn Wig On This God Damn Night"

Their dance cards full, the evening was playing out like a Cinderella Ball for Tia. In honor of the glamour of the Cinderella Ball, she had adopted the name Cindy for the evening.

And Tia's, rather Cindy's, dance card was the hottest ticket at The Adams Theater.

Nika had the niggling distraction of not knowing where Kaleb had gone off to and much attentive consternation was aimed in the direction of the club's entryways. Nika, too, had seen the pair of bruisers that had been tailing them. She had recognized them and she knew their business. Fat Tony and Jimmy-Jimbo. The brothers Rubble. Nika had often traded her womanly favors for the arm juice that the brothers trafficked.

For Tia's part, she was being courted and charmed by Detroit's money elite. The debonair and dashing were in a constant swirl tableside in hopes of gaining the favor of this new and enchanting beauty who had fallen into their midst. The sculpted blonde beauty, Cindy, had become the most popular artifact in The Adams Theater.

And Tia was going to milk it for all it was worth. These white boys, these bogus lovers, were going to buy her drinks all right. And dinner. And any other thing she might finagle through the night. It wouldn't be much in the grand scheme of things, but Tia would cut her quarter pound of white flesh before the night was out.

Ma Rainey and The Rabbit Foot Minstrels kept the theater's dance floor hopping and bopping while a constant parade of suitors was keeping Tia and Nika busy cutting the rug.

When the women managed a breather, they sat down at their table and admired the selection of drinks proffered upon them like so many chaliced offerings to an altar.

Tia was aware of Nika's distraction. "He'll be okay, honey. He's jes off somewhere with some buddy musician that rounded 'im up. You know they all know him down 'ere 'n they all want ta be jive-jammin' with him. He be okay."

Nika's pouty lips lifted in a half-hearted smile at Tia's attempt to comfort. But Nika's eyes did not join in the merriment. She changed the subject. "You seem to be having yourself a time."

Tia managed a scowl between them. "With these crackers? Making time, not having time. Jes seein' how far I can fool the fools. Lord, these white boys is a bunch of blubberin' suckers for a cheap wig."

"But didya ever rub shoulders with so much money in your life?"

Tia had a robust laugh at that. "Sure, darling. I've rubbed shoulders with many of these sophisticates. Shoulders and a good deal more."

There was a time when, just up from Alabama and working her way through Mercy School of Nursing that Tia had needed to turn tricks for the tuition.

Nika studied Tia's face to understand what she was saying. Then the light bulb lit. "You mean ...?"

"Yep. Same men that used me as a two-dollar whore are now courtin' me like I'm the Queen of England."

Nika looked around the room with new wonder. "Some of these same men had been your clients?"

"Sure. Ain't that a hoot!" In great gaiety Tia began nodding her head in the direction of various men. "That boy over there, the short one with the bad toupee, he is kinda afraid of women and he hides under the covers and never takes off his T-shirt and socks." Nodding again, this time in the direction of a man standing at the bar, she said, "That one that is all puffed up like a rooster owning the hen house? Why he's got a pecker the size of a your baby finger that you can't barely touch before it goes off."

Nika muffled a laugh and for a moment, only for a moment, she did not think about Kaleb and the Rubble boys.

All eyes in the Adams Theater were constantly scanning Tia in hopes of eye contact. As she had been nodding in their direction for Nika's benefit, they caught Tia's nod and thought that it was all about them. They nodded a return acknowledgement and smiled warmly at Tia. "Them crackers sure got some stupid."

As the girls were sharing stories and belly laughs on the lowdown of the men of this select nobility, they failed to notice a young man come up to the table from the dance floor. When he spoke the two women blushed at what he might have overheard. "You ladies seem to be enjoying the evening."

Nika spoke, "My, but you do have a way of stealth about you."

"Oh, I'm sorry ladies, I meant no untoward intrusion," and he aimed his attention at Tia. "I was just hoping that I might be able to land a place on your dance card this evening."

Tia shyly flushed. This man was tall and athletic and blonde with high cheek bones and piercing blue eyes. Eyes that could push a lover off of a cliff and a soft manner to catch the lover in free fall.

Nika had never seen Tia blush so and found it amusing. Strong Tia. Hard Tia. Tia full of vengeance. Tia full of hate.

Tia's response was slow in coming so Nika answered for her. "You'd like a swing with my friend here?"

With great formality, the young man bowed with his head. "Yes. I would very much enjoy the opportunity to accompany the young lady in dance."

"And you are?"

"My name is Edgar and I am just one of the many admirers of this young lady."

Nika was in great humor. "Yes you are."

Edgar was confused. "Yes I am?"

"Yes you are one of her many admirers." This seemed to fluster Edgar as Nika continued. "My name is Nika and my many admired colleague here is Cindy."

Edgar nodded to Nika and smiled at Tia. "I am Edgar Land. Edgar Nicholas Land," and he waited for Cindy to offer her surname. When it was not forthcoming, Nika said, "Rella. Cindy's last name is Rella. Cindy Rella."

Edgar fit the name onto his tongue. "Cindy Rella. Rella. Of the Chicago Rellas?"

"I don't believe so."

Something was happening to Tia in the presence of this white boy. She was having a difficult time finding her verve so Nika continued to speak for her. "I think that Cindy would enjoy a dance with you very much. When Ma Rainey's band comes off break, come back here for the first dance."

Although he was answering Nika, Edgar nodded his head and addressed Tia. "Thank you very much Cindy Rella. I look forward to the twirl," and he slightly bowed at the waist and melted into the direction of the bar.

Nika watched him walk half way across the club before she said, "Client you knew?"

Tia had been watching Edgar walk away as well. She had been admiring the way he moved with the ease of an athlete.

Nika prodded again, "Do you know him?"

Coming back to earth, Tia responded, "Know him? You mean as a meal ticket? No. No, never seen 'im before."

"Quite a specimen, yes?"

Tia was feeling things that were unfamiliar to her. Unchartered territories. Slowly she turned to Nika and whimpered. "What ... what am I gonna do?"

Nika had to laugh out loud. "Why, you're gonna dance with him, of course."

***

And Tia did dance with him of course. Tia danced with him to the swings and to the ballads and Edgar even made a silly attempt at dancing the "Black Bottom" dance. He had no rhythm in his bones, and he looked more like a writhing worm on a fisherman's hook, but he made Tia laugh with the effort. Tia loved every movement of the gawky attempt.

Edgar Nicholas Land, was second cousin to Dr. Charles Henry Land, third cousin to Evangeline Lodge Land Lindbergh, and as such, distantly related to Charles Lindbergh III.

Edgar and Tia spun the night away on the dance floor. Tia, the blonde goddess of elegance, nimble on her toes and managing to avoid both of Edgar's left feet. Edgar, dumbstruck with infatuation and giddy with the romance of the hour.

The rowdy songs were fun and funny, especially Edgar's flailing efforts with moving to the "Black Bottom," dance but for Tia, it was the slow numbers, the heartfelt ballads, that allowed her to linger deep into Edgars arms and waxed poetic for her.

***

Tia tried to slow down, to reflect. This was just another cracker hoping to crack another nut.

When Edgar pulled Tia into his arms, into his chest, into his heart, the world around Tia melted away into a surreal background of too many shadows and too much fog.

Tia cozied into Edgar's embrace like a hand in a glove; like affixing the last piece in a jigsaw puzzle; like fitting the round peg into the round hole. Or, maybe, fitting the heart shaped peg into the heart shaped hole.

Edgar's warm breath against her cheek, his strong arms pulling her into his breast and his attentive interest to her every need made

Tia feel like a queen. But it was Edgar's scent mostly, sweet yet salty - sultry - that set Tia's metronome clicking to the beat.

Lost in the infatuation, in the passion of the moment, Tia initially failed to notice that Nika hadn't returned from a restroom visit. Eventually, as the evening progressed, Tia did notice. It was difficult to leave Edgar's arms, but finally Tia excused herself and left him to hunt up Nika. And she found Nika.

Nika was on the floor of the bathroom in the Adams Theater in the stall at the furthest end of the lavatory. Deep in the bowels of the restroom, where the washroom matron could not see her and the shadows reached out to the dark. Nika was sprawled across the toilet and splattered with her own vomit.

The needle stuck out of Nika's forearm like a graveside spade.

***

It was meant to be a quick dash back to their table to retrieve their purses, but Edgar had been watching for Cindy and he intercepted her as she found her way to the door.

"So soon to the night? I was hoping for another round on the dance floor."

Tia did not look up into Edgar's eyes and she fumbled for words. "I'm sorry, Edgar, pressing concerns. I need to dash off," and she angled her body to slip past him.

More hurt than angry, Edgar reached for her arm and spun her to him. "Dash off? Or brush off?"

With that Tia stopped full throttle and turned to look into Edgar's eyes. She did not want to hurt this man. "No. Not a brush off Edgar. My friend Nika has taken ill and I need to get her home."

Edgar accepted this and his face drew concern. "Then let me drive the two of you home."

Too quickly Tia said, "No," and then she caught herself and softened her voice. "No Edgar, that is sweet of you but I think it's probably best that we say good night here and now."

Accepting this, Edgar nodded in compliance. "I understand. Take care of your friend. But can I see you again?"

Tia raised her hand and gently rested it along Edgar's cheek, her eyes pained. "I'm sorry. I just don't think that it would be right for us to see each other again." Tia's thoughts were racing. All of the equations of white boys and colored people and segregation and a lifetime of hate jumbled up in Tia's thoughts in a flush of anger. She swore to herself, "God damn black and god damn white and god damn wig on this god damn night."

Edgar was crushed with the thought of not seeing Cindy again and his hand squeezed tighter on her arm. "What have I done? Whatever it was, I'm so sorry, really sorry."

It hurt Tia to see Edgar crushed. "No, baby, no no, it's not you," and she played her hand across Edgar's face and looked into his blue eyes. The blonde wig had snookered the Adams and had snookered the bar patrons and now the blonde wig had snookered Tia.

On a wild night of passing at the Adams Theater, Tia was falling in love and all that she could think was, "God damn black and god damn white and god damn wig on this god damn night."

Edgar reached for her other arm and holding fast he pulled her to him. "I won't let you go you know. Not now. Not without a promise of a second chance."

It was everything that Tia could do to not melt into Edgar's arms and fold into his breast. Into his soul.

Tia did not want to postpone the inevitable but she did not want it to end like this either. Tia, Cindy, Cindy Rella, did not have a glass slipper to drop on her escape, and she'd be damned if she'd drop the blonde wig. Maybe one more cocktail across a quiet table would be better than this.

Edgar was insistent. "I won't let you go, you know."

Bodies close now, Tia could smell Edgar's sweat from the dancing and it gave her pause. Never before had a man's scent thrilled her so. A pheromonal connection that spoke to Tia's innermost and, innermoist, regions. Chemical amore.

Relenting, she drew her hand from his face and placed it upon his chest, upon his heart. "Do you know Carolina's Cup O'Joe?"

Hope sprung into Edgar's face. "The coffee café on Ledyard Street?"

"Yes. Ledyard at 3rd."

"I know it. When?"

Tia was once again working on her blush. "When are you available?"

"Now and for the rest of my life."

This made Tia laugh and she reached up and kissed Edgar on the cheek. "Is next Tuesday good?"

"Tomorrow is better."

"Tuesday is a quiet night at Carolina's and I'd like to talk to you."

"I'd love to listen. Tuesday it is. Shall I bring the preacher?"

Again Tia laughed. She had not laughed often in her time in Detroit and it felt good to laugh.

That is when Tia remembered Nika on the washroom floor and she pressed her hand against Edgar's chest and pushed off. "I need to go now."

Releasing his grip he said, "Of course, but Tuesday..."

"Yes. Tuesday, 6 p.m."

"Carolina's Cup O'Joe."

"Yes." Tia pushed away from Edgar and she was gone. He stood there momentarily, his arms still cupping the contour of Cindy's shape as she slipped off into the crowd and into the night. Eventually he lowered his arms to his side and turned back into the theater. The dancing gaiety that spun the dance floor, stomping to the "Black Bottom," never looked so empty.

As Tia hustled back to the washroom to Nika, she could not drive the thought from her head. "God damn black and god damn white and god damn wig on this god damn night."

45

Kaleb Confronts The Rumbling Rubbles

Kaleb had left Tia and Nika at the Adams because he had sniffed out a tail. Two big bruisers were following him and he didn't want the girls to be endangered. He had crossed The Grand Circus Park, stopping momentarily at Eddy's newsstand where he confirmed he was being followed.

A calmness settled over Kaleb. One would suppose that this threat, this potential danger, would make one's blood run hot, if not with fear then at least with anger. But Kaleb felt none of that. This risk, this menace, only served to calm Kaleb and he relaxed into a quietness within. A coolness. A place of the familiar and a place of habit.

The four blocks down to Michigan Avenue were all half blocks, and Kaleb led the bruisers on a zigzag through the streets and alleys of Clifford to Shelby to Wilcox to Washington and back to Shelby and State Street, and again back to Washington. As Kaleb turned each corner he surreptitiously stole a glance back to make sure that the hoods were there. They were there all right. Their bulk was proving cumbersome and they were panting to keep up. They were losing ground but they were there all right. Kaleb slowed his pace so he wouldn't lose them.

Crossing Michigan at Shelby, Kaleb headed due south to the Detroit River. To the docks. At Atwater Kaleb turned the corner and slipped into the shadow of a warehouse entry foyer and he waited. He could hear the pursuers huffing and puffing as they hustled to catch up to Kaleb. When they rounded the corner one of the beefs said, "Shit, now where did the little kike go?"

As they passed the alcove that Kaleb was in, he stepped out behind them and locked into their stride just a few feet to their rear. The brunos huffing and puffing and wheezing kept Kaleb's steps on the sly.

At Wayne Street the shorter one of the pair peered around the corner and said, "God damn it, we lost 'em."

Kaleb answered from behind, "Maybe he turned up to Griswald."

"No gad-damn way. We woulda seen him cross the street an'… hey…!" As the realization sank in, the big men turned around to look at Kaleb.

The shorter fatter one offered, "Funny man," and took a swing at Kaleb. The taller man spent moments trying to catch up with the revelation that they were being trailed by Kaleb. Each of these goons doubled Kaleb in weight, but the pursuit that Kaleb had led them on had exercised their blubber and had spent their strength.

Kaleb easily sidestepped the punch and as the man's follow-through punch whiffed by, Kaleb kicked out his back leg sending him sprawling to the cement.

Kaleb did not give the second mug an opportunity to attack. He drilled his foot into the man's knee, and the mug collapsed onto the sidewalk beside the first goon.

From the ground the two men began fumbling in their jackets for weapons, but the leather lining of Kaleb's jacket pockets allowed his guns to flash into his fists. "Leave the gats be." The men, seeing the guns in Kaleb's hands, eased their hands away from their coat pockets.

"You must be the Rubble boys."

As they caught their breath they glowered at Kaleb. The older, shorter, fatter one managed to wheeze, "What cha gonna do? Shoot us?"

Kaleb had a gun trained on each of the men and he took his time responding. "That's a tempting prospect. Reason I shouldn't?"

The younger one of the two began rubbing the knee that Kaleb had kicked out from under him. "I'll kill you. You mother-fucker, I'll kill you."

That made Kaleb smile. "That's not a real good argument why I shouldn't shoot you."

The fatter man said, "Shut up, Jimmy."

Kaleb went with that and said to the one rubbing his knee. "So you're Jimmy-Jimbo," and he looked then to the other, "and that would make you Fat Tony."

Sarcastically Fat Tony answered, "Pleased to meet your acquaintance," and he began to push himself up from the pavement. Kaleb put a foot on Fat Tony's chest and pushed him back down to the cement. "Suppose you just relax there for the moment. Catch your breath."

Fat Tony scowled, "You got some beef wit' us?"

"You tell me. Why'n you putting a stalk on me?"

Jimmy-Jimbo offered, "We were just out for an evenin' stroll when…."

Fat Tony cut him off. "Shut up Jimmy." He said to Kaleb, "Okay kike, you got the drop on us, now where you gonna drop us?"

"Why were you following me?"

"Just want to barber, is all."

"We've got something to barber about?"

Fat Tony measured this. "You don't know? You really don't know?"

Kaleb had nothing to say and that's exactly what he said. Fat Tony continued, "This some dizzy shit, this amnesia thing they say you gots, it's on the level?"

Again Kaleb had a whole lot of nothing to say.

"Lookit 'ere boy. We got no personal beef wit' you, it's jes, we..."

Jimmy-Jimbo could not control himself. "Ma 'n us want The Temp and we gonna god damn well git it."

"Shut up, Jimmy." To Kaleb he said, "Lookit 'ere, Kaleb, we don' mean you no harm. Jes bizness is all. We'd be glad to buy out The Temp all amicably like."

Kaleb did not lower his guns. "Ma? You mean Mizzy Rubble."

"Sure. Ma, Mizzy, an' me an' Jimmy-Jimbo 'ere. We got a sweet little joint out west 'a Detroit an' we jes lookin' for an opp'tunity to move uptown. We're willin' to pay a fair an' decent price for The Temp."

"And all the fixin's?"

"And all the fixin's."

"And the staff?"

Fat Tony hesitated at that and looked down the barrel of Kaleb's gun. "Why sure. Bucky can stay. And clubfoot Hollie's a good mop man. We'd even keep Beethoven Jones and Jazz du Jour on payroll if'n that would seal the deal."

Kaleb thought this over. "If Mizzy and you boys are so on the up 'n up, why'r you following me down alleyways?

Again Jimmy-Jimbo couldn't control himself. "'Cause I'd rather beat that speak out of you."

Fat Tony was more tired of Jimmy than he was angry. "Please shut up, Jimmy." Fat Tony turned back to Kaleb and said, "But there is some truth to that, Kaleb. Mizzy 'n us ain't gonna wait much longer for you to muddle on. One way or t'nother, The Temp is gonna belong to the Rubbles."

***

Trouble seemed to follow Kaleb like a bad penny rolling downhill. On roller skates. How was it that wherever Kaleb turned, trouble was there waiting for him and doubling down? Beatdowns and shakedowns and down in the mouth and down in the dumps. Always one step forward and two steps down.

Detective Morane was the first to note it. Morane had pointed out that Kaleb's first beatdown had to be a setup. Kaleb's caution had been legendary, and for him to be waylaid so easily spoke of an inside job. The tossing of both his apartment and the office at The Temp, and now this play by the Rubble boys. How had they known where to find him?

The only intangible character that Kaleb could figure in was the hatchet-faced man in the navy blue duds who seemed to track his every move. Certainly a good candidate. But how would this character know Kaleb's movements ahead of time. Even if the hatchet-faced man were the set-up man, how was he getting his information?

There was something inside going on, but what was the motive and who was the conspirator? Who knew enough of Kaleb's movements to be able to alert an intercept? Who knew of Kaleb's movements beforehand and might be in a position to share this information with unsavory elements?

Bucky? Could Bucky somehow, financially maybe, be induced to betray Kaleb? Hollie was omnipresent at The Temp and could pick up information. Could Hollie be duped into divulging Kaleb's designs? Hard to believe that Kitty or Tia were involved. Nika was out. But how about the boys of Jazz du Jour? Pini or Oldham or Doctor Dan or even Beethoven Jones? Could one of these brothers of the beat be the traitor?

Someone had to be tipping the goons, but Kaleb could find no good candidate for the turncoat.

***

After having the Rubble boys unload their guns on the sidewalk and kicking them away, Kaleb let the boys get up from the asphalt. But he kept his guns trained on the men.

As Fat Tony and Jimmy-Jimbo dusted off and unfolded to their full worth, Kaleb got a more complete assessment of the boys' girth. Each of the brothers topped 300 pounds on a slim day. Fat Tony, the elder brother, fit the 300 pounds into a squat, square frame that topped at just under 6 feet tall. Jimmy-Jimbo was half a foot taller and a goodly amount of his weight was carried in his shoulders. Each of the Rubble brothers wore a characteristic low brow, Neanderthal fashion, which spoke of a DNA brotherhood.

Casually Kaleb waved his guns at the Rubbles, "You didn't pick up my scent until I got to The Grand Circus Park. How'd you know where to find me?"

Fat Tony and Jimmy-Jimbo looked at each other and then Fat Tony spoke, "Jes lucky I guess."

Kaleb stifled a laugh and countered, "Com'on boys, you're better'n that."

Jimmy-Jimbo jumped in and said, "Maybe we got more ears on you then you know."

"Shut up, Jimmy."

But Jimmy-Jimbo pressed on. "Maybe all the chickadees don't jes sing for you."

Fat Tony cuffed Jimmy-Jimbo across his ear. "Shut up Jimmy." To Kaleb he said, "Lookit 'ere, Kabe, it don't matter how we find you. We will always find you. You can make it easy on yourself and give up The Temp simple-like or you can die tryin' to keep it. Makes no matter to Mizzy Rubble and it make less matter to me."

Kaleb took a minute to consider this and then he waved a gun in the direction that the boys had come. "Dust off."

"You sayin' you ain't interested in a buy-out?"

Again Kaleb waved the gun and again he just said, "Dust off."

"Okay Kabe, you take the gamble."

The Rubbles picked up their hats from the dirt, slapped them on their respective legs and fixed them to their heads. When they reached for their guns Kaleb suggested, "How 'bout we leave those pieces be."

"You gonna keep our guns?"

"Not likely. But if you want to retrieve them, you'll find them in there," and with a wave of his own gun Kaleb indicated the Detroit River.

Fat Tony looked at his gun and then he looked at Kaleb and then he looked at the Detroit River. With a wicked smile he offered. "Why, sure, kike, there's plenty of gats where 'dose come from."

Kaleb said, "I'm sure there are. Now, dust."

46

Memory Holds No Mortgage On The Moment

There were two good reasons for Kaleb to return to Baldy's speakeasy in the Black Bottom.

First off, Kaleb needed to be alone. Everybody needs some time alone. Alone to digest and reflect and accept and reject. Mental time and mental space where the background noise of the mundane might quiet and the distractions of the exotic do not demand attention. Alone to be autonomous. Alone to sit and to ponder over a boilermaker and suck on a twig or two and let his mind settle into the wherewithal with his foggy recollect. Reflection without the commotion offered by the familiar and the attention demanded by the foreign.

Alone time.

The second reason Kaleb sought out Baldy's Speakeasy was a more personal, innate reason. There had been an itching, a twitching in his fingertips and in the deepest reaches of his psyche. A wail from deep within his breast that cried to Kaleb every time he heard the music, every damn time he was near a piano.

Kaleb heard the cry, the shout-out, with every gasp that Nika crooned and with every bow drag across Beethoven Jones's bass fiddle. He heard the music in the melody of a child's laughter and in the rhythm of the city streets as it hummed to the beat of industry. Everywhere was the music and the music was everywhere.

To find this man Kaleb, he would need to follow the path of Kaleb. And the path of Kaleb was music.

Turning the T south onto St. Antoinette and across Gratiot Avenue, Kaleb drove into the 1927 Detroit night toward the beckoning of the music. The beacon of the piano. The beckoning beacon that was Kaleb Kierka.

Kaleb steered the T downward to the nether reaches of Detroit's black ghetto. Down among the shacks and the tracks and the blue-collar blacks.

Down into the Black Bottom.

***

Baldy's Speakeasy had settled into the quiet bustle of a joint wrapping up for the night when Kaleb slipped through its doors. Again Kaleb was the only white face there, and again the patrons gave Kaleb a cursory study as he walked to the bar. This time Baldy recognized Kaleb right off and set a shot and a shell of beer in front of him. Kaleb nodded a thanks and plopped the shot glass into the beer.

Baldy busied himself with a task below the bar, offering Kaleb a globed view of his expanding forehead. "Ya jes made it fer last call," he said.

**

It is known as "being in the moment." Some might refer to this moment as a spiritual place, a space unencumbered by thought and by reflection. Movement and action are designed by the confluence of the kinetic and the cerebral. It becomes difficult to discern when in the moment, whether time stops or whether time is eternal.

Memory is of no matter in this place called the moment as the moment is only of the now, existing in the slimmest margins between the before and the after. In the moment is always on the precipice of what comes next with no measure given for the mirage of time.

Memory holds no mortgage in this moment.

Athletes can experience this moment when every muscle, every sinew, is charged to the physical task before them. Scientists can experience these moments when their attention is lost in the absentmindedness of the theory. Hunters focused on the track of blood, woodworkers attuned to the swirl of the burl, and young mothers with breasts swollen from suckling new life. These are moment-less moments. Timeless time.

And memory holds no mortgage on these moments.

**

The bar was closed and the doors barred at Baldy's. The musicians were trickling from the stage like a late summer seasonal creek, packing up their instruments along the drying creek bed to wait for the next surge of the spring rains of jazz to replenish the songs ravine.

It had been a good night of music for the instrumentalists and they were reluctant to let the feeling go. The house had been packed and rocking from the jump and the musicians had a taste of the "moment" as they swam in the swollen spring creek called jazz.

While the musicians packed their wares, Kaleb slipped up onto the stage and tucked himself into the piano. He had knocked back the boilermaker and was working on a second shot, sans the beer. He did not go unnoticed by the trickling musicians as they packed away their watercraft of instruments. But they allowed Kaleb a private moment.

The musicians docked their collection of watercraft: saxophones and trumpets and drums and accordions, the full complement of floating vessels that had been bobbing on the rivulet of jazz. As they did, they sneaked sidelong glances at the piano as Kaleb began to noodle on the piano ship. Musicianship.

Not a word was offered as Kaleb plunked his first tentative bass notes with his left hand. The bass notes fell into line on nimble fingers, into a pattern, and began walking to a rhythm of swing. Of jazz. 12/8 and four to the bar.

As the musicians stole longer peeks at him, Kaleb skimmed his thumbnail down the piano through a cascading glissando waterfall of a chromatic swell and landed with a backbeat, comping chords against the steady walk of his left hand rhythm. 12/8 and four to the bar.

Kaleb had taken to the stage tentatively and self-consciously knowing that, despite the veil of autonomy, he was being studied. But as his body warmed to the piano, as his consciousness let go of the ego, the backdrop of the bar and the stage and the other people melted away into an ethereal milieu.

The fingering and the phrasing became fluid under Kaleb's digits. This was a familiar and fantastic domain; Kaleb let go of time and he let go of the id. As he slid deeper and deeper into the moment, as the sham of time and the ego of self melted away, Kaleb become one with the piano. One with the music and one with the cosmos. One.

A full measure of time. A full measure of the man.

***

While the feral cat was telling the midnight sax-man what to play, the lightest of fog was settling on the streetlamp's glow, quietly shrouding the pair in a misty, ethereal reality. Ethereality.

The silhouette blackness of the duo stained the grey light while the lamppost that the sax-man leaned upon, slump-shouldered, sucked the darkness out of the night, leaving a vaporous glow. Other worldly. Other otherly.

The black cat spoke within a soft whisper with the conviction of a half-remembered Edgar Allan Poe sonnet. He told the sax-man what to play and the sax-man interpreted the words into the low end of the Bb scale.

Black asked Blew, "Play me a tune about the now, will ya?"

Blew repeated, "The now?"

"Now."

"Now?"

"Yes. Now."

Blew shrugged his shoulders and put the saxophone's mouthpiece to his lips. He wet the reed and the music that Blew blew sounded like this:

Another Round Of Coffee Grounds

There's nothing to remember,
There's nothing to forget.
There's only now or never,
Right now is all you get.
Right now is all you get.
Right now is all you get.
Just another rest stop,
Alongside the road.
Another round of coffee grounds,
'Fore I have to go.

Don't you hurry, don't you worry,
'Cause here's that simple caveat,
"It's all about the journey,"
It's the getting not the got.
It's the getting not the got.
It's the getting not the got.
Just another tightrope,
Another sideshow,
Another round of coffee grounds,
'Fore I have to go.

There's nothing to remember,
There's nothing to forget,
There's only now or never.
(There's only now forever),
Right now is all you get,
Right now is all you get,
Right now is all you get.
I see the light above me,
I see the path below,
Another round of coffee grounds,
'Fore I have to go,
'Fore I have to go.
'Fore I have to go.

***

The musicians gave up their covert survey of Kaleb and turned full attention on him as he keyed into his moment.

It is easy to recognize when one is in the moment and it is a beautiful and compelling moment. Every athlete and scientist and mother and farmer and toolmaker who experiences the moment would trade a hundred years for a singular moment of being in the moment. Everyone would like to have a piece of that moment, and the musicians admiring Kaleb were not to be excluded.

First it was the saxophone player, wetting his reed and adjusting the embouchure as he slipped quietly back onto the stage, sliding warm saxophone stabs under Kaleb's piano licks. Next came the trap-man with just a snare drum and a high-hat to tap tap tap into the triplet rhythm of Kaleb's moment. 12/8 and four to the bar.

When the bassist slipped the sheath off his bass and began thumping a bass walk it freed Kaleb's left hand, allowing Kaleb to explore, to improvise, the full breath of the piano. The full breath of the song. The full breath of the now.

The moment.

Kaleb did not need to retrieve his lost memory in this moment, in this now. In the moment there is no want of memory or of history or of saga. Time and ego are relegated to the bleacher section when one is in the moment. The nose-bleed section.

For memory holds no mortgage on the moment.

47

Kitty Lips

It was late when Kaleb rapped lightly on Nika's apartment door. The music jam at Baldy's had been exhilarating. Liberating. He was still juiced from the music, from the jazz. When the blowoff had blown off and the band had quit, Kaleb still had adrenaline to burn. Talking would be a good outlet and maybe Nika was still awake.

He did not want to awaken Nika if she was asleep so he tapped softly on the apartment door. Kaleb heard immediate stirrings in the apartment.

Bare feet shuffled to the door, a moment's pause to listen, then, "Party's closed down for the night. Go away." It was Kitty.

There was no sleepiness in Kitty's voice so Kaleb pressed on. "Kit, it's me, Kaleb, is Nika in?"

One lock, two locks, three locks clacked free and then a sliver of the door opened and Kitty's eye appeared. When recognition was confirmed she flung the door open and gave Kaleb a hug. "Come in, come in, come in," she said and gave Kaleb a kiss on the mouth. Although the kiss surprised Kaleb, he did not find it unpleasant.

Kitty was wrapped in a pink robe and her feet padded barefoot on the hardwood floor. The pinkness of the robe gave her milk chocolate skin a russet tone.

The Murphy bed was up and tucked into the wall. There was a cup of coffee trailing steam and a cigarette trailing smoke in an ashtray on the table in the kitchenette space. Kitty's work uniform, hoo-doo-dress, dark seamed nylons, pink panties, high heels, were strewn about the pillowed easy chair.

There was evidence on the towel at the sink that Kitty had washed her mascara from her face. With the make-up on, Kitty offered a festive and devil-may-care presentation. With the make-up removed Kitty was unadorned, russet-hued, and plain. And beautiful. Kitty had a face that was bullet proof.

"Sorry so late, Kit. I was looking for Nika."

Kitty was beaming. "Not at'all. Glad for the company. I just set up a pot a grounds. Ja like a cup?"

Kaleb nodded the affirmative and Kitty guided him to the sofa-chair, splashing her work outfit to the floor. She went to the kitchen area to scrounge up a cup. As she passed the kitchenette table she reached for the smoldering cigarette, gave a final deep draw, and snuffed it out.

Sinking into the welcoming softness of the pillowed easy chair, Kaleb said, "'Spect you don't know where Nika is, then."

"'Spect not. Ain't seen the girl in a couple of days. Last I heard, you 'n Nika 'n Tia be steppin' out to the Adams t'night. Say, how was Ma Rainey. She 'member Nika? Now she's got that chart toppin' song she play she must be the howl."

"Can't say how Rainey was. Never got to the show."

Kitty paused and said, "No, why not?"

Kaleb shrugged his shoulders. "Got distracted by the Rubble boys. Last I saw Nika and Tia were heading stage side."

"The Rubble boys? There goes some butt-ugly. You okay?"

Kaleb pulled the guns from his pockets and set them down on the floor beside the chair. It felt good to unload the weight. "Minor distraction, is all," he answered.

Kitty noted the hardware as she returned with the cup of coffee. She reached over and flicked off the kitchen light leaving only the soft glow from the table lamp. Sitting on the puffy arm of the chair, she rested her feet on Kaleb's lap. As she handed him the cup of coffee, she repeated, "Sorry. Ain't seen Nika in a couple of days. 'Course, I been busy, too. She coulda come 'n gone 'ere and we never seen 'another."

As Kaleb tested the brew, Kitty leaned in and softly pet the scar that dove under his eyebrow. "I see's you always strokin' at this damage. Do it hurt you much?"

Kitty's touch was professional and Kaleb felt warmness in the stroke. "Hurt? No, can't say that it hurts. Kinda tingles, actually. Just a prickling recollect that something happened there." Kaleb reached to stroke the scar. "And I can use all the recollect that I can get."

Noting the hootchie-gal clothes strewn on the floor, Kaleb asked, "How was the night?"

"Slow and lonely." And then adding a playful wink, she said, "I gots lots of lovin' left over...."

Kaleb set the coffee down. He caught the innuendo but ignored it.

Kitty persisted. "I'm warmed and ready to ride."

Again Kaleb let the flirt pass. Again Kitty pressed forward.

When Kaleb reached for his coffee again, he touched Kitty's hand, and she took this opportunity to grasp his hand and bring it to her chest. With her other hand she took Kaleb's cup of coffee and set it on the side table beside the chair. As she did this, she reached across Kaleb and her left breast slipped out of her robe, exposing a dark brown areola against her mocha breast.

Before any awkwardness could be exchanged, Kitty leaned forward and lightly touched Kaleb's mouth with her lips. When she detected no resistance, she planted a full puckered kiss on Kaleb's mouth.

Kitty's lips were soft and warm and had the fullness of her African ancestry behind them. In them. Through them.

Kaleb could taste the coffee and the cigarettes in Kitty's kiss. He also tasted the richness of Kitty's affection and the magic of her African ancestry. There was an element of beguiled eagerness in Kitty's kiss.

But Kaleb tasted something else in Kitty's kiss. There was yearning and loneliness in Kitty's kiss. Perhaps there are no lonelier kisses than those from lips for hire.

Kaleb accepted the full breath of Kitty's kiss, but as the kiss subsided, he gently held her head in his hand and nudged her lips away from his. For long moments he looked into her soft brown eyes, and Kaleb recognized in those eyes a chronicle of pain and of longing and of hope. And maybe, maybe, love.

Acknowledging Kaleb's hesitation Kitty smiled a sad smile. "You don' wanta go there?"

Kaleb took a moment before answering, "Where's there?"

The narration in Kitty's eyes was of a candor that spoke a language unencumbered by the confines of mere words. It was a language of heart and it was a language of tenderness. Soul to soul.

This conversation had been a long time coming for Kitty, and now that it was here, she was uncertain of the course. She had long admired the man Kaleb Kierka and envied his relationship with Nika. Although she held no ill feelings toward Nika, she often played with the thought about Kaleb being with her. Her man. Kitty and Kaleb. Even off of the tongue, the bond rang true. Kitty and Kaleb. Kaleb and Kitty.

When no answer was forthcoming, Kaleb bought time. "I need to hit the head, where's…?"

Kitty popped off the chair, off Kaleb, and flicked her thumb toward the hallway. "End of the hall, follow the smell, can't miss it." As Kaleb pushed off the chair, Kitty planted a full mouthed kiss on Kaleb's lips. "I be waitin'."

***

When Kaleb returned from the bathroom the apartment door was slightly ajar and he pushed through. The single table lamp was now extinguished and replaced by a half a dozen flickering candles, shadow dancing with the room. The Murphy bed was down, center room, and Kitty lounged across it. Unadorned. Naked.

Kitty was beautiful. Her skin had a light reddish glow in the candlelight and the dark brown areolas gave an exclamation to her full breasts. Hearty hips framed a dark patch of pubic curls that gave promise to a celebration of primal passions.

But Kaleb's smile was a sad smile. He came over and sat on the edge of the bed and his weight, pressing against the mattress, drew Kitty to him. Breath to breath, their eyes locked. "I'm sorry, Kit, I can't...."

Kitty stroked the eyebrow scar gently and cut him off. She used the tip of her fingers to outline his mouth, "Shhhh. I know."

"I'm not so sure if Nika needs me...."

"I know."

"...Or if I need Nika."

"I know."

"I just can't get a handle on our crossing...."

"Or cross, anyways."

This surprised Kaleb and he looked into Kitty's eyes to grasp the meaning. Kitty looked away and shrugged her shoulders. "Seems like both ya crucified to each other. Spiked with different kinda nails but hanging on the same damn crucifix."

Kitty did not press the point. Pulling away, she feigned a quick laugh. "S'alright, honey, I'm just testin' my limits." Kaleb could hear the sadness in her words and in her laughter.

She could love this boy. This Kaleb Kierka. This Jew boy. Kitty had been with enough men to know the real deal.

Even if Kaleb didn't know it himself.

***

On the street Kaleb tried to collect his thoughts on Kitty. And on Nika. And on who the hell Kaleb Kierka was. Is.

Will be.

It was not a comprehensive collection of thoughts.

48

Beat Me, Daddy, Four To The Bar

It was warm and dark when Kaleb made the street. On the stoop he turned and looked back up toward Kitty's flat. Is this what the old Kaleb would have done? Walked away from a beautiful lover.

Was this exchange a step to the rear or to the fore? To the dark or to the light? Who the hell was this man veiled in Kaleb Kierka's amnesia?

What can one derive from our involuntary actions? What character trait can be estimated as we move reflexively through this plane?

Pulling out the sack of Bull Durham, Kaleb absently began to work up a smoke while he wandered the Black Bottom in the general direction of north. North towards Paradise Valley.

***

Black was waxing poetic:

"What is the true measure of a man's worth? Of his esteem? Of his reason to exist?

"If a man begins his life in poverty and achieves affluence, should this be the deciding factor in the equation of the man?

"Or maybe it would be the growth of the spirit, of the man's character. If one were raised in the hideous but achieved the inspirational, or, conversely, if a man is given every opportunity but wastes his life piddling away the prospects, should these, then, be the sum of the equation that is the man?

Blew warmed up his horn.

Black yowled on. "Is the growth or decay of one's character the true aggregate that justifies the tally?"

Blew blew a refrain:

"There's an itching in my heart,
That I don't know how to scratch.
A torch in the darkness,
But I ain't got a match.
But sometimes,
Sometimes,
SOMETIMES THE WOLVES ARE SILENT."

***

Cupping his hands to flame the cigarette was an automatic and absent gesture. Kinetic memory drew the cigarette smoke into his lungs and kinetic memory triggered the leg muscles mechanical momentum north. North to Paradise Valley. North to home.

Walking Riopelle Street and deep in deliberations of the who and the what this Kaleb Kierka was and is, he crossed Gratiot and passed the House of Corrections at Alfred. The Grand Trunk Railroad line was two blocks to the east, and Kaleb could hear the rumble of the tracks as a trainload of commerce made its late night delivery to the warehouses at the rivers wharf.

As he shuffled down the sidewalk, Kaleb examined his visit with Kitty. Especially the part about he and Nika hanging on the same crucifix. Understanding the nails that secured Nika was easy. But what of his own nails? What were the pegs that kept Kaleb nailed to the crucifix? The cross that Nika and Kaleb shared.

Lost in this thought, Kaleb failed to notice the black Buick that had quietly tucked into his trace. And he failed to make note of a second black Buick that had parked at the corner of the dead end of Erskine Street, directly across Kaleb's path.

As Kaleb began to cross Erskin Street, the doors of the now parked Buick were flung open and two hunks of beef jumped out. Awakening from his inward deliberations, Kaleb was quick to estimate the situation. Turning for escape, he now saw the following Buick spill two more masses of beef. Kaleb had been herded into the dead end street and he scolded himself for the folly with a quick and breathy. "Dammit."

Their hats were tilted low to impede facial detail, while saps and clubs jumped into the hands of the interlopers. The four brunos were backing Kaleb deeper into Erskine Street. Into the dead end.

Reflexively Kaleb dug into his pockets for his handguns but came up empty. He left the guns on the floor at Kitty's.

Swiftly scanning the alley for an instrument of war, a rock, a two-by-four, anything, Kaleb came up empty.

The four-crew gang formed a half circle and bore down on Kaleb. Their silence was the most intimidating. These were businessmen attending a symposium and crushing Kaleb's skull would be the order of business on tonight's agenda. This beatdown, this manner of doing business, was to be a painstaking and hostile corporate takeover.

Beat me, daddy, four to the bar.

It was time to stand his ground, and if Kaleb only had his fists against the saps, he would pick one target, one of the gangsters, to focus his defense. That target, that gangster, would be the one crumpled body left to lie beside his own crumpled body in the afterburn.

The hoodlum to his right was closest, within swinging range, and this was the man that Kaleb would mark.

As he shifted his left foot forward to get power into his right cross punch, a fifth figure appeared at the rear of the attack. He was coming up behind the four gangsters from Riopelle Street and he was coming fast. He appeared from the shadows beyond the reach of the streetlight and beyond the darkness of the dead end.

This new attendee, this extra constituent, did not veil his identity. He was tall and he was thin and he wore a dark blue suit. His long, lanky legs were churning real estate in an effort to join the fray.

And he had a face like a hatchet.

The recognition of the hatchet-faced man distracted Kaleb just enough to slow his assault on the hoodlum to his right. A critical distraction.

When the blow hit Kaleb it came blinded from his left side. It came with thunder and lightning and it came with a finality that rocked Kaleb to a heap.

49

Too Many Shadows And Too Much Fog

Kaleb awoke to a searing headache, and at first, he dared not open his eyes. When he finally ventured the light, the brightness flooded in on the thunder of a rolling tympani.

He blinked his eyelids. Focusing. Unfocusing. Focusing. It took a few moments for Kaleb to squint the light into a point where he could regulate its illumination. And another few moments before he could actually make some use of the light.

Detective Morane sat in a chair across from Kaleb's bed. One of the detective's stubby legs was casually angled over the other, and he was dug into the chair like he was expecting to be there for a while. He was deep in the study of his knuckles as he rolled a silver dollar through his fingers, back and forth, forth and back, and he did not notice when Kaleb's eyes fluttered against the light.

A cursory sweep of the room and Kaleb knew that this, again, was a hospital. The clock on the wall suggested 2:30 but, as the drapes were drawn, the nighttime or the daytime remained elusive. Worse, Kaleb was unaware of how many days had again elapsed in his comatose world. One? Two? Another five weeks?

A panic set in. Not again. Not another cycle of questions with no answers and tomorrows with no yesterdays. He broke into a cold sweat as he began a review of the circumstances as he remembered them.

He remembered being Kaleb Kierka; and he remembered that he had had amnesia and he remembered he had begun to piece his life back together; and he remembered Detective Morane; and he remembered The Temple Bar Speakeasy And Play Nice. He remembered Nika and Kitty and Tia and Bucky and the Purple Gang and Grand Circus Park and Model T's and the hatchet-faced man and….

The hatchet-faced man. The last man Kaleb recognized as he succumbed to the hammering blackjack. The last memory before awakening in this bed; in this hospital. The hatchet-faced man. The progenitor of all things fatal. The hatchet-faced man.

"We've got to stop meeting like this." Morane suspended the silver dollars journey across his knuckles and was looking into Kaleb's eyes. He offered a smile but the smile was just this side of sad.

Kaleb cleared his throat, testing for phlegm, testing for words. "How long?"

Morane caught the reference. "Can't say exactly how long but you were discovered by a milk man on an early morning delivery in the Erskine alley. More specifically, the Golden Jersey Milkman's horse found you. Pair a horses was nosing up fresh grass along the alleyway while the milkman was runnin' butter 'n eggs."

Morane eased back into the chair, his frumpy suit spilling over the chair's edges.

"How long?"

"Doc figures you were there for a while as the blood under your scalp was dried brown. You been out eight, nine hours we figure. Max, maybe ten."

Kaleb was working at his memory, feeling it out, seeing what might be available. "I thought Detroit outlawed horses on the city streets last year. That is, if last year was 1926."

Detective Morane smiled at what Kaleb was able to recollect. "Sure. Illegal on the streets. Alleyways are still fair game. And this milkman was a teamster, had a two-horse buggy. They's grandfathered horses to the teamsters rigs."

Kaleb nodded to this, pleased with himself that he could draw on memory, disappointed that there wasn't more draw. "And what's Doctor Stein's estimation of my condition."

Morane was in a coy humor. "Can't rightly say. Haven't been to the Henry Ford Hospital in a good spell."

Kaleb let that sink in and again surveyed the room, the bed, the chair and the detective. It was a hospital all right.

"Then where the hell are we?"

"We're on Frederick. At the Parkside."

Kaleb leafed through the filing system in his brain. "Parkside. Parkside. Parkside?" and recognition caught. "We're in the colored hospital?"

***

Doctor James Ames was the attending physician. Ames was also the Parkside Hospital's medical director, so Kaleb Kierka, this Jew boy from Paradise Valley, was attracting quite a bit of attention from the hospital hierarchy.

"It ain't the wound that concerns me." Doctor Ames spoke with a measured self confidence in a warm voice. "The cut was not so deep, just bled plenty because, well, that's what head wounds do. No, the blood doesn't concern me. What concerns me is how it might have scrambled up your brains."

Detective Morane offered, "Won't be the first scrambling."

Doctor Ames shot Morane a gratuitous smile and continued. "I've spoken with Doctor Stein at Henry Ford. Says you've had some memory issues. Says you've had a bout of amnesia."

Kaleb found some humor in this. "Sure, I can remember having amnesia. There's a conundrum. I can remember not remembering."

This time Doctor Ames shared his gratuitous smile with Kaleb and asked, "How deep goes the memory?"

Kaleb took a moment to do a deep scan of his memory banks. He could remember everything that had happened since the coma. But back behind those memories, on the other side of his life, there were still many holes and many shadows. Too many shadows and too much fog.

***

There were long moments of silence after Doctor Ames left the room before either Kaleb or Detective Morane spoke.

Morane retrieved the silver dollar from his pocket and began again to spin it through his fingers. Kaleb watched Morane roll the coin absently across his knuckles.

Not looking up from the rolling coin, Moraine queried, "What were you up to last night?"

Kaleb thought about it and was pleased that he had the memory. "Uptown to the Adams. Had a little gum flappin' with the Rubble boys.

"Rubbles? Maybe them, then?"

"Maybe. I relieved them of their hardware and sent them on their way. But I didn' mention to them where I was headin'."

Any place else?"

"I swung by Nika's apartment visiting…."

"Nika live alone?"

"No. It's Kitty's and Tia's apartment as well. But Nika and Tia weren't there."

"Stay long?"

Wistfully Kaleb remembered Kitty's soft lips and generous offer. "Just long enough to get out of there in time."

Morane considered that, then asked, "Anybody besides you and Kitty know you were there?"

Kaleb thought about that. "I might have mentioned where I was going at The Temp. I made Baldy's juice-joint later. But I didn't really talk to anyone there."

"Okay. Who was in the Temp when you might have yakked it up?"

Kaleb tried to envision the night before. "Most the gang. Bucky, certainly. Hollie, Granma and Jones were there. Most regulars I guess."

Morane considered this and he gave Kaleb time to consider it as well. "...'member anything about this mugging?"

Kaleb switched gears. "Four, maybe five, brunos. And Buicks. Two black Buicks."

The coin rolling across Morane's knuckles was mesmerizing. "Buick's are a dime a dozen with the street goons. What else?"

Kaleb resisted following the trace of the rolling silver dollar. "I remember the hatchet-faced man."

This interested Morane and the coin ceased rotating. "What hatchet-faced man?"

"Seen 'im a few times now. Twice outside of my apartment. Once down at The Temp. And last night. Last night he was the last thing I remember seeing before the lights went out."

Morane considered this as the coin resumed its journey across his knuckles. "Hatchet-faced? Like a thin, long, face you mean?"

"Yep."

"What else?"

Kaleb shrugged, buying time to remember. "Sharp long nose, like the leading edge of an axe. Tall. Dark hair. Dark navy-bluish suit. Too spiffy for the Paradise Valley."

"Packin'?"

Kaleb tried to recall if there was a bulge under the man's arms. "Can't say for sure. Maybe yes, maybe no."

Silence again as the silver dollar resumed its journey from the pinky finger to the thumb and back again.

"Could you pick 'em out of a line-up?"

"Yep."

"Could you pick 'em out of a morgue drawer?"

"Preferably."

"Here's what bugs me...." Morane was working out the thought as the silver dollar rolled on.

After a moment, Kaleb coaxed, "What bugs you?"

"Well, first off, you're alive. You ain't dead. That first beatdown, that beatdown that lay you to waste for a five-week coma, that beatdown was somebody out to kill you."

Kaleb let that lay.

Morane continued with his thought. "But this beatdown, this beatdown is different. Ya got yerself a swell bump on the noggin' to wow the dames, but that's all you got. One sap upside the head and it was over. One sap. Don't seem likely that any gang would send three, four, five mugs to do the task of one mug. One sap."

Detective Morane knit his brow tight and chewed on his bottom lip before he continued. "Whyn't they kill you last night?"

Kaleb let that sink in but it didn't offer any insights.

Morane added, "But something else bothers me about this whole game. Been bothering me from the jump."

When Kaleb again offered nothing, Morane continued, "Both these beatdowns, the first that lay you up for five weeks and now this one, well, both these beatdowns don't make sense."

"Don't make sense how?"

Morane looked uneasy in the chair, in his skin. "They don't make sense because I been going over your history the same way you been going over your history and there's one thing about Kaleb Kierka that has always been consistent...."

"That I absorb abuse regularly?"

There was nothing in that for Morane and he pushed on. "One thing about Kaleb Kierka that comes again and again is that Kaleb Kierka is a cautious man, a man not prone to letting his guard down. A man that is difficult to fool and more difficult to surprise."

Kaleb's fingers began a slow stroke on his scarred eyebrow as he let that sink in. "And your conclusion is...?"

"My conclusion is that you are gettin' set up. There is a Benedict Arnold in your circle that is giving you up."

When Kaleb did not ask the obvious, Morane continued. "Who knew where you were last night? You were coming from a rendezvous at Kitty and Nika and Tia's apartment. Who else knows about that apartment?"

This was not a pleasant thought, that someone who was a friend or a colleague, someone close, was aiding and abetting his enemies.

"Think about it, Kaleb. You know you well enough now to know that you are not easily ambushed. Your eyes go full circle.

Maybe one time you get caught off your guard. Maybe. But two times? Two times? Not likely."

Someone in Kaleb's inner circle? Bucky? Granma? Kitty? Jones? Maybe one of the musicians? It didn't seem right but Kaleb had considered this before and he knew that Morane had a point.

The coin stopped and Morane looked dead into Kaleb's eyes.

"Someone privy to your playlist has been circulating the bulletin."

It did not leave a good taste in Kaleb's mouth but it was a flavor that needed to be tasted.

50

Conundrum On Conundrum

Doctor Ames was reluctant to discharge Kaleb but he couldn't tie him down. Instead, he sent a nurse in to try to sway him.

Nurse Tiana Strickland, Tia, was a seraph in her nurse-whites. Her nurse's cap on her short cropped and kinky hair fit like a halo.

"Boy, we were wonderin' where you'd a run off to. Your noggin' seems to become a magnet for clubs and saps."

Kaleb didn't want to talk about it. "How was the Adams? How was Ma Rainey?"

Tia fogged, turning the memory over in her mind like kneading warm bread dough said, "Ma was hot, she had the nightclub hoppin' and stompin'."

But Kaleb heard something else in her voice, in her knead. "And…?"

Tia abruptly took her hands out of the dough. "And jes a bunch of white boys tryin' to make time…."

Kaleb did not want to talk about the beatdown, so he added yeast to expand the dough and said. "White boys give you a full dance card, did they?"

"I guess."

"You guess? What does that mean? Any particular boy on your card?"

Tia thought about that particular white boy. Matter of fact, there were few moments since the Adams that she had not thought about that particular white boy.

"Maybe one. But that was then, this is now."

"And…?"

"And that was night, this is day."

"Who was the maybe one?"

Tia saw that Kaleb was not going to let this go, so she resigned to just get it over with. "A Edgar somebody. Edgar Land, I think,"

Kaleb was surprised. Surprised that he had a memory coming on and surprised who had filled up Tia's dance card, "Edgar Land? Edgar Nicholas Land?"

***

Psychology is an iffy proposition. And amnesia compounds the iffy. What can an amnesia patient remember and why? As electrical charges flit across the synaptic gaps, memories are lit. Or not.

But where is the rhyme and what is the reason? Why do some memories hide deep in the cerebellum while other memories spark?

Doctor Stein at Henry Ford Hospital suggested that this might happen. "Memory might find a foothold at the furthermost reaches and work their way back. Or maybe at the closest and work their way out. Or maybe no foothold at all. We just don't know."

Kaleb had a memory of Edgar Nicholas Land but he'd be damned if he knew why. And the discipline of psychology was likewise flummoxed.

For from the front to the back or from the back to the front, Kaleb did not know why the memory of Edgar Nicholas Land sparked memory but spark memory it did.

***

In the Detroit of 1927 the unions were in their infancy and they were taking a beating. Figuratively and literally. Henry Bennett was Henry Ford's point man and he led with the tip of a bludgeon. Figuratively and literally.

When a line-worker went to work in a Henry Ford factory, Henry was of the opinion that he owned the worker's blood and bone.

While Ford built for himself mansions and art institutes and recreational playgrounds with the sweat of the laborer, the laborer could look forward to 10-hour shifts, six days a week. And benefits? If a worker became ill, he was dismissed and replaced by another husk of blood and bone and the assembly line droned on.

Such was the design that Henry Ford had on the blood and the bone of the factory working class.

Edgar Land took exception to Henry Ford's design.

Henry Bennett took exception to Edgar Land's exception.

Battle lines were drawn and the young barrister, Edgar Nicholas Land, found himself in a union battle of blood and bone and grease and guns.

Figuratively and literally.

***

Tia thought about it. "Yeah, I think that's what he said. Edgar Nicholas Land."

Letting a soft whistle waft 'twixt his lips, Kaleb offered, "Whew, Tia, you sure picked a doozy."

First with an angry charge she lashed out, "I didn't pick no one. Just another white boy tryin' to get in my drawers, is all." And then she softened and asked, "Hey, how the hell do you know this Edgar guy? I thought you was wit-giddy?"

Kaleb tried to ascertain where this memory had come from but he was left with shrugging his shoulders. "Jes come up. Don't know from where. Don't know from why. But, well, there it is."

Tia thought about that for a moment. "So what about this Edgar Nicholas Land? What's his legend to me?"

Kaleb took his time, attempting to piece together as much memory of Edgar Land as he could collect. Finally he said, "Something about a high stakes lawyer."

"A lawyer?"

And more came to Kaleb. "A lawyer. Represents the new unions or somethin'. The auto unions. As I recall, he's been going up against Henry Ford's union-busting goons. Walkin' the line, getting his head busted in with the rest of the union organizers, takin' 'em to court. That sort of thing."

Tia did not enjoy the thought of Edgar getting his pretty little blonde head busted open, and she didn't enjoy the thought that she cared about the white boy getting his pretty little blonde head busted open. Conundrum on conundrum.

As memory came, Kaleb spoke it out loud. "Edgar's gone toe to toe with Henry Bennett, Ford's top goon, in smack down after smack down. Edgar always comes up on the losing end of the club."

Again, Tia didn't enjoy that thought nor the thought that she didn't enjoy that thought. Absently she tried to block out Kaleb's recall, reminding herself that Edgar was just another white boy.

Kaleb pushed on adding, "An' he's sued Henry Ford many times."

Tia feigned disinterest as she busied up the bandage on Kaleb's scalp. "Edgar sued Ford for what, 'xactly?"

Kaleb winced at Tia's touch to the wound. "Ow. Easy on the dome." And then back to Edgar he said, "Seems our boy Edgar's been suing Ford to make him pay the colored workers same wages at the white workers."

"What?" Tia exclaimed, but she had heard Kaleb all right. "He's the white boy that sued Ford over colored wages?"

"Best I can remember. Ow, ow, ow, easy on the noggin'!"

51

Rats Is Rats

As it turned out, the 2:30 time that Kaleb read on the hospital clock registered post meridiem. Now dusk, Kaleb was already back in his flat. The headache from the sap slap was waning and the wound's throb was subsiding.

This time the apartment on Hastings Street felt like home. More to the point, it looked like home. It was a recognizable element and that spoke to Kaleb Kierka's grasp of memory. He didn't have it all yet - big fat blanks were yet a part of the structure - but he had a foundation on which to start the brickwork.

Mechanically Kaleb moved to the kitchen and busied up the coffee pot. The making of the cigarette from the Bull Durham sack was perfunctory. These efforts, the coffee and the cigarette, were tried and true and moved with the grace of dancing with a long-time partner.

With coffee in hand and the cigarette suspended from his lips, Kaleb stood at the front bay window of his apartment and surveyed Hastings Street. He rocked his head northward in the direction of Parkside Hospital and then rolled it south on Hastings Street in the direction of The Temple Bar Speakeasy And Play Nice. Kaleb's domain.

Toting fractals of memory, Kaleb summed that he was a piano player and an owner of a speakeasy and a confederate of hookers and mobsters and artists. And he was a man who was easy with a gun. All part of the grand total that was his promenade of roaring along in the Detroit of 1927.

Relationships held more of a challenge: Nika and Kitty and the Purple Gang and Ma Rainey and even the sharp-faced man in the navy blue blazer. And these relationships, these fogged memories, were where the danger held fast.

But one relationship, one player who held center stage for the second act was a somebody somewhere hell-bent on destroying this Kaleb Kierka.

Lost in the thought of jumbled memories, the cigarette had burned ashes to his lips and the coffee had gone cold.

***

A light rapping on the apartment door coaxed Kaleb out of his musings. He set down the cold coffee as he crossed the room to the door. He hesitated at the door and listened against the door panel. He had abandoned his guns to a drawer in his office at The Temp. Looking toward the kitchen, he considered a butcher knife when that rap-rap-raping began again.

Quietly sideling the door he pressed his ear to the wood but there was nothing to be gained there.

"Open the door, kid." It was Detective Morane.

Morane followed Kaleb into the room. "I smell coffee."

Over his shoulder, Kaleb offered, "Coffee's ablaze on the stove. 'elp yourself."

Coffee in hand, Morane tossed his hat on the coffee table and dumped his full complement of pudgy into the easy chair. Wherever Morane sat himself - be it a hospital stool, a car bench, or in Kaleb's easy chair - the detective's dumpy proportions flowed like liquid that squished into every crevasse offered by the host furniture.

Morane said, "You know I once knew a guy that kept pet mice. White mice. Little guys. Can't say I cared for 'em, kinda creeped me out, but they kept the man entertained enough."

As Kaleb studied the detective he absently rolled a smoke. "Is this your attempt at being folksy?"

Morane smiled at that and continued. "Seems the man's wife didn't appreciate the rodent roommates and she left him. His friends got tired of him talking about the vermin like they were children and they melted away as well."

Kaleb flamed the coffin nail and shook out the match. "Is this story going anywhere or you just flappin' gums?"

"Eventually the landlord had his fill and kicked the man to the street."

"Fun story. It'd make a nice dime novel."

Undeterred Morane added, "So the man ends up on the street with his clutch of mice, but the clutch of mice interbreeds with the street rodents, and sure 'nough, he ends up with a gang of rats. Big brown ugly rats."

"And the moral is, I suppose, that sometimes you just can't tell the mice from the rats. Subtle. Like a circus barker."

Morane had nothing to add to that so he let it lay there.

Kaleb took a long draw on the cigarette and blew a plume of smoke toward the ceiling. "You suggestin' that I got a rat somewhere in my mice family?"

Detective Morane adjusted his weight, oozing into more nooks of the chair. "What all was on your calendar yesterday 'sides the Adams and Kitty's 'partment?"

"And that's pertinent, how?"

"Where you went, who you saw, and who knew where you were all figure in. Somebody trapped you up Erskine alley. That's plain."

It made sense to Kaleb and Morane continued. "Who else you been seein' lately?"

Kaleb saw no gain in being deceptive. "I had a rendezvous with the Purples."

The detective thought this through. "Hmm. Where'd they find you?"

"I hunted them up."

"You huntin' trouble?"

"Huntin' information. Had to find what the Purples mean to me."

"Did you find out, all right?"

"I filled in some blanks."

"The Purples relieve you of your guns?"

"Didn't take guns."

Morane gave an unintentional shudder, and his body fat seeped a little deeper into the easy chair. "Boy, you sure can shake up the garbage can. Think the Purples had anything to do with last night's muggin'?"

"Nope. The Purples could have had me any time. They're businessmen. If they wanted me out, I was convenient enough; they needn't follow me up any alleyway."

The detective bought time by sipping on his coffee. "Tell me more about this hatchety-faced man."

Kaleb finished his smoke and stubbed it in an ashtray. "Not a lot to tell. Like I said, I seen him at The Temp and I seen him at a colored speak in the Black Bottom." Nodding over his shoulder, Kaleb offered Hastings Street. "And I seen him down there."

"And you seen him last night, right?"

Kaleb remembered the entrapment. "And I seen him last night, right. Just before the lights went out."

Morane's silence led to Kaleb repeating, "Like I said, tall, maybe six-two, slender, appreciates darker threads. He's got a sharp face, nose 'most like a beak, recessed chin, and eyebrows that bush out under the fedora."

"Not a bad spotlight for a civy."

"Civy?"

"Civilian. Not the law."

That's when another memory caught as Kaleb's mind saw the man as he leaned back against Kaleb's T on the street below. "And a bulge of a gat under his left arm. So's he's probably right-handed."

"Jesus, boy, you sound like a cop. What was the brand of his underwear?"

They both let that lay there like dust settling on a mantel clock. A dead mantel clock.

After a spell of silence, Detective Morane set down his coffee cup and pushed his weight from the easy chair. Compressing his hat over his slick dome, he headed for the door. At the door, he turned back to Kaleb and concluded, "White mice is pretty but in the end, rats is rats."

A wisp of a smile turned the upper edges of Kaleb's lips. "Sell it to the pulps."

52

Needle To Needle

It is a wry irony that the word needle begins with need. And those riding the heroin horse will be the first to admit that the need of the needle will ultimately usurp any other basic need, be it food or shelter or physical safety. Love, too, will take a slow canter to the gallop offered by the horse.

Heroin holds fast like a vice. An ever-taut vice of vice. And every moment without heroin becomes another twist of the vice until your guts are gutted and your head shatters in a million pieces of blood stained glass.

Hanging onto the edge of reality, high on the cliff of heroin, these zombied souls fill their veins with an elixir that can only deliver them as far as their next appointed inoculation. They move in a foggy netherworld of pain and release, pain and release, pain and release.

Needle to needle.

***

Kaleb Kierka was on the stage, at the piano, and on cloud nine. It was a shade beyond midnight and the band had settled into groove after groove of glory. Oldham was in lock down on the traps; Beethoven Jones was thumpin 'n pumpin' on the bass; and Doctor Dan on the saxophone was praising the Lord.

As for Kaleb, he was lost in the crush of this new blues note, this flat 5 hammering against the grain of the scale, this brave new world of the blue sun.

The band had been in jam orbit for more than an hour before Kaleb returned to earth. When he did manage to look up from the piano, he saw that the bar was full and the patrons were hanging on every flat 5. The band was in a 12/8 swing and The Temple Bar Speakeasy And Play Nice was swinging low sweet chariot with every backbeat triplet that Oldham and Jones laid down.

It was well nigh 12:50 a.m. and Kaleb realized that Nika was late. Scheduled to join Jazz du Jour for the midnight set, Nika should be center bash by now. Nodding to Doctor Dan to take over the maestro task, Kaleb slid from the piano, from the stage, and ambled to the end of the bar where Bucky was boilermaker busy. Kaleb needed only to tip his head toward the clock, and Bucky understood the question, squeezing his shoulders upwards in uncertainty. With a quick tilt of his head towards the back door, Bucky offered an option.

Kaleb slipped to the rear door and into hallway, past the restrooms and the office, and out the back door to the alleyway.

He didn't see her on his first scan of the alley. Kaleb was looking for a slinky little Jew girl in a tight number with probably a needle in her arm. Upon a second and more intent examination of the alley, Kaleb noted a heap of black clothing bundled at the base of a garbage can.

The heap of black clothing was a heap of Nika Nightingale.

Slapping the needle out of the unconscious girl's vein, Kaleb collected Nika to his chest. Waif-like in his arms, she was cold to the touch as he placed her in his T. The six block drive up Hastings Street to Kaleb's apartment kept his right arm busy gear mashing the T while keeping a check on Nika's aorta. By the time he carried her up the three flights to his apartment, she was beginning the long and steep climb into consciousness.

Kaleb's first thought had been to deliver her to the closest hospital, The Parkside. But as her pasty flesh began to warm in the car next to him, he recognized that the worst had passed, and now it would just be a matter of her long and painful climb into the realm of the undead.

Two hours of pacing, two pots of black coffee, and the constant rubbing of Nika's pallid skin finally brought some semblance of cognizance to Nika's eyes. The vomiting was the best of the antidotes.

Nika puked buckets of antidote.

Sitting across from her now so he could study her eyes he said, "You ain't doin' yourself any favors, sweetheart." He used the word sweetheart like a truckload of trouble. "...And you ain't doin' me no favors neither."

Climbing out of the pit of bad drugs is a climb out of hell. The stomach churns in rebellion, the skin creepy-crawls with cold sweat, and the damned light spits and sputters in the brain like oil on a hot skillet.

Nika focused on Kaleb, on his face, on his eyes. She was up on the score and she was sorry for it, but the demand of the drug craving would always be the primary default.

And she loved Kaleb for standing between her and the heroin. And she hated Kaleb for standing between her and the heroin. And she loved him. And she hated him.

There were no words to exchange. Kaleb went to Nika and lifted her to her feet. With her under his guidance, they began another slow round of toddling the apartment, wall to wall and back again. Wall to wall and back again. And again. And again.

Walking and coffee and puking and walking and coffee and puking and walking and coffee and puking would be the order of business well into dawn's early light.

Walking and coffee and puking. Walking and coffee and puking. Needle to needle.

53

THE BALLAD OF TIA AND EDGAR:
The Feral Moans Of Pheromones

They met, Tia and Edgar, at Caroline's Cup O'Joe on Tuesday evening at 6:00. He arrived at 5:30 with great anticipation. She arrived at 6:15 with great trepidation.

When Edgar arrived, his fedora and summer jacket were wet from a summer rain, and he slung them on a coat tree next to the front door of the café. It was warm in the café and Edgar found a table where he could keep an eager vigil on the entrance. As he sat transfixed on the front door, he could see the steam rise from his drying coat and hat on the coat rack at the door.

The summer rain had begun with the bluster of thunder and lightning but had waned into a light mist. In the heavy rain's aftermath came the humidity. By the time Tia arrived at Caroline's Cup O'Joe, it was difficult to discern if there was more moisture falling from the sky or evaporating from the pavement.

Tia had had some difficulty wresting the blonde wig onto her nappy locks, and the humidity made her scalp itch miserably under the wig's cap. She carried a flowered umbrella that she dropped absently in the umbrella urn by the coat rack at the front door. She was miserable with the heat and the humidity and the itching scalp. But mostly she was miserable with what she would need to tell Edgar. What Edgar deserved to know.

After dropping the umbrella into the urn, Tia turned to scan the room for Edgar and she was met with a full frontal assault of his beaming smile as he jumped from his seat and pulled out a chair for her.

He was a full 6'2" of everything that Hitler had envisioned of the master race. Blonde and blue with a leanness that suggested action and a determination that would get the job done. But then, he had a smile that glowed like the beacon of a safe harbor in a storm-ravaged sea.

When Tia saw Edgar pull the chair for her, her knees softened under her weight, and if she had been in anything taller than the one-inch sling-back pumps, she would have crumbled to the floor.

Steadying her gait, Tia crossed to Edgar and they exchanged a light peck on the cheek. As she leaned into Edgar she caught a whiff of his scent, and if it was not for the chair already extended, her knees might finally have delivered her butt to the floor.

Transported on the heat and the humidity of the day, Edgar's perspiration, Edgar's pheromones, clung thick to his body and hung in the air like the howling from a feral animal in heat. The feral moans of pheromones.

With Edgar's sultry aroma came the release of Tia's trepidation as her thought processing gave way to other regions in her woman's body. Gone was the misery of the heat and gone was the misery of the humidity and even gone was the misery of the itching blonde wig.

These were two beautiful specimens of this lineage known as humanity and they sat, transfixed on each other's eyes, on each other's chemistry, across a cup of coffee in Caroline's Cup O'Joe on a sultry summer evening in 1927 Detroit.

***

They met again, Tia and Edgar. And again and again. Secretly. Sometimes they met back at Caroline's Cup O'Joe; sometimes they met on the outskirts of Detroit in a country café north on Woodward; sometimes they would just stroll the Grand Circus Park among the old men and the baby strollers. But Tia and Edgar's favorite spot to rendezvous became Belle Isle, the green island of sanctuary between Detroit and Windsor, Canada.

And with each rendezvous, with each clandestine meeting, Edgar would press for a more open affair. Tia, for her part, would promise herself that this would finally be the time that she would tell Edgar that she was not a blonde and she was not white and that her only hob-nobbing with high society mucky mucks had been at the salacious end of a twenty dollar bill. She would inform him that she was a colored nurse at the colored hospital, The Parkside, and that her home was in the Black Bottom.

But then they would walk and talk and laugh and the pheromones would tweak and the next thing Tia knew, she was back home in her ghetto apartment, swearing that next time, next time for sure, she would give Edgar a full account.

***

Edgar would speak of his union work, of his legal battles with Henry Ford and of the physical confrontations with Harry Bennett. Harry Bennett, Ford's anti-union goon, the muscle behind Henry Ford's war on the unions. Harry Bennett, the thug who became more important to Henry Ford then Ford's own son, Edsel.

When Edgar spoke of the unions, he spoke with a zeal that seeped from his core, bubbling up in passion for workers' rights and honest wages and blue-collar dignity. He spoke of an honest day's pay for an honest day's work. Lost in the passion of equitable wages and of justice, Edgar spoke, preaching from the pulpit of the egalitarian.

Egalitarian. When Edgar spoke of the unions he was driven by a fervor for a classless and a colorless society. A society based on merit. A society based on open and democratic principles.

Hand in hand Tia and Edgar would stroll the green shores of Belle Isle. Edgar, lost in his passion and his principles, and Tia, marveling at this rich white boy's compassion for the working man's plight.

***

"You've just got to tell him." Kitty pressed Tia.

Tia, eyes unfocused, ringing her hands and answered, "I know, I know. It's just so, it's just so hard. When I'm with him it seems that time stops. Or time quickens. Or something. I get the words all formed, and I've sucked in my stomach for a big breath to spill it all out in one gush and then...."

"And then?"

Refocusing her eyes back on Kitty she said, "And then I am sitting here again in the Black Bottom telling you that I didn't tell Edgar."

"Gotta tell 'em."

"I know."

But then they were back on Belle Isle, hand in hand with no color between them. They would stroll through the Botanical Gardens or rent a canoe for a cruise around the canals of Belle Isle and count the white fallow deer that roamed the island's forest. Or clamber through the reeds at the river's edge and collect eggs from the migrating duck nests. They would visit the half-mile long swimming beach along the western waterfront of Belle Isle and dip their bared toes into the white sand at the rushing rivers shore and talk about everything and laugh about nothing.

With each meeting, with each covert rendezvous, they would talk less and kiss more and the hormones would kick in and rush the time or still the time or something. And then, again, Tia was a working black girl back in this apartment in the Black Bottom wringing her hands and promising that the next time...

"Gotta tell 'em."

"I know."

***

Edgar Nicholas Land, of Detroit's Land and Lodge and Lindbergh families, was an up and coming young lawyer. He had concerned himself with facilitating the fledgling union movement of industrial Detroit, and by doing so, had not endeared himself to the political and corporate foundations of Detroit. But his family name gave him some measure of cache in the privileged community, and his passion for the working man earned him some rapport with the blue-collar everyman. He was thusly known to every quarter of Detroit whether in the capacity of an adversary or as an advocate.

Cindy, or Tia, had never concerned herself with the comings and goings of Detroit's political landscape, but as she came to understand Edgar's omnipresence in Detroit, she realized that it was only a matter of time before someone in some quarter of town, be it uptown or downtown, would recognize her for who she was. And what she was.

Tia was playing on borrowed time and, at some point, times debit would come due.

***

" You gotta tell 'em."
"I know."

***

Tia, or Cindy, came to own the white.

When Tia donned the blonde wig she became Cindy and Cindy was white with a white persona and a white demeanor. At first the guise was forced, unnatural, as Cindy tried to blend into the white backdrop like a prey's camouflage against the teeth. But, eventually, Cindy settled into the white like she was born into it.

Cindy's warm black voice, the voice indebted to her African heritage, came to articulate with a harder, crisper clip while shedding the southern drawl. The gentle southern sashay of Cindy's hips, owing to the slow sizzle of the Alabama heat, squeezed into a tighter and more purposeful pace.

Ever vigilant against discovery, Cindy coaxed Edgar away from crowds, away from the light and into the veil of the shadows.

All the while, Edgar was becoming impatient. He wanted to bring their affair to the light. He wanted to walk arm and arm with Cindy and announce his love for her to the world. Edgar wanted to cry out his love for Cindy from the top of the newly constructed Leland Hotel on Bagley Street to the lowliest alleyways of the ghetto tenements of Paradise Valley. Edgar had fallen hard for this coy blonde woman. Fallen hard and fallen deep into the raging waters of love. Plunging into the deep end with a lover's anvil tied tight around his neck.

And Cindy promised time and again - next time... next time I will tell him everything. I will tell him that I am colored; I will tell him that I am a nurse and a used to be prostitute. I will cast off this god damn blonde wig forever and I will let the chips fall where they may. I will take whatever consequences that might come. Next time.

But the next time came and the next time went, and again Tia fell under the spell of the dastardly pheromone. Tia's heart soared with love and the words were stifled in her throat and the moment was lost.

But, certainly, Tia promised herself, next time....

***

One would think that Cindy and Edgar would have nothing to talk about. No history in common to share. But this was not the case. Conversation flowed easily between them as dialogue explored an intimacy of the spirit, of the soul, and banter became a conduit to character rather than the blather of the frivolous.

When Cindy did share a history, it was more of an abstract chronicle as she would talk about the ills and pains of the world in general, alluding to, but never owning, the pain of her own history.

They had yet to be physically intimate, Tia and Edgar. Six weeks they had been ducking from shadow to shadow and Edgar never pressed his desire for a corporeal bond. It was enough to just be with this woman of intrigue, this woman of intelligence and of beauty.

For herself, Tia had never been this long in a relationship without being physically intimate. From her youngest years on the farm in Alabama, when she had lost her virginity to a field-mate behind the cotton gin, Tia had always assumed that sex was the precursor to love. And now her world was being turned topsy-turvy.

Tia was discovering that sex was a compliment to love, not the consummation of love.

And Tia thrilled to the discovery.

54

Flat 5

The band was smokin'. It was 1:30 in the morning and The Temple Bar Speakeasy and Play Nice was jam-packed with black-and-tans. The dance floor was hopping and the party was on. And the band played on.

This revelry would be going until the wee hours. Until the weeee hours.

There was a new face sitting at the piano, and he was banging on the ivories in a new-fangled style. Or maybe an old-fangled style.

The black man had come up from Mississippi to The Temp via a house party gig in the Black Bottom. And he was bringing with him a new attitude to the piano.

Using the minor blues scale as the underpinning, this new blood pounded two dissonant blue notes together in a hard, rhythmic percussive solo on the piano, slamming the discordant pitches against the rhythm section. The trick was to play the flat 5 of the scale simultaneously with an abutting note on the piano, either against the four or the five, pounding triplets hard against the tune's groove. The resulting tension gave a taunting timbre to this mode of music called the blues.

This method of piano improvisation, this "crushing" of the tones, would eventually become a standard bearer for playing blues piano but for now it was new and fresh and scary and inspiring.

Billy Oldham on the traps and Beethoven Jones on the double bass were locking down the rhythm section. Under their guidance, the groove dynamics swelled and retreated, swelled and retreated. Swelling and retreating like a tide in a storm as wave after wave of the surge crashed the shore. To the dance floor.

On top of this aural surf, and under her shock of black hair, rang the soaring vocals of Nika. Petite Nika, in tight black midcalf-cut slacks and a low-cut black top that clung to her hard little nipples like a bobbing boat on wave after wave of music splashing the shore in the melodious eye of the storm.

Behind the bar Bucky was filling shot upon shot and beer mugs and beer shells of uncut Canadian hooch to wave after wave of swelling and swilling partiers. Swelling and swilling.

Kaleb was on his stool at the end of the bar next to the short hallway that led to the restrooms, his office, and the back door. He was sucking on a cigarette and enjoying the vista.

It was a good scene for Kaleb. The crowd was toned and the till was turning and Rubble's gang and the Purples and the beatdown and the hatchet-faced man and Detective Morane were all but forgotten.

Forgotten? What is forgotten to a man with amnesia? Even Kaleb's forgotten was forgotten as his body and his cognizance relaxed on the surging wave after wave of the music.

But mostly it was a good scene for Kaleb because of Nika.

***

When the band broke for a breath at 2 a.m. the party was just beginning. They would be back.

Billy and Leon, the sax-man, broke out reefers and headed for the bar. Nika slipped past Kaleb to the hallway leading out to the back door and into the night. She blew a cursory puckered kiss to Kaleb as she flit past his stool.

By the time that Kaleb made it to the alleyway, the needle was already in Nika's arm. She looked up from the needle work, smiled demurely, and resumed the booster.

Sitting back on a garbage can, Kaleb folded his arms and looked on as Nika finished her inoculation. When she was done, she quickly tucked the spike into a small hand bag and looked at Kaleb.

As he watched her go through her needle routine, he rolled a smoke, fired it up, and said nothing, scrutinizing Nika's handiwork while dragging on the cigarette. He continued to say a very loud nothing.

Finally Nika spoke, "And...?"

"And what?"

"And, what you got to say?"

Kaleb's lips smiled but his eyes were sad. "I got nothin'. Nothin' that ain't been said. Nothin' you don't know."

Even in this dim alley light, Nika was electric. Her jet black hair caught every flicker of every sliver of starlight. A petite perfect little Jew girl. Except, maybe, for the needle tapestry tattooing her arm.

Nika was defiant. "No lecture? No 'bad bad girl'?"

Kaleb drew hard on his smoke and looked away from Nika and up into the night sky. This seemed very familiar to Kaleb. The night, the needle, Nika's defiance. He was still recovering his memory and he didn't know his place and he didn't know his boundaries.

Even so, it was familiar. Here was the pox of their relationship. Nika and Kaleb had been in this rodeo many times before. Nika wanted Kaleb, Kaleb wanted Nika. Kaleb wanted Nika clean.

Nika wanted to ride the bronco. The horse. Heroin. Same rodeo, different bronco.

Horse, smack, skag, junk, hero, dope, dragon, no matter the tag, there was the consequence. You may yearn for love or fame or fortune or happiness, but, whatever your yearning, whatever your want, you always want that needle just a little bit more.

Heroin is the illness and heroin is its own remedy.

Nika looked up to share the night sky with Kaleb. As the heroin surged through her, it warmed Nika's complexion to a soft pink. The drug eased the craving, and as the defiance slipped from her shoulders, she moved to Kaleb and folded quietly into his arms. Strong arms. Welcoming arms. Familiar arms.

Reaching up with her lips she kissed Kaleb's cheek and then her lips reached his mouth. The kiss was relaxed and Kaleb, ever so gently, held Nika's lower lip with his teeth. He could taste the sweet brandy on her lips and he could feel her body draw tight into him.

"I can blow off the next set," she whispered.

"Not hardly. I'm sittin' in with the band. 'N I've got that new piano lingo 'n I'd like to give it a go."

Nika rubbed at the veins on her arm to push the heroin into her blood stream. "Ya heard that piano man from Missi'pi way? The way he pound out dose blue notes on the keys?"

"Sure. I heard 'em. Thought I'd try a slammin' on the flat 5 myself."

The drug was reaching Nika's tongue and the words were at the edge of slurring.

Kaleb heard the slur. He held onto Nika's head, drawing her under his chin and softly kissing her forehead. In Nika's slur, Kaleb heard how the flat 5 of the blues scale crushed against the four and the notes cried together in a dissonance of misery. In Nika's slur. In Nika's flat 5.

Nika felt so good, so right, in his arms that it almost made Kaleb forget about the drugs.

Almost.

***

"You can't make 'em quit ya know," Black said, "...it don't work that a way."

Blew had a sticky sax valve and, while he was dragging a dollar bill through the valve to clean it, he was forced to listen to Black ramble on.

"Addicts. Ya can't make 'em quit. They gotta come to it on they own. You only piss 'em off and they dig in they heels. Then all you got is a pissed-off addict."

Blew tapped on the valve. It seemed clear and so he blew a riff that sounded something like, "Enabling, enabling, enabling."

Black listened to the refrain, then he said, "Sure. Maybe that sounds like enabling to some folk but if'n you've ever dealt with an addict; drugs, cig's, liquor, sex, you know they ain't nothin' you can do but bide your time 'n wait for the fall."

Black was warming up the riff. "Enabling, enabling, enabling."

"Ain't nothin' you can do but wait for the fall. And they will fall. Jes a matter of time." echoed Black.

In a falling glissando, Black cascaded the riff down. "Enabling, enabling, enabling."

"Sure it's down," said Black, "But down is where they will go until they decide theys had enough. If you're there to catch 'em when they fall then it might work out okay. If you ain't there to catch 'em, well, you ain't there to catch 'em."

Blew stopped playing and listened to Black finish his thought.

"If you ain't there to catch 'em then you ain't there to catch 'em. If you is you is. Simple as that."

Blew considered this and he put the horn to his mouth but this time he played a dirge that sounded like the walls of Jericho tumbling down.

The saxophone sounded exactly like this:

Joshua fought the battle of Jericho,
Jericho, Jericho.
Joshua fought the battle of Jericho,
And the walls came tumbling down.

As an afterthought, *Blew blew the darkest of blues:*

You see the sufferin', you see the pain in her eyes,
You want to help her but it's best just to let her cry.
Well there you go, another World of Woe.
There you go, another World of Woe.

***

Love and woe.

Kaleb had the need to crush the blue notes together. Crush the flat 5.

55

What The Matter?

The night was sticky with the heat of passion. Love and love's sweat dripped between Kaleb and Nika like a juice, like an elixir.

They twisted their bodies in every which direction in their fervor; the physical options were exposed and explored and explained.

Infinite lovemaking: The resulting exposition of lovemaking had mathematical improbabilities written in the exponent to the power of Pi. The power of love.

Kaleb and Nika's lovemaking ballet pirouetted toe to toe and toe to nose, and nose to groin and groin to groan; from the front and from the behind and from the top and to the bottom. A wild lovemaking of passion and purge. Fervor and fever. Ardor and harder.

***

As Kaleb lay in the aftermath of the passion with a Bull-Durham hanging from his lip and a spent Nika asleep in the crux of his armpit, he reasoned that maybe this, maybe the act of lovemaking itself, is the only measure of humankind.

***

Black had this to say to Blew:

"Maybe the physical, this performance of the body, of the matter, is all that truly matters. For when one comes to the core of man, to man's place in the cycle of life, is man really nothing more than a breathing and farting and fucking animal? Does man's breath keep him upright as methane farts push him forward while copulation generates a progeny to carry on the constant and chronic cycle of the animal?"

Blew trilled the flat 5 like a bovine's cry in the slaughter yard. Just one more bovine's cry in the slaughterhouse. On the flat 5.

***

As Kaleb lay in the semi-glow of the leftover light from the kitchen, he closed his eyes to the blush and his mind reached for the man within.

***

Black had plenty to say:

"Beyond our simple collection of skin and bones, how best might a man be estimated, be measured?

"Could our best hope for an accurate judgment of our worth be found in the absence of light? In the parameter-less darkness?

"In the darkness, the assessment of man is not distracted by pretty eyes or strong and sinewy muscles. In the dark, in the cast of the shadow, no quarter is given for the flow of one's tresses or the cut of the jowl, and no information can be gleaned from the tone of complexion. In the dark, stark naked yields no curriculum."

Blew shrugged his shoulders and blew cobalt:

EASE AWAY WALK

1.
There is nothing to say,
There are no words to talk.
Ease your feet
To the street,
And walk,
And walk.

2.
Your ears are like clay,
Your eyes are like a wall.
Ease your feet
To the street,
And walk,
And walk.

3.
With nothing up your sleeve,
And your bluff has been called.
Ease your feet
To the street,
And walk,
And walk.

4.
Your heart is to break,
Your knees are to crawl.
Ease your feet
To the street,
And walk,
And walk.

In the absence of light, the measure of matter becomes moot.
Quality and quantity are given no matter.
No matter. Nomatter.

***

Somewhere down below, on the broiling streets of 1927 Detroit, a judgment had been made on the worth, on the value, of Kaleb Kierka's life. And the tally was that Kaleb's dying was a more desirable sum than his living.

Kaleb understood that these tallies would sometime need to come due. He would need to face up to the balance due on Kaleb Kierka.

There would come a time, coming soon, when the full sum of this Kaleb Kierka would need to be paid. A time when the debit is calculated and the invoice is served.

But in this moment, in this passion, with Nika, was where he would need to stay for now. In the moment. In the matter.

***

The dawn's light filtered as it passed through the bedroom curtains, stirring dust particles before settling on the soft features of the little Jew girl as she slept quietly, wrapped loosely in the sheets. Her breath held a peaceful rhythm that only the orgasm of love can deliver.

On the bed next to her was an empty hollow where Kaleb's contour lingered.

56

Rubble's Bubble

Mizzy Rubble's speakeasy, Rubble's Bubble, was on the far west side of the city, out in farm country. Kaleb took his time driving along Grand River before turning north on the dirt road named Livernois. This area had been annexed by Detroit the year before, in 1926, and although the city was beginning its inevitable crawl-sprawl to this end of the county, it was yet a mostly rural and farming community populated by dairy farms and open fields of alfalfa and wheat and corn.

Holstein cattle, the black and white splotched dairy cows, were held fast behind the barbed-wired fences, and the red barns where milk would be sucked from their teats sporadically dotted either side of Livernois. The road itself was a gravel affair with enough washboard ruts to rattle the T and jar the liver. Liver noise. Livernois.

There was a dusky dusk with a dirt-hazy sun setting over the flat farming landscape like a gauze. Dust and dirt kicked up from the T's wheels, curling over the air current of the car's slipstream and back into the car. The dust gave the air a gritty, suffocating, breath. Although it was cooler out here, out away from the brick and cement of the city, the air still held fast to summer's swelter.

Kaleb thought about packing his pockets full of iron for his meeting with Mizzy Rubble, but he decided against it. If he brought the artillery he would be suggesting a different sort of conference. And Kaleb needed information. He needed to talk.

Rubble's speakeasy was a grand old farmhouse on the west side of the road, and when Kaleb turned left into the dirt drive, the low sun blasted his eyes. A road-grimed windshield diffused the sunlight into a dirty smear. The parking area was an earthen affair that would be a muddy pond during a rainy spell. Squinting against the low sun, he angled the T onto a grassy lump near the front door of the farmhouse. There were a few vehicles parked in the lot. Farmers vehicles mostly - funky and pitted Model T pick-up trucks and field buggies. A couple of new coupes seemed incongruent among the alfalfa fields and the dairy barns. Parked along the side of the building was an International Farmall tractor with a manure spreader in tow. The manure spreader was empty but held fast to the odor of its business.

As he climbed from the T, Kaleb's eyes were still blurred and splotchy from the low western sun that had blasted his eyes through the dirty windshield. A black Buick spitting dirt from spinning wheels nearly crushed Kaleb's toes as it tore out of the driveway and jumped onto Livernois. Even as the Buick covered Kaleb in the wash of its whirling wake, he managed a quick glimpse of the driver.

The plume of dust from the car's wake, his sun-spotted eyes, and the swiftness of the car's acceleration out of the driveway, all would have been good reasons for Kaleb to doubt his identification of the driver of the Buick. But it was him all right. It was Kaleb's old nemesis. The hatchet-faced man splashing Kaleb with dirt and dust and grit.

The Buick had been parked under a canopy of oak with a brushy understory that kept it hidden from the Rubble's speakeasy-cum-dope den.

Running to the road, to Livernois, Kaleb squinted against the lowering sun's light but could not catch a license plate number through the plume of powdered soil that the Buick was kicking up.

This was a new development. This was a new twist. Too many times this man, this ghost, had haunted Kaleb's shadows. Outside of Kaleb's tossed apartment. To the rear door of The Temp. When last Kaleb was conked and sent to the hospital. And now. Now as a visitor to Rubble's Bubble. This was no coincidence; this was no fluke.

As Kaleb stood in the settling dust of the Buick's spinning wheels, he considered the hatchet-faced man's connection to the Rubbles. Was he a part of this collection of no-good? And if he was a part of the Rubble rousers, then why had he been veiled in the foliage? But Kaleb had little time for these considerations, for as he turned to his car he was intercepted by two hunks of beef that had rolled from the farmhouse.

Again, then, the matter of the sharp-faced man in the neat cut navy blue suit would need to be rescheduled.

Kaleb turned to the two hunks of beef. He knew these boys alright.

Fat Tony and Jimmy-Jimbo. The bulges under the men's armpits suggested fortification. Kaleb nodded to the armpit bulges. "I see you've restocked the artillery."

Neither man smiled. Fat Tony slid his gun out of his coat. "Fair is fair. How 'bout this time we take your gat?"

"Ain't carryin'."

Fat Tony waved his gun at Kaleb. "Suppose you reach the clouds and let us be the judge of that." Fat Tony said to Jimmy-Jimbo, "Pat 'im down. Pat 'im down real good."

Kaleb raised his arms and Jimmy-Jimbo went around and searched Kaleb from behind. He was thorough, slapping Kaleb from his shoulders right down to his ankles. Kaleb lifted his arms and while the bruise brother thumped him down, he was glad he had left his hardware at home.

Walking back to Fat Tony, Jimmy-Jimbo said, "He's clean."

Fat Tony thought this over a moment. "Kinda brave of you to come into our garrison empty fisted. What's the game?"

Kaleb took his time answering, going from one face to the other. The men were walking walls of meat, and with the sun to their backs they cast a deep shadow on Kaleb.

There was something familiar about the ugliness. Something beyond his earlier encounter outside the Adams. Something familial and foreboding. He scoured his memory banks but to no avail. Even so, there was a kinetic memory that tweaked at every muscle in Kaleb's body.

"I'm here for your mama. Where's Mizzy?"

The brutes were slow-witted at letting that sink in. Finally Jimmy-Jimbo sneered through yellowed teeth. "You want Mizzy? What bizness you got wit' mama?"

Kaleb did not respond; he just stood there letting the moment drag on. Despite the intimidation suggested by the sentinels, Kaleb felt relaxed in his skin. This was not a foreign encounter for Kaleb, and he felt comfortable against the intimidation offered by the hulks. For a quick moment Kaleb reflected on this comfort level, this ease.

In the hub of the threats and the guns, Kaleb relaxed. Like pulling on an old and warm coat, Kaleb's comfort level rose in diametric opposition to the hostility. He marveled at what history he might have had that left him so cozy in the presence of peril.

Again Jimmy-Jimbo demanded, "What for with mama?"

Kaleb's eyelids half closed against the lowering sun and against the danger. Casually he said, "I want the boss. I don't speak to the help."

Jimmy-Jimbo balled up a fist and took a step toward Kaleb. If it were possible, Kaleb eased into an even greater tranquility. This potential violence was home cooking to Kaleb (Who in the hell was this Kaleb Kierka?).

Before Jimmy-Jimbo could take another step, Fat Tony caught his arm. "Let 'em be."

"But...."

"Butt yer own self. Let 'em be. He wants to speak to ma 'n ma wants to speak to 'im." Then Fat Tony said to Kaleb, "Follow me, rube."

Fat Tony turned to the farmhouse and Kaleb followed. Jimmy-Jimbo tucked in behind Kaleb with his hands balled into fists.

***

It was the smell, initially, that hit Kaleb while his eyes adjusted to the darkness of Rubble's Bubble. The smell of opiates and heroin and booze. And vomit. The cacophony of stench assailed his nostrils like a slap in the face.

As his eyes tuned to the darkness, Kaleb beheld a barroom of a dozen or so tables and a collection of slumping bodies propped against the walls and dripping from the chairs.

The first floor of the farmhouse had had its walls knocked out to offer a grand room with plenty of pillars and corners to accommodate the shadows. The bar, nothing more than a plank of board on a series of saw-horses, ran across the back wall. Just another drug den on just another Podunk heroin highway to hell.

The lumps of bodies were sitting, heads bowed to the table, lost in the stupor of the heroin. Somewhere there would be a room for the heroin intake, the shooting room, where these lumps of flesh would crawl off to receive another potion portion. Then again, back to their table, heads hovering dully over their inebriant of choice.

Behind the bar was a staircase to the second floor and this is where the bruisers escorted Kaleb. Up the stairs and to the first door on the right. To Mizzy Rubble's office.

Mizzy Rubble was a big woman and wore the same pug nose and thick brow as Kaleb's escorts. Although she did not quite make it to six feet tall, her girth gave her dominion over her sons and over Rubble's Bubble.

Out here in the boonies Rubble's Bubble catered to the locals and the locals were few and far between. Farm boys had early morning cows to milk and late evening hay to pitch and precious few moments in between to spend their paltry earnings at Rubble's Bubble.

Why Mizzy Rubble wanted to move into the big city was obvious. It was the *how* that Kaleb was here to ascertain.

***

"I'll give you this, kike, you got some balls walkin' into Rubble's Bubble." Mizzy Rubble's mouth was an ugly affair and seemed to move independently of her words. Her lower lip hung loosely letting the tarred and yellowed lower teeth of her jaw chatter, while the philtrum was graced with a thin, black mustache. The smoldering cigar in the ashtray on her desk gave some explanation to the splendor of her rotting teeth.

The office was small to begin with and the three big bodies of the Rubbles squeezed the space with flesh and sweat.

Mizzy was to the point. "I really ain't got no chatter left. I laid out for you my intentions."

"Humor me. Tell me your intentions one more time."

Mizzy Rubble took her time, sizing Kaleb up and down. Leaning back in her chair, she shoved the cigar into her mouth and drew on the stogie until the cinder flamed. "I heard you went brain sloppy. Can't 'member for shit. 'Zat right?"

There was nothing in that for Kaleb, and he let the silence hang like another body in the room.

"How 'bouts we sloppy up 'is brains a little bit more, mama?" This was the larger beef, Jimmy-Jimbo, speaking to the back of Kaleb's head.

Mizzy was still estimating Kaleb. She was fat and she was ugly but she was not stupid. "You 'n Tony leave 'im be." She sucked at the stumpy roll of tobacco again and added, "For now...."

"But mama..."

Mizzy Rubble silenced Jimmy-Jimbo with a quick glare and then she was back at Kaleb. "Okay, kike, let's play your game. Let's assume you don't know the weather. Here's the layout. I want The Temp and I'm a gonna have The Temp. I'll give you a market price and I will determine the market price." Mizzy Rubble's lower lip undulated independent of her upper lips giving Kaleb a panoramic view of the tartared maw.

"That's your design *on* The Temp. What's your design *for* The Temp?"

"Aww, ma, let me *design* 'is ass...," and again Jimmy-Jimbo was nipped with a glower from Mizzy.

Kaleb had never seen anybody inhale cigar smoke, but that is exactly what Mizzy Rubble was doing. Sucking deep, filling her lungs with the smoke and then exhaling a blue plum into the already stuffy room. She held the cigar between two fat fingers and pointed the embers at Kaleb like she was pointing a gun.

"I *design* on doing with The Temp whatever the god damned *design* I want to do with The Temp. I've had enough of bein' out 'ere in the boonies caterin' to bumpkins. Real money's in town and The Temp is real money. And I'm gonna have it. You can sell out and I move in or you can die and I move in. But I'm movin' in."

Sucking in and then blowing out another billow of blue burn, Mizzy Rubble concluded, "That is the *design* and that is the whole of the contract negotiations."

Kaleb considered this. He could hear Jimmy-Jimbo behind him wheezing in anticipation of redesigning Kaleb's face. "And what do you plan for the workforce at The Temp?"

"I really don't see as that's any of your business." She shared another ugly teeth vista with Kaleb.

"No mo' bohunks, mama. You promised no mo' bohunks and no mo' jigaboos in da Temp," said Fat Tony.

Fat Tony must have been the favored child as Mizzy shared a smile with him. The smile pulled her bottom lip over her rotting teeth hiding the tar-caked lower incisors. Kaleb thought that she really ought to smile more to hide that mouth, but he doubted that anyone would ever tell her that.

"Sure Tony, sure. No more bohunks an' no mo' jigaboos in the bar." And then with her attention right back on Kaleb she said, "Like I says, what we do with The Temp is none of your affairs. I'll give you a week to close up and turn the keys over to the boys 'ere."

Kaleb could smell the boys' sweaty bodies behind him, as they pressed close. The three big Rubbles seemed to fill the room like a liquid, pouring fat into every corner of space.

"And if I don't like the offer on the table?"

Mizzy Rubble did not smile. Her lower lip slackened into a scowl but she did not offer any words. Sucking the cigar into her face she blew a plume in Kaleb's direction. Pointing the tip of the burning cigar at Kaleb, she slowly crushed the cinder tip into her desktop until the embers were extinguished.

The metaphor was not lost on Kaleb.

***

Jimmy-Jimbo and Fat Tony escorted Kaleb to the parking yard under strict orders of safe passage from Mizzy Rubble.

The cool of the evening had brought more of the farm vehicles to the dirt parking lot. The Farmall tractor with the manure spreader was gone, but, fittingly, the odor of manure lingered.

57

Victimless Crime Of Love

It had been a tough night on Kitty's body. The pummeling of her profession had taken its toll and left her with battered inner thighs and a bruised spirit. Some nights the weight of her profession were more grueling than other nights. The weight of the men, physically and emotionally, pounded their passion and their pain into Kitty's body until they exploded, leaving Kitty drenched in their ache.

When Kitty opened the door to her apartment, she caught the scent of Nika and warmed to the fragrance.

Nika was asleep on the Murphy, but the kitchen area light had been left on and there were flowers, tulips and roses, and a shot glass left on the counter. The shot glass offered a taste of peppermint schnapps and the flowers held a note that said, "To Kitty, my sweet baby. I love loving you." It was signed simply, Nightingale.

Nika understood. Nika knew. Nika had needed, at times, to suffer under the weight of the prostitute. To prostrate her body in the servitude of fulfilling a need. Whereas Kitty's service was for the betterment of her children who were still in the muddy poverty of Alabama, Nika's service was rendered as a slave to the needle.

Kitty sniffed at the flowers and looked at little Nika cuddled under the blanket, and Kitty's eyes misted in the moment. Again she sniffed the flowers and then sipped at the schnapps. The peppermint burn cleansed her palette of the leftover pong from her mouth. The warmth of the liqueur soothed her throat and the alcohol calmed Kitty's abused body.

Tulips and roses. Kitty's favorite flowers, favorite scents. Tulips and roses. Two lips and roses.

Another snuffle at the flowers and another sip of the schnapps and Kitty dropped her dress and underclothes and crawled into bed with Nika. Gently, so as not to wake her, she slid an arm under Nika's head and pulled her to her breasts. Nika's breath was deep and calm in her slumber. Her delicate scent reached a place in Kitty that no amount of tulips and roses and peppermint schnapps would ever access.

Kitty had known love before. The giving of love leastways. It was not reciprocated but it was love none the less. He had been a good lover and a good provider until one day... he wasn't.

Kitty was young and Thom had come to Kitty on a rush of infatuation and passion and Thom had left Kitty on a rush of infatuation and passion for somebody else. But in that brief spell of infatuation and passion, in that time allotted to Kitty, Kitty had found within herself the capacity of devotion and affection, of giving without the need to receive. Kitty knew that she was capable of, and deserving of, love.

Kitty had learned. It was a painful lesson but it was an important lesson. Kitty had learned that there is always a silver lining if you are a willing student. Kitty was not a victim. Even the loss of love is a victimless crime. A victimless crime of love.

***

Black's tail went clickety click click click and he said, "Without the tally of debit, no summary gain can be measured."
Blew blew blue. The saxophone sounded like this:

VICTIMLESS CRIME OF LOVE

1.
Kitty understood the rules,
And it didn't come as a shock of something new.
And she knew that Thom would leave,
But as he got what he wanted she was getting what she need.
And she did Victimless Time
For a Victimless Crime
Of Love.

2.
Benny never really cared,
As Kim spent his money like she was breathing air.
And he saw through all the greed,
But as she got what she wanted he was getting what he need.
And he did Victimless Time
For a Victimless Crime
Of Love.

BRIDGE:
Prepare yourself,
Then dare yourself,
To take a fall.
It's better to have loved and lost
Then never have paid the cost
At all.

3.
And we've all been up that street,
And maybe if we're lucky someday it will repeat.
If we just land on our feet,
They can have what they want 'cause we'll be getting what we need.
And we'll do Victimless Time
For a Victimless Crime
Of Love

***

Kitty cozied Nika into the crux of her arm hollow and lightly kissed the sleeping girl's forehead. This stirred Nika and her eyes slit open through the fog of slumber. She gave a thin smile to Kitty and whispered, "Hiya baby, how was work?"

Kitty planted another peck on Nika's forehead. "Got lots better when I got home. Thanks, sugar, for the flowers. The roses and the tulips."

Nika smiled, kissed Kitty's two lips, and drifted back off to sleep.

Kitty lay awake for a long time in Nika's arms and felt the soft rise and fall of Nika's bosom against the still of the night. Eventually slumber came to Kitty in the Black Bottom of 1927 Detroit.

58

Body Of The Band

They were dueling vernaculars as the Armenian Krikor was trying to explain to the bar-swabber Hollie how the music ensemble of the jazz band was like the human body. Their conversation was playing hide-and-seek among the consonants and the vowels - dodging behind the tree trunks of accents and ducking down the hollows of lisps.

Granma was innocently sitting in front of the radio waiting for the Tigers game and doing her damnedest to ignore the jousting dialects as Krikor would thrust a verb and Hollie would parry an adjective.

Thrust and parry went Krikor's broken English. Parry and thrust answered Hollie's maligned vocabulary. Back and forth, forth and back fenced Hollie and Krikor's respective argots.

"Goddamnittohellandbackagain." spit Granma.

"What do ya mean, Kreek? Where 'fore is a band is like a body?"

Most folks knew better than to engage Krikor when he went off on one of his theoretical musings about music. Most folks did not encourage Krikor's abstract dissertations and incantations on his theories of music. But Hollie was not most folks. Hollie enjoyed the attention and Krikor enjoyed the audience.

Granma, not so much a fan exclaimed, "Goddammnittohellandbackagain, Hollie, don't get him started." Today's spittoon for Granma was an old pea tin, and as an exclamation point, she exercised a healthy spittle of chaw into it. *Ting* went the spit cup.

***

Hollie was standing near Krikor and Nika's table while quietly swishing the broom under their conversation.

Krikor had offered that the jazz band was just like the human body. Nika paid no heed. Granma, at the bar, ignored him.

Hollie was puzzled and asked, "Why'n'cha wherefore is dis jazz band like pebble's body?"

"Pebble's body?" asked Krikor.

"People's body," corrected Granma.

Swish swish went the broom. *Ting* went the pea can.

Small, gray, and wild of mane, Krikor looked more professorial, akin to one who might be developing theories on relativity at a university rather than one waxing poetic about the particulars of jazz in the dive bars of 1927 Detroit.

Krikor set his accordion on the table and sipped on a ginger ale. No alcohol for the professor. Nika was sipping on a 7 'n 7 highball.

***

It wasn't often that Krikor enjoyed an audience and he was enjoying this one now. "Sure sure. Like de-a-body. Performing band is just-a-like-a human body."

Krikor, a refugee intelligentsia of the Armenian Genocide of WW I, had been smuggled out of the Ottoman Empire and shuttled to Detroit by an Italian scholar. The scholar, architect Nicholas Sarno, and Krikor were part of the flood of European refugees who had landed in Detroit's Paradise Valley.

That was the good. The bad was that Krikor had learned to speak English from the Italian Nicholas and Nicholas was not a linguist.

If English was a second language to Nicholas, then English was a second-hand hand-me-down to Krikor. Nicholas imparted just enough of the English language to Krikor to make Krikor's dialect a hodgepodge of runaway syllables. There were never enough "a's" in the English language for a good Italian immigrant and Krikor became a good progenitor of the "a." In the broken English of the Italian model, the letter "a" was inserted generously, filling in the noun gaps, in a lilting sing-song manner.

"Just-a-like-a-de human body. With a-de-bones and-a-de-muscle and-a-de skin." Krikor's dialect was taking the A Train.

Granma said to Hollie, "Don't encourage 'im. Best jes to give Kreek the Greek a no never mind."

"He's Armenian," reminded Nika.

"What?" said Granma.

"Krikor's not Greek. He's Armenian." said Nika.

"Goddamnittohellandbackagain," said Granma. *Ting* rang her spit-cup.

For her part, before and between the bouts of opium, Nika was a forever student. Although never registered formally, she was a lecture hound at The College of The City of Detroit north east of Paradise Valley on Warren Avenue at Cass. And she was one of the few who got a kick out of Krikor's ramblings.

Hollie probed, "So, then, Mr. Kreek, how is the jazzy band like pebble's body?"

Krikor took another draw on his Vernors Ginger Ale and studied for the words in English. "Well, first off, let's-a-look at a-Jazz du Jour. It all-a-starts out a-with-a-Beethoven on-a-de-bass fiddle. 'kay?"

Hollie pictured Beethoven Jones thumping up a bass line. That was an easy vision. "'Kay."

"Jones is a-like-a-de-skeleton in-a-de-human-a-body. Jones is-a-providing the framework for-a-de rest of a-de-music to-a-a-a-how you say, to take shape on?"

Nika was getting sucked in to the idea. "You mean like a scaffold? Like a frame?"

Krikor appreciated the help. "Sure, sure. Like a-de-frame. On'y in a-de-body. A scaffold in-a-de-a-body."

"He means a *skeleton*, Goddamnittohellandbackagain." *Ting ting.*

"Yes. That is a-good, Granma. Beethoven Jones is-a-like-a-de skeleton-in-a-de-body. De skeleton. Dat is-a-good. Very good."

"Beethoven Jones? Jones the bones?" offered Nika.

"Oh, brother." Granma shook her head. "Don't you start now."

Hollie swished the broom. "Okay, Mr. Jones is plaguein' the bass."

Granma was becoming overwhelmed by the language mutilation, and shaking her head to her beer she said to herself, "Playing the bass. Not plagueing. *Playing* bass."

Hollie was not deterred. "Jones is the bones plaguein' the bass, go 'head."

Still struggling for words in English, Krikor stumbled on, "After Jones on-a-de-bass, on-a-de-skeleton well then, next come-a-Oldham wit' de-a-muscle."

"Billy drumbling? The drumbling is the muscal of the band?"

"Muscle," murmured Granma to her beer. "Billy is the *muscle* of the band."

"Yes, yes. De-a-*muscle*. After Jones a-come-a-with-a-de-skeleton, Billy put de-muscle on-a-de-bones. He a-move-a-de-bones. Push 'em 'round. Listen as he drumming-a-de counters on-a-de-skeleton."

Hollie asked, "Cowards on the skeleton?"

"De-a-counters," said Krikor.

"Cow herds?"

Granma had resigned herself to conversing with her pea can. "He means *contours*. Not counters. He's talking about the muscle on the bones giving the bones shape. *Contours*." The pea can had nothing to say.

Krikor overhead Granma's avowal to her pea can. "Yes, yes, I-a-meant *contours* a'right. But counters is a'right too because Billy counts time on-a-de drums. But *contours* is-a-de-best, yes. Thank you-a-Granma."

Granma rolled her eyes. Nika nipped at the highball. Hollie swish swished the broom.

Krikor took a moment to collect his thoughts before he clickety-clacked down the track on the A Train. "Notice a-how-a-de drums give muscle to Jones's bones? Listen to de-a-movement to de-music. Wit'out de-a-drumma, de-a-muscle, dem-a-bones-a-gotta-no-a-place to go."

Nika was in the game now. "Okay, then, we have Billy on the drums providing the muscle and giving propulsion to the bones of Jones's bass fiddle. What next?"

It was not often that Krikor enjoyed such a grand audience for his ramblings, and he glowed with the attention. "Den a-after-de-a-bones and-a-de-a-muscle, what do you t'ink in a-de-a-human-a-body?"

"I give up," said Hollie.

"I give up," said Granma and she meant it.

Besides the plethora of *a-a-a*'s, another attribute of the Italian-English that Krikor had assumed from Nicholas Sarno was the wild hand gesticulations as he spoke. The more excited he became, the greater the hand gesticulations. Krikor's arms began to whip up a breeze.

"After de-a-bones-and-a-de-a-muscle, then we have to-a-wrap it up-a-all in de-a-skin. And that is-a-what-a-Kaleb a-do on-a-de-piano. Wit' de-a-harmonies, wit' de-chords-a-and-a-such, Kaleb puts a-de-skin on-a-de-muscle and-on-a-de-bones. Kaleb is de-a-memorybrane on de-a-body."

"Memory bran?" Hollie was confused.

"... De-a-memery*brane*," Krikor corrected.

"Memory *brain*?" Hollie was more confused.

Chagrined, Granma could not control herself any longer and cried, "Oh, for god's sake, he means the membrane. Membrane! Kaleb puts the *membrane* on the muscle and bones. He's talkin' about the skin. Kaleb puts the skin on Oldham and Jones's muscle and bones."

Granma looked to the radio behind the bar, but the sanctuary of the Tigers ballgame would not come on for a couple of hours. *Ting ting ting.*

"Yes, yes, the memorybrane. De-a-covering. De skin!"

Nika was not sure which she was enjoying more: Krikor's theory or Granma's exasperation. "So, let's see what we have here, Kreek. Jones on the bass is the skeleton and Billy on drums is the muscle. Then Kaleb on the piano is the skin that covers the body?"

"Yes, yes, dat's-a-right. But it ain't-a-de everything."

Underneath the conversation, the swishing of Hollie's broom was providing a rhythm to the conversation. "'An then? Then what?" Granma mumbled facetiously to her pea can, "Oh yes, yes, please tell us what comes next in the body of the jazz band."

Krikor overheard Granma's dialogue with her pea can, but his grasp of the English language was not equipped to catch facetious. Encouraged, he went on. "Well, after de-a-bones an' de-a-muscle an' de-a-skin we-a-have our-a-coope-de-grass, of course."

"Coope-de-grass?" asked Nika.

"Poop the grass?" asked Hollie.

"*Coope*-de-grass." explained Krikor.

"Coup de gras!" exclaimed Granma. "Coup de gras!" Granma was in a fit. "Goddamnittohellandbackagain! You can't even speak English and now you're attempting French? The phrase is *coup de gras!*"

Krikor was excited now and his arms were awhirl. "Yes, yes! The coo-a-de-a-gra! On top of de-a-bones an' de-a-muscle and de-a-skin, you get-a-de-character of de-a-band. De personality of de-a-band."

"Don't ask, don't ask, don't ask!" pleaded Granma.

"What is the personality in the band-body?" asked Nika.

"Goddammittohellandbackagain," spit Granma.

Krikor took his time now, swirling the Vernors and watching the tiny carbonated bubbles fizzle to the top.

"The character of-a-de-a musical body is in-a-de *I*'s."

"In the *I*'s?"

"Yes, yes."

"Or in the eyes?"

"Yes yes. In-a-de eyes and in-a-de *I*'s. De *I*'s are in-a-de eyes."

Nika had no option but to pursue the metaphor. "And what are the eyes of the band's body?"

"De eyes are a-de instrument dat is-a-playin' de melody. Coulda be-a-saxophone. Coulda-be-a-trumpet. Coulda be-a-violin. Coulda be-anyt'ing. De a-personality of a-de band-a-body is in a-de eyes. Like-a-Doctor Danny on-a-de saxophone. He's-a-givin' sight to-de-music. He a-give-a-personality to-a-de music."

Nika considered this. "So a music ensemble has a skeleton of bass, muscles of drums, skin of a piano, and the eyes of the saxophone."

Swish swish went the broom. *Ting* went the pea cup.

"A-sometimes-a-de-a saxophone, yes. Eyes can be any-a-instrument. Even you, Nika, when you a-singin'. You is de-a-eyes of de-a-band when you is a-singin'."

"Goddamnittohellandbackagain," Granma told the pea tin.

Nika summed it. "Let me understand this, then. The band is like the body in that the bass provides the skeletal structure, the drums provide the muscle to move the skeleton, the piano provides the chordal skin to keep it all together and the melody instrument provides the personality, the character, of the music?

"Yes, yes, yes. De-a-jazz-a-band-is-a-like-a-de-a-human-a-de-a-body."

Hollie had a tenuous grip on the ledge of understanding. "But what of music misseggs?"

"Missed eggs?" said Krikor.

"Miss *stakes*," said Hollie.

"Miss steaks?" said Krikor.

Exasperated, Granma could contain herself no longer. "Mistakes! Not missed eggs. Not miss steaks. *Mistakes*. What happens when the musicians fuck up?"

"Mistakes? Oh. What a-if-a-body goes sour?" Krikor said.

"Sure. What if a body goes sour?" Nika reiterated.

Granma was sorry she had said anything. "Let it go, Nika, let it go." Granma did not want to know.

Hollie had his own agenda. "Yes. Whyin' if the music body stinks?"

"When a-de-body-of-a-de-music stinks?"

Nika found this funny. She had been in the middle of many stinky musical mistakes at one time or another. "Yes, Kreek, what happens when the body of the music stinks up the place?"

Krikor shrugged his shoulders. "Sometimes a-body-a-farts."

Hollie's broom stopped swishing while Nika choked on her drink, spraying The Temple Bar Speakeasy And Play Nice with the 7 'n 7 highball.

"Goddamnittohellandbackagain!" concluded Granma and rang the pea cup with a *ting ting ting.*

***

Kaleb marched through the bar doors, shoulders squared to purpose, brow tucked in resolve. Blowing past Krikor and Nika and Granma, he tramped directly to his office.

Krikor looked at Nika. Nika looked at Granma. Granma looked at the radio and said, "Goddamnittohellandbackagain."

59

A Whole Lot Of Nothing

Sliding off of her stool, Nika followed Kaleb to the back room. She passed through the office door in time to see Kaleb flick the .45 Colt's cylinder closed and give the chamber a spin.

Nika stepped inside the room, leaning back against the door, letting her weight softly close the door with a shush. Kaleb looked up from the desk and acknowledged Nika with a nod but he did not smile. Jamming the .45 into his right coat pocket, he reached into the drawer for the .38.

Nika watched quietly as Kaleb checked the chambers of the .38, fully shelled, slapped it closed and spun the cylinder. When he finished the inspection, Kaleb shoved the gun into his left jacket pocket. Only when the coat was fully loaded did Kaleb give full attention to Nika.

"Can I help you?"

Nika nodded to Kaleb's pockets, to his guns. "I thought that you don't play with artillery no more?"

Kaleb said, "It don't concern you."

Nika pushed off from the door and came around the desk. She stepped behind Kaleb and began absently rubbing his shoulders. After a moment she said, "You concern me. So's those gats you're totin' concern me."

Kaleb reached up and stilled her hands. Swiveling the chair, Kaleb spun into Nika, and in the same motion, gently pulled her into his lap. It was the sweetly pungent scent of Nika that broke through Kaleb's resolve. "Look, Neek, circumstances change. I got to evolve with the change."

"Or?"

"Or become extinct."

Nika thought about that before she proceeded. "What circumstances changed?"

"I'm a hunted man."

Nika knew the answer but she asked it anyway. "Hunted by who?"

Kaleb knew that Nika knew the answer and he looked away from her eyes. He began a slow stroke to the scar under his eyebrow.

Nika substituted her fingers for Kaleb's and began to stroke his damaged eyebrow. She spoke softly, gently, "Why'n'cha jes quit this place. You got money. You got talent. Hell, why'n'cha jes light out for New York. Pull together a jazz band out there. What the hell, you know

Jazz du Jour will go along if you ask. Jones at least. Beethoven would runnel along."

"I considered that. But then I'd be leavin' The Temp to a gang of no-goods."

"So what. You're a piano player. You got no business dancin' with no-goods."

There was something in Kaleb that got that. Something that screamed at him to get the hell out of Detroit and don't look back. But there was something else, something deeper. Something in Kaleb that would not run and something in Kaleb that would not cower. Besides all that, the Rubbles just pissed him off.

"It's just comin' up my time to make a stand."

Nika would have none of it. "For what? For honor? For principle? For god damn principle?"

Kaleb wasn't even sure himself. Who the hell was he anyway, that he needed a showdown with these thugs? What the hell was in it for him to draw gats with hoodlums?

There was a deep familiarity, a foreboding bawl, in Kaleb's chest that was bursting to get out. But what? Little by little, Kaleb had uncovered a past of personal violence. A history of guns and gangs and booze and carnage. He was not happy with these discoveries, but he did not recoil from the unveiling either. To the contrary, this past that had been unfolding had felt inherent. Inborn. Violence was instinctive to Kaleb and the greater the threat, the more he relaxed into an innate calm. As the danger swelled, so too did the coolness that settled into Kaleb's breast.

Kaleb did not know from whence these sensations bubbled. He had a whole lot of nothing to grasp onto.

He offered, "The Rubbles think that they can come down here and enforce their dress code on the skin and the blood of the Black Bottom. I say they can't."

Nika challenged him. "What makes it your fight anyway?"

"Beethoven Jones makes it my fight. And Bucky makes it my fight. And Granma and Kitty and Krikor and Hollie make it my fight." And then, quieter, "And you make it my fight."

Nika jumped off his lap and aimed her fists hard down at her sides. "Don't you go pullin' that crap on me, bud. If you're gonna get yourself killed, don't come layin' that shit on me."

Kaleb looked to the floor, sadly, and asked without looking up to her, "What are the Rubble boys to you, Nika?"

60

Kitty's Song

Detective Morane was probably wrong. But he might be right. It would behoove Kaleb Kierka to at least give some entertainment to the idea that his beatdowns were a setup.

And, if the beatings were a setup, this would be a new and vexing rub added to the mix. The first beatdown was designed for maximum damage, to maim severely if not to kill. This second beating though, so much muscle for a singular pop upside the head, was a niggling proposition. One would think that once the goons had Kaleb unconscious, at their mercy and at their boot-heels, they would have delivered the decisive verdict.

Could it be this muscle crew was interrupted mid-hammer by a power greater than themselves? Or could they have been called off? Interrupted? Or maybe they had all found Jesus at the exact same moment. Whatever the cause for the reprieve of this second beatdown, Kaleb was still alive to marvel at the deliverance.

Whatever the purpose and the result of these beatdowns, Kaleb knew well that he lived and breathed in a culture of violence. The meeting with Mizzy Rubble had sealed the deal. No matter his present desire for amity, Kaleb had to resign himself to the fact that people were out to severely damage him.

The first order of business had been to retrieve his guns from The Temp and re-stuff his pockets with the ironed mayhem. If violence were hoisted upon Kaleb, he would be ready for the war.

Kaleb would not have to wait long for the Rubbles to make their statement. There would be no warning shot across the bow. The first shot would be a shot of death.

***

Hollie was emptying trash into the garbage cans behind The Temp in the oncoming dusk of a hot and sticky alleyscape of 1927 Detroit.

He could hear Hastings Street abuzz with vendors shuttering their vegetable stands as shops rolled in the awnings above the storefronts. A time when men would be slipping out of their suit, finger-hooking their jackets over their shoulders as they scurried about in the city maze. Mothers would be bringing their children out of the swelter of the apartments to fill the porches with busyness and noise. Hastings Street was alive with the banter and the sweat of a city in motion. A city charging headlong into tomorrow.

Kaleb walked to The Temp, leaving the T at the curb outside of his apartment.

In the evening's muggy heat, the alley was an odiferous bouquet of garbage, reeking of the frothing filth of putrid meats and gooey garbage. The decaying discards from this thing we call civilization. The night's sweltering heat gave a full measure to the scent of a city's disposable bits and pieces of refuse and rubbish and waste.

While Hollie exited The Temp's back door, a new and disturbing odor reached Kaleb's nose. More stringent than the familiar garbage, the cadaverous stench demanded attention. Following his nose he joined Hollie and they walked to a garbage can set away from the other containers of human waste. Reaching for the lid, Hollie hesitated, recognizing the stench even as he lifted the cover.

It was a dead body all right. A woman. She was naked and she had been stuffed headfirst into the garbage can. Hollie stifled the vomit reflex.

The dead and naked woman was crammed upside down in the garbage can and in the evening's summer heat had begun her decomposition back to the earth from whence she had come. This garbage can served as the coffin to escort this woman's soul to her spirit's next appointment.

The garbage can was Kitty's urn.

***

Black had no words.
Blew blew blue.

KITTY'S SONG

I open my door to another anxious date,
Who'll use my body to masturbate.
But I won't let it show, I'll hold back my tears,
Or else I'll jeopardize the money that he bears,
That he bears.

He wouldn't feel right if I were to cry,
And he'd probably feel sorry but he'd have to lie
About how he's late for an appointment he made,
And then he'd rush off and I wouldn't get paid
For my pain.

And my door bell rang,
My heart start to pain,
'Cause it's only the man,
Come to use me again.

So I'll just hold my feelings inside,
And let him think he took me for a ride,
Because they say it's better to love and to lose,
And besides it pays my gas bills and my dues,
And my dues.

And my door bell rang,
My heart start to pain,
'Cause it's only the man,
Come to use me again.

And if I'm an old woman thinking back on my ways,
I hope I'll understand that I had to get paid,
'Cause someone is the bottom and some is the top,
And it's really not my fault that I deserved what I got,
What I got.

And my door bell rang,
My heart start to pain,
'Cause it's only the man,
Come to use me again.

***

Kitty never made it to that last verse.

***

Black the Cat let Blew blow his peace. He looked out past the glow of the streetlamp to the deep emptiness of the cosmos.

Finally Black flicked his tail once and conjectured, "Maybe death is the ultimate arbiter. The last word. The definitive measurement. And it really doesn't matter if you are 8 years old or 80 years old because once deceased all measurement is tallied. Whatever value your life has accumulated, whatever significance you squeezed out of your time allotment, then that will be the sum of the you.

"Your earned urn.

"The full measure."

***

After the years of comfort and relief that Kitty had bestowed upon her fellow mortals, there were few mourners at the funeral to celebrate the life of Kitty. Kaleb was there. Nika and Tia were there. Granma and Bucky and Hollie were there.

Although he had sent a beautiful bouquet of tulips and roses, Beethoven Jones did not want to get involved.

There was a smattering of folk who might not have known Kitty but attended funerals as a matter of principle. And there was one tall young blonde man, most German looking, sitting alone in the back pew, blue eyes seeing red.

Kaleb had to hire pallbearers to carry Kitty to her final niche in the dirt.

The tall, blue-eyed stranger in a back pew followed the procession to the Elmwood Cemetery.

61

The Mountain Of Black And The Mountain Of White

There had been few mourners at Kitty's funeral and fewer still made the trek out to the Elmwood Cemetery for her final planting. Kaleb, Tia, and Granma were graveside but Bucky had to get back to the bar. Nika was distraught but steeled by the flush of the needle.

It was a community plot in the north-east back corner of the Elmwood Cemetery, near the crossing of Waterloo Street and Mt. Elliott. Kitty would be potted in the same plot of soil that had sopped up little Sammy Cohen's blood so many years before.

They stood graveside as the pine coffin was lowered to the dirt and Kaleb had the honor of tossing the first fistful of dirt into the grave. The splash of dirt onto the pine box gave a soft whispering scuffle like the farewell of so many little hands waving adieu.

A smattering of people was there as Kitty was lowered into her final bed. A tall German-looking man went unnoticed as all due reverence was directed toward Kitty's burial cavity. When Tia moved her eyes from Kitty's final parcel of peace, she caught Edgar's eye and gave a start. Her first inclination was to reach up and adjust her blonde wig. But Tia was not wearing her blonde wig and she came up with a fistful of nappy for her effort.

Quickly Tia's eyes shot to the ground and she tried to make her way out of the cemetery without further eye contact. But Edgar was having none of that and he blocked her path to the gate.

Not looking up at Edgar, Tia said, "Excuse me." and attempted to walk around Edgar. Again Edgar blocked her exit.

Still without looking up, "Mister, if you don't get out of my way I swear I'll scream for help."

"No you won't, Tia. Or Cindy. Or whatever you want to call yourself today." There was no anger in Edgar's voice. Maybe a little sadness. Maybe a little hope. Maybe even a little encouragement. But there was no anger.

Now Tia looked up into Edgar's face, into his eyes. She was embarrassed, ashamed, "I'm sorry. I wanted to tell you so many…"

Edgar put his hands to her shoulders. "It's okay."

"…So many times but then you would kiss me and…."

"It's okay. I knew. I knew. I was okay with it."

Tia was surprised but she did not shake her shoulders free from Edgar's grip. "You knew?" She scoured her brain for any evidence of her giving herself away. "When did you know?"

"Almost from the beginning. I knew at Carolina's Cup O'Joe and I knew on our walks on Belle Isle. I even suspected the night that I met you at the Adams Theater."

Tia was stunned, "B-b-but h-h-how...?"

Edgar smiled at that, but the smile was cautious because he did not want Tia to be embarrassed by the revelation. "I may not be as provincial as my skin tone might suggest." Even so, Tia blushed as Edgar forged ahead. "I was always okay with it. I was just waiting for you to be okay with it."

Tia began to mist and a tear drop, gaining weight before the plunge down her cheek, formed in the corner of her eye. The color, the black and the white, was like a mountain between the couple. But the mountain began its slow erosion as Tia's tears washed down the mountainside.

Edgar reached his arms around Tia and pulled her close into his chest. Holding her head to his breastplate, he kissed her nappy locks once. Twice. And again.

With a finger on her chin, Edgar tipped Tia's head up. Leaning down, he kissed her tears and Tia felt then that the mountain, the mountain of black and white, would wash away in the deluge.

62

On The Brink Of The Graveyard

They had little to say as they crossed the threshold of the Elmwood Cemetery.

Kaleb and Nika left the cemetery hand in hand. Kitty's death ended any pretext of happily-ever-after for the lovers. Kaleb was loaded with cannons and out to hunt bear. Nika was empty of contraband and out to hunt horse.

There were no words.

Nika slipped a piece of paper into Kaleb's hand. There was an address on the paper. Nothing more.

Kaleb studied the paper, not recognizing the address. "Does this mean something to me?"

The little Jewess turned her sad brown eyes up into Kaleb's. "This is the key that you have been missing." With one hand she softly stroked the scar under Kaleb's damaged eyebrow. Kissing Kaleb a soft farewell on his check she quickly spun and left him standing there on the brink of the graveyard.

***

Kaleb watched Nika walk away until she was smaller than a punctuation period at the end of a lover's eulogy.

When he could take the eulogy no more, he looked down at the paper that Nika had slipped into his hand. On it was an address. She said it was the key he had been looking for. What key…?

Then it struck him and he reached into his pocket and pulled out the set of keys that he had been carrying. Four door keys and one car key. The model T was the car key. His apartment, Nika's apartment, and The Temp accounted for three keys.

Kaleb looked at the fourth key and then he looked at the address on the paper.

Nika was long out of sight by now, but even so, Kaleb gave one more desolate look across the threshold of the necropolis.

63

We Have Met The Enemy And He Be We. Too Much Too Much. Too Much Much.

Kaleb busted through the door with both guns drawn. The hatchet-faced man did not have time to draw his guns or to stand up. Instead, he sat, relaxed, on a hard-back chair flipped around, legs splayed over the sides, with his arms casually draped over the chair back and a welcoming smile. A welcoming smile?

"'Bout time."

Kaleb had been waiting outside the door in the hallway for long moments with his ear pressed hard against the apartment door. No words had been spoken inside the apartment, but feet had been shuffled and a chair was heard scraping the floor. Somebody was in there all right and most probably alone.

Something was wrong here. Kaleb had the drop on the man, both guns to his fists, and the man, casual-like, like he had been waiting for Kaleb, sat relaxed and genial.

Before Kaleb lowered the guns he did a quick scan of the room. It was a studio apartment and Kaleb had full scope of the room's corners. The sole potential hideout in the room, the corner closet, had its door flung open and it was empty.

Like the empty closet, the room was bereft of any sign of habitation. No pots in the kitchen, no clothes in the closet, no dresser, no table, no sign of a life lived within these walls. There were two hard-back kitchen chairs, one of which was occupied by the hatchet-faced man. The man's casual and welcoming smile was disconcerting.

Lowering the guns, Kaleb was trying to get his bearing. "'Bout time? What's 'bout time?"

With one foot the hatchet-faced man pushed the second chair at Kaleb, "Tuck in your gats and we'll talk a spell.

The man's voice was a good match for his face. A sharp, hard, voice that cut vowels like a sharp knife through hide.

Wary, Kaleb waved the guns in the man's direction. "Stand up for a dustin'."

The shape of the man's face, thin and drawn forward, gave his slow smile an incongruent and unnatural turn. He stood up and held his arms out, crucifix style. "Go 'head, Kabe, I've got one gun holstered in my left pit and another tucked in my belt at the small of my back, and if I wanted to burn powder I would have had you when you busted down the door."

This made sense. "Even so."

Kaleb slipped his own .38 into his pocket and dusted the man with his left hand, keeping the .45 to the ready. When he was satisfied he set the man's guns in the closet and closed the closet door. Pulling up the second chair to face the man Kaleb sat down. He lowered the .45 but kept it ready on his lap.

The man's body echoed his hatchet face. He was drawn and tight with a long axe handle for a body that looked like it could hack a cord of lumber without breaking a sweat. Splayed around the chair-back, he pulled his careworn face into another uncomfortable smile.

Kaleb was direct. "Now who the hell are you and what are you to me?"

"To the point then?" Though hard and taut, the man had an easiness about him.

"Yes. Get to the point."

Again the drawn smile. "My name is Gillian Comesky. *Captain* Gillian Comesky. But you've always called me Gil." He let that idea settle into Kaleb's face before continuing. "I'm a cop with The Bureau of Prohibition." Indicating his breast pocket, Comesky said, "May I?"

Kaleb nodded an affirmation and Comesky reached into his breast pocket, pulled two billfolds from his jacket, and tossed one of them to Kaleb.

Kaleb caught the wallet with his left hand, flipped it open, read the license and studied the badge. "You're the Feds?"

"Yep."

Something familiar, something known. The memory banks were beginning to flutter deep in Kaleb's cerebellum, the fog was thinning. "Okay, Gil, I'll bite, how do I know you?"

The smile was withdrawn. "You know me because I'm your boss, Kaleb. You work for me. You are *Detective* Kaleb Kierka: Special Unit, Drug Enforcement," and with that Comesky tossed the second billfold to Kaleb. When Kaleb reached to catch the second billfold the .45 fell from his lap to the floor with a metallic thud. When the gun hit the floor both men looked at it. Neither man bothered to retrieve it.

Kaleb flipped open the second wallet to reveal a federal badge with an ID. Kaleb Kierka's name and picture were imprinted on it.

Recall slammed Kaleb with the ping of a sledge to the anvil. Too much information flashing across too many synaptic gaps. Blazing sparks of recall and recognition and recollect of the whos and the whys and the wherefores.

Too much memory flushing in too abruptly sent Kaleb's body shuddering to the remembrance. Spasming in memory, Kaleb quaked to the recall, wilting to a lifeless comatose as his bones melted from the chair to the hard floor.

Too much too much. Too much much.

64

Whereas

Captain Gil had helped Kaleb back into the chair in the empty studio apartment as memory continued to flush in like a bursting levee in a spring flood. Slumped forward in the hard-back chair, face in hands, Kaleb let the waters flow. As wave after wave of the memories came on, he was swamped with a boatload of yesterdays.

"I am the owner of a speakeasy *and* an agent for the Feds?"

"Yes."

"That reads like sham tabloid copy."

"I hope so. That's what made it such a good cover."

What Kaleb could not retrieve, Captain Gil was able to fill in the gaps.

"Outside my apartment, at The Temp, out at Rubble's Bubble, you were watching me because?" Kaleb still had his face in his hands. The flood had not subsided.

"Yes. I was watching you. I was trying to ascertain your memory and your safety. You were my recruit for the Bureau and I wanted to be there if your memory returned. You weren't playin' with a full deck and you didn't even know the wild card."

"That time I saw you when I was ambushed in the Erskine Street alley, you were there. I saw you comin' on to join the fray."

"Yep, I joined the fray all right. Late."

It was beginning to come together for Kaleb. "I remember you running full tilt from behind the gangsters. Then the lights went out."

"Yep, I was to the battle. Too late to save another pop to your skull, unfortunately."

More to himself then to Comesky, Kaleb said, "…That explains why I wasn't beaten to death. It stumped me why the brunos didn't finish the job once they had me down."

"I got the brunos all tied up in the hoosegow if you'd like to bring 'em cupcakes."

***

Kaleb read and reread the badge and the Bureau ID. "This is what you were looking for when you tossed my apartment and office? Why didn't you rustle up my apartment when I was 5 weeks down?"

"I didn't know it was missing at first. I assumed that the hospital had your ID. Then I just got too busy rousing the Rubbles, trying to keep them off of The Temp."

"You roused the Rubbles?"

"Mhhm. Kept 'em busy with raids. Damn thing is, I couldn't catch 'em with anything to stick."

"When did you realize that my Fed ID was missing?"

"When you didn't contact us or... somebody. No mention to Detective Morane who would have contacted us right away. Big mystery. It wouldn't have been healthy for you if that badge had fallen into the wrong hands before you got your memory back. You picked one hell of a place to hide it."

Kaleb tucked the billfold into the inside breast pocket of his jacket. "Where'd you find it?"

Comesky took his time. "I had to do some god-awful backtracking, and some of my best detective work, to find that damn badge."

After a moment, Kaleb asked, "And...?"

"You hid that badge where you hid your history. You hid that badge at the place that Kaleb Kierka turned his back to the life of the street tough. You can't remember?"

"Where the hell did you find the badge?"

Comesky fit in the final piece. "That badge was left in the Elmwood Cemetery. In the Elmwood Cemetery on the little rise of a hill toward the back of the graveyard, just over the fence from Mount Elliott Avenue. Planted up there like a tombstone, like a memorial to something. Maybe you can tell me."

As recall caught, Kaleb's face shadowed gray to the memory. "I remember now. Little Sammy Cohen. The blood. The mud. I remember little Sammy Cohen's graying face as the life slipped out of his body. I remember." He had heard the story from the Purples but only now did the weight of the emotion hit him.

Kaleb's face drew mask-like in the wretchedness of the memory of little Sammy Cohen hanging on Kenny Still's butcher knife. A whispering whimpering began in Kaleb's throat, but too quickly the whimper sunk into a deep and cavernous sob into the chest of the man.

Comesky reached over and rested a hand on Kaleb's knee, but he said nothing as he allowed Kaleb the full breadth of his grief.

When the sobbing subsided, when the sorrow had been spent, Kaleb asked, "My badge was buried on the hill at the Elmwood Cemetery?"

"Not buried, Kaleb. The billfold was folded back on itself and propped up on the rise that, I suspect, was the exact plot that he had bled out; where little Sammy Cohen had drawn his last breath on this earth."

Again Captain Gillian Comesky shared the drawn unnatural smile, but this time the smile was repainted in the shades of Picasso's Blue Period. "The badge was propped up like a tombstone on the dirt where little Sammy Cohen died."

***

Little Sammy Cohen's death had impacted each attending member to his demise in their own way.

The Bernstein brothers and the Keywell brothers and the Fleisher brothers united forces into the Purple Gang after the death of little Sammy Cohen, the Purples had became the force to be reckoned with in the gang wars of prohibitioned Detroit.

The death of little Sammy Cohen on the knife of Kenny Still turned Beethoven Jones inward, into himself, with only his personal moral fiber to answer to. Forever more would Jones not get involved.

It was the death of Sammy Cohen in the Elmwood Cemetery that turned the course of Kaleb's life. That same knife-thrust that opened Sammy's gut cut Kaleb from the street gangs. Cleaved from his boyhood pals, the Purples.

Kaleb spun full circle to the battle against the drugs that surged in Kenny Still's veins. The drug that drew the sieve into Kenny Still's fist and the drug that thrust the butcher blade into Sammy Cohen's chest.

Kaleb, sickened by the death, spun opposite and turned instead to the fight against the drug that enabled Kenny Still's action. Kaleb turned to the enforcement of the law.

***

Black said to Blew:

"Maybe that's the final and cumulative sum of a man's measurement; a measurement that can only be tallied by the individual. A measurement of one's own fortitude, of one's own weight.

"And character can never be measured from the perspective of looking out but, rather, of only by looking within."

Black snapped his tail to the beat as Blew blew blue:

Are your senses suddenly reeling?
Do your feet feel anchored in clay?
Are you finally left with the feeling,
There's nothing left to do but walk away.

***

When Kaleb first approached the Bureau of Prohibition he was seen as a piece that could best serve clandestinely, a covert piece to the puzzle of law enforcement.

As Kaleb's underground connections were deep, he was deemed most valuable as an underground agent, so on the outside, he would continue his path as a piano player in the underground speakeasies, eventually even owning a speakeasy.

Kaleb, sickened by Sammy's death, spun opposite from the Bernsteins and the Fleishers and the Keywells and turned instead to the law enforcement. And with Kaleb as one of their own in the game of illegal commerce, the Bureau could keep a keen eye on the sieve of alcohol that was the Detroit River.

Kaleb had laid down two prerequisites when he agreed to the arrangement with the Bureau. The first condition that he would not be a part of any clandestine operation concerning the Purple Gang. Although he had taken a different path, these were his childhood chums and he would draw no quarter against them.

Kaleb's second condition was that he would focus his energies on drugs, more specifically heroin. It was the narcotic heroin that had jerked the knife into Kenny Still's hand, and it had been heroin that drove the blade into Sammy Cohen's chest.

For Kaleb, heroin was the enemy and heroin was the battle that he would engage.

65

Kaleb Remembers

"You came to us, Kaleb."

"I remember."

Kaleb did remember. He remembered it all. He was just a boy but he remembered it all.

Kaleb remembered seeing Zuggy Murk, the piano player, overdose on bad heroin and Kelly Bandon the 'bone player overdose on good heroin. He remembered backstage at the Adams Theater where the needle was handed off from arm to arm, and he was onstage with Boots Bedough when he tumbled dead over his drums from an opiate soaking.

Kaleb remembered it all.

These memories of heroin and opium were witnessed by the teenage musical phenomena Kaleb Kierka and Beethoven Jones, The Jew Boy and The Colored Boy, as they toured Kunsky's Circle.

Each boy bore witness to the carnage of the drug, of the heroin. Beethoven Jones hid in the refuge of his bass, never again to get involved. Kaleb wanted to kick heroin's ass.

But mostly it was the death of little Sammy Cohen on the small lump of a hill on a back plot of the Elmwood Cemetery that had left the deepest scars in Kaleb's psyche.

Kaleb remembered it all. He remembered The Temple Bar Speakeasy And Play Nice, and he remembered the Purple Gang; and he remembered the Model T's spinning tires in muddy ruts and shots of schnapps with Kitty; and he remembered waking from a post-sexual slumber with Nika in his arms and a needle in Nika's arm. The flood of memories, good and bad, gushed to Kaleb on a torrent of recall.

Kaleb remembered the beatdown as well, the beatdown that had left him brain-crippled and in the hospital for five weeks. It was the Rubbles all right. It was Jimmy-Jimbo and Fat Tony and a couple of their button men.

Mizzy Rubble wanted The Temple Bar Speakeasy And Play Nice as a channel for the heroin that she and her boys were pushing. A heroin highway to Paradise Valley and the Black Bottom. And Kaleb Kierka was standing in her way.

It took all four of them, the Rubble thugs, with two saps and two baseball bats. They didn't just want to rub out Kaleb; they wanted Kaleb's death to be a lesson and a warning. Mizzy Rubble would use the ugly death of Kaleb as an advertisement of her dominion over the Black Bottom.

But Kaleb didn't die.

***

"Do the Purples know?"

Comesky shrugged his shoulders. "I 'spect they know. You let them be, they let you be. I 'spect you boys understand each other better'n anybody has a right to. The Purples 'n you share the moment that sent you boys spinnin' in different directions. But you shared the same moment. The same measure."

Kaleb nodded his head and thought this over. There was nothing to say to that, and Kaleb let it lay there like a warm wool blanket on a cold afterthought.

***

"And how about me? Do you remember me, now, Kabe?"

Kaleb gave a slow study to the Fed's mug. "Yes. I remember you now. Did anyone ever tell you that you have a hatchet face?"

The hatchet face furrowed into unfamiliar smile lines on Captain Gillian Comesky mug. "Only you, Kaleb. Only you."

***

"Why haven't you taken out the Rubbles?"

Somberly, Comesky shook his head and answered, "Wish we could. We know their game but that Mizzy, that Mizzy she's good with the veil. Can't bust down the door without a warrant and every time we get a warrant, her place is clean of junk."

"What about records? She's got to have records of her junk coming and going."

"Her commerce records would be better'n the dope itself. But the place is clean whenever we been there. I'm pretty sure that Mizzy's got it all, dope 'n records 'n all, buried somewhere back in that cornfield behind Rubble's Bubble, but I'll be damned if we've got the manpower to tear up that acreage."

Comesky let that seep in before he continued. "Place is always spic-'n-span when we serve the warrants."

Kaleb thought about this for a moment. "Think Mizzy has an inside ear in The Bureau?"

"I'm certain of it. But until we snare the inside ear, I'm afraid that we ain't gonna catch Mizzy with much of anything."

***

This had been a lot for Kaleb to digest, but there was one more pressing point that he needed cleared up.

"Do you know who has been setting me up?"

Comesky looked away. "Yes."

"So tell me."

Comesky's hatchet face looked like it wanted to be anywhere else. "You're not going to like it."

"So tell me."

Comesky took a deep breath like he was pumping up the cylinder of a shotgun. "It ain't pretty."

"It's never pretty. So tell me."

"It was Nika Nightingale."

Kierka began to laugh in disbelief, but seeing that Comesky was serious, he stifled it.

"Nika?" This was a kick to the gut. First Kaleb was stunned and then he was angry. "Nika. Nika? You're lyin'."

"I'm not lyin', Kaleb."

Kaleb's eyes glazed momentarily and seemed to focus on an object on the other side of room, on the other side of the world. Softly, "Nika? But why do you suspect Nika?"

"Sorry, Kabe. Not a suspicion."

Kaleb's body shuddered at the thought. "But...but, how? When? Why?"

"The how is easy. Nika always had a direct line to Rubble's Bubble through the junk in her veins. The when? The when is a little more ambiguous. My guess is when you took the conk that waylaid you comatose, Nika became part of the Rubbles' furniture. The how is easy because the Rubbles had a first class ticket through Nika's arm."

Yet stunned, Kaleb could only manage, "Rubbles' furniture?"

Comesky did not pull the punch. "Sure, the furniture. Or maybe the bedspread."

Kaleb: "So she's been hookin' at Rubble's Bubble?"

Comesky: "At, for, to, with. It ain't a pretty picture. There's always a surcharge on drugs."

Kaleb let this sink in while Federal Agent Comesky worked up a cigarette. Sucking a deep draw on the nicotine stick, he blew a cloud of smoke and added nothing more.

The slightest of shudder belied Kaleb's thoughts. Collecting himself, he asked, "That's the how. And the why is?"

"The why is a little more complicated. Nika Nightingale has been turning tricks for Jimmy-Jimbo Rubble and the Rubbles have been keeping Nika's veins streaming heroin. The Rubbles either juiced her to the point that she did not know what she was doing or..."

"Or?"

"Or she gave you up as a trade for the junk." Comesky's hatchet voice sliced a deep gash in Kaleb's psyche. The thought of Nika trading Kaleb for the drugs infected the gash.

Kaleb was stunned. "But you don't know that as fact."

Comesky's face sharpened to the task. "Took me a while to figure it out. That's why I had to keep my distance from you. If you'd have found out that I was a Fed but you didn't remember that we were working together, you might have given up my veil. Here's the rub, Kaleb, you were just way too clever a man to keep walking into ambushes on a regular bases. Clever and careful. So I knew that someone close to you must be giving you up. But your circle was wide. Musicians, bar patrons, Bucky, Kitty, the Purples, and, of course, you made a lot of enemies with your stubbornness."

"But Nika?"

"I know, Kaleb. It was hard for me to measure that as well. Does she love you? No doubt. But the junk is a more demanding lover."

Kaleb didn't say anything so Comesky continued. "Heroin is like that. When you are juicing junk, junk is all that matters. The juice becomes your lover and your partner. Your world. You live for the rush and you die for the rush. When the veins are full you exist to plod comatose through your existence. But when the veins go dry..."

"...When the veins go dry?"

"...When the veins go dry you will sell your soul to soak them again. At first Nika just swapped tricks with Jimmy-Jimbo to get the junk. After a time, after he had soaked her up with the juice, it was an easy matter to get her to give you up."

Comesky sucked on his cigarette and blew smoke at the ceiling. When he continued it was with a sour taste in his mouth. "One way or another she was giving you up. Whether she gave you up in the fog of full veins or the torture of empty veins I do not know. But she gave you up."

Slowly it sank in like a slow slap across the face. "She gave me up?"

"She gave you up."

With a slight shake of his head Kaleb cleared his eyes. "Where is she now?"

Comesky hesitated and then he said, "It's not her fault."

"Where is she now?"

"It's not her…"

"Do you take me for a fool? I know it's not her fault. It's the drug's fault. But beyond the drug's fault, it's Jimmy-Jimbo's fault and it's Mizzy Rubble's fault, and I will deal with them in due course. But first I need to get Nika out of the way. Out of the game." Unconsciously, Kaleb punched his right fist into his left palm. "Then I'll deal with the Rubbles and I'll be dealing with a loaded deck."

Comesky was hesitant. "Maybe you let this cool for…"

The wrath in Kaleb's eyes shut down Comesky's maybes.

Comesky wavered. Then he said, "Last I knew, she's out at Rubble's Bubble."

Kaleb spun on his heels and headed for the door. "Where you going now, Kabe?"

Over his shoulder Kaleb snapped, "I'm going after Jimmy-Jimbo."

Urgently Comesky said, "You can't take him out, Kaleb; you're a federal officer. You can arrest him but you can't kill him."

This froze Kaleb and he turned back into the room to face Comesky. Taking the billfold with his ID and badge out of his pocket, Kaleb flipped it to Comesky. "Consider this my resignation."

Comesky snatched Kaleb's badge out of the air and they stood there with a whole lot of nothing to say. After a moment of a deafening nothing, Kaleb turned and slipped out the door.

66

Our Little Secret

Dusk was settling on the metropolis of Detroit when Kaleb arrived at The Temp.

Bucky was mucking around behind the bar, and Krikor had just finished his violin lesson with little Joe Louis Barrow. Joe Louis, dressed clean and spiffy in his tattered Sunday best, was packing up his violin. Krikor was swapping button bass riffs on his accordion with Beethoven Jones.

Kaleb made a beeline to the stage and said to Jones, "We got to talk." Then, to Krikor he said, "Give us some space."

Krikor looked up at Kaleb and put on a grin. "Hey Kabe, me 'n-a Jones worked out-a-de riff on-a Hoagy's Stardust. De-a beginnin' is-a…."

"Not now, Kreek, drift." He then called out to Bucky, "Hey Buck, give Kreek a couple Vernors. Paint it on my bill." Returning to Krikor he repeated, "Drift, Kreek."

Krikor looked from Kaleb to Beethoven Jones and back to Kaleb. Acquiescently, he squeezed the billows into the accordion case while Joe Louis slipped out of the bar doors, his mother waiting for him at the curb.

Beethoven Jones turned into the bass and began to draw a slow bow across the catguts.

Kaleb dug out his tobacco satchel and worked up a smoke, watching Jones slowly pull through a somber dirge. Keeping his eyes tight on Jones's face as he flamed the cigarette, he sucked hard and deep, flaring his lungs with the burn.

Exhaling a blue and smoky affront, he said, "You knew, didn't you?"

Jones stopped the bow in mid pull and, from under his brow, looked into Kaleb's face. When he got what he needed out of Kaleb's mien, Jones sat up from the bass. "That you were Fed?"

To discover this himself was one thing but to hear it actually voiced from the outside was like a slap in the face. It took Kaleb a moment to understand the slap.

"You knew I was a Fed and you didn't tell me?"

Jones turned back into the bass but Kaleb pressed the point. "You knew I was Fed and you didn't tell me?"

This time Jones turned his full attention to Kaleb, looking him directly in the eye. "I don't get involved, man, I don't get involved."

"How long have you known?"

"From the jump."

"You knew I was wearing tin from day one?"

"Day one."

"How?"

At this Jones looked Kaleb directly in the eye. "Man, Kaleb, me 'n you, we ain't never had no secrets. You do your thing, man, I do mine." He patted the bass strings with his long digits. "...But we ain't never had no secrets."

Kaleb considered this, pitching his cigarette to the floor and twisting his toe into the butt with more vigor than the butt deserved. "Who else knew?"

"Just me, far's I know. You might have told someone else but I'm kinda doubtin' it." And then Jones added, "She's a surrogate for Sammy, ya know?'

Kaleb was caught off guard. "Now what the hell are you talking about?"

"Nika's a proxy, a stand in, for little Sammy Cohen. She's jes an understudy for the role of Sammy. A surrogate fatality for what you couldn't do for Sammy."

Kaleb was trying to fit this piece in. "Nika an understudy for Sammy?"

"Sure, man. You couldn't save Sammy from dyin' in your arms. That's the guilt you wear. Now you got Nika in your arms. Savin' Nika seems to be a good fit for your savior complex."

Kaleb was chagrined. "My savior complex? You a psychoanalyst now, Jones? Your bass is a couch, now?"

Jones slackened and shrugged his shoulders but his eyes never left Kaleb's eyes.

"Fuck you," said Kaleb. Sometimes the truth is like a steamroller on hot asphalt. On the hot ass fault.

Jones shrugged his shoulders again. "I'm jes sayin'."

"Fuck you."

Moments passed. Jones was a somber cool, while Kaleb tried to tally this new equation.

In the end Kaleb pulled the piece of paper that Nika had given him at the cemetery. The paper with the address of where he had found Federal Agent Comesky. Holding it up to Jones, he asked, "Know anything about this?"

Jones took the paper and studied the address. "Pretty deep in the Black Bottom. But can't say I know the crib. What's it to you."

"Nika gave it to me. She called it the key. And it was the key. She knew."

A soft sigh of a whistle escaped Beethoven Jones lips. "Whew, brother. So Nika knew, then. That's some heavy shit."

Kaleb was turning over stones and he wasn't thrilled with the understory. But he had to figure this man named Kaleb Kierka out. "I ever tell you why I became an underground Fed?"

"Yes."

After a moment, "And...?"

"Part ways that boy dyin'."

"Sammy Cohen."

"Thet's the boy. Him dyin' in that graveyard rumble when we was jes kids. You didn't want no part of the Bernstein and the Fleisher scrap. Neither of us coulda cared less for who the top dog on the street was. You was always a wise egg and I jes followed 'long, I guess. You didn't need no gang crutch to keep you upright and movin' forward. You jes happened upon the tribe and got recruited to the battle. You were my bud and I went along for the ride. When that little Sammy Cohen got gut-stuck something clicked in your dome. Messed wit' yer head. Changed yer perspective."

Jones looked into Kaleb's eyes and saw a storm brewing. He continued, "Messed wit' my head too, I guess. I went into my bass and didn't come out. I don't get involved no mo' nohow. But you, you wanted to right the world. You wanted to kick that heroin's ass. Found yourself on the right side of the law, wearin' tin."

This was familiar terrain to Kaleb but he let Jones talk. "I guess when you couldn't save the Cohen kid you just started looking for another war on drugs. Becomin' Fed was the first ways."

"And my second war on drugs?

Jones shook his head. "Now we's back to Nika. Nika, man, Nika. You went hell bent on saving Nika. If you couldn't pull the shiv out of Sammy's belly, you were gonna pull the needle out of Nika's arm."

Synaptic gaps were charging in Kaleb's memory as Jones continued. "That boy with the knife, that Still boy, Kenny, he was juiced on the heroin and primed for the kill, and you took on heroin as a personal nemesis. Almost like heroin had a body and soul and you wanted to see that body in a grave and that soul in hell."

Eyes focused elsewhere Kaleb murmured to himself, "I remember the rumble."

"Sure you remember the rumble. It changed your whole life. The Purples never tried to recruit you because of that rumble, and they gave you a wide berth because of that rumble. Baseball became nothing to you and even the piano became a secondary passion. You hated heroin like a mouse hates a cat."

"So I became a rat?"

Beethoven Jones cringed at the word. "I never thought of you as a rat, man. I understood what that Cohen boy dyin' in your arms done to you. Can't 'magine what it'd do to me but I warn't surprised at what it done to you. And you might cut yourself some slack, boy. Loosen up on that self-floggin' shit. Draw up a new sketch."

But Kaleb did not have the opportunity to cut himself slack or to draw up a new sketch as the back door of The Temp exploded with a fury of noise and battle.

***

Fat Tony and a posse of a couple of hired goons blasted through the door, gangbuster fashion, hammering Bucky across the forehead with a pistol before he had a chance to set himself. Kaleb met the three men in the middle of the dance floor, but the men, with fists full of artillery, had the drop on Kaleb.

Fat Tony offered his celebrated rotten teeth in a sour smile. "Drop your hardware." He waved his gun at Kaleb's bulging coat pockets.

Kaleb eased the rods out of his pockets and let them fall with a dull thud to the floor. This gave Fat Tony another opportunity to share his rotten-toothy smile.

"Your time's up, meat. No more negotiatin'. You will now sign off title of The Temp over to ma. Write it out to Mizzy Rubble."

In an unexpected move, Kaleb advanced on Fat Tony with his hand outstretched in a gesture to indicate that he wanted to shake Fat Tony's hand. Confused, the three gangsters let Kaleb come on, but as he reached Fat Tony, Kaleb grabbed Fat Tony's fisted gun hand and jammed his hand, gun and all, back up and into Fat Tony's face. Fat Tony's face exploded, splashing blood and teeth.

As Fat Tony went down to the floor, Kaleb braced himself for the inevitable surge of the other two gangsters, either by sap or by bullet.

Ducking and sliding sideways, Kaleb hoped to defray the wrath of the bruiser's retribution.

But wrath never came.

When Kaleb turned to meet the posse, the boys were suspended, feet dangling, against the speakeasy's wall. They were held high in place in the grasp of Beethoven Jones's big, hard fists. Jones had grabbed the men by their throats, digging muscular fingers deep into each mans larynx, and held them suspended high against the wall.

Wrapped around the double bass, Jones's true length was hidden, but as he unfolded and stretched his frame, pinning the thugs to the wall, the full complement of Beethoven Jones could be appreciated. Just shy of seven feet tall and with his arms extended, he had elevated the men and plastered them 10 feet up the wall. His black hands were digging deep vice grips into the white of the gangsters' throats.

With that threat removed, Kaleb turned once again to Fat Tony who was still sitting on the floor using both of his hands to hold together his busted-up face.

Reaching down, Kaleb pulled the fat man to his feet by his coat collar, and cuffing his ears as he pushed Fat Tony against the bar, Kaleb demanded, "Where's Nika?"

Fat Tony managed a gory smile with a gooey mixture of blood and saliva dribbling from his rotting teeth. "Jimmy-Jimbo own 'dat pussy now."

Kaleb did not measure the blow, but it hit the back of Fat Tony's skull, passing through Fat Tony's face.

When Fat Tony crumbled to the floor, Kaleb turned to Beethoven Jones. "I need to get out to Rubble's Bubble."

Pinning the goons high to wall, Beethoven Jones repeated, "You need to get out to Rubble's Bubble."

Kaleb nodded at the dangling goons. "You got those boys covered?"

Jones turned to his quarry, beaming and replied, "Oh yes I do. Me 'n da boys, well, I got some dirge arrangements I'd like to run over wit' 'em." He turned to Kaleb and said, "You best git 'long now. Nika needs you."

Grabbing his hat, Kaleb made the door in two strides. As he reached the door he stopped short and turned back to Beethoven Jones and said, "I thought you didn't get involved?"

The toothy white grin was exaggerated by the blackness of Jones's face. "Dis'll be our little secret."

Kaleb smiled, nodded, and he turned to the door.

67

Double Trouble At Rubble's Bubble

Desperation can make a man run. Running to, running from. From, to. Desperation is in the subject matter, not in the direction.

Desperation can make a man run *from* other men. Or from women. Or from the law or from jobs or from themselves.

Still other men are running desperately *to*. To salvation, to shelter, to sanctuary.

But when the shoes are slapping the pavement, desperation does not know betwixt the *from* from the *to*.

It's all a measure of matter. It's all a matter of measure.

***

Kaleb lead-footed the T up Grand River Avenue and was spitting gravel north along Livernois before he remembered that his guns were left on the floor of the bar. He had let them clatter to the floor when Fat Tony got the drop on him. And he hadn't picked them up. He was too distracted by the sight of Beethoven Jones plastering two goons by their throats high up against The Temp's wall.

Without the hardware, Kaleb would need some element of surprise at the Rubble's place.

Realizing that the clouds of dirt and dust that were billowing behind the T would announce his approach, Kaleb turned into a hedgerow tractor lane along a cornfield just south of Rubble's Bubble. He guided the T into a row of trees that outlined the cultivated fields.

The cornstalks were mid-summer tall, not quite to Kaleb's shoulders, and he had to slump hunchback into the rows as he hoofed the final quarter of a mile to the farmhouse. The cornstalks slapped at his face as he clandestinely approached the farmhouse.

The trek through the cornfield took Kaleb to within twenty-five feet of the rear of the old farmhouse. Resting on his haunches, with his butt on his heels, Kaleb rolled a cigarette, flamed it, and appraised the house, a two-story turn-of-the-century structure that had been retrofitted with plumbing. The water pipes and sewage drains clung to the outside walls like leafless vines. On the north side, the rear of the building was a staircase reaching to a small porch on the second floor that had a door. Although the first-floor windows were boarded over, the top-floor windows were glassed and gave a panoramic vision encircling the farmstead, offering an overview from above. The proximity of the cornfield to the building gave Kaleb good cover to within twenty-five feet but from that point forward he would need stealth and a good dash.

The heroin crowd that Rubble's Bubble catered to would be too lethargic, too slothful, to be of any real concern. Kaleb reasoned that with Fat Tony knocked loopy and Beethoven Jones pinning the two bruisers high to the wall of The Temp, there would only be Mizzy Rubble and Jimmy-Jimbo to deal with inside.

Someone would need to be manning the bar and the needle room. That would be Jimmy-Jimbo. With luck, Mizzy would be engaged in the books or tending the till, or maybe, just distracted with plugging her fat cigar into her face. With luck.

Setting his sights on the second-story staircase, Kaleb hoped to take Mizzy Rubble off guard.

The sprint from the cornfield to the house did not raise any alarms, and Kaleb pressed his body against the house to reassess the stalk.

The side stairs to the second floor of Rubble's Bubble were old, ancient old, and the weathering they had sustained left them decayed and squishy. Rubble's Bubble fronted Livernois Road from the east side leaving these side steps on the north side in the shade of the building, and the rotting wood was beginning to sprout mushrooms. Climbing the steps, Kaleb was grateful that the sponginess of the wood offered a quiet approach, but the fortitude of each step was suspect and the going was slow.

Gaining the top landing, Kaleb tried the door. It was unlatched. But even as he pushed gently through the door into the dark hallway of the second floor, he realized that this had been too easy. Too simple. When the sap fell across the back of his skull he was not as much surprised as he was disappointed in himself. But that disappointment was momentary as the blackness of unconsciousness reached out with shadowy arms, coaxing him to oblivion.

***

Even as Kaleb realized his blunder and the sap was falling across his skull, he ducked quickly enough so that the sap grazed his shoulder before hammering his cranium; the blow's impact was mitigated ever so slightly. Not slightly enough to save a good thumping but at least enough to save his life.

Straining against the ghost of the Id, of the unconscious self, Kaleb fought to keep the comatose at bay. He knew that if he surrendered to the blackness all hope would be lost. In the half stupor of the blow, he felt himself being dragged from the corridor and down the inside staircase of the farmhouse. Little care was given as his body was thump-thumped down the stairs and tumbled down a hallway before finally being dumped rashly into a dimly lit room.

The smells that greeted Kaleb in the room bespoke of opium and heroin and blood and vomit. With his face flat to the floor, the reek of the room filled his nostrils with the putrid stench of lives in waste. The only redeeming virtue was that the odor acted as a sort of smelling salt, bracing Kaleb against the wheedle of the blackness.

This would be the shooting den at the end of the bar, and through half-closed eyelids, Kaleb stole a peek at the surroundings. He had been dumped on the floor near a small bar. A dispensary, of sorts, for the distribution of the narcotics. Above the bar hung a collection of needles and rubber tie-offs while glass tubes and pestles and a Bunsen burner were sitting on the top of the bar; this was paraphernalia for the whisking of potions.

Someone was moving behind the bar; it was Jimmy-Jimbo, busily concocting concoctions.

They were alone in the room, Kaleb and Jimmy-Jimbo, and when Jimmy-Jimbo finished his labor behind the bar, he returned to Kaleb. Dragging him up to the bar, he dumped Kaleb, sack-like, onto a chair. Kaleb, feigning unconsciousness, let himself be manhandled. Jimmy-Jimbo was almost twice Kaleb's weight, and when Kaleb made his move, he would need the benefit of surprise.

Inwardly taking stock of his body Kaleb tried to estimate the firepower in his muscles without alerting Jimmy-Jimbo. He found his head was clearing rapidly, but his shoulder that was stung by the brunt of the sap was sore and resisted reflex. When Kaleb made his play, he would be going into battle without a full battalion.

Through pinched eyes Kaleb could see Jimmy-Jimbo filling a spike with the poisoned inoculation and then testing the needle for service. The needle squirted a splash of the solution into the air, testifying to its serviceability.

Returning to Kaleb, Jimmy-Jimbo smiled ugly at Kaleb. He was enjoying the moment. "Well, nighty night, kike. Can't say it's been a pleasure. Have a safe trip to whatever god-shit you Jew-boys call the Lord." He gripped and lifted Kaleb's limp left arm for the inoculation.

As Jimmy-Jimbo brought the needle to Kaleb's arm, Kaleb fought through the lethargy of semi-consciousness, and twisting suddenly, he grabbed Jimmy-Jimbo's wrist and guided the needle past his own arm and into Jimmy-Jimbo. The needle drilled into Jimmy-Jimbo's thigh. Thumbing the needle's pump, Kaleb punched a full discharge of the inoculation into the big man's leg.

Shock first, then comprehension flashed across Jimmy-Jimbo's face. "Why you son-of-a-bitch," he screamed, took a full round house swing at Kaleb's face. But Kaleb had already planted his feet on the floor and, pushing off, was tumbling away from the blow. When Jimmy-Jimbo's fist caught Kaleb, it caught him on the backside and pushed Kaleb further away, sprawling Kaleb across the room. As Kaleb toppled to the floor, Jimmy-Jimbo kicked the chair out of the way and went after Kaleb. Still groggy, Kaleb knew that he would have to buy time until the elixir's effect arrested Jimmy-Jimbo's attack.

As Jimmy-Jimbo threw punches and kicks at him, Kaleb continued to roll about the room, managing to stay just out of the reach of the full freight of the pummeling.

The needle had dug deep into Jimmy-Jimbo's thigh and the circulation of the potion soon slowed Jimmy-Jimbo's advance, tempering his blows.

When Jimmy-Jimbo genuflected to one knee in submission to the drug, Kaleb pushed himself from the floor and stood over the big man as Jimmy-Jimbo continued to slowly succumb to the inoculation.

Jimmy-Jimbo was now at Kaleb's mercy and within the easy cuff of Kaleb's fists.

But Kaleb did not want his pound of flesh. He scrutinized Jimmy-Jimbo's eyes as they clouded under the drug's advance. Kaleb bore witness to Jimmy-Jimbo's last flicker of clarity to a life that was nigh spent. And it was a fear, even horror, that plastered Jimmy-Jimbo's face in his last moments of lucidity, of life. Jimmy-Jimbo was not very keen on meeting whatever maker might lie on the other side.

Just another life measured in increments of feet. Six feet. Down.

It was not Kaleb's desire to beat down Jimmy-Jimbo nor to watch Jimmy-Jimbo die.

Kaleb was here to find Nika. Now the information would need to come from Mizzy Rubble, and Kaleb turned his attention to the door, leaving Jimmy-Jimbo alone to grapple with his maker of choice.

68

The 5th Edition

Mizzy Rubble was in her office all right and she was waiting for Kaleb, but this time Kaleb did not barge headlong into the room. He entered the room crouched low and the sap, swung hard from behind the door, missed Kaleb as he twirled to face her. But Mizzy was well versed in the craft of sap whacking and quickly backhanded another blow, aiming now at Kaleb's face.

Leaning away from the blow left Kaleb off balance, and Mizzy quickly took advantage. With her full 300 pounds of ugly she shoved Kaleb to the floor and pounced, pummeling away with the sap. Screaming as she brandished the sap, Kaleb could smell her sweat and her cigar stained mouth. Her fatness was squeezing the breath from Kaleb's lungs.

What blows Kaleb could not avoid he was able to deflect enough to dull the impact, but pinned under the obese woman, he needed an out. He needed an out fast.

Rolling hard against Mizzy's left leg Kaleb was able to tip her onto her right side. She caught her tumble with her right elbow, silencing the sap momentarily. As Kaleb spooled to his knees, Mizzy pushed off with her elbow and was set to begin another cycle of battering. Kaleb was quicker. Although he was on his knees, he was able to get enough torque into a blow to splatter Mizzy's nose.

The nose strike sent her off her knees and back onto her butt. The automatic reflex of her splashing nose caused her to grab for her face, for her beak. Her problem was that she still had the sap in her hand when she grabbed for her face. When the palm of her hand jumped to collect her nose, the sap slapped her forehead knocking her prone and unconscious.

With Mizzy Rubble knocked out on the floor and Jimmy-Jimbo dead or dying in the shooting room, Kaleb pulled himself from the floor and scrutinized the room. He began to rifle through the desk. In one of the drawers he found a .45, loaded and with the safety filed off. He spilled the chambers, tucked the bullets into his coat pocket, and set the gun on the desk.

The file cabinets proved to be more obliging. The drawers were chock-full of evidentiary data regarding drug commerce. Heroin and opium importing and exporting; the whos, the whys, the wheres and the how much. This was the full tally of the Rubble's heroin commerce. This was the mother lode.

Filling three waste baskets full of the files, Kaleb trucked them down the mushrooming back stairs of Rubble's Bubble and set them alongside the garbage cans under the stairs. When he got back up to the office, Mizzy Rubble was beginning to moan a moan that suggested the long climb out of the blackness. Boy, could Kaleb relate.

Kaleb sat down behind Mizzy's desk and dug a business card out of his pocket, picked up the phone and dialed a number.

On the other end of the line a voice said, "Bureau of Prohibition, how can I direct your call?"

"Comesky. Captain Gillian Comesky."

"Please wait."

There was the clicking and scratching of circuits, of plugs being pulled and pushed and rerouted, and, finally, "Comesky here, what's the blow?"

"Still looking for the Heroin Highway, boss?"

Silence as Comesky worked on the voice. "Kaleb?"

"Yes." Mizzy Rubble added some groaning and moaning in the background.

"Whatcha got, kid?"

"I got the main artery, you want it?"

Mizzy began to add some motion to the moaning and the groaning. Kaleb almost felt sorry for her. Almost.

Comesky was all business. "Spill."

"You know Rubble's Bubble?"

"Of course!"

"On Livernois."

"Sure. On Livernois. What's the 5th Edition?"

"There's trash cans lousy with butter 'n cream out back waitin' for you."

"What kind of butter 'n cream?"

"Names, dates, amounts, tallies, you want it, it's all laid out plain and simple."

There was a silence on Comesky's end. Kaleb filled the emptiness by watching Mizzy writhe around on the floor.

"It'll take me some time for the warrant if I want anything sticky."

"Don't need a warrant. Somebody seems to have emptied the whole butter churn out back with the garbage cans. It's anybody's business now."

Again silence, then Comesky said, "I can be out there in half an hour."

"I can give you twenty minutes."

This was answered with a click on Comesky's end.

***

Kaleb hung up the phone and turned his attention to the now awake Mizzy Rubble. As she sat up she brought her hand to her face, assessing damage. The damage had gushed across her mug in a splash of a crimson smear.

Gingerly she prodded her face, her nose, and then she addressed Kaleb. "You fuckin' kike, you's is a cadaver. A fuckin' walkin' cadaver."

Kaleb ignored that and asked, "Where's Nika?"

This brought out a display of Mizzy's heirloom yellowed teeth, the yellow being tempered by the crimson blood. "Don't know 'bout your little canary cutie, do ya?" This pleased Mizzy.

"Where's Nika?"

The blood from Mizzy's busted nose spilled over her yellow teeth giving her smile a green cast. "Tell you what, kike, you slide me that gat," she indicated the .45 on the desk, "and I'll give up the text on Nika."

Kaleb's silence gave her the answer so Mizzy continued, "I 'magine she's jes 'bout offin' the deep end by now."

Again Kaleb had nothing to say and let Mizzy continue with her revelry. "She left here so juiced I 'spect she's already cold."

This sent a chill through Kaleb and he leaned forward in the chair. "I'll tell you what, Mizzy, you give up Nika, I'll give you Jimmy-Jimbo."

The smile leeched off of Mizzy's face and sobered her humor. "You hurt that boy, I'll kill you."

Kaleb smiled at that. "You gonna kill a walking cadaver?"

"Where's Jimmy-Jimbo?" Mizzy demanded.

"Where's Nika?"

This had her and she knew it. Spitting blood through her teeth, Mizzy gave up. "We juiced her, juiced her good, and delivered her to her 'partment. Same 'partment where we off'ed that jigaboo girl. Don't want no dead Nika found at Rubble's Bubble." She spit the word 'Nika' like she was spewing phlegm.

Kaleb jumped to his feet and headed for the door.

"Where's Jimmy-Jimbo?" Mizzy bellowed at Kaleb's back.

Kaleb stopped at the door and turned to Mizzy still sitting on the floor. "You'll find Jimmy-Jimbo down there." said Kaleb and indicated the direction of downstairs. Or maybe Kaleb was indicating the direction of hell.

"He seems to have sampled a bit too much of the Rubble's Bubbles specialty." With that, he was out the door and down the stairs, three steps at a time.

***

The cornstalks slapped at Kaleb's arms as he dashed across the cornfield, making the tree line in moments. By the time he turned the T around in the hedgerow and made it back to the road, Livernois was a cloud of spraying dirt and dust as police cars and paddy wagons were churning the gravel of the road into powder.

Waiting for the last of the police vehicles to pass, Kaleb could see Rubble's Bubble half of a mile away as the police vehicles spun around the heroin house like Indians around a wagon train.

When the posse finished passing Kaleb's hedgerow, he turned the T south onto Livernois and slammed the accelerator full throttle.

69

The Final Measure

It was a hot mid-summer evening. Hot. Swarthy. The kind of hot where the muggy air brines neck hairs with perspiration and the cats prowl with their claws to the ready. A swelter where sweat is part of the air that you breathe and the slightest motion carries with it the weight of an iron lung.

Nika was in her studio apartment. Alone. Stoned.

From the outside looking in: Nika was a messy heap of dirty laundry. Heroin will do that. Sluggish in movement, slothful in reposition, Nika's comportment was more roll than walk; a body dribbling in motion and leaking futility.

From the inside looking out: Nika's senses were inverted. Nika heard colors and saw music. She could taste with her fingertips and reality was waving goodbye from the caboose of the last train to Auschwitz.

Drawing herself up to the windowsill, Nika sat with her feet dangling three flights up over Mullet Street. Over the Black Bottom.

***

It was early in the evening and shops were still busy with the bustle of bodies and the hustle of commerce. On the pavement below her dangling toes meandered the city's running dialogue: newspaper hawkers hawking, "Mayor John C. Lodge starts rocky second term;" grocers calling out "...potatoes 3 cents a pound;" and the general murmur of neighbors exchanging, "... streets as hot as a skillet..."

On her windowsill perch above the fray, Nika witnessed the flush of humanity beneath her toes. A shallow tributary with the tumbling rapids of humanity. The jumbled street sounds below, the river of humankind roiled together in the turbulence of one babble, one voice, "Mayor John C. Lodge starts potatoes on a hot skillet."

Listening absently to the babbling flow of the torrents tumbling below her, Nika leaned further out over Mullet Street from the perch of the window ledge.

The drag of the Black Bottom unfolded underneath Nika and with the aid of the surging heroin, she could discern the colors between the sounds and the taste between the touch of the street soundscape below. The Black Bottom.

The sudden shouts of "My god, that girl's gonna jump," and "Somebody grab her..." rushed to Nika in a kaleidoscope rainbow of energy, and she leaned out further from her roost to better examine the vista and see just what the gathering crowd was so anxious about.

Nika was familiar with the blackness of the bottom below. And with familiar comes some measure of comfort. Of console. The devil one knows...

The black bottom. The Black Bottom.

***

The coroner listed it as suicide. And maybe it was suicide. But if it was suicide it was a long and tortuous suicide that stretched a lifetime. It was a suicide that began when a molested seventeen year old girl lifted a shotgun to her abusive step father and blew a hole in the middle of his chest. And then, against the weight of the long, heavy double barrels, she blew another hole in his chest.

The coroner listed Nika's suicide as a drug-induced suicide. And maybe it was a suicide from drugs. But if it was a suicide from drugs, then it was a suicide from a drug that was the only antidote that the tiny and exploited child, Nika Nightingale, had known.

***

Kaleb elbowed through the fluttering rush of people to get to the crushed body of the used-to-be Nika Nightingale. She looked so small in a broken heap of former humanity on the sidewalk of 1927 Detroit.

Nika's skull was hemorrhaging, and as liquids will do, gravity channeled the blood down. Down slope. Downstream. Down to the gutter. Down.

She recognized Kaleb and when he held her, she gave a wisp of a smile and managed to mouth, but not voice, "Sorry." The effort bubbled blood to her lips.

Her final breath was quiet, too quiet to hear, but Kaleb could feel it in his arms as she gave up her last gasp of life. Her final measure of air.

No more would Nika be tortured in nightmares of rape and of murder. Never again would the haunting of might-have-beens torment her quiet moments. The little Jew girl's devils were finally and forever silenced.

Gently, tenderly, Kaleb bent to the girl and lifted the shattered body to his chest. He knelt there embracing Nika's now empty vessel while the crowd hushed in respectful deference to a body drained and a life exhausted.

70

Closing Time:
Epilogue For The Temple Bar
Speakeasy And Play Nice

The Prohibition years had been very good for the honky-tonks and the speakeasies and the blind pigs. And the Canadian distilleries flourished and the gun makers made a killing.

With the end of Prohibition, the honky-tonks and speakeasies and blind pigs cleaned up and moved uptown. Jazz put on a tuxedo, big band style, and followed the clubs uptown. The American distilleries resumed their craft and the gun industry continued to make a killing.

The Roaring Twenties had proven to be a very lucrative bridge for the gun industry in the lull between world wars.

Things began to happen fast and furious in the United States and between Wall Street's collapse in 1929 and the end of Prohibition in 1933, the roar of the '20s was relegated to an ethereal echo of a long ago revelry and mayhem.

Drift: intransitive verb: to move gradually from one state
or situation to another in an unintentional, casual, or aimless way.
Encarta Dictionary

Sure. Drift. That's the word. Intransitive drift. Empires don't crumble and mountains don't tumble and seasons don't turn and people don't die.

Places, times, people…just…drift.

The Temple Bar Speakeasy And Play Nice closed shop in 1928. Bucky drifted on to another barkeep position and Hollie drifted his broom to another floor. Tia and Edgar drifted off to Paris where their color scheme was not an issue.

Granma drifted on to whatever heaven hosts the disciples of baseball and a golden pea-can spittoon. Goddamnittohellandbackagain. Certainly backagain.

Krikor and his squeeze box continued their theoretical drift on-a-whatever-a-podium-a-'dey could-a-cajole-a.

Captain Gillian Comesky drifted his hatchet face to Chicago where he was celebrated in a hail of gunfire for his efforts. Detective Morane drifted into a peaceful retirement oozing into the crevices of his rocking chair.

Little Joey Louis Barrow gave up the violin and drifted into becoming the gentleman pugilist: the Brown Bomber. Thanks Mama Lillie.

Kaleb Kierka and Beethoven Jones drifted as well.

With Kaleb as a full-time piano jockey now, they worked their way west, first through the haunts of the South Side of Chicago and then to St Louis. Eventually they drifted south onto the westward artery of Route 66, the Blues Highway, which, finally, dumped them into the Los Angeles basin.

When the silent movie gigs dried up, Kaleb and Jones mucked around the Venice Beach dives, playing on any stage that offered a full-toothed piano and headroom accommodations for Jones; adrift with the flat 5 on the rivulet of a paradise valley.

Or maybe drifting down the flat 5 into a black bottom.

No matter, paradise valley or black bottom, it's always dust to dust.

The time spent between the dust to dust is all in how you frame it. How you measure it.

Go ahead and pick whichever metaphoric measurement helps you to crawl out of bed tomorrow morning.

THE ENDless

About The Author

Born and bred on the hard-scrabble streets of Detroit, Theo left home at seventeen riding his thumb from sea to shining sea to see what he could see. He served time in the cityscapes of New York, Los Angeles and San Francisco before landing on the coastal shores of Oregon.

The personification of a storyteller, Theo explores life, love and loss through literature, poetry, and songwriting as well as in live performances.

Theo's first novel, *HEART-SCARRED*, won the LARAMIE Book Award for Best Literary Western before he turned his attention to writing this novel-noir psychological thriller, *THE BLACK BOTTOM.*

A Renaissance Man, Theo has written and released critically acclaimed songs in a myriad of genres including jazz, rock & roll, blues, R&B, gospel, country, folk and heavy metal. As a novelist, Theo has written in the genres of a western and a psychological thriller and is presently crafting a science fiction novel. As a musician, Theo has performed professionally as a vocalist, pianist, guitarist, bassist, saxophone player and harmonica player.

Today Theo and his wife, Pi, reside high on a perch overlooking the Pacific Ocean.

The crosspollination of the novel and the music album:

The novel, *THE BLACK BOTTOM: The Measure Of Man,* concerns itself from whence jazz sparked. The time before the flame.

The music album, *THE BLACK BOTTOM: The Full Measure,* concerns itself with where the blaze of jazz has flamed. Jazz has dotted the landscape of every genre of American music. This album connects the dots.

Theo presents:

A working musician, storyteller, humorist and lecturer, Theo is available for music performances, lectures, house concerts, book club discussions, and various other events.

Treat your event guests to a rare and unique presentation by this singular artist.

Visit Theo at:
https://www.tedczuk.com
https://www.facebook.com/theoczuk
Contact Theo at:
theoczuk@gmail.com